BOOK V

The Old Grey Wolf:
The Southern Campaigns of
Captain Jacob Clarke

BOOK V

The Old Grey Wolf:
The Southern Campaigns of
Captain Jacob Clarke

Erick W. Nason

Strategic Book Publishing and Rights Co.

Strategic Book Publishing & Rights Co., LLC
USA | Singapore
www.sbpra.net

For information about special discounts for bulk purchases, please contact Strategic Book Publishing and Rights Co. Special Sales, at bookorder@sbpra.net.

ISBN: 978-1-68235-708-8

The hour is fast approaching, on which the Honor and Success of this army and the safety of our bleeding Country depend. Remember, officers and Soldiers, that you are Freemen, fighting for the blessings of Liberty - that slavery will be your portion, and that of your posterity, if you do not acquit yourselves like men.

George Washington

Three million people, armed in the holy cause of liberty, and in such a country as that which we possess, are invincible by any force our enemy can send against us. Besides, sir, we shall not fight our battles alone. There is a just God who presides over the destinies of nations and will raise friends to fight our battles for us.

Patrick Henry

"These are the times that try men's souls. The summer soldier and the sunshine patriot will, in this crisis, shrink from the service of their country, but he that stands it now deserves the love and thanks of man and woman. Tyranny, like hell, is not easily conquered; yet we have this consolation with us, that the harder the conflict, the more glorious the triumph."

Thomas Paine, The American Crisis, No. 1,
December 19, 1776

This book is dedicated to the men and women, those who have served and those who gave the last full measure, from Operation Infinite Justice to Operation Enduring Freedom, 07 October 2001 - 31 August 2021
You will not be forgotten

ACKNOWLEDGMENTS

I want to thank the best daughter in the world, Samantha Botros, for the great photography and editing to give the book its flair. Thanks, Sammy!

I want to thank Sandra Rose for being my second set of eyes, catching mistakes I have overlooked, and making the book that much better. Thanks, Mom!

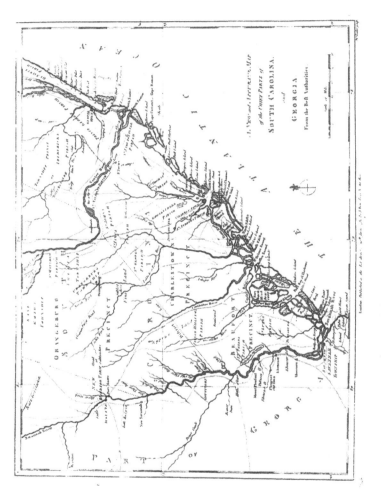

Area of Operations: South Carolina

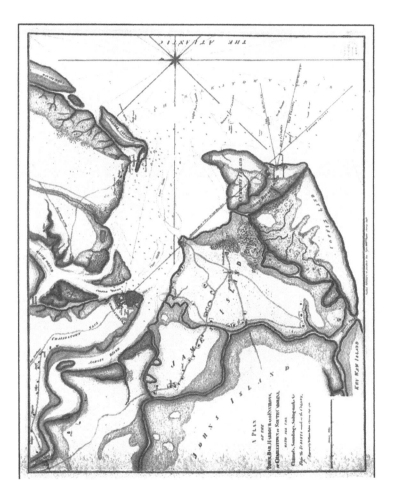

City of Charles Town

TABLE OF CONTENTS

PROLOGUE

Jacob sat at his table, sewing his breaches as he had torn a hole in the knee while demonstrating kneeling firing positions. He wished his wife Maria was there; she was better at sewing than he was, not to mention he missed his wife. While it was January, he could have taken leave while the army was on winter quarters, but as they received new men, he was busy getting them trained as the enlistments of the initial volunteers of the regiment were up.

The only sound was the crackling fire in the fireplace, as Samuel, Jean, and the others were out on other details, leaving Jacob alone at the moment. Outside, the cold wind whistled through the barracks, winter having placed the city in its icy grip.

As Jacob pulled the needle and thread through his breaches, he recalled the hundreds of times he had to repair his clothes and moccasins during his military career, which now spanned three wars. This one, which had just started as local uprisings, turned into an all-out revolution.

Mainly, the war focused on the north, ignoring them for a short period. Then their chance came when an invasion fleet arrived off of Charles Town in June of 1776. Behind the stout walls of the half-finished Fort Sullivan, then men of the 2nd and 4th Regiments were victorious, and the city was safe, for the time being.

The focus of the British remained centered and constant in the north, working on a campaign of maneuver to split the colonies, and stop General Washington and his Continental and Patriot Army. Jacob had learned that General Washington suffered a defeat near Brandywine Creek and the British marched into Philadelphia. Reforming the army, he attacked again near Germantown but was defeated by General Howe again.

Jacob put down his sewing; he recalled Lord George Howe, who many considered the best general in the British Army during the French and Indian War. General Howe had been very receptive to the Ranger ways and created his light infantry regiment based on the Rangers. It was a sad and significant loss when the French killed him on the opening days of the attack against the French Fort Carillon.

It was his brother, William Howe, who now, Jacob learned, was the overall British commander for the colonies and the commander giving General Washington a run for his money. Then they received some good news that at the same time that Washington was being pushed around, in upper New York near Saratoga, General Gates and his army soundly defeated British General Burgoyne and his army.

While all the fighting was up north, it didn't mean it was all safe and cozy in South Carolina. Jacob was concerned about what the old allies of the British, the Cherokee, and the Shawnee would do during this fight. Jacob had tried working with Nancy Ward and the other Cherokee clans. They wanted peace to influence those Cherokee clans being courted by the British to attack the Carolinas and Virginia.

Jacob's efforts and attempts, along with the "Most Beloved Woman" of the Cherokee, he learned that the Cherokee, Shawnee, and other tribes, along with Loyalists, all well-supplied from the British, attacked all across South and North Carolina. There were even some reports from Virginia and Georgia. Many frontier villages were attacked and burned, driving the people to forts or towards the coastal regions and larger towns or cities.

Jacob pricked his finger with his needle, causing him to curse, sucking on the injury before returning to the sewing. He believed the attack was supposed to coincide with the British invasion of Charles Town; while they stopped the British, the Cherokee attacked anyways. Jacob knew that John Stuart, the Indian Agent for the Southern Colonies, was behind it, along with his agents, stirring up the Cherokees, Shawnees, and Delaware with promises and supplies of arms.

When he thought of John, the old scars from the Cherokee gauntlet would twinge, reminding him of what he did to save John's life, to only find out he was using Jacob for his means instead of South Carolina. The Catawbas were still friends to South Carolina, with no love for the British who forced them off their lands and relocated them. In Jacob's opinion, the whole Anglo-Cherokee Campaign was a massive concealed land grab for the wealthy.

Still, during this campaign, he met William Moultrie, Francis Marion, Henry Laurens, and a good portion of the men that now serve within the 2nd Regiment. Another man he had met, Thomas Sumter, was now a Lieutenant Colonel and commanded the newly raised 6th Regiment. Colonel Moultrie, now a Brigadier General, and Colonel Motte now commanded the regiment. Francis Marion had been promoted to Major and soon to Lieutenant Colonel and was second-in-command of the unit.

Their overall Continental commander had been Major General Charles Lee, but he had been recalled back to New York; most South Carolina men did not like that a northern general commanded them. So instead, Colonel Robert Howe of North Carolina was promoted to Brigadier General and assumed overall command. The men in the ranks seemed to feel better with a Carolinian commanding them, then General Lee.

1777 arrived, which was the army's only significant action. After that, the army settled into the routine grind of an army in garrison. Jacob's concern was the men were becoming too complacent, and the lack of action and constantly needing to be prepared for battle was dulling the men's skills.

Jacob knew from experience that the private soldier left to their own devices would find mischief, and the 2nd Regiment was no different. There had been several instances of men firing their muskets from the barracks windows, and then the naked footraces bothered the local ladies. In addition, drinking and being drunk was becoming a significant distractor, tarnishing the reputation of the regiment it had earned at Fort Sullivan.

The companies rotated to different guard posts around the city, out on Fort Sullivan, and up at Dorchester. Still, the boredom was seeping in, unlike all the action they read or heard about up north. Even as the winter transitioned to spring, the warmer weather worsened the situation, as more men were found drunk in the city of Charles Town. Not only were the men being found drunk, but there were so many drunk in the streets that it became a safety concern as a few had nearly been run over by wagons and carts.

For most of the first half of 1777, the men of the second regiment remained on guard duties in and around Charles Town and Dorchester. Jacob was still on the staff for special responsibilities, so he went to Dorchester with Jean and Samuel to drop by and see their families. The training continued when they served at Dorchester and presence patrols around the region due to the Loyalists. At least he was out, and they would bring their wolves with them.

Even Jacob had to admit that the lack of activity made him concerned and anxious; even the Loyalists seemed to have gone to the ground and become silent. He was beginning to miss the action, and the inactivity was getting to him, Samuel and

Jean. It even affected some company officers, who resigned their commission from a lack of activity.

They did receive good news when the word arrived that a Continental and Militia Army under the commander of General Gates up in New York not only stopped but defeated a British, German, and Loyalists force under a General Burgoyne near Saratoga.

Jacob chuckled to himself, recalling his earlier days near Saratoga. He had run the first Ranger School there to train a cadre of British officers. He had met Abigail from Saratoga, which filled a hole in his heart for a short time before her father, Phillip Schuyler, came to find her and return home.

1777 transitioned to 1778, but the problems continued within the Southern Army, rotting from the inside from inactivity. Lieutenant Colonel Marion met with the regimental officers, indicating the growing problem. He identified that the men had been in the city too long and inactive; all of the work they had done before the fight against the British in 1776 was lost.

Jacob stopped sewing, recalling what Marion had told the regiment's officers. "Gentlemen, we need to stop this downward spiral," directed Marion, "I am calling on all of you fine gentlemen to help me bring the regiment back to a well-drilled, well-disciplined unit like before. We had earned our honor, gentlemen, but now that honor is tarnished."

Jacob was one of the few original officers from the regiment; many had transitioned to other battalions and brigades in the army or resigned and left. As the army continued with its garrison life, General Howe continued to plan for a strike against the British in Florida. He was becoming concerned that his requests for authorization to conduct the expedition from General Washington's headquarters had not been supportive. General Howe was also not getting any support from the civilian government of South Carolina. Undeterred, General Howe continued to plan his expedition against British Florida.

Jacob snickered as he pulled the thread through once more before starting the next stitch. Jacob had followed the planning for Florida, as General Howe wasn't getting any support from General Washington. Still, Georgia didn't want to provide any soldiers, for it was concerned about the British and Loyalist activity they faced. Then there was Governor Rutledge, who still had a say on what the state troops would do, even though they were considered Continentals.

One of the reasons Governor Rutledge was not supporting any expedition into Florida was his concern about the British blockade off of Charles Town. He wanted the Continentals to support his naval expedition by providing one hundred and fifty men to serve as marines aboard the small South Carolina Navy. The British had four Royal Navy frigates lurking off the shore, which kept all of the Charles Town merchants' ships stuck in port. The governor continued to pressure General Howe to the point that Howe held a council of war to determine what they should do.

General Howe had proposed his plan to take the fight to the British in Florida, which currently were the only ground threat to his army and Charles Town. However, the city leaders did see his point and considered it valid. Still, they believed the soldiers were needed here in South Carolina to stop raids from British or Loyalists from Georgia or Florida. They wanted soldiers to serve as marines and remove the threat closest to their shores. General Howe realized he would not get his way, so he relented and agreed to provide the soldiers to serve as marines.

While Jacob was by no means a maritime man, he had seen his fair share of action on schooners during the French and Indian War and the early days here in South Carolina. The South Carolina Navy consisted of the frigate *General Moultrie*, armed with twenty-six guns; three brigs, *Notre Dame* with sixteen guns; the *Polly* with sixteen guns, and the snow *Fair American* with twenty guns.

The governor tried to convince the captain of the frigate *Randolph*, which had its hull scrapped and repairs made. The *Randolph* belonged to the Continental Navy. However, her captain was interested in taking more prizes and indicated he was willing to support their naval expedition to remove the British naval threat. The captains began planning their strategy to clear the shore of South Carolina, counting on the Continentals from General Howe to give them the extra punch.

Jacob finished his sewing and tied off the stitching. What bothered him was the lack of Loyalist activity where they had been a constant threat upcountry. Now, they all seemed to Jacob to have gone to ground as instructed. Even his eyes and ears, long hunters who roamed the mid-country and sometimes near the Cherokee lands, heard and saw nothing. Jacob was bothered by this the most.

Jacob held up his breaches, looking at his handiwork. It may not be perfect or pretty, but it would keep the hole close. He placed it back on the table, took up his pipe, and sat down next to the fire, thinking. The British campaign up north also stopped maneuvering; they had not received any word on significant battles, only some skirmishes.

Some more good news they heard, which Jacob debated, was that France was considering joining the war on the colonies' side. However, even though he was now friends with Jean Langy, a former French Canadian partisan leader who was their most significant opponent of the Rangers, he still didn't know how he felt about the French.

While Jacob understood they needed help; muskets, shot, powder, and supplies, Jacob wondered what the price would be. He suspected they were upset with the loss of Canada to the British following the French and Indian War and were looking for revenge. Were they doing this with a clear conscious, or were they looking at a means of getting back at England?

Jacob sat and thought, the glow of his pipe washing over his face before Jacob gave a deep sigh and blew out his pipe smoke. The door banged open, and Jean and Samuel entered, wrapped in their heavy blanket coats. Jean still wore his distinct French Canadian White, Samuel, in his distinctive Ranger Green.

Jacob smiled, looking at the two former adversaries, now friends. The two looked up at Jacob smiling, and Samuel responded with, "What is so funny?"

"Brings back old memories of New York, doesn't it?" Jacob responded. Samuel looked at Jean, who looked back, before responding with, "No, New York was much worse!" The three started to laugh as Jean and Samuel took off their blanket coats and joined Jacob at the fire, warming their hands.

"How did the company do?" Jacob asked; Jean and Samuel had taken one of the companies out for training north of the city, as it had about three-quarters of new men in the ranks. Only the captain and the sergeants were part of the original veterans of 1776.

"They did well; they did well." Then, as he lit his pipe, Samuel commented, "No one died, which is a good thing."

The three sat in silence, listening to the snap and crackle of the fire, lost in their thoughts. "Well, time will tell, I guess," Jacob replied, and the other two nodded.

"Yes, but when, I am ready for some action," returned Samuel.

"Be careful what you wish for, my friend," Jean commented, "You might just get it."

CHAPTER 1

1778: THE RETURN OF ARIES

Jacob was sleeping soundly in his barracks room when suddenly awakened by the long roll reverberating through the barracks. Kicking his heavy wool blankets off, Jacob pulled his winter moccasins on, pulled his old blanket coat around him, and ran out into the parade ground. Jean, Samuel, and the others quickly followed behind.

Instead of hearing about an enemy force heading towards him, the shout of "Fire, Fire!" drew his attention. "The city is on fire!" shouted through the barracks. Beyond the barracks, the sky was aglow from the reported fire. Jacob ran into the parade area and yelled for everyone to fall out without their arms.

Once the companies formed, Jacob dispatched them running to the city to assist; their primary concern was protecting the quartermaster yard and the barracks. Jacob directed the companies as they came out, sending them in different directions. Jacob then moved into the inferno, jogging through a veil of sparks as numerous buildings burned around them on the street.

The citizens were in a panic; fear etched in their faces as they pulled their belongings out of their houses and piled them in the street or areas they thought would be safe from the flames. It was difficult for the men to jog through, as they had to weave around the piles of belongings while dodging men and slaves carrying bundles, firefighters, and helpers.

The sound was deafening, the roar and crackling of the fire as the dry wooden homes went up and the brick homes' wooden roofs caught. Then, moving through the grey smoke, Jacob with two of the companies arrived and began helping citizens in bucket brigades near the wells.

The men jumped right in, helped move buckets from the well, and began throwing the water onto the fire and a few hand-pump firefighting gear. The water started extinguishing some of the fire, changing the smoke from black to grey and making it thicker.

Soon, Colonel Motte and Marion arrived, taking stock of the situation. "This is different!" shouted Marion over the fires' roar and men's shouting.

"I've sent two companies to protect the quartermaster yard; the other two were brought here to stop any movement towards the barracks," Jacob explained.

Colonel Motte nodded, "Good Job Captain Clarke! Francis, head over and take charge of the situation at the quartermaster yard. If they can't stop the fire, save what you can!"

Marion nodded and took off towards the quartermaster yard. Motte moved to intercept the next company trotting towards the fire to direct them to where they were needed.

As Jacob was supervising his men, a civilian came running out and grabbed Jacob by the arm. "Please, please help! My wife is in our house, and I can't get to her!" Jacob began to follow the man who was pulling him towards his house.

"Samuel, grab some men and follow me!" Jacob yelled out, and Samuel nodded, grabbed a few of the men, and followed quickly behind. Jacob followed the man into the vortex of the fire storm until he stopped in front of a house, heavily burning on the second floor. The front door was blocked by burning debris, and Jacob heard a woman screaming from inside.

The man was hopping from foot to foot, begging Jacob to rescue his wife. Looking over, Jacob spotted an ax, which he grabbed and raised over his shoulder. Running forward, Jacob threw the ax through a large window, shattering it, and dove through the window. Hitting the floor and rolling to his feet, Jacob saw he was in a sitting room and a hallway to his left. As he began to move forward, Samuel and Jean came through the same window, following Jacob into the burning house after getting to their feet.

Wiping the tears from his eyes and coughing on the smoke, the three men crouched and moved forward towards the sound of a woman's voice yelling for help.

"Where are you?" Jacob yelled, and the woman's voice responded, "Thank God, I am in the baby's room!"

They found the room; the door was blocked by burning ceiling timbers. Twisting his body, Jacob got his shoulders under the burning beams and pressed with his legs, shouldering the burning beams out of the way. Samuel and Jean quickly patted out the flames on Jacob's shoulders and, with a nod from Jacob, pushed through the door.

Sitting in a corner, a woman cradled a child in her arms. Through the smoke, Jacob could see the relief on the woman's face. "Get the child!" Jacob yelled, and Samuel moved and took the child into his arms while Jacob and Jean helped the woman with an injured leg.

Jacob held her right side, Jean her left; she hopped on her good leg as Jacob began to lead the woman out, following Samuel behind sheltering the crying child. They made their way to the sitting room, where men were waiting.

Jacob and Jean helped the woman jump through the window to the waiting hands of the men outside, and then they passed the child to the helpers. Then the three of them jumped out of the burning house and took in deep breaths of fresh air.

They heard the ceiling cracking outside, followed by a loud groan. Quickly there was a thunderous crash as the second floor fell onto the first floor, and the house went up with a roaring flame. Eyes watering and coughing from the smoke, Jacob looked over to see the man hugging his wife and child, who looked back at Jacob and mouthed "thank you" to him.

Still coughing, Jacob, Jean, and Samuel sat on the street as they tried to clear the smoke from their lungs. Finally, with a smile, Jean looked at Samuel and asked, "Was this the action you were wishing for?"

Samuel coughed, shaking his head, "No, no, it wasn't." Then he looked at the happy family, "But we did our duty, and that works for me."

Smoked smeared faces streaked from their watery eyes, they stood up and headed back to help where they could. Most of the fires appeared to be under control. From where they could see, the barracks were safe.

By noon, the city was covered by a cloud of thick smoke from the hundreds of fires. Having done what they could, the tired men of the regiment returned to the barracks. Colonel Motte was waiting with Marion and the quartermaster sergeants, handing out a gill of rum to the men as they passed by; he said, "Well done, men, well done!"

***

Maclane watched from his perch on the top of the South Sea Mercantile warehouse near the Cooper River. Using a telescope, he scanned the city and smiled to himself. He then lowered the telescope and slowly closed it.

"Well, it almost worked," he whispered to himself, "had the wind been more robust and haven't shifted, not only would he have burned the section of the city where he felt were more of these supporters of the rebels lived, but nearly burned their damn barracks and almost their supplies.

Spotting men moving in large groups, he reopened the telescope and focused on them. He could recognize the sailors from the rebel warships by their slops and shirts. Then he spotted other groups, which had to be these bloody leather helmeted men of the infantry he had been observing.

"If it hadn't been for these soldiers and sailors, perhaps the fire would have been successful."

Closing and returning his telescope into his pocket, he watched and thought about how he could still use this to his advantage. He had found the abandoned house over on North Street; when he started the fire, the wind was strong enough and in the right direction to cause the damage he desired.

Then the wind died, which slowed the fire's pace, and the alarm went out and, through the concentrated efforts of the city dwellers and the soldiers, stopped it. He had to admit that had been impressive grudgingly, but he guessed from what he scanned that a good two hundred or more homes had burned.

Maclane scratched his chin, then turned and headed back to his office to see if he could find an angle to exploit.

***

It was learned that over two hundred and fifty houses and five hundred businesses burned. By noon, rumors spread that British saboteurs had infiltrated the city and caused the fire. This rumor seemed to take control of the city, and soon the people of Charles

Town were yelling for vengeance and for South Carolina to take the fight to the British.

A few days after the "Great Fire," Jacob was called to the orderly room to see Colonel Motte and Marion. After reporting, Motte began with, "You are aware of the need to remove the British naval threat from the area by the governor and the desire for men from the regiments to serve as marines?"

Jacob nodded, having a feeling where this was heading. "Yes, sir, I am well aware of it."

Marion smiled, "As we're not heavily engaged in training right now, and you have experience with naval operations, we would like you to lead a detail of hand-picked men to serve as marines for a short period."

"I would like to have Lieutenant Langy and Sergeant Penny with me," Jacob asked, and Motte nodded.

"We wouldn't have it any other way," He responded. "Return here tomorrow morning to receive your section of men."

Jacob saluted, turned, and returned to his room where Langy and Samuel were sitting, playing cards. When Jacob entered, Samuel looked up and tossed his cards onto the table. "Ok, by the look on your face, where are we off to?"

"We're off to sea again, my good friend,' Jacob replied, "We're going to see if it's the pirate life for you," Jacob explained they were leading a group of selected men to be marines, and they were to report in the morning.

Jean tossed his cards on the table and started packing his gear. "Good. Honestly, garrison life is not suitable for me." He looked at Samuel, "I want some action like our dear friend Samuel here."

Samuel nodded, then turned to Jacob. "Will it be a real ship this time, unlike the last one? While I love swivel guns and all, it would be nice to have some larger guns, especially if we're going up against the larger British warships."

Jacob chuckled, recalling their mission to support the sinking of hulks in the channel and the small schooner they were on, the *Hawke.* She had only been armed with swivel guns and their muskets. They had a quick engagement with the *HMS Tamar* during that fight.

"We'll have to see when we get to the harbor, but from what it sounds like, we may be serving on one of our new frigates," Jacob explained; in which Samuel smiled and started packing his knapsack.

The following morning, they headed to the orderly with their packs over their shoulders. Captain Poor and his section from the 1st Regiment were already there. Next to them was a section of about twenty men, with a sergeant standing out front. When they saw Jacob approach, they all came to attention and had smiles on their faces.

Jacob stood before the sergeant, David Conner, who saluted. "Sir, the section is formed!" Jacob returned the salute and had the men stand easy. As Jacob looked over the men, Sergeant Conner stated, "Most of these men hail from the Georgetown area, all served on local fishing and cargo vessels."

Jacob nodded and looked at the faces of these men, stern faces, wrinkled and lined from time out on the water. It appeared they liked the fact they would be under Jacob for this mission. Jacob recognized several who had previously served with Jacob on the Hawke as marines. They smiled and nodded when he looked at them. Jacob smiled and nodded back in return.

"Also, we ensured they are all good in a fight, especially close quarters."

"Good job," Jacob remarked, "Excellent!"

Two more sections arrived from the 4th and 5th Regiments. Jacob entered the orderly room, leaving Jean and Samuel in charge of their team, and reported to Colonel Motte.

"So, do the men meet your approval?" Motte asked, and Jacob nodded.

"They indeed do, sir, my thanks."

Motte nodded, "Good luck out there; I know you will do well. Hopefully, we will have more to do when you return than just guard duty."

"Sir?" Jacob asked.

Motte chuckled, "General Howe is still working on his campaign against Florida, so he feels as we are supporting the naval aspect for the governor, he will relent and allow his land campaign." Motte shook his hand before returning to his work.

After signing out in the orderly book on detached duty to the South Carolina Navy, Jacob rejoined his section. When all was ready, the four teams marched to the harbor and broke out to the respective ships they would be serving on. Longboats would shuttle them out to their ships.

Captain Poor from the 1st Regiment was assigned to the *Randolph*; Jacob's men were assigned to the *General Moultrie*, which he thought was appropriate; the volunteers from the 5th were assigned to the *Fair American*, and the 4th was given to the *Polly*.

As the men stowed their gears below deck, Jacob introduced himself to the captain of the *General Moultrie*, Captain Sullivant. Shaking hands, Captain Sullivant asked about Jacob's experience as a marine, in which Jacob summarized his naval experiences during the last war and this conflict.

"Ah, you were part of that night engagement supporting Captain Tuft then." Captain Sullivant commented, and Jacob nodded.

"Yes, sir, we were on the *Hawke,* and when the sun rose, realized we were fighting the *Tamar*."

Satisfied, Captain Sullivant welcomed Jacob and his men aboard and went over his expectations, roles, and duties during sea duties and battle. They spent the next day drilling their duties as marines, Jacob's men practicing climbing up the masts to take up firing positions, and the other men taking up supporting places along the bulwark of the frigate.

While smaller than her British counterparts, she was armed with twelve short barrel 6-pound cannons and six long barrel 6-pound cannons split nine per side. More of a light frigate, much smaller than the British, but Jacob expected she would be faster and hoped they would use that to their advantage.

Jacob explained how a naval engagement worked, with the naval crews operating the guns, and they would be acting as marines, providing musket fire. He warned them that splinters were their worst enemy during the opening cannon engagement. Their best shots would be up in the masts, engaging the British gunners. Once they closed enough to board, they would take the fight to the crew.

Most of his men recalled how to handle cannons from their fight at Fort Sullivan, so they practiced crew drills on the ship's smaller 6-pounders, to the crew's delight, who now realized they had experienced marines serving with them, and it bolstered their morale. Captain Sullivant nodded and smiled as he observed.

He strode up to Jacob, who was observing their training under the direction of Samuel and Jean. "Your men seem very experienced for landlubbers," he commented, and Jacob looked to see he had a twinkle in his eye.

"Aye, sir, most of them are sailors from around Georgetown and serve on our regiment. Many of them were with us on the *Hawke* and fought against the British back in '76."

Captain Sullivant nodded, "Would it break your heart if I offered them positions on my ship, always looking for experienced crewmen."

Jacob shrugged, "I can't stop you, sir, though I think General Moultrie and Colonel Motte would be rather put out."

Captain Sullivant chuckled deeply, patted Jacob and the shoulder, and continued observing the training and moving about the deck.

The men quickly settled into their new quarters, some of them taking longer getting used to sleeping in hammocks instead of a bed, but many found it more comfortable than the barracks. One thing for sure, they were all happy to be out and away from garrison duty and were looking forward to the new adventure. Then, finally, the signal was given when the fleet was ready, and the fleet raised its anchors and set sail.

The *Randolph* led the way out of the harbor, followed by the *General Moultrie*, then the smaller vessels. The *Moultrie* rose and fell with the swells as she passed into the open ocean. Along with their men, Jacob, Jean, and Samuel lined the ship's side and watched Fort Sullivan slide past.

The blue flag and its silver crescent flapped in the breeze; Jacob and the men of the Second Regiment raised a cheer, waving their caps in the air at the fort as they passed. Then, as the fort began to shrink in the distance, the men returned to milling in small groups and staying out of the way of the ship's crew.

Jacob stood on the quarter deck with Captain Sullivant, who watched the wind and gave orders to the quartermaster to trim the sails. With the chilly January night, Jacob wore his blanker coat while the captain wore his cloak, which flapped around him. The fleet turned southeast and began making its way towards the West Indies, where the British were reported to be operating their privateers and merchant ships.

"Our orders from the governor are to engage the British merchant ships and draw the British fleet that had been hovering outside of Charles Town away to the West Indies. Hopefully, along the way, we will take some prizes," Captain Sullivant explained, then he turned to Jacob and winked, "We promise we'll share some of the prize money with you and your men from the Second Regiment."

Life aboard the warship had its similarities but both advantages and challenges. Of course, one of the biggest challenges was getting their sea legs. Even though most of the volunteers had served on vessels before, it took some time to get used to the rolling ship, but at least they weren't horribly sea sick.

Samuel, Jean, and even Jacob took a little time to get their sea legs; they were not horrible sea sick but a little bit sea queasy. Then, like in garrison, the men drilled, except this time Jacob showed them how to fight on the tight quarters of a ship's deck with the ax, the smaller cutlass, and belaying pin.

They also learned how to use a new weapon, hand grenades. Small iron balls, filled with gunpowder and fuse, would be lit and thrown onto the deck of the enemy warship. Sometimes, they dropped from the masts of their ship. Finally, Jacob, Samuel, and Jean divided the section and showed their men hand-to-hand combat.

Jacob also spoke to them about the unique method of using their muskets at sea in battle. First, they must compensate for the enemy ship's rise and fall. So they had to time it right when the two would be aligned before firing at close range.

The fleet arrived at their patrolling area near the West Indies; Captain Sullivant doubled the watch in the crow's nest to look for targets. Jacob and his men helped where they could, and with much sailing experience, the ship operated more smoothly than before, which pleased Captain Sullivant.

Jacob even took his turn standing watch, though he realized he seemed always to draw the late night watch. Jacob ran his men through crew drills when they could, beating out the long roll as his men took up their battle stations as quickly as possible.

Samuel stood the watch with Jacob one evening, looking out over the empty ocean.

"Well, it does beat garrison life," Samuel stated, "Air is fresher at least, and you can feel the wind on your face."

Jacob chuckled, "As well as the feel of the spray and salt."

The two stood for a moment in silence, just taking in the quiet of the sea compared to the hustle and bustle of being in Charles Town or the barracks. There was peace on the ocean, but Jacob knew it would not last.

While they cruised off of the West Indies, they spotted no prizes. So when they were able, the Second Regiment men fished to augment their rations. During the day, just like back in garrison, the men formed into their mess, but instead of cooking their rations, they would stand in line with the crew with a pot where the ship's cook would ladle out enough food for the entire section.

The men would sit in a circle on the deck with biscuits or hard tack and eat their rations. As an officer, Jacob would eat with the ship's officers, but only after he made sure his men ate. Jean and Samuel selected to eat with the men, teasing Jacob about "privileges of rank."

When not on duty, the men relaxed the best they could, mostly trying to stay out of the way of the ship's crew. However, the most challenging part was when it came to relieving themselves. Instead of a privy, they were used to, on the ship, it was called a "head." Located in the vessel's bow, consisting of a couple of holes over the bowsprit, you could see the ocean flowing below.

It could be challenging if the ship was pitching and rolling, but with most of the men former sailors, it didn't take them long to adjust. Soon, they were adjusting to the routine of ship life; at least they had fresh air versus being stuck in tight quarters in the barracks, enjoying the aroma of men who haven't bathed regularly.

After a week or so, when they thought their luck wouldn't hold, the lookout shouted, "Sail Ho!" The men ran to the bow as Captain Sullivant pulled out his telescope and looked in the direction the lookouts were pointing.

On the horizon, a brig's sail was moving in their direction. "At bloody last," Captain Sullivant shouted, "beat to quarters!" Men began running to their battle stations; the ship's crew handled the guns while the Second Regiment men climbed up to the crow's nest, while Jacob, Samuel, and the other half of the men took up their post near the quarterdeck.

Opening the gun ports, the crew pulled on the ropes to run the guns out after being loaded, eagerly bending forward in anticipation of action. Jacob used his telescope and saw the *Randolph*, a quarter mile ahead, turn towards the unknown brig.

"Two more vessels sighted!" were shouted from the lookout. Looking through the telescope, Jacob observed the brig raise the union jack; the other two smaller vessels were starting to raise more sails and turn away.

"The brig must be the escort," commented Captain Sullivant, "the other vessels must be cargo. So, helmsman set a course to intercept the merchant vessels, and the *Randolph* has the brig."

As the helmsman spun the wheel, the ship healed with the wind and began to race after the prizes. As the captain kept his eyes on the running merchant vessels, Jacob observed the *Randolph* close with the brig, and then her side exploded in grey, billowy clouds of smoke, followed by the roar of the cannons firing on the brig.

From this distance, Jacob could not see any effect of the guns on the enemy brig, so he turned to observe their approaching targets. Using his telescope, he watched the lead merchant vessel, a large sloop with a large mainsail, trying to turn herself and run away. The chase was on, and the crew readied themselves for action.

The *Moultrie* had the wind at her back, her bow slicing effortlessly through the sea, and closed the distance between the vessels. "Starboard batteries take care to fire!" bellowed Captain Sullivant, and the gun crews bent to their guns.

The distance quickly shrunk to only a few hundred yards, and she caught the sloop in a perfect "T" by crossing her bow. "Fire as she bears!" commanded Captain Sullivant, and as the guns aligned with the sloop's bow, boomed as the gunner fired.

Having been caught by the bow, the enemy sloop could not defend herself, and the cannon shot tore through the length of the vessels. Nine cannons barked one after the other, their balls screeching through the sloop, smashing into the enemy crews, the balls skipping along the deck, spraying splinters and shattering bones, tearing flesh into a bloody pulp.

Some of the shots tore through the sails and lines; a lucky shot hit the stays that held the main sail aloft, causing it to crash onto the deck. The crew raised a chair as the enemy sloop slowed to a stop.

Seeing the sloop was dead in the water, Captain Sullivant ordered the helmsman to make for the second ship, a larger two-masted schooner. The crew was loading the cannons and pulling them back out into position to fire.

Using his telescope, Jacob could see the *Randolph* and the enemy brig clinched in combat. He turned, and he could see in the distance the rest of the small South Carolina fleet, the *Polly* and the *Fair American,* were in pursuit of two more enemy sloops; it must have been the rest of the enemy convoy they had engaged.

The new target was making as much speed it could muster, but the *Moultrie* was gaining on the schooner, the crew once more ready for action. The *Moultrie* raised and fell with the swells, sails snapping and popping from the strain of running with the wind behind it.

The schooner may have been slightly smaller, but the *Moultrie* had more sails, giving her the advantage of speed. "Take care port side batteries to fire broadside, boarders stand by grappling hooks!" ordered Captain Sullivant.

Some of Jacob's men and the crew grabbed large grapples tied to thick ropes, crouching next to the ship's bulwark. Jacob checked his weapons, his trusty tomahawk in the small of his back and a pair of pistols that Captain Sullivant had given him. Jacob preferred his tomahawk over the traditional sword or cutlass.

The captain angled the ship as she caught the sloop; she would fire a broadside, all nine cannons firing at once. Captain Sullivant was angling their approach so the mass of their shot would catch the schooner by the flank.

The gunners were bent over their cannons, sighting along the barrels of their guns. They were close enough that the gunners could see their target through the gun ports. "Stand by!" bellowed the captain, and the crew held their breaths, waiting for the order to fire.

"Fire!" was ordered, and all nine cannons boomed as one, the guns slamming back from the recoils, the grey and black billowy smoke blowing before them at the enemy sloop, blinding them. The ropes that held the guns in place went taunt from the recoil, and the crews automatically began to reload. At this range, they loaded grapeshot instead of round shot.

The Captain waited for the distance to close; the effect of the broadside was evident by the flapping sound of the enemy's damaged sails. "Away grappling hooks!" commanded Captain Sullivant, and the men threw their hooks.

The crew began to pull on the ropes, and Jacob had his men ready their weapons, axes, and cutlasses. Jacob pulled his tomahawk under his coat, preparing to leap across to the enemy ship. Other crew members were ready themselves, swords and boarding axes ready.

The men stationed on the tops of the masts began to fire their muskets down onto the enemy's deck. A few hand grenades were lit and tossed down on the enemy deck to explode with loud cracks. Samuel moved up next to Jacob, his blunderbuss ready for action. Jean also had his tomahawk in hand, a determined look on his face.

As the crew pulled on the gabbling lines, and when there were only a few feet between the ships, Captain Sullivant gave the order "Away boarders!" Jacob looked over to his men and the crew, who were watching him, and waved them over with "Follow me!" Then, leaping, Jacob cleared the distance between the ships and landed on the enemy's deck, his men and crew following, shouting and yelling.

The deck was strewn with splinters, torn sail, and damaged ropes, and the bodies were riddled with long barbs of bloody shards. The shock of the broadside, the grenades, and the smoke helped mask their boarding, but silhouettes soon headed towards them as the enemy crew attempted to repel the boarders.

Jacob launched himself into the fight and met one of the charging crew members who had a cutlass in hand. As he raised his sword, Jacob blocked his sword arm with his free hand before cracking him in the head with his tomahawk, dropping him like a rag-doll. Jean was next to Jacob, engaging another sailor with a loud "clang."

Samuel can aboard and covered the backs of Jacob and Jean, and when he spotted an enemy crewman charging, he let loose his thunderous blunderbuss. The enemy sailors crumbled to the ground, and their sailors followed through the smoke.

The melee crashed and surged as the enemy crew tried to stop the charging men of the regiment and team who had followed

Jacob over. His musket men in the crow's nest were firing down but soon had to stop firing because they were all mixed, and they were afraid they would hit their men, even though they were wearing their blue regimentals.

The thick smoke blotted their colors, so the men held their fire and became spectators in the fight. The fight on the deck was quick and brutal, and many enemy crew members began to surrender.

As the deck appeared to be cleared, Jacob called out, "Jean, secure the quarter-deck, Samuel and the rest with me!" Jacob led his men below decks to clear it in case some sailors were still resisting. Then, shoving his tomahawk back into the small of his back in his belt, Jacob drew his pistols and, with each hand armed, led his men down the steps into the ship.

There was a severe change in light, going from bright to the dim darkness below deck. Just like the top deck, debris and splinters were strewn all over the deck, so Jacob moved to the side and forced his men to wait after they got on the deck, allowing their eyes to adjust to the different light.

Samuel, with his blunderbuss, was next to Jacob, waiting. Then there was a shout, and the enemy crew members came running out of the dimness to attack. Samuel pulled the trigger without hesitating, and his blunderbuss roared with a loud blast, spraying the ship's interior with shot.

Like a small cannon, the blunderbuss shredded three of the charging crew members who caught the shot at nearly point-blank range. Then, using the shock, Jacob charged forward, his men yelling a war cry, even Jacob shouting a war cry.

Seeing motion to his right, Jacob dropped to his knee as an enemy crewman jumped out from behind some crates, swinging his saber. Using his pistol in his right to block the sword, he shot the enemy sailor with his left pistol. He had no sooner discharged his shot and was standing when a second sailor appeared; Jacob smoothly transitioned to his right, pointed, and fired, dropping the enemy sailor.

The fighting below decks was more brutal, much more up close and personal, but it had the same effect. After a few enemy sailors fell to the deck, the rest stopped resisting and raised their hands, yelling for "Quarter!" Jacob ordered his men to stop fighting and to secure the enemy sailors.

Having climbed back up into the brightness of the main deck, Jacob moved forward towards the quarterdeck, moving past his men guarding the captured enemy crew, who kept their hands up in surrender.

Climbing the splintered quarterdeck, blood running down a small waterfall down the steps, Jacob spotted Jean standing over the captain. The captain was slumped over, dead with a large wooden splinter through his arm and shoulder.

Jacob quickly surveyed the quarterdeck, trying to find someone who would be in command. Jacob's men and the *Moultrie*'s crew had rounded up the remaining enemy crew, and eventually, the second officer was found and surrendered to Jacob.

The crew of the *Moultrie* cheered as Jacob brought the now dead captain's sword to Captain Sullivant. Jacob and his men helped clear the dead from the now captured schooner *Biscayne Bay*. Captain Sullivant scanned the area and saw the *Polly* capturing the first sloop they had damaged. In the distance, he could see the enemy brig burning, the *Randolph*'s sails furled and clearing the captured brig.

With a few of their men, Jacob, Samuel, and Jean went below the *Biscayne Bay*'s deck to see what her cargo was. Her hold was full of rum casks, spices, and cloth, which would bring a healthy sum of prize money.

"Better put a guard on the rum casks," Samuel and Jacob agreed. So Captain Sullivant sent a prize crew over to take charge of the sloop, and he asked if five of Jacob's men would sail on the sloop back to Charles Town.

After he detached the five men to serve with the lieutenant from the *Moultrie* who would serve as the prize captain, Jacob watched from the *Moultrie* as the *Biscayne Bay* raised its repaired sails. A small blue South Carolina flag with a silver crescent in the corner flapped in the breeze from the captured prize's mainmast.

The fleet reformed; the *Randolph* took the lead, followed by the *Moultrie*, the *Polly*, the *Biscayne Bay*, and the *Fair American*. After a few days of sailing, and no other contact, Captain Sullivant began to wonder if their plan of drawing the British fleet away from Charles Town would work. He finally received his answer a few days later.

Jacob was below deck with his men, playing cards, when the drummer began beating to quarters. Leaping to their feet and scattering cards everywhere, the men threw cartridge boxes, haversacks, bayonets, and canteens over their shoulders, grabbed their muskets, and ran on deck.

Jacob was settling his tomahawk in the small of his back and then checked on the brace of two pistols he received from Captain Sullivant as he stood next to the captain. "Well, we did it now," Captain Sullivant stated, "we've called for the beast, and it has arrived."

Jacob pulled out his telescope and looked to where Captain Sullivant was looking. On the horizon, a large three-masted ship was bearing down on the fleet. Soon, Jacob could see she was a large ship-of-the-line, a double-decker warship. As he watched, the gun ports opened, and large cannons emerged from the ship.

"A sixty-four, she has more guns than this entire fleet," remarked Captain Sullivant as he lowered his telescope, "If we're smart, we'll run." However, as they watched, the *Randolph* turned towards the enemy warship. Captain Sullivant gave a deep sigh, "we're not smart.

Signalman, order the other ships to head away; we'll support the *Randolph*." So the smaller ships began to head away while the crew of the *Moultrie* readied for battle. The deck was cleared for action, the guns loaded and ran out, and Jacob's men again took up their battle positions.

Jacob stood next to Captain Sullivant, telescope to his eye to watch as the *Randolph* turned to wait for the enemy warship. She was bearing down on the smaller frigate, a giant red flag with the union jack in the corner blowing in the wind. "I'll give him some credit; he's in a good position to rake the enemy ship as she approaches," commented Captain Sullivan, "but she is outgunned almost four to one, and the enemy has bigger guns, probably; twelve and twenty-fours."

Jacob nodded his head in understanding, recalling the action against the British Navy at Fort Sullivan. "We'll intercept her after she closes with the *Randolph*," explained captain Sullivant, "we'll try to catch her in a cross-fire."

The *Moultrie* continued to close; the *Randolph* raised her flag, red and white stripes that could be seen from their distance, and fired a broadside into the approaching enemy man-o-war. The enemy ship was beginning to turn towards them to give her side to the *Randolph*; Captain Sullivant directed his helmsman to steer their ship so they could rake across the enemy's bow.

The double-decker gun deck belched in fire and smoke, obscuring their view of the fight. Jacob thought that with the sure weight of all those guns firing in a broadside, the *Randolph* would be disabled.

As the wind blew the smoke away, both Jacob and Captain Sullivant were surprised to see the *Randolph* was nearly unscathed.

"Well, I'll be damned, they missed, and at that range no less. Starboard gunners, make ready!" Captain Sullivant turned to the helmsman and the quartermaster, "We'll put shot into her bow, then swing wide so we can rake her with the portside guns while the starboard loads," instructed Captain Sullivant and his men nodded in agreement. The captain turned and was rubbing his hands together with a smile on his face. "This is going to be a good fight!"

The *Randolph* was already returning fire as the *Moultrie* began her attack against the bow of the enemy warship. "Fire as she bears!" the captain ordered. Jacob looked at the looming enemy, which towered a full deck and a half over them.

"Well, at least we won't miss at this range," commented Jacob, and Captain Sullivant nodded his agreement. Then, as the *Moultrie* slipped past the enemy warship's bow, her guns unable to fire on her, *Moultrie*'s guns began to bark as they passed the bow. They were less than fifty yards from the enemy ship, and Jacob could watch their shot run true and smash into the forecastle and bow of the enemy ship.

Whenever a ball hit the enemy ship, wood chips and splinters flew, and damaged parts of the bow flew up into the air. It was a rhythmic firing as they passed by the enemy ship, and the crews began reloading quickly. Then, as they passed the bow and began to make the large turn back towards the enemy ship, her guns began firing on the *Moultrie*.

The lower deck of guns was the larger twenty-four pounders, and their balls came screaming over and around them, some landing in the water with a large splash. Some large balls tore through the sails, leaving a large circular hole, and a few lines snapped.

The upper gun deck of the enemy ship had the smaller twelve-pounders, which all seemed to have fired over the

Moultrie, passing harmlessly by or through the lines without touching them. Jacob looked at Captain Sullivant, who looked back and smiled, "that was close!"

The *Randolph* was pouring fire into the enemy warship, which they discovered was the *HMS Yarmouth*, when they could finally see her nameplate. "Port side, make ready!" commanded Captain Sullivant, and the gunners prepared to fire. But, just as the captain ordered the port side guns to fire, the enemy fired.

The sound was deafening as both warships fired; the difference was the *Yarmouth* had bigger guns, and now they were close enough that it would hurt. As the *Moultrie*'s guns recoiled back and her shots began to smash or bounce off the enemy hull, the British shot began to tear into the *Moultrie*.

Jacob, who had taken his place with his men on the deck and Samuel, ducked as the balls smashed into the bulwarks, shattering the wood as they crashed through, sending woodchips and hundreds of splinters into the air.

Two gun crews absorbed the hundreds of splinters that showered them from the impact, blood and entrails spraying over the deck. Then, as blood sprayed over the deck, numerous men fell from the splinters screaming. Two men had arms severed from their bodies; they sat on the deck in shock as their lives drained out of them onto the deck.

Without hesitating, Jacob moved the injured away from the guns, his men moving them to sheltered areas on the deck where the crewman tried to stop the bleeding. "Man, the guns!" Jacob yelled, and his men took up gun crew positions on the two empty guns.

Jacob took charge of the section of guns, Samuel on one gun and Jean on the second. Jacob could see that Samuel's regimental sleeve had a large tear and a damp, dark edge to the rip. "Samuel, are you alright?" Jacob yelled, and Samuel replied with an absent wave, "Just a scratch, I'm fine!" he yelled back.

Jacob nodded and gave the command of "Load!" His men took up the implements and began loading the long six-pounders, much smaller than the massive thirty-twos they had manned at the fort. Jacob found the linstock and started blowing to get the spark glowing before handing it to one of his men.

Jacob's men pulled the rope to run the guns out, and Jean looked over the barrel to ensure the gun was clear. Samuel's gun was also run out, and his men readied for firing. Just like before, Captain Sullivant was going to bring one side of the ship alongside to fire before he would turn and make a second approach for the other side to fire.

Jacob turned to watch the starboard crews ready to fire, and as they came alongside the enemy ship, Captain Sullivant gave the command to fire, and the guns belched and roared. Some of the *Yarmouth*'s guns returned fire, some of the larger balls again tearing into the side of the *Moultrie*, sending wood chips and splinters, killing and injuring a few more crew members.

It only took a few minutes for Captain Sullivant to bring the ship around for the port side gunners to get their chance to fire. The *Randolph* had not moved, standing toe-to-toe with the larger *Yarmouth*, a constant roar of guns as she fired almost five broadsides to the *Yarmouth*'s one.

Jacob could see that the *Yarmouth* was beginning to suffer from the *Randolph*, the sails had many holes through them, and the topmast of the main mast had been shot away. "Port side make ready!" ordered Captain Sullivant, and Jacob raised his hand that he was ready, Jean and Samuel watching.

"Fire!" was given, and Jacob repeated the command to fire. Their cannons barked and rolled back in recoil. Jacob could not see whether they had done any damage or not, as the smoke of battle obscured everything. Then, "Load!" was given by Jacob and his men automatically went into action.

The *Moultrie* had moved about five hundred yards away to make her turn when there was a volcanic explosion of fire and smoke, the shock wave striking the *Moultrie*, knocking most of the men from their feet. "What in the hell was that?" Samuel yelled, and Jacob climbed onto the quarterdeck to see a stunned Captain Sullivant.

Looking in the direction of the battle, the *Randolph* was gone; hundreds of pieces of wood, masts, and sails rained down on the *Yarmouth* and the surrounding sea. "She's gone; she's all gone," mumbled Captain Sullivant.

There was no sign of the *Randolph* except for smoke and burning chunks of wood floating on the water. Even the *Yarmouth* was rocking from the shockwave. "They must have hit her powder magazine," remarked Captain Sullivant in disbelief. So they had the *Yarmouth;* she was suffering from their cross-fire, and Jacob and the captain thought they would take a British man-o-war. But fate was fickle, and their luck had run out.

"Time to get away while we have the wind," muttered Captain Sullivant, "we have no chance against that ship." Then, with the smoke and shock of the explosion, Captain Sullivant decided to get away from the monster. They had the wind, and he was going to use it.

"Helmsman, make for home; quartermaster, secure from quarters and begin repairs," commanded Captain Sullivant, and the orders were passed. The *Yarmouth* fired a few shots at the withdrawing *General Moultrie*, sailing harmlessly behind them.

Jacob and his men secured their guns, then began to help move the injured and clear the ship after stowing their gear. It had been a hard fight; six of the crew had been killed or would die from their wounds. Another twenty were wounded. The deck was strewn with debris, splinters, and pieces of canvas.

Jacob didn't lose anyone but had seven wounded, including Samuel. Jacob helped Samuel get his regimental coat off, his white linen shirt bloody and a tear near Samuel's right bicep where a large splinter had torn his arm but had not embedded itself. Eventually, a surgeon's mate sewed up the wound and placed a bandage around it.

Jacob and his men assisted in making repairs to the *Moultrie*, removing the damaged sections, and helping the carpenters fix the bulwarks and other parts of the ship. Captain Sullivant kept double lookouts, more for any more enemy warships than looking for prizes.

As they sailed back, they held a ceremony where the dead were buried at sea. The dead were sewn into their hammocks, and a cannonball was set at the bottom of the sewn hammock so it would sink. The crew was assembled; Jacob had his men drawn up in a small formation.

The captain read from a bible and said some words about the crew before they slid down a plank and into the arms of the ocean. Jacob had his men present arms, saluting as the dead were given to the sea.

The week sailing back to Charles Town was uneventful, and the men felt relieved when they turned into the harbor and saw Fort Sullivan in the distance. Samuel looked over to Jacob and then slapped him on the back. "By God, we made it back in one piece!" yelled Samuel, and the men began to cheer once more as they passed the fort and the blue South Carolina flag hanging from the pole. Even Jacob had to smile in relief; though sea duty was a nice change of pace, it was good to see land and home again.

The *Moultrie* pulled into port, and Captain John Blake from the Second Regiment was waiting for Jacob; his men would be relieving Jacob. But, first, Jacob had his men gather their gear and get ready to march. Then, Jacob reported to Captain Sullivant, who instructed the quartermaster on the ship's disposition and work priorities.

"Captain Blake here," Jacob introduced Captain Blake to Captain Sullivant, "is our relief. I am taking my leave of you, sir, and wanted to shake your hand before we go." Captain Sullivant smiled and shook Jacob's hand. "You're a good man Captain Clarke, and you have good men. I asked them to join my crew, but they said they much rather fight with you. You can sail with me anytime, but until then, best of luck."

After shouldering their gear and bags, Jacob led his men off the ship as Captain Blake's men waited on the dock to take their place. Then, they marched through the city towards the barracks; a few people called out if they had been lucky or if they had driven the British away. When they arrived at the barracks, Jacob had Jean and Samuel take charge of the men while he reported to Marion.

Jacob told Marion of their exploits, the taking of the enemy sloop, and the fight with the *Yarmouth*. Marion cringed when he heard of the loss of the *Randolph*, including the men from the First Regiment. "A heavy price to pay," replied Marion before he dismissed Jacob.

A few days later, an officer arrived at the barracks and asked for Jacob and his men, who had served on the *General Moultrie*. Jacob, Samuel, and the men who had served as marines were formed up and true to his word; Captain Sullivant had sent their cut of the prize money.

The official had the men sign for their share, including Jacob, whose portion was slightly higher due to his rank. Then, after they were dismissed and maintaining proper discipline, the men shouted with joy for their share. Samuel was tossing and catching his small bag of clinking coins in his hands, "Not bad, not bad at all," was all he said, "perhaps serving in the Navy isn't so bad."

CHAPTER 2

THE STALKING LION

When Jacob returned to his barracks room, Richard Shubrick, John Walter, and Frederick Fuller updated Jacob, Jean, and Samuel on what occurred back in garrison. Shubrick began explaining what had happened while they were away.

"While you all were at sea, General Howe got his wish and led an expedition through Georgia to Florida. We heard that Governor John Houston of Georgia passed that he believed that only five hundred Loyalists held Saint Augustine, which could be easily taken. So General Howe ordered the Georgia Continentals to intercept."

John Walter continued. "It was the 1ˢᵗ of April, and General Howe marched with about three hundred men of the First South Carolina Regiment to East Florida to link up with the Georgian Continentals, along with eleven hundred militiamen under Colonel Williamson."

Jacob nodded, "Any word from General Howe?" The three men shook their heads.

"Nothing other than they had crossed into Georgia and were still marching into Florida. They had no contact with either Loyalists or British forces."

Jacob shrugged, "Well, I guess no news is good news, I guess."

Jacob and the others returned to everyday garrison life of formations, drills, and work details. Many of the men asked them to tell about their adventure on the ocean. A lot asked about the battle with the British warship.

The garrison life did not last long, and by June, Jacob, Jean, and Samuel were directed to the orderly room. The three arrived and were shown immediately into Colonel Motte's office.

"Sir, you summoned us?" Jacob asked.

Motte looked up from a report and motioned for the men to stand easy.

"Gentlemen, we have just received word that several Loyalist attacks and murders occurred in a short time up north. Naturally, this concerned the governor greatly, making it over to us."

"Our instructions, sir?" Jacob asked, and Motte chuckled.

"To the point, I see Captain Clarke, always ready to answer the call."

"Yes, sir," Jacob smiled, "It's from too many years as a Ranger and serving under Major Rogers."

Colonel Motte nodded in understanding. "We want you to head north, determine what is happening and put a stop to it."

"Will it be the three of us, or will we have a company?" Jacob followed up.

"As we still have not heard from General Howe, then you will head to Newtown; Captain Allston said he had a mounted Catawba and some mounted Rangers waiting for you."

Jacob nodded, "When shall we depart?" asked Jacob, and Colonel Motte replied, "As soon as you can."

Then he followed up. "Captain Clarke, use what you must stop these blood-thirsty Loyalists from attacking the good people up there. We'll lose their support if we can't take care of them."

***

Captain David Fanning and his company of Loyalists were fanning out and slowly advancing towards a group of patriot militia. He had learned that the Patriots were watching a bridge next to a grist mill and, as he suspected, were not paying attention to their surroundings. Instead, they were standing in groups, talking instead of watching the road or, luckily for him, the woods.

Following his frozen trek back up into Cherokee land and then returning to North Carolina, Loyalist Lieutenant Colonel Thomas Brown mobilized local Loyalists. Fanning, having recuperated and wanting to get back at the patriots, joined back up and was elected captain of his own company.

They were to join the Loyalist activity in Southern Georgia, So Fanning marched his company to the Savannah River. They could move along trails that prevented their detection by Patriot patrols. Still, Fanning kept his eyes and ears open, just in case.

They had been successful in a few skirmishes with the Patriots, but when ordered to head towards East Florida, half of his company refused to go, Fanning included. So he decided to stay behind to apply his personal justice to the upcountry South Carolina Patriots, primarily due to the thrashing he received at Long Cane.

As Fanning led his men forward, he looked over on his left at "Plundering Sam" Brown and his men, who were moving crouched and at the ready. There was anticipation in their eyes. Looking to his right, William Cunningham, having decided to head back to South Carolina from Georgia, led his section of men.

Fanning raised his hand when he felt they were close enough, and they all stopped, bringing their muskets to shoulder. Then, looking left then right, seeing everyone was ready, Fanning dropped his hand with a loud "Fire!" The Loyalists' muskets barked, catching the Patriots by surprise. They charged through the smoke, checking to see if any of them were alive.

The attack was quick and vicious; one of the men knocked over the stacked muskets for a group who had been standing around a small fire. Two men started running down the road; Cunningham stopped and aimed and fired with one of his other rifled-armed men. The two runners collapsed into the dirt, a dust cloud rising from where they fell.

The few wounded or who tried to surrender were tomahawked, so there would be no survivors. So plundering, Sam and his men went to work stripping the dead, even seeing if any of the dead's shoes would fit. Cunningham joined Fanning as their men spread out, going through the belongings and gathering muskets.

"Nicely done," commented Cunningham to Fanning, "Dead men tell no tales." Not taking his eyes off the activity, Fanning smiled and nodded. Cunningham finished loading his rifle, then cradled it in his arm.

"Aye, it works better that way; it sends a clear message."

Once everything of value or use was taken from the dead, Fanning gathered the men and headed back to where their horses waited. They secured the captured muskets, bags, and booty and then returned to their camp. The men joked and scoffed about the attack on the hapless Patriots. "We were just doing our duty for the Crown, eh?" one of the men commented.

When they arrived at their camp, a messenger was waiting for Cunningham, whom he seemed to know. He headed over after dismounting from his horse.

"Robert, what are you doing here?" Cunningham asked.

"It's your dad and brother, Cousin William," Robert answered slightly. Cunningham gave him a stern look.

"What about them? What happened?"

Robert shook his head, "It was Captain Ritchie; he came looking for you again. He came to the house, dragged your poor father out, and threw him out of his home. He only had what was on his back."

A cold, harsh look came over Cunningham's face, a growing rage. "What about my brother?"

Fanning could see the conversation between Cunningham and this young man appeared it wasn't good news, and moved over to see what was going on with Cunningham.

Robert began to weep as he continued his tale. "Captain Ritchie had your poor brother whipped. Whipped him so bad that he died. I tried to stop them, but his men grabbed me, and they laughed as he pleaded with them, and they laughed harder when he died."

Cunningham was livid, breathing heavily with his face in a scowl. "That's bloody it! I am going to make that damn Ritchie pay this time!" After quickly securing his gear, Cunningham turned and went straight to his horse and mounted up.

Fanning met him at his horse; when Cunningham looked down on him, it was like Death was looking at him.

Through clenched teeth, Cunningham stated, "I have to leave David; there is some business I need to take care of!"

Fanning knew he couldn't stop him and nodded. "Go take care of business; we'll be at the western rendezvous in about two weeks. Meet us there."

Cunningham gave a curt nod and rode off. Fanning moved over to speak with Robert. "What did you tell him, boy?"

"Sir, Captain Ritchie, a Patriot Leader up in Saluda, has been after Cousin William since he escaped a couple of years ago. Well, sir, they threw his father out and killed his invalid brother; neither could defend themselves."

Fanning nodded, "So I take it he is heading up there to make things right?"

The boy nodded, "Yes, sir, and Hell is going with him."

***

Jacob was speaking with a couple of the lieutenants when he spotted a familiar face ride into the barracks area and headed to the orderly room. Lieutenant Colonel Peter Horry, who, like Marion, had been promoted and given the command of the newly formed 5th Regiment, stood there. After tying his horse to a post, Horry turned and smiled as Jacob came up to shake his hand.

"It has been some time, sir," Jacob said pleasantly, "how is the new regiment shaping up."

Horry shook Jacob's hand warmly and shrugged. "Well, they are not like the 2nd, but they are getting there." Then he looked up with a mischievous look in his eye. "Do you think Moultrie would release you to me for a bit to shape up my regiment?"

Jacob chuckled and shook his head, "Probably not, sir." Then he asked, "What brings you to our happy corner of the city?"

"Problems upcountry again, some man named Fanning is raising all sorts of Hell there, and I am to send some of my companies to go quell this problem before it gets worse."

Then Horry gave a solemn look. "We even heard about a deserter from the 3rd, and I believe his name was Cunningham. From what we heard, he rode right up to Captain William Ritchie and shot him in front of his wife and children. Can you believe that? Right there in front of the man's family. A cold-hearted murderer, that's what's going on up there, and that's where we're going."

Jacob took on a look of concern and slowly nodded his head. "Good hunting, sir, but it will be a challenge. They fight by the hit and run and hide in plain sight in the middle of the good people. So keep your eyes and ears open."

Shaking his hand again, Jacob wished Horry luck before turning and heading to his barracks room, and Horry entered the orderly room. Although Jean, Samuel, and the other three men discussed a training plan in the barracks room, they stopped and looked up as Jacob came in.

"Please tell me that Moultrie found you, and we have a scout to do or something," Samuel moaned, "I am bored and getting tired of garrison life!"

Jacob sat down with them, took out his pipe, and after getting it lit, nodded in agreement. He told them what Horry told them about the activity up north, with Fanning and this cold-hearted murderer Cunningham.

"See, they need to send us Jacob," Samuel thoughtfully stated, "We could take a company and clean all of that business up in a short time."

Jacob leaned back, smoking his pipe, and sighed. "I agree, Samuel; I, too, am growing tired of just drilling and garrison life. But, we all know, the longer we sit here, the softer we become, and our skills lessen."

The men all nodded in agreement. Shubrick added, "The only word I have heard is from Georgia. A relative of mine sent me a letter; he told me there is a good deal of skirmishing between Patriots and those Loyal to the Crown. There is even word they will form their own Continental Regiments."

The boredom and lack of activity impacted the regiments, with court martials held every day for numerous offenses. General Howe finally received permission for his expedition against the British at Saint Augustine, Florida, and the men were overjoyed to see action finally. But unfortunately, his expedition was not supported by the Governor of Georgia, and except for a few skirmishes with Loyalists, he did not make it to Florida.

Howe and the Southern Army limped back into Charles Town at the end of July, demoralized, exhausted, and sick from numerous diseases. Jacob watched the column of men march by, as he did not participate in the expedition, and shook his head slowly. Jean stood with him, watching as well.

"This does not bode well for us, no?" he remarked, and Jacob nodded. "A situation like this, we can expect desertions to increase here."

***

The rain beat against the glass of the tall window; the British Secretary Lord Germain looked out at the dreary, grey London. The weather reflected his mood, the situation in the colonies was not favorable, and there was even a growing sentiment in the Parliament and local British citizens striving for peaceful resolutions, granting their independence.

Lord Germain shook his head in disgust. This rabble pushed their forces out of Boston. At least Howe drove General George Washington out of New York, which had become their main base of operations, but put down this rebellion.

The wind battered the window, driving the rain harder as Lord Germain reflected on Lord Howe. His 1777 campaign to split the colony ended in not only a complete failure but a strategic win for these rebels. France was supporting them, more and likely seeking revenge from the Seven Years' War.

They lost a good portion of their army when Burgoyne surrendered, and the only bright side, if there was one, was that Lord Howe captured Philadelphia but was nearly defeated at Germantown.

"At least he did the honorable thing and resigned before any more damage could be done," Lord Germain spoke to the glass, "But at what cost?"

Sir Henry Clinton, who has been of such nuisance since arriving in the colonies, constantly sent him letters. He had been assigned Howe's Second in Command but did not approve of Howe or his plans and continuously threatened to resign but was appeased due to politics. Finally, he was awarded a knighthood and presented the Order of Bath. Lord Germain shook his head in disgust.

"These damn rebels have fought us to a stalemate, and I have to deal with politics!"

From behind Lord German, his secretary asked, "My lord?"

Lord German turned and waved his hand in dismissal, "Never mind, read back what you have so far."

The secretary nodded and held up the parchment and read aloud.

"To General Sir Henry Clinton, Commander-in-Chief, North America. You are directed to abandon Philadelphia and secure our holdings in the Caribbean. You should be aware that France is supporting this insurrection, and we have received word a French fleet has departed and is en route."

The secretary stopped reading and looked up at Lord Germain, pacing with his hand scratching his chin in thought. Then, hearing nothing, he returned to reading the letter.

"Therefore, you are ordered not to engage the rebels but instead secure our strongholds and maintain our lines of communication. Additionally, they no longer conducted raiding expeditions into rebel-controlled areas to preserve what British forces were available in the Colonies. As we may become more engaged in other locations with the French, we may not be able to provide additional forces to your campaign in the colonies. Use your forces at your best discretion.

The secretary looked up, and Lord Germain nodded. Then, folding the letter and dripping hot wax to seal it with Lord Germain's signet, the secretary hustled away to get the message on the next ship heading to the colonies while Lord Germain looked out once more over a gloomy London.

***

Since the army returned from their failed expedition, the mood around Charles Town was bleak. But unfortunately, the same could be said when the news arrived at the Continental Congress up north. Due to the miserable results in East Florida and Georgia, General Howe lost favor with the Congress, his popularity at an all-time low.

Jacob, along with most of the leadership in the 2nd Regiment, wondered when the eyes of Britain would shift towards them. They knew there had been no progress up north, and from all of the reports they were seeing of Loyalist activity in South Carolina and Georgia, it made military sense.

Summer quickly transitioned into fall; along with Jean and Samuel, Jacob and the other officers sat on benches around a fire, smoking their pipes. The barracks had its typical sound of life, men laughing or discussions reverberating off the buildings' stones and logs.

They may be at war, and they may not be doing any actual fighting, but Jacob admitted he did enjoy these times with his comrades in arms. He admitted he did miss his wife and his family, but these times around a fire made him feel at home. He smiled around his pipe stem, and Samuel looked at him from across the fire.

"What's on your mind, Jacob?" Samuel asked, "Seems odd you would be smiling now."

Jacob chuckled lightly, "Recalling all the times we have done this, my friend, sit around the fire with comrades and tell stories. We have been doing this forever, and this feels like home."

Samuel snorted, "We have been doing it forever, but you're right; this always feels like home, no matter what war or location. It's always the same."

The following morning, Marion called for Jacob, who could see Samuel with a look of anticipation of a mission. Even Jean appeared to have the hopeful expectation in his eyes. However, when he arrived in the orderly room, he received a task he was not expecting.

After reporting to Marion and dropping his salute, Marion smiled at Jacob.

"I have a special mission for you, Jacob, as well as Sergeant Penny and Lieutenant Langy."

Jacob braced for it and nodded his head. "Yes, sir, we're always at your service."

"I am releasing you three on leave, head back home and see to your business and family. The regiment has been performing well. All due to the hard work the three of you have done. Go get some rest, as we may see some action finally."

Marion smiled at the surprised look on Jacob's face, which quickly turned into a smile.

"We have heard rumors that the Lion may be looking this way again," Jacob replied, and Marion nodded.

"We have heard the same. Right now, we don't have anything solid. What information we have from up north is General Howe has departed and is being replaced by General Clinton. We also heard he is marching away from Philadelphia, heading north."

Jacob nodded, "When should we return, sir?"

Marion gave Jacob a quick look, then replied with "December. Will you be able to take care of your family and business by then?"

Smiling, Jacob nodded, "Then settled. Go on leave, Captain Clarke; you deserve a break."

Jacob turned and returned to the barracks where both Jean and Samuel were waiting.

"Well, do we have a task? Where are we off to? Samuel asked.

Jacob shrugged and dragged out the anticipation before replying, "Home. We are going on leave until December."

The shock washed over Samuel and Jean, who looked at one another, then back at Jacob before smiling.

"When can we leave?"

"As soon as we're packed and signed out, we can be on our way," Jacob answered.

Compared to when they packed for a mission, they packed quicker with less as they headed home. Once packed and signed out of the orderly room, they headed to the stables to get their horses. Then, with their rifles resting across the pommels to their front, they rode through the northern gate and followed the road home.

***

General Clinton read the newest letter once more from Lord Germain before tossing it on a table with distaste.

"Who is he to direct me from England how to fight this war here in the colonies," scoffed Clinton, "they have no idea what we are facing here."

The first had been his orders to withdraw from Philadelphia, which he accomplished though faced with logistical challenges. When the Loyalists heard of the evacuation, they took all the water vessels, leaving him to go overland. Nevertheless, not only did he lead the army successfully to New York during a hot summer march without losing a single wagon or man, but he was also able to bring Washington to a pitched battle near Monmouth Courthouse finally.

Granted, it could be considered a draw, as this General Washington arrived just in time to rally and withdraw in good order when victory was so close. But, at least the damn rebels did not bag his army like they do good old Gentleman Johnny Burgoyne. Compared to Lord Howe, he was fighting instead of sitting.

Then the French Fleet arrived outside New York Harbor, anchoring outside the bar. The fleet never crossed, though Admiral Howe was waiting for them. Instead, they raised anchors and sailed north to Newport. Dispatching Admiral Howe to pursue the French, he led the army northward to deal with any French landing force.

By the time he arrived at Newport, neither fleet was present. There was no French to engage, and any rebel forces in the area did not appear. So instead, he had ordered raids against local communities, which he knew contradicted the orders he had received from Lord Germain.

He left the raiding to his subordinates and returned to New York. He had acquired a new house on Broadway across from the bowling green, which he used for his headquarters. In a sitting room that he turned into an office, Clinton looked at what maps he had of both the northern colonels and the southern ones.

Along with Clinton were Major General Alexander Leslie, Admiral Howe, Lieutenant Colonel James Webster, and Major Peter Traille of the Royal Artillery Train. In addition, a few aids and secretaries were waiting on General Clinton's directions. Nodding to himself, Clinton turned and faced the assembled officers from his staff.

"Gentlemen, he is our quandary," Clinton began, "Our illustrious Lord Germain had directed during the evacuation of Philadelphia that we were to maintain our hold of what colonies we control, Canada, and reinforce our holdings; in the Caribbean."

He paused as the officers listened patiently. "I have received new guidance that we are to focus our new efforts in the southern colonies due to the stalemate. So this, gentlemen, is what we must determine. With what forces available, can we secure our positions and launch an expedition to the south?"

Clinton looked at the officers as they thought about the question. Admiral Howe answered first.

"Do we know where the French fleet is? We hadn't seen them since the chase towards Newtown before the storm broke up the pursuit. If we don't know where that fleet is, I can't guarantee the expedition's safety unless you plan to march down there."

There was a low chuckle from Leslie and Webster, with Clinton shaking his head no. "How do we stand with the army?"

"We do not have the available manpower to be in two places, sir; unless we can get reinforcements, there is nothing we can do," Leslie stated, and Clinton nodded.

"So, how do we meet Lord Germain's directive to move against the southern colonies without losing our army as Burgoyne did or any more of our positions to the rebels?"

"Sir, if I may," replied Webster and Clinton nodded. Then, Webster walked over to the map of the southern colonies, followed by the rest of the officers.

"Florida, sir, we can direct General Prevost to move northward and start pushing through Georgia and into South Carolina." Webster drew a line from Saint Augustine up through Georgia and tapped it on Charles Town with his finger.

Clinton rubbed his chin in thought and began to nod his head in agreement. "If I request reinforcements and can confirm the location of the French Fleet, Prevost can already be on the move and launching the expedition from there. Then, once we receive our reinforcements, and with Admiral Howe, can strike between our two forces, crush them between us!"

All of the officers nodded in agreement. Next, an orderly was called for, and the first order was written for General Prevost to launch his expedition through Georgia, take Savannah, and, if able, begin operations in South Carolina. The second was the request for reinforcements to be used in the second part of the expedition.

Looking at the map, Clinton looked to the west, and an idea began forming in his mind. "What information about the Native support in the south? Have we been able to secure their allegiance?"

"Our last report from the Southern Superintendent for the Southern District Stuart indicated negotiations with the Cherokee and Creek Nations are favorable and should be able to support our expeditions when necessary."

Clinton nodded, "It's necessary. Send a dispatch to Stuart and tell him to have our native Allies ready to support by attacking from the west, catching these rebels in a harder vice!"

"Sir, what do we know of the rebel strengths in South Carolina?" Leslie asked.

Reflecting on the question, Clinton had to admit that his information concerning the rebels' strength was inaccurate. He had previously considered their army a rag-tag collection of militia until he faced them at Monmouth Courthouse, and they performed well.

"Send a dispatch to our intelligence network in South Carolina; we need detailed information on any sightings of the French Fleet, regimental strengths and locations, defenses, and militia forces in the area."

The orderly nodded and began writing the dispatches, his quill dipping in his inkwell, his mouth moving as he wrote out the general's instructions.

As the officers chatted amongst themselves, Clinton stared at the map. First, he visualized Prevost's forces moving northeast into Georgia and investing in Savannah. Then Clinton envisioned his expedition crushing the southern rebels like a hammer and anvil. Finally, he'll show them in England how a war can be fought.

***

Maclane watched as another section of soldiers marched past, heading off on some details. Once they moved down the street, Maclane continued to the South Sea Mercantile office. When he entered the main room, a couple of the local plantation owners arranged transportation of their goods to trading ports.

Opening the door to his private office, Maclane froze as Bedlow was there, wearing a set of plain clothes that allowed him to appear like a local farmer.

"Ah, Bedlow, what brings you to a fair city this fine day?" Maclane stated, only with a slight edge of mockery in it. Both men worked in their unique ways in gathering information, had their agendas, and did not have a fondness for each other.

"I have business for you," Bedlow answered.

"You, or the Crown?"

Bedlow raised an eyebrow and nodded, "The Crown. We require information as we did before, troop strengths, movement, defenses, and any militia units in the area. We also need to know if the French Fleet has been seen."

Maclane nodded, "That's an easy one; I can tell you where we last saw the French Fleet."

Bedlow sat up quickly, "You can?"

Maclane shrugged like it was nothing, knowing it would get under Bedlow's skin. "One of our trading ships arrived in Savannah and saw the French Fleet anchored there, making repairs."

Bedlow sat back and nodded. "I assume your rates are still the same; we can't simply call on your loyalties to the King and country?"

Maclane held up his hands. "Well, sir, while I may be a loyal subject, it takes more than that to get my eyes and ears to gather the information you are looking for, with so many rabid patriots roaming the city, eager with heated buckets of tar, feathers and a noose."

Knowing full well that while Captain Maclane was a member of the British Army, he had been immersed so long as a gatherer of information within these provincials, he had become one of them. Sometimes the lines of his loyalty blurred between King and coin. Bedlow sometimes wondered where his true loyalties lie.

Nodding, Bedlow pulled out a bag of coins and tossed them to Maclane, who caught it and brought it up to his forehead as a salute.

"Same means of passing information; you're still up at the Black Widow's place?"

Bedlow nodded as he put a plain farmer's round hat on. "I am." He then looked directly at Maclane. "Plans are afoot to take back the south and this city. When the time comes, we may need the services of your cutthroats, troublemakers, and bandits. Be ready."

Nodding his head, Maclane gave a half-smile. "Aye, sir, we'll be ready."

***

John Stuart ensured his British uniform was straight, clean and what expected of a British officer. Helping was his assistant, Alexander Cameron, also wearing his British uniform. Today was an important day, as both southern and northern tribes of different native nations have arrived to determine if they would side with the British or not.

Looking at himself in a small mirror, Stuart was satisfied, placed his officer's tricorn, and headed outside their hut. A small cart of gifts was waiting, two of their aids waiting to pull the cart.

"Well, sir, this will either make us heroes or failures in the eyes of the Crown," Cameron stated simply to Stuart, who nodded—taking a deep breath, Stuart led them to where a great council had been laid out, with the chiefs and warriors from the southern and northern tribes.

As Stuart and Cameron entered the council area, many voices spoke in different dialects, their assistants pulling the cart behind them. They stopped at the edge of the center of a large semi-circle, and in the center were blankets on the ground where the chiefs and war chiefs sat. Dragging Canoe, the leader of the Cherokee saw Stuart and Cameron and motioned for them to join them on the blanket.

They took a seat to the side, taking off their hats and sitting cross-legged. Both men had spent many years living with the Indians, Stuart with the Mohawks and Cameron with the Cherokee. They were waiting for the northern tribe representatives.

A short time later, the delegation of the northern tribes arrived with their war chiefs. The Shawnee Cornstalk led the delegation, with war chiefs from the Shawnee, Lenape, Iroquois, and Ottawa. In the circle were Cherokee, Muscogee, Chickasaw, and Choctaw.

Cornstalk strode with pride and stopped before Cornstalk and greeted him. He then turned and faced Stuart and Cameron. "The Royal Governor of Detroit Henry Hamilton sends his greetings and welcomes these warriors with the same desire and purpose."

Both Stuart and Cameron bowed to Cornstalk, who bowed back in return. He then turned and joined Dragging Canoe in the center. Dragging Canoe rose and strode before the assembled chiefs and warriors.

"Hear me, brothers, for the time has come to make the decision! How long will we allow these English to take our lands and break the treaties we have agreed to? These settlers don't listen to their fathers," Dragging Canoe stated by pointing to Stuart and Cameron, "taking the food from our families and driving us from our homes?

Then Cornstalk stood and addressed the assembled warriors. "I share my voice with our southern brothers, the Cherokee. We, too, have seen the same long knives enter our lands in the Kain-tuck-ee, taking what is not theirs. They have total disregard for treaties, for our lands and people. This must end now!"

The warriors rose their voices in a war whoop, agreeing. Cornstalk turned and, when he faced Dragging Canoe, presented him his war belt. "I Cornstalk and the Shawnee join our Cherokee brothers in driving these squatters from their lands." Then, after pulling his tomahawk, he struck the war post before standing off to the side.

Once more, the crowd of warriors rose in celebratory whoops. Following Cornstalk, the Ottawa and the Iroquois leaders presented their war belts to Dragging Canoe and struck the war post with their tomahawks. The other war chiefs filed by, hitting the war post. Stuart and Cameron rose, smiling. They had their Indian Allies.

They motioned for the cart to come in and began to hand out gifts to the assembled war chiefs and leaders.

"I guess we're not failures after all," Cameron whispered to Stuart, who only nodded as he handed out shiny brass gorgets and armbands. Then, finally, the different warriors came up to accept their gifts, and joyful cries echoed around the meeting area.

Cameron nodded, "Yes, sir, not failures after all."

CHAPTER 3

THE BRITISH ARE COMING, AGAIN

December arrived, and Jacob had to return to Charles Town and report back to duty. It had been a welcome break, though mainly from the boredom of garrison life, and it was great to see his family. Jacob admitted he loved his wife's cooking and felt she went out of her way to fatten him, constantly muttering, "The army doesn't feed him right."

Jacob's eldest son Patrick was now a strapping fourteen-year-old, standing a good six feet tall and had his broad shoulders. His younger brother Richard wasn't that far behind for a twelve-year-old. Constantly growing out of his clothes and, with the working of hides and around the compound, was filling out.

Helga was becoming like her mother, wearing men's clothing and not acting very "lady-like." She was learning how to cook from Maria, her aunt, and her grandmother. She also learned to be a crack shot from Peter and can hold her own against her brothers when it came to shooting.

As what had become routine, Maria packed Jacob's bags, ensuring he had new stockings, a new shirt, and even a new pair of moccasins. "I made them for you," Helga said with pride, "do you like them?"

Jacob smiled at his daughter and nodded. "They are well made, much better than what South Carolina would provide."

Helga beamed before she came over and hugged her father tightly.

"Stay safe, papa," she said, the words muffled by Jacob's shirt. Then she looked up and had that same determined look on her face as Maria's. "Come back safe and sound, and as mom keeps asking, no holes in you!"

Helga gave her father a light smirk before walking away. Maria watched her go with a smile on her face.

"She's growing up fast," Jacob stated, then he looked at Maria, "She is just like you."

She smiled and patted Jacob's cheek, "Of course, she is learning from one of the best."

Continuing with another tradition, their last night home was a family feast where everyone came over to Jacob's house. Again, the men sat around the fire to stay out of the women's way, as they controlled the kitchen area and would chase anyone out, including the wolves who came by to see if they could get some scraps.

The wolves padded over and joined, sitting with the men near the fire, as they discussed and talked about what news they had heard. Of course, the news came differently, but most often, word of mouth from waggoneers and merchants.

"Getting a lot of news that there is no some major activity in Georgia, and it's not Loyalists either," Samuel said from around his pipe stem. "Spoke with a team of wagons they came back from Savannah, said British regulars were raiding on the border between Georgia and Florida."

Jacob's forehead creased as he concentrated. "Did these waggoneers indicate anything else? What was done during the raid?"

"Cattle mostly, then they burned the farms and headed back into Florida. Then there were a couple of skirmishes right after along the border." Samuel answered but could see Jacob's mind was busy.

"What do you think, Jacob?" Jean asked.

"I think we may be facing the invasion everyone has worried about, but it's not coming from the North. It's coming from the south."

Samuel's eyes opened as he had a thought. "I must be getting old like you, Jacob, or bloody daft."

Jacob's eyebrows raised at the comment, but he waited to see where Samuel would take the conversation.

"They're gathering supplies for provisions ahead of the invasion instead of during like they normally would."

Nodding his head, Jean added, "If they are coming across the border, it would also be smart to remove anyone who could see and report it. So you chase off the farmers and burn their homes, no?"

They all nodded, "Well, lads, I think we'll be busy once we get back to Charles Town." Jacob indicated, and they all nodded. Their discussion was interrupted when they were called to dinner, putting the border issue away for the moment. Then, tapping out their pipes, they all gathered at the table piled high with freshly roasted venison, wild boar, fresh loaves of bread, and gravy.

It was a great feast, and after a while, everyone returned home. In another part of the farewell routine, Jacob and Maria enjoyed their last special time together, embracing the tender moment before Jacob returned to duty. They held each other close, focusing on the moment and not worrying about tomorrow.

The morning did arrive, and Jacob dressed in his uniform. He had a good breakfast before heading out to his horse, which had already been loaded with his bags. Jean was already there on his horse, and Samuel was mounting up saying goodbye to his family. Jacob said his farewells, hugging Maria and Helga and shaking Patrick and Richard's hands. Then, mounting up and after Patrick handed up his rifle, laid it across the pommel.

Looking over his shoulder, Jean and Samuel nodded, and Jacob motioned to head out. To a chorus of "Farewells and come back safe and sound," they rode out the compound. Peter, their old trusty Ranger Comrade, saluted them with his pipe as they trotted past and headed out the gate for the road.

While the day was clear and sunny, it was rather cold, and the three wore their well-worn blanket coats. The cold winter breeze tugged at their coats, pulling them back towards Charles Town. The fields were empty, except for cows and other livestock, with no other travelers on the road.

"So what do you think," Samuel asked Jacob. "We have been gone for a month; how many changes are waiting for us?"

"Maybe peace broke out?' Jean answered quickly, but the three chuckled as it was unrealistic expectations.

"I'm sure there has been," Jacob replied, "We may have taken a break, but I am sure the war marched on without us. We'll just have to catch up." Jacob's words provided to be prophetic as they returned to the barracks and reported back to the regiment. Marion updated them on what had happened while they were away.

"It seems the Continental Congress lost favor with our old commander General Howe and, in their infinite wisdom, will be sending a new one," Marion briefed, though a slight distaste look was on his face.

"I take it, sir, it's another general from up north?" Samuel asked.

Marion nodded. "He is coming from down from New England, so general Howe will remain in command until our new commander arrives."

"Which is who, sir?" Jacob asked.

"Major General Benjamin Lincoln is our new commander," Marion answered. He could see that both Jacob and Samuel's faces showed they knew the name.

"Do you know him?" Marion asked.

"The name is familiar; I'm trying to recall where," Jacob replied as he pondered.

Samuel snapped his finger. "Remember that ass of a man up in Massachusetts that we ran into during the recruiting trip for Rogers? How arrogant he was, and if it wasn't for our quick action, the man he was chasing nearly killed him."

Jacob's eyes open as he recalled the moment when Lincoln, whose horse had been shot and when it fell, pinned Lincoln's leg under it, trapping him and making an easy target for the highwayman. Had Jacob and his men not intervened, Lincoln would have been a dead man.

Jacob nodded, "Yes, sir, we had a run-in with a younger Lincoln back in his sheriff days in Massachusetts. He nearly got himself killed, and we rescued him."

Marion nodded, "What is your opinion of him?

Jacob responded, "Arrogant fool unless he has matured over these years."

"Which is highly doubtful," Samuel added, followed quickly with "Sir."

Chuckling, Marion shook his head. "Well, there may be other reasons our illustrious General Howe may have been relieved of his command, and it may have nothing to do with his prowess on the field."

The three looked at each other and turned back to Marion, Jacob asking with a "Sir?"

"Ah, that's right." Marion replied, "You may not have heard about our General Howe's prowess in the bedroom."

Again, the three gave Marion an enquiring look, who shook his head and chuckled.

Unfortunately, our General Howe didn't understand the tactics and concealment of his operations and had a rather public affair with an esteem Charles Town lady. Enough so that not only did our delegates of South Carolina ask for his removal, but it was public enough that even the Georgia delegates asked."

Samuel raised his eyebrows and whistled, "I see your point, sir, I see your point."

***

General Clinton stood on the quay, watching the assembled fleet raise their sails in the cold, biting northern wind. His cloak flapped about his legs like blue wings as he watched the white sails rise into their positions, catching and filling with the same cold wind.

The reinforcements had arrived, but he decided to say "To hell with orders" and changed them though he was following the letter of the orders. He created three expeditions to meet Lord Germain's intent. The first expedition included thirty-five hundred men loaded on fifty ships under the command of Lieutenant Colonel Archibald Campbell.

Clinton specifically instructed Campbell that he had already sent messages to General Prevost in Florida. Accordingly, Prevost was directed to work directly with and coordinate activity with Lieutenant Colonel Campbell on the combined campaign to take Georgia.

"Georgia will be the first stepping stone towards our victory," Clinton stated. Besides his aids, a man in civilian clothes standing next to Clinton watching the departure turned and asked, "Sir?"

The gentleman, William Eden, was a member of the Carlisle Peace Commission that he had met during his time in Philadelphia. Eden was part of a commission trying to negotiate a peaceful resolution to the crisis.

"If our campaign is successful, we will place you and your commission in a position of power, perhaps forcing these rebels to negotiate more to our terms."

Along with the expedition to Georgia, a second expedition under Major General James Grant with five thousand men to take Saint Lucia in the Caribbean from the French. Additionally. A third expedition Brigadier General John Campbell with thirteen hundred men to take the Spanish holding of Pensacola, Florida.

"We will hold three key positions in the southern colonies and demonstrate to France and Spain not to interfere in an English problem. Thus will, your peace delegation will have a strong position."

Eden nodded, then looked back into the harbor as the ships began to sail out of the port. First were the sleek frigates moving first as the sails were flapping of the larger troop transports as they turned and filled their sails with a boom. Then, finally, the wind was with the fleet for a change, pushing it out to sea.

Taking in a deep, cold breath of air, Clinton nodded and smiled to himself. The campaign was on its way that would bath him in glory.

***

Lieutenant Colonel Archibald Campbell paced the deck on the flagship for the Georgia expedition, watching the crew raise the sails and secure the lines. The ship's bow rose and fell with the waves as she moved out of the harbor and into the ocean. Campbell's mind was focused on the task at hand.

He was ready, wanting to get revenge on these damn rebels. So in 1776, his regiment, the 71st Highlanders, was sent to reinforce the garrison in Boston. But unfortunately. They had not learned that the garrison had been pushed out of Boston, and these rebels captured them.

Sitting in prison, he was not treated according to his rank or position, the courtesy the English would have shown their prisoners. Instead, he sat in a cell like a common criminal, the rebels showing disrespect and heaped ill-treatment upon him.

Freedom would come in May of 1778 when he was exchanged for a rebel officer, some man named Ethan Allen. He went to New York to recuperate, and there he was able to rejoin his regiment, the 71st. So when Clinton offered him the opportunity to lead the expedition against Georgia, he readily accepted the command.

Seagulls flew alongside the warship as she cut through the steel-grey ocean. Campbell walked along the gundeck, moving towards the bow of the warship. Campbell suspected that Clinton had a feeling he was looking for revenge on the rebels and offered him the command. But, when he was informed that General Prevost was to coordinate with him and not the other way around, he showed his understanding of his desires.

"Yes, I will make them pay for the disrespect and dishonor they showed me as a prisoner," Campbell spoke to himself, two sailors ignoring him as they coiled lines as Campbell walked by. "They will suffer the same indignity as I did."

***

The regiment faced a significant crisis as most of the men who enlisted in 1775 as provincial troops or in 1776 as Continental troops' time was up. Their enlistments were about to expire. General

Moultrie with Marion met with all the officers and asked them to stay on. For Jacob and Jean, that was an easy ask as they would remain committed until the end, whichever it may be. However, some officers chose not to stay and would have to be replaced.

The men in the ranks, mainly the private soldiers, were concerned. A good portion of the veteran sergeants and corporals remained, but about a quarter of the private soldiers ended their enlistments and headed home. Jacob, Samuel, and Jean worked with the company officers to identify who in the ranks should be raised to corporals and which corporals to become sergeants.

Recruiting details were sent out to the parishes to recruit new volunteers, and luckily Jacob was spared this duty. He recalled his time with Rogers; having been sent out on recruiting duty, he could see the countryside, but that's it.

On one of these recruiting trips, they ran into Sheriff Lincoln in Massachusetts in pursuit of dangerous highwaymen. He had met them at a local tavern where he had asked for their assistance. His disregard for good tactics and not thinking nearly cost him his life if it had not been for Jacob, Samuel, and a few of the Rangers who had accompanied them on the detail.

Instead, as the regiment's Drill Master, they remained behind to take in all the new recruits and begin drilling them so they could at least march and handle their muskets safely. In addition, Samuel ran training for the new corporals and sergeants. Still, as many recruits they were getting in, they were not filling their ranks to the required numbers. A sad note included the number of dissertations that were still occurring.

During one of their evenings, sitting around the fire and smoking their pipes after a full day of training, they discussed this recruitment problem.

"What do you expect, Jacob," Samuel said as he puffed on his pipe, lighting it from a flaming brand from the fire. "With all the fighting appeared to be occurring in the north, and no Loyalist activity in the south, getting volunteers to join the army is going to be tough."

"There is also the Cherokee," Jean followed, "some raiding going on upcountry and in North Carolina. So they are going to be afraid to leave their homes."

The men sat, looking into the fire, reflecting. Shubrick spoke up.

"I heard that we may not be recruiting well, but the port privateers are doing very well. At least money could be made as a privateer, something most of these volunteers could live with; there is no profit from joining the army."

"True," answered Samuel, then pointed with his pipe stem as he made his point. "Some of our illustrious volunteers are here because we're not in action. They like the garrison life. They have food, clothing, and a place to sleep. Better than being in jails. What will happen when the British return and they get their taste of combat?"

Jacob thought on it, his pipe smoke circling his head caught in the evening breeze. When the British tried against Fort Sullivan, the regiment was ready and well trained. But, as time wore on, their edge was slowly dulling from the lack of combat or activity. Samuel made the point he was concerned about the most; the regiment had lost its edge.

"Hate to admit it, Samuel, but you're right as always," Jacob commented, "we've lost our edge. We all have, and even I admit garrison life had softened me some, not used to the rigors of campaign and the threat of attacks. But, unless something is done, I fear we as an army won't be very effective."

"Our new general, he won't seek battle?" Jean asked.

Jacob stared into the fire and thought about it but could not come up with an answer. No one pushed it but sat and watched the flames dance and the wood snap. The fact that Jacob couldn't answer made them all concerned.

It wasn't just Jacob who was concerned about the strength of the army, but the government of South Carolina as well. So they passed the Vagrant Act, which allowed for the pressing of anyone who the city's authorities would consider idle men, beggars, or anyone considered riff-raff could be ordered into the army to fill the ranks of the six regiments.

When Jacob learned of this act, he became concerned. These types of men the army didn't need would only cause problems with discipline in the ranks; many recruits were being drawn from the local area jails.

When the first batch of these recruits was brought to the regiment, Jacob, Jean, and Samuel watched them enter the barracks area, and all three shook their heads.

"Bloody hell, this is much worse than what we have," Samuel grumbled as he pointed. "Look at them!"

It was a rather pitiful sight for the group of men being herded into the compound. Disheveled looking, dirty, unkempt, with a depressed look in their eyes. Unlike the fevered volunteers at the beginning, men who knew they were at the bottom of the barrel. Join the army, or stay in jail.

"Discipline is going to be a major problem, no?" Jean asked, and both Jacob and Samuel nodded.

"We had this before, back during the last war," Jacob explained, "was like a disease that once it got into the ranks, it ate from within."

Jean looked surprised and asked Jacob, "You had this problem with the Rangers?"

"They tried once, and we needed more men to fill the ranks because you and your friends did a good job teaching us humility. So they asked for volunteers from the British line and local provincials, and all we got were the hand-offs and bad apples. Most did not last, we saw to that, and even a couple came around. When the line units did it, discipline was a major issue."

As if on cue, Jacob's name was called, and the three went over to where the new regimental recruits were standing. Ten men stood in two ragged lines, held in position by six men from the local provost. In charge was a sergeant, who saluted when Jacob arrived.

"Sir, we have been directed to provide you with these volunteers for the regiment. Do you acknowledge receipt?"

Jacob returned the sergeant's salute. "I acknowledge receipt and take charge of these men. You are dismissed to return to your duty."

Returning the salute, the sergeant turned and headed back into the city with his men. The ten men just stood there and stared at the three. All of them had different eyes as Jacob looked at everyone one of them. Some had depressed eyes, some had wild eyes, and one man had defiant eyes. Jacob approached him.

Standing before the defiant man, he gave Jacob a disgusted look and grumbled, "What are you looking at?"

Jacob snorted and stared back, "What were you in jail for?"

The man smirked, "Murder and highway robbery. It seems you all don't have enough men, and they have too many of us in jail, so they just cleared us all out. You can't change me, and I won't listen to no uptight landowner giving me orders. So you might as well just let me go as I will be nothing but trouble."

Then he smiled a big smile, though he had control of the situation. Jacob walloped him so fast that he never saw it coming. The impact caught the man in the jaw, crumbling to the ground, seeing stars flash before his eyes. Twisting, he hit the ground face-first and sprawled out. The other recruits were shocked and stood there, not moving.

Jean was about to move, but Samuel held his arm and kept him in place. "Don't interfere," Samuel commented quietly, "Jacob is showing who the Alpha Wolf in this pack is, and they had better listen."

Also observing was Marion, who chuckled to himself when he saw the blur of Jacob's arm and could hear the sound of the "smack" as the recruit was struck and fell to the ground. Captain Baker, who happened to be standing next to him, was shocked by what he saw.

"Don't worry," Marion answered the unasked question, "Captain Clarke, who, like myself, believes in discipline. He knows the direct way to get their attention with ruffians like that. I've seen him in action, though not by the book, is compelling.

"Yes, sir," Baker responded, "very effective and to the point."

"We have no choice," Marion grumbled, "if this is the riff-raff, we will be sent for recruits.

Jacob stood over the dazed recruit, who had rolled over and laid on the ground holding his chin. The other recruits looked nervously at one another. Jacob's face was a thundercloud. And they all knew another lightning bolt could come at any moment.

"You can't do that to me," the recruit said as he struggled to his feet, "you're an officer and a gentleman."

Once again, Jacob's arm flashed out and cracked the recruit on the other side, dropping him to the ground. Then Jacob knelt on the sprawled recruit and pulled his knife from within his coat, holding it against the recruit's throat.

In almost what could be considered a wolfish growl, Jacob replied, "I am an officer, but I am no gentleman."

He then looked up at the recruits staring back at him in shock, the knife not moving an inch from the fallen recruit.

"We have been told we must take you recruits; if I had my choice, I would let the lot of you rot in jails. Instead, I am charged with molding you into members of our regiment. We must work together, or we will all die, understand?"

The recruits looked at each other and nodded. Jacob stood and helped pull the fallen recruit to his feet. He continued without taking the recruit's eyes, "Know this, Lieutenant Colonel Marion is a strong believer in discipline, and he learned it from the British. We hold daily court-martials, and many men who failed to perform their duty have received their punishment with lashes. Do you understand?"

Again, the shocked recruits nodded their heads in understanding. Jacob took a deep breath and then nodded. "Sergeant Penny, Lieutenant Langy, see these recruits to the quartermaster and get them outfitted."

Herding them together, Samuel and Jean led the recruits over to the quartermaster, and Jacob watched them go. Shaking his head, if this is what the government would send them for recruits, how could they stand up to the British?

It won't be like it was back in 76," Jacob thought, then taking another deep breath, heading over to his barracks to get ready to train another set of recruits for the regiment.

***

Maclane sat in the corner of the Six Mile Wayfarer House tavern. As the locals considered him one of the regulars, he was ignored, which worked well for him. He was reading notes and dispatches from his network before sending his report to New York concerning the situation in South Carolina.

There was raucous laughter coming from the bar area, and Maclane looked up to see the tavern owner Lavinia Trout speaking with a waggoneer who was clanking his mug with hers. Maclane shook his head and mumbled "Poor bastard" to himself as he went back to reading his notes. That waggoneer may be the "Black Widow's" next victim, needing some more coin for her other activities.

A note from Little Harpe upcountry reported that he and his brother, Big Harpe, are getting restless and, unless something happens soon, may have to rob or kill something because Big Harpe's murderous tendency was becoming difficult to control.

Maclane placed the note on the table and thought. He had to admit, for once, they were following his instructions and staying out of sight for now. He had been told of the impending campaign, in which he was to release his brigands and bandits to sow chaos to keep the South Carolina government off balanced.

Picking up another note, it was from Richard Pearis, his spy in the South Carolina government. The message confirmed his suspicion that there was no love between the government and General Howe. Maclane had heard a new commander, and General Lincoln had been selected to assume command of the Southern Army. He also knew it would take time for this Lincoln to get here.

He dropped the dispatch on the table and thought, rubbing his chin as he looked around the tavern. He had another task, to confirm that Stuart had successfully brought the Cherokee and other Indian Nations as Allies so they could attack from the west. Unfortunately, though he had sent dispatches to John Stuart, he had not received anything back. Maclane dropped his hand from his face to the table, landing on the notes, shaking his head. He knew he couldn't leave his post to head up into the Cherokee lands, so he had to wait for a response.

"I hate waiting," he said to himself softly before hearing some more loud laughing. Looking over, it seemed the waggoneer had passed out from too much drink, and two of Lavinia's men supported the unconscious man. There were numerous comments: "These old waggoneers can't hold their drink!"

Shuddering, Maclane knew better. The Black Widow had struck, adept at using poisons she grew in her garden out back of the tavern. It was where she also buried all of these victims that fertilized her garden. After that, her men would see the wagon and its content, selling off the merchandise and the horses and wagon itself.

Once again, Maclane shook his head as the laughter continued within the tavern, most of the patrons not realizing the murder that just happened right under their noses.

"If this is how we must fight and win this war," Maclane thought, *"Have we become no better than they?"* He looked down at his tankard of ale and decided to push it away from him, not knowing if or when the Black Widow may come after him.

***

While the privateers were out, they had no significant impact on the Royal Navy. Instead, Mother Nature decided to give it a go. A massive winter storm barreled across the eastern seaboard and caught the British expedition on the open waters. The high winds and crashing waves pounded the fleet, scattering the ships to the four winds. Nevertheless, a small, ten-ship column was pushed towards the shore and could be seen from South Carolina.

A coast watcher spotted the ships, lit a warning fire that the other coast watchers picked up, and got the word to Charles Town. Word was being spread by horse messengers that the British were coming down the along the coast.

Jacob, Samuel, and Jean had joined a company doing a rotation at Fort Sullivan to escape the barracks. As they did before, they joined one of the shorthanded designated gun crews. They were discussing with one of the sergeants by the powder magazine when a rider came in the fort at a gallop. In a plume of dust, the rider skidded to a halt in front of the commander's hut. Soon the officer of the day came out and yelled for the duty drummer.

"Oh, this can't be good," Samuel and Jacob watched expectantly.

As they suspected, the drummer began beating the long roll, calling the men to arms. The duty officer, Captain Goodwin, yelled, "The British fleet has been spotted up the coast and heading this way to your posts!"

Jacob, Samuel with Jean in tow, headed to the left front corner of the defenses, operating a large thirty-pound cannon as they did back in '76. As they manned their guns, a rider was sent to the island's northern side to serve as an early warning.

Jacob and Samuel helped the crew pull the ropes and run the large gun out of the embrasure, while Jean helped get the shot. Once the guns were in position, the linstocks were lit and glowing; the crews waited for the coming battle. Then, as he did in the battle back in '76, Jacob climbed to the top of the northeast rampart, pulling out his telescope, and began looking for the ships.

In the city, the word of the approaching ships spread like wildfire; some residents ran to the harbor to watch the action, while others began packing to evacuate the city. Major General Howe, who was still in command, as General Lincoln had not arrived, dressed, hoping to bath himself in fame and glory so he could regain the support from Congress like he had before.

The sun had set, yet the men stayed at their guns. They had extinguished their linstocks to save what they had. Lanterns were brought out, and Samuel had gone to their quarters and returned with their blanket coats and furred caps. Jacob leaned on the gun, looking out to the cold, black sea. His breath curled as steam in the cold night as he breathed out.

"Almost as cold as up at Carillon, no?" Jean asked as he joined Jacob by the gun. Smiling, Jacob chuckled and shook his head.

"No, my friend, you should know much better it was much colder up there than here."

The two men laughed, able to laugh about it now when Samuel joined them with three steaming mugs of mulled wine. "What's so funny?"

"Jean asked if this was as cold as Carillion," Jacob answered as he took the warm mug.

Samuel started to sputter, "Cold as up there? Bloody Hell no! I thought I would never thaw out from all those scouting expeditions around Carillion. No sir, no way!"

Jacob raised his cup of steaming mulled wine, "To not being as cold as we used to be!" Three veterans from the north smiled and clinked their mugs together, giving Samuel a resounding "Hear, hear!"

The boredom began to set in, and the men on the ramparts had just about lost all interest in a fight when a rider came galloping through the gate, which recharged the men.

"The fleet was spotted; at least ten ships were seen moving south following the coast!" was shouted by the messenger. Then, everyone was back to their alert state, waiting for the command to be given.

"Easy lads," remarked Jacob to his men as he walked along the rampart behind the gun crews. Then there was a cry from the lookouts on top of the rampart, "Ship sighted lights on the horizon!"

Jacob stopped, moved up to one of the gun ports, and, having pulled out his telescope, began looking for the ships. The sun had not risen yet, though there was a faint pinkish glow to the east.

Sure enough, a black silhouette of a large, three-masted ship was seen, its stern lights helping to detect it. Jacob looked and then lowered his telescope. The ship was not moving towards them; it appeared to be heading out to sea away from them. Then, a second ship was seen, moving away from them and out to sea.

Captain Goodwin joined Jacob on the ramparts, and Jacob pointed out the enemy fleet was moving away. "It appears, sir," Jacob informed Goodwin, "we're not the target, and they're heading down the coast."

Captain Goodwin nodded, "Then it seems Georgia must be their new target, not us yet." Jacob nodded, slowly closing his telescope, wondering what the British were up to.

The report of the fleet passing Charles Town and continuing southward was enough for General Howe. "Inform General Moultrie," instructed General Howe to his orderly, "he is in command and to continue preparing the city's defenses. I will take some of the army to meet the British when they land and drive them back into the sea."

The word reached the barracks that General Howe had marched from the city. He was heading to Georgia with about a third of the army. He had the Third and the Fifth Regiments, supported by four guns from the Fourth Regiment, marching quickly to get ahead of the British so they could meet them when they landed. Jacob, Samuel, and Jean rotated back to the barracks with Captain Goodwin as a company from the 1st Regiment had relieved them.

General Moultrie began inspecting the city's defenses, knowing that eventually, the British would be back to try and take Charles Town. So he asked Jacob and Jean to accompany him as he headed north of the city to a place known as the "neck." It was a narrow part of the peninsula north of the city that could be defendable, with both rivers and swamps protecting the sides.

Standing on a slight rise, it was close to where Jacob had been part of the embarrassing duel between Middleton and

Grant, and Jacob started laughing to himself. Both Moultrie and Jean gave Jacob an odd look.

"Are you feeling well?" Moultrie asked; Jacob explained about the completely glossed-over duel, and the paper reported how "Grant had allowed Middleton live."

"I remember that story; it was right after the fight with the Cherokee. Now that makes more sense than what we read in the paper afterward. Moultrie even chuckled, having no love of Middleton, having been a company commander under him during that expedition.

They returned to the matter at hand, looking over the land. The three men looked over the terrain with experienced eyes, taking in every roll, defile, high grounds, and swampy areas. Moultrie pursed his lips, thinking deeply as he scanned.

"What do you think," Moultrie asked, "Could we hold off a major land attack by the British?"

Jacob looked over the terrain, deep in thought and after scratching his chin, nodded. "Yes, sir, I do."

Moultrie turned and gave Jacob a puzzled look as it was a quick answer. "Tell me your thoughts; what do you see that can help us?"

Jacob pointed his thumb over his shoulder at Jean, "He could probably tell you better than I, as he did more defenses than I. I was mostly on the attacking side of a siege."

Moultrie gave them both a puzzled look.

"Back in the last war, Jean here was on the opposite side, leading the French Partisans against the British and us," Jacob explained. "Jean gave us a good fight, taught us humility as he nearly defeated us in some actions and did in others. Kept Rogers on his toes."

Jean simply shrugged, "Especially at that fight back in 57, south of Carillon in the snow."

Jacob looked at Jean, "You mean the Battle on Snowshoes?"

Again, Jean just shrugged, "We didn't give it a name, only that we nearly bagged you all, especially Rogers. I have a souvenir; I have Rogers' coat and his orders promoting him to major."

Jacob's mind flashed back to that fateful and ugly battle. From the captured Ranger being tortured by the Ottawa to draw them out, they were nearly encircled and wiped out. Yet, they were able to escape and evade back to Fort William Henry under cover of darkness.

Shaking the thoughts from his head, Jacob continued the conversation at hand. "I was speaking back in the summer of 58."

Jean looked at Jacob, trying to recall the fight he was talking about, and then he remembered.

"Ah, Carillon! You are speaking of Carillon, no?"

Jacob nodded; Moultrie watched with amazement at the discussion between two former enemies, now working together. Then, finally, Jacob explained the action to General Moultrie.

"General Abercrombie, with a large force of British and Provincials, traveled to the north end of Lake George to attack the French Fort Carillon. We heavily outnumbered the French and had heavy artillery. There, they had built a defense of redoubts and a large abatis across the peninsula before the fort. We never made it up to the redoubt before the attack was crushed."

Moultrie nodded, then looked at Jean, "Was you there?'

Jean smiled and, with a modest nod, confirmed it had been. "I commanded the fight from within the redoubt."

Jacob's eyes grew wide as he looked at Jean, "That, was you? I thought it was the Marquis who was in command."

Jean shrugged, not showing any real emotion, "He was, but he was back in the fort; I was there with the men fighting at the redoubt. Those men with the bagpipes would not stop even though we shot them to pieces. They frightened us so, very determined, very brave."

Jacob had another flashback to the hot, horrible day. General Abercrombie gave no direction, the poorly coordinated attack and waste of good men. They kept attacking the abatis and being shot by the French musketry and cannon fire. The 42nd Highlanders, The Black Watch, continue to throw themselves into the abatis, hacking with axes and trying to get through.

Then the horrible screams as the dry wood of the abatis caught on fire, many of the wounded burning to death. Shaking his head, Jacob returned to the present. The sound and smell were etched in Jacob's memories from that day.

Jacob had mixed emotions, knowing that Jean may be responsible for the deaths of several of Jacob's friends and fellow Rangers. Then he shook his head as he wondered how many of Jean's friends he had killed.

Looking up, he could see Jean looking at him, understanding. "It is better to leave old wounds closed, no? What is in the past should stay in the past, and we look to a better future, oui?"

Taking a deep breath and letting it out, suppressing the rage that had started to build, Jacob smiled and nodded. Then, reaching out, Jean took Jacob's hand, and they shook, nodding. Moultrie seemed to give a slight sigh of relief.

Jean continued. "If we build good, strong defensive works anchored by the rivers and use abatis as we did at Carillon, we have a good chance of holding them."

"The only problem would be if they bring siege artillery," Jacob replied. "They won't have to close with the redoubts and abatis; they can sit back and throw heavy shot at us."

Moultrie nodded, then pointed out onto the rivers. "We could place our navy out on the rivers; cover the approach as we did on Sullivan's Island, just with more ships."

The three looked out over the terrain, visualizing in their own way what the defenses could look like. Then, all three began to nod their heads, having an idea about what could be done.

"We'll have to clear the fields of fire, use the trees for the abatis, but gentlemen, I think that we can do it," Moultrie commented, and both Jacob and Jean nodded in agreement. The construction began the next day as companies from the regiments were sent as work details to start clearing the land while the other guard duties and drill were conducted.

A messenger arrived, and word quickly spread across the city and in the barracks. General Howe had taken a beating and had been soundly defeated by the British. The civilians began preparing to evacuate while Moultrie and the rest of the army prepared for the British's eventual arrival. The South Carolina Government was wrestling with what they should do next.

General Howe returned with very few men, and Jacob watched the dejected men march into the city. A good portion of the army was missing.

"Do you think they were all killed or captured?" Samuel asked as he watched the survivors march by, all with that defeated look in their eyes.

Jacob slowly shook his head, "Probably lost most of them on the march back, deserting and heading home. Hard to say, though, but I do suspect desertion."

***

Brigadier General Augustine Prevost walked around his new headquarters in Savannah, a large, well-built manor house near the center. Even in this southern weather, his bones ached, and he was tired. Staring out of a large window and looking at the people moving along the street, General Prevost was considering retiring and letting one of his younger officers assume command.

While he had achieved General Clinton's desired objective, he had enough of this war. He had already sent a letter to General Clinton, requesting that he wished to resign, and the command passed to Lieutenant Colonel Campbell, Lieutenant Colonel Lewis Fuser, or even his younger brother, Major James Prevost.

"Sir, the commanders, are here," a voice said behind the general. Prevost turned to see one of the orderlies standing there. Nodding, he followed the orderly into a converted large room where they were planning the next stage of the campaign.

A large fire crackled at both ends of the room, and in the center was a large table covered in maps. Standing around the table were Lieutenant Colonel Campbell, Lieutenant Colonel Fuser, Major Gardiner, and Major Prevost. Their engineer Major Moncrieff and Captain Johnstone of the Royal Artillery were standing off to one side, chatting.

In another corner stood four Loyalist commanders who would be supporting the campaign. Lieutenant Colonel Allen, with his New Jersey Volunteers, Lieutenant Colonel Brown that he knew and his East Florida Rangers, Lieutenant Colonel Robinson and the South Carolina Royalists, Lieutenant Colonel Daniel McGirtt and his Georgia Light Dragoons.

They all stopped talking when the general entered and waited for him to begin. But instead, General Prevost centered himself on the table and looked at the map of the eastern seaboard of Georgia and South Carolina. Then, picking up a pointer, he nodded and began to explain his plan for the campaign's next step.

"Gentlemen, as we have secured the city as a base of operation, we can now work on our next objective, taking the City of Charles Town," Prevost began, circling the City of Savannah with the pointer, then drawing a line up the coast to Charles Town.

"Lieutenant Colonel Campbell, you will lead an expedition to secure Hudson's Ferry." Once again, he drew a line from Savannah to Hudson Ferry using his pointer. "Leave a detachment to secure the ferry, continue north, and take Augusta if feasible."

Prevost turned to face the Loyalist Lieutenant Colonel Brown.

"Colonel Brown, I will provide a detachment of light infantry and secure the crossing here at Briar's Creek with your Royalists." The pointer moved and circled again. "This will give us three crossing areas to move the army across when we invest in Charles Town."

"To support our initial movement and keep the rebels off balance, Major Gardiner and your 60th Regiment will make a landing on the coast of South Carolina, here at Bull's Island." The pointer circles Bulls Island, southwest of Charles Town.

"I will attach a company of light infantry from the 16th, and Captain Johnstone will provide howitzers to support." Then, Prevost looked directly at Gardiner, "This is strictly designed to be a feint to draw the new rebel commander, this Lincoln, I believe, to come towards you and not react to either Colonels Campbell's or Thompson's expeditions."

There was a moment of silence as Prevost thought; the other officers waited patiently. Then, nodding once more, Prevost looked to Gardiner. "If you feel you have superiority over the enemy and feel the risk is worth it, invest and take Port Royal as a base of operations against Charles Town."

General Prevost looked at the assembled officers, faces showing intent and a desire to take the field. "Any questions?"

There were none, "Then gentlemen, see to your commands and prepare to march in four days. Coordinate your activities and support when you can. Good hunting!"

General Prevost stood back as the commanders looked at the map and spoke amongst themselves as they used their fingers to draw routes, circle objectives, and look to the operation's future. As he scanned the room, he saw the face of the cavalry commander, McGirtt. However, his face was set differently than the other.

His face showed a fanaticism, a desire for revenge instead of serving King and Country, putting this rebellion down and restoring order. Prevost studied the man's eyes, hard, cold like the dead. Prevost recalled when his executive officer explained what Loyalists they had. This McGirtt had been one of those rebels who killed an officer and escaped to Georgia.

"While seeking revenge may be something we can use to recruit more Loyalists, is it the right way?" Prevost thought as he watched the planning. *"Can we rely on forces more interested in vengeance and blood instead of true loyalty? Clinton better approves my resignation, as I don't want any part of this if this is how we're going to fight."*

***

As December transitioned to January of 1779, General Lincoln finally arrived, and General Howe was relieved of his command and told to report to General Washington's headquarters in the north. With what the government thought was the impending attack against the city, the defenses took higher priority than drill or training. Most of the regiments, including the second, were digging earthen redoubts across the neck. Jacob, Jean, and Samuel helped with taking turns digging and organizing the redoubts and abatis.

Three new militia brigades were called up as scouts and sent south to keep an eye on the British. But, instead of coming north, they were consolidating their hold on Georgia. Victory after victory, remnants of the Georgia Continentals, militia, and even South Carolina survivors from the Howard expedition were flowing across the border into South Carolina.

General Moultrie was sent to Beaufort with a militia brigade under the command of General Bull, as word of the British army approaching the border of South Carolina frightened the government and city officials.

Fear was heightened when a rider galloped into the city and reported to the government that British movement was spotted coming up the coast. Governor Rutledge received the report, nodded, and looked at what few assemblymen were there.

"Gentlemen, I feel I have been sitting out long enough! It is time for action, and we'll see this matter firsthand by thunder! Send for General Lincoln at once." Rutledge instructed, "Go get me a map of the coast."

Sitting off to the side like he always does, Richard Pearis sat at his desk, keeping the assembly's journal and all the details to send back to Maclane.

Fifteen minutes later, General Lincoln arrived with his adjutant and approached Governor Rutledge.

"Sir, you asked for me?" Lincoln asked, and the governor nodded.

"Yes, the British are on the move, coming up the coast. We must stop them before they can close on Charles Town."

Rutledge showed the coast with his finger, circling the area near Beaufort. Lincoln looked down, then nodded.

"I am ordering General Stephan Bull with his militia brigade from here, and I will personally lead the Up Country Militia. I would also like some of your Continentals to have them ready to march by tomorrow."

Governor Rutledge stared directly at General Lincoln, waiting to see if he would refuse like the other Continental generals. But, while South Carolina does have its own Continentals, they belong to him as Governor-General, not to some northern general.

Lincoln looked at the map, thought for a few moments, and then nodded. "I'll dispatch General Moultrie to bring Continentals to support your expedition. I'll continue to monitor the development of the defenses here."

Rutledge was satisfied, primarily as Moultrie was assigned to the mission.

"If that is all," Lincoln concluded, "I'll send a runner to notify General Moultrie to be ready to march on the morrow."

Bowing to Governor Rutledge, General Lincoln departed and headed back to his command headquarters. He wrote the orders and sent a runner to General Moultrie.

"At least the governor will be out of my hair, and I can get down to business in shaping up this army and getting ready for the coming fight," Lincoln thought. Then, standing, he decided to go out and see how far the defenses had been completed.

General Moultrie received his orders and headed to the barracks, where Jacob was instructed to report to the orderly room. Samuel's eyes began twinkling as Jacob departed, and he started rubbing his hands together. Jean gave Samuel a strange look.

"Why do you do that?" Jean asked.

Samuel pointed at the orderly room, and Jacob headed towards it. "Because I feel we're going to see some action soon!"

Jean took off Samuel's hat to look at the bald spot, the remnants of the old scalping he survived. "I think they did more damage up there than just taking your hair."

Samuel grabbed his hat and placed it back on his head, "trust me, you'll see."

A few minutes later, Jacob returned, and Samuel beamed with a smug look at Jean by the happy expression on his face.

"We are to pack and report to General Moultrie," Jacob informed as he headed to his bunk area. "We are marching with him to Beaufort. It seems the British are on the move, and we are looking to stop them."

The three packed their backpacks with warm gear as it was the end of January, moving into February. Their roommates came in while packing, giving them a surprised look.

"I guess the rumors are true," Shubrick commented, "We heard a British expedition coming; are you heading out to face them?"

Jacob nodded as he cinched down his pack. "We'll be advising General Moultrie, who is leading an expedition with General Bull's Charles Town Militia Brigade, and even the governor is coming with the Up Country Militia."

The three roommates looked at them with envy but knew they had to stay behind with their companies. Jacob looked at them and understood how they felt, having been left behind on several operations.

"I hate to say this, lads," Jacob consoled, "Your time is coming for action soon, so make sure your companies are ready. But, to be so eager to meet death on the field, that time will come soon enough."

After they were packed, they headed to the quartermaster to get their horses, and then Jacob led them out of the city to where Moultrie had instructed them to meet. Just before the redoubts and near the second one being built behind the main line, they found Moultrie.

He spoke to his staff and turned when the three rode up. After talking to his staff officer, who mounted his horse and headed back to the city, Moultrie approached Jacob.

"Captain Clarke, remain here and receive the militia and artillery I have ordered to join us. They will arrive later today, so we can depart early in the morning to start on our way. Any questions?"

"Yes, sir, our role in this upcoming expedition?" Jacob asked.

Moultrie smiled. "I am steeling you from Marion for this one. You are to assist, advise, and be ready to assume command if needed. There may be a situation where I'll need experienced field officers to take charge."

Jacob nodded; he understood, and Moultrie mounted his horse and rode back towards the city. Then, moving over to a stack of barrels, Jacob, Samuel, and Jean made themselves comfortable as they waited for the first units to arrive.

"Do you think this is a wild goose chase, or are the British really coming?" Samuel asked.

Jacob shrugged, using a stick to draw designs in the dirt as he thought about it. Then looking up, "I don't know, Samuel, I really don't know. Of course, the British are there, and we know it makes strategic sense to take Charles Town, but if this is the main push, my gut is saying no."

Samuel nodded, satisfied with the answer. "Let me know when your gut tells you this is the big one."

Smiling, Jacob nodded, "I sure will, Samuel, I promise."

After an hour, the first companies of the Charles Town Militia arrived, followed by Brigadier General Bull himself and the Beaufort Company of Volunteers. "Is there we are to meet with General Moultrie?" General Bull asked, and Jacob responded he was.

The militia companies were commanded to rest and sat down on either side of the road. The men relaxed while waiting for the arrival of General Moultrie. It wasn't much longer when the sound of wooden wheels and jingle equipment when Moultrie led an element from the 4th South Carolina to move a 2-pound brass field piece with a horse.

General Bull had his militia assemble and, after a quick consultation with Moultrie, led the column out. Jacob, Samuel, and Jean mounted their horses and took a position behind the gun. The column moved all day until the sun went down when Moultrie called for a halt, and the column set up camp for the night.

Jacob, Jean, and Samuel helped set up pickets around the camp and worked with the militia company commanders for guard rotations. Once set, they went over to join Generals Moultrie and Bull sitting near a small fire. Moultrie looked up when the three arrived.

"Pickets all set?" Moultrie asked, and Jacob confirmed they were. "Well, find a comfortable place to sit and relax; we'll meet Governor Rutledge and his militia here at first light. Then we'll find a suitable defensive position to block whatever British column is coming this way."

"Bah, it's no column." Grunted General Bull as he tamped down his pipe, "Probably more of those thieving raiding parties coming to steal cattle." Then, taking a burning stick from the fire, he lights his pipe, blowing a stream of smoke. "Won't be much of a fight."

General Moultrie looked into the fire and shrugged his shoulders. "We don't have much information, only that British are coming this way. I hope it is a simple raiding party. We're not ready to defend Charles Town yet; we're just not ready."

***

The sound of whistling balls flew past the section of running light infantry as they moved to get into better firing positions against the rebel militia. Having landed his force on Hilton Head Island, Major Gardiner was now moving inland when they ran into two houses with militiamen garrisoning them. The 60th Regiment was sweeping around the other side to catch the houses in a crossfire. If that doesn't work, he could always roll up the howitzer and blast them out.

Once the light infantry and the 60th were in position, they took the two houses under heavy fire. It was effective as the sound of the militia returning fire slackened until one of the flanking light infantry shouted, "They're running out the back!"

Nodding, Major Gardiner gave the order, "Light torches, burn those two houses down! This is a way to start if the general wants us to draw attention." Once both houses were fully blazing, Major Gardiner moved the column inland, following the road towards Port Royal Island. The naval vessels supporting the landing continued to sail up the broad river to anchor and take a supporting position across from one of the large plantations.

When Major Gardiner arrived near some of the large homes where the owners had evacuated, he ordered Captain Murray to take a detachment, burn these homes, and meet back up with the expedition near Port Royal.

"Hopefully, this Lincoln is getting the message we're sending," remarked Gardiner to Major Graham of the light infantry from the 16th.

"We burn enough of these rebel plantations, sir; should make this General Lincoln pay attention."

As the column approached the location of Port Royal, they could hear musketry and rifle fire in the distance. In a large mansion, unknown people were shooting at the British brig anchored in the river. Major Gardiner pulled out his telescope and could see that the shooting from the estate was more harassment than causing any actual harm.

"We'll camp here and see what develops in the morning," Gardiner commanded, and the expedition made camp. Captain Murray arrived with two captured slaves as the men were cooking their rations.

"Sir, as we were about to put to the torch, a mansion we later found belonged to a rebel named Captain Thomas Heyword attempted to stop us. First, they demanded we go away from a distance, then opened fire. They caused no harm, mounted their horses, and rode away. We placed the mansion to the torch."

Major Gardiner nodded, then pointed to the two captured slaves. "And these two?"

"These are two of Heyward's slaves. They attempted to ambush us, but our advance guard easily noticed them, and we could quickly overtake them and secure their muskets before they could fire."

Major Gardiner asked, "How many mansions or homes did you burn afterward."

"We burned two larger plantation homes and six smaller homes before we began our march here."

"Good job, captain, see these prisoners are secured and see to your men." The captain nodded, then turned and escorted the prisoners away. He stood and walked to the edge of the camp, looking at the mansion in the distance. Major Gardiner thought about how he would handle the following morning and settled on the plan.

"Captain George, take the longboat and row out to the brig. Inform them that we plan on a morning assault. Then, the brig will open fire on that plantation as soon as the sun rises."

The captain took the message and, with some sailors, rowed out to the brig, *Lord George Germaine*. Major Gardiner finalized the plan in his head and got some rest before the morning. The only action was the shooting between the mansion and the brig, so Gardiner slept easily.

In the morning, the expedition was up and formed, Major Gardiner waiting for the sun to rise. The brig opened fire on the mansion as soon as the sun crested over the world's edge. Soon the guns were booming, and the balls screamed across to smash through large windows and pound the walls.

Drawing his sword, Major Gardiner gave the command to fix bayonets. Once the bayonets were ready, Gardiner gave the order to form a column, with the lights in front, followed by the 60th, then the howitzer. Once everyone was in the column, Gardiner raised his sword, "To the front, march!"

As the column exited the woods, Gardiner deployed the light infantry to his right, the 60th to the left. Supporting, he deployed the howitzer in the center. He ensured they were more to the flank to avoid the naval gunfire. A few muskets were fired at them from a second-floor window, but they were ineffective.

Once the expedition was in line, Gardiner raised his sword and yelled "Charge!" the trot, the British flowed around the mansion, the brig ceasing fire when they saw the charge go in. What few militiamen who had been in the estate fled out the back door, and the light infantry was sent in pursuit.

Major Gardiner entered the large mansion as elements of the 60th ensured no other militiamen were in the building. It was a well-built house, nicely furnished, though now there were splinters and broken plaster from the brig's cannon shot. He went over to look at a large painting of a distinguished-looking man. There was a brass nameplate that read "Stephan Bull, Esquire."

Once the area was secured, the men moved the furniture outside the mansion, except for the billiard table that Gardiner would use for his maps. They found a well-stocked wine cellar of several hundred bottles of wine and liquors.

"See that the man get all of the ale, send the wine to the men on the brig; the rest will be us for later this evening," Gardiner instructed, and the sergeants quickly saw the distribution to the pleased men. Then, as the men celebrated their advancement into South Carolina, Gardiner held a council of war to determine their next move.

"Gentlemen, a toast to our victory so far!" he said, raising a bottle, and the assembled officers raised theirs. Then, once everyone was paying attention to him, Major Gardiner began.

"Gentlemen, based on what little to no resistance we have faced since we landed and the orders from General Prevost, we will coordinate our attack with the navy and invest in Port Royal."

He looked around the room and was surprised that not everyone was smiling. Instead, Major Graham of the light infantry was shaking his head. "Your thoughts Major Graham?"

"Sir, we've been lucky so far," Major Graham explained, "We have no idea where their main army is, and we truly do not fully know the town's defenses. So we could be walking into a trap or larger force that could jeopardize our mission."

Major Gardiner shrugged and nodded, then asked, "Anyone else have reservations about attacking Port Royal?"

Lieutenant Mowbry, one of the gunners for the howitzer, raised his hand. "Sir, do we even know if they have fortifications or not? Our one howitzer only has so much shot."

Again, Major Gardiner nodded, then looked up. "Gentlemen, I appreciate your advice, but we will attack Port Royal. If we need more artillery support, then the navy will supply it. I do not believe there is any real threat other than another small company of these local militiamen. We depart tomorrow."

The officers murmured and talked amongst themselves. "Sir, what of this mansion when we leave in the morning?" asked Captain Mowbray.

Major Gardiner looked at him and stated, "Burn it."

***

After an uneventful evening, in the early morning, the militia was packed and formed up, and in the distance, the sound of marching and the sound of rolling wheels could be heard approaching. Then, finally, Governor Rutledge arrived with his Up Country Militia and two 6-pound cannons pulled by teams of oxen. Both generals saluted when the governor arrived.

"General Moultrie, you will remain in overall command; I'll remain with the Up Country Militia. General Bull, your militia will lead out."

Both officers saluted, and orders were issued. The companies were formed for the march, and once ready, Bull led his men forward. Moultrie waited for them to pass and rode with the governor, while Jacob, Samuel, and Jean rode in the rear with the cannons.

Samuel looked at the 6-pound cannon and nodded with approval. He always had a fondness for big guns that fire many projectiles. "Do you think they'll let me help crew one of those? Samuel asked, and Jacob shrugged.

"As General Moultrie said, we here advise and assist, and if asked, assume command of an element. Well, those guns are an element, so maybe." Samuel smiled with the response, and Jacob simply shook his head.

As the column approached the Port Royal area, the column halted, and the men were told to take a rest break off to the side, followed by "Officers to the front" passed down the line. Jean and Samuel looked at Jacob, who shrugged, then trotted forward. When they arrived at the front, Generals Moultrie and Bull were there, along with the governor and several black men and women.

"Thomas, what happened? Why are you all here?" General Bull asked one of the black men, part of the group consisting of six men and three women with two children.

"The British came, sir; we couldn't stop them. We could see the smoke in the distance, knew they would come."

Bull looked at the man with a very concerned look.

"General Bull, who is this? What is saying about the British?" Governor Rutledge asked.

"This is Thomas, one of my field hands from my plantation," Bull explained, "Go on, Thomas, what else happened?"

"Well, sir," Thomas continued, holding his hat in his hands, "we hid in the backfield, watched them British ships anchor out in the river. Then some militia men came running up the road and went into the house, shooting at the ship."

Bull nodded, "Go on."

"We stayed hidden until the sun came up, then the British came in their redcoats, and the ship shoot big guns at the house. The British came out of the woods, walked in a line, and attacked the house. The militiamen ran away, and the British chased them."

Bull took a deep sigh and nodded his head. "Anything else?"

"Yes, sir, the British entered the house, took out all the furniture, and piled it up outside. We stayed hidden and watched. They took all the bottles from the cellar and gave them away to all the soldiers."

"All of them?" Bull asked, and Thomas nodded. Then, after a few moments, Bull asked in a quiet voice, "Did they burn it?" Thomas nodded his head.

"Yes, sir, in the morning. They set the main house, cook house, and even our houses on fire. Everything was burning." There were tears in Thomas' eyes.

Bull nodded. "Thomas, take these hands over to the Petersons; stay with them." Thomas nodded, placed his hat on, then led the group down the road through the column and back up the road. General Bull's face was a thundercloud, his hands shaking as he stared into the distance, trying to see his house from afar.

Instead, a group of riders came into view and began trotting towards the head of the column. The lead platoon quickly came to their feet, muskets at the ready. Governor Rutledge waved them down, "Easy lads, easy. I know them. That's Thomas Heyward and his boys."

The three rode up and nodded to the assembled commanders. "Governor, you are a sight for sore eyes!"

"I take it you had a run-in with the British?" he asked, and Heyward nodded.

"We tried to convince them there was no need to burn our place, and it had nothing of any importance. They wouldn't listen; as they put it, we are rebels and will be treated as criminals for going against the King. The punishment for treason is confiscation of all personal property. So instead, they put my place to the torch."

Rutledge nodded. "We off to see to this matter; you're welcome to join if you like."

Heyward sat straight in his saddle, "Sir, Captain Heyward, and sons report for duty!"

Rutledge smiled and pointed to one of the militia companies before turning to General Bull and Moultrie.

"Well, at least we confirmed it is not a wild goose chase; we better push on and get to Port Royal ahead of them, or we could lose the port."

The column reformed; Jacob, Samuel, and Jean waited for the column's rear to march by before retaking their place behind the cannons. After that, the column moved quicker. Some men were eager for action, some for revenge after hearing that homes were burned. It was going to be a race to see who could get to Port Royal first.

***

Major Gardiner stepped out of the longboat onto the shore as the navy transported them quicker down the river and safer from rebel ambushes. After he came ashore, Captain Murray was waiting for him.

"Sir, permission to take a section over to the Pocotaligo Bridge. We learned that these rebels have a hospital with over three hundred sick people. So we could bag the whole lot of them without much of a fight."

Gardiner thought for a moment, then shook his head. "Captain Murray, I applaud your initiative, but we must take Port Royal; that is more important than some sick rebel prisoners. Moreover, that port is capable of an anchorage for ships of the line, a need for taking Charles Town. Besides, what is the sickness at this hospital? We need not bring sickness into this army to prevent our objective."

Captain Murray nodded, understanding the more significant, bigger picture of the expedition than just capturing some six prisoners. He stood with the major and watched as the rest of the troops came ashore. They only landed the three light infantry companies plus one of the howitzers, which was manhandled onto the shore.

Once everyone was ashore and organized, Gardiner gave the order to march, and the column started towards Port Royal. They had only gone two miles when the "Cavalry!" call was sent back from the front of the column. Gardiner quickly ordered the other two companies from either side of the lead company and to have the howitzer rolled up.

As Gardiner and Murray reached the front to see what they were facing, a mounted force of militia cavalry had stopped and raised their muskets. The horsemen fired, turned, and rode into the woods, then another section of cavalry rode out a different area of the woods and fired.

The light infantry deployed into open order and advanced towards the skirmishing cavalry, whose musket balls only whistled by, not striking any advancing infantry. Gardiner ordered the howitzer up and to commence fire on the cavalry. "That should change their minds about skirmishing with us!"

After being loaded, the howitzer barked, a smoke ring flowing up and out as the shot rose and then crashed down on the woods near where the cavalry had been riding out from. Then, Relading quickly, the howitzer barked again, along with the crash of musketry from the light infantry.

As Major Gardiner had predicted, the cavalry faded into the woods and stopped their small skirmishing action. The column reformed, except now he formed them into small platoon elements and continued their march.

Major Gardiner, with Captain Murray and Captain Bruere, rode from the center, a smile on Gardiner's face. "Well, that was a nice way to start the day," he remarked, and the two captains nodded, "it's a start to a nice day."

***

There was a loud explosion in the distance, Jacob listening intently for the sound of musketry in the distance. "What was that?" Samuel asked.

Jacob shook his head, "I don't know, but we'll know soon enough!"

The column kept up the quick pace, and soon the road broke out of the road into an open area, and in the distance was both a large black column of smoke and the Town of Port Royal. Then, finally, the column stopped, and Jacob with Jean and Samuel rode to the front.

Moultrie and Rutledge were already there, along with General Bull. They had their telescopes out, looking to see if the British were there.

Jacob pulled out his telescope and focused on where the column of smoke was coming from. It was coming from the middle of a fort near the town.

"Sir, it appears that fort is on fire," Jacob reported, and the other telescopes looked over.

"Fort Lyttleton," General Bull remarked in a melancholy tone. "Someone just blew the powder magazine."

"Men are approaching," Samuel stated as a group of men wearing Continental uniforms walked towards them. When they arrived, they were shocked to see the column sitting, and even more so, that Generals Moultrie, Bull, and Governor Rutledge were standing there.

Leading the group of twenty men, a captain who once saw Moultrie quickly approached and saluted.

"Sir, Captain Treville reporting!"

"Captain, could you explain why the fort is on fire?" Moultrie asked with an edge in his voice.

"Well, sir, we learned the British are coming and in a good size force. We also learned they had naval support as well. But, unfortunately, we didn't have enough men to hold against such a large force." Treville explained, turning and showing the size of his unit.

"Go on," Moultrie pressed.

"We didn't want the fort to fall into enemy hands, so we spiked the guns and blew the powder so neither would be used against us."

It seemed to have satisfied Moultrie, who asked, "Are they here? Have the British arrived?"

"No sir, not yet, but a militia cavalry unit rode through, said they skirmished with a British column near Roupelles Ferry. They're coming, sir, and they'll be here soon."

"Thank you, captain, join the column," Moultrie commanded as he looked out over the terrain before him.

"Well, gentlemen, it seems we have won this race; now we must be ready to receive our British friends warmly." So Moultrie stated as he looked for infantry and artillery positions. He turned and looked at Jacob, Samuel, and Jean. "Come with me; let's find a good place to fight," Moultrie instructed, then turned to Bull, "Get the men ready for action!"

As the four rode towards the town, General Bull, with a very determined look, began issuing orders to prepare for action, check muskets, and prime and load. As they rode closer, there was a decent wooded area off to one side of the open field, then the town itself, which could protect their flanks.

They stopped just before the town, near where the fort was burning, with a snapping and crackling sound coming from inside. As they were looking, three militia cavalrymen came galloping out of the woods, and when they saw Moultrie and Jacob, they rode directly over and skidded to a halt.

"General sir, the British are only about five miles out," the lead rider stated as he pointed over his shoulder from where they rode, "If you're going to do something, you better do it now!"

The rider nodded, and the three rode toward where the column was waiting. Moultrie quickly scanned the area and took a deep breath before letting it out. "Well, we may have won the race, but we didn't buy much time. What do you think, Jacob?"

Jacob quickly scanned the terrain. "Sir, I would use the woods for cover, have the artillery cover the open area where their shot would cause more harm."

Moultrie nodded, "Makes sense." He turned his horse and headed back to the column, with Jacob, Jean, and Samuel behind.

When they stopped before the column, Moultrie began shouting out orders.

"Captain Clarke, take this advance company and move towards the wood line. General Bull, deploy your men into line here and advance behind Captain Clarke. Position the 6-pounders here on the road; the brass cannon will advance with you, General Bull. Governor Rutledge, you will support General Bull from his right. We will advance until we contact the British and give them a warm welcome to South Carolina!"

The men cheered and quickly moved into action. First, Jacob, Jean, and Samuel dismounted from their horses and handed them to one of the Heyward boys. Then, with their rifles at the ready, Jacob moved to the front of the advance company and gave the signal to advance. As they advanced, General Bull began forming his line on the left side, Governor Rutledge on the left, and the two 6-pounders rolled into positions on the road as the oxen team detached and headed to safety.

With Jacob leading from the front, jean on the left, and Samuel on the right of the company, they extended the lines into open order so they could move easier through the trees. When they entered the trees, they quickly found the ground was swampy and wet, slowing their movement. Using his hands to single for slowing, the company slowly pressed forward.

As in the past, Jacob's gut warned him that an enemy was nearby. Raising his hand to halt, the company stopped and slowly sank to a knee. In the distance, there was a soft sound of feet crunching through trees and down limbs. Once more, using his hands, Jacob motioned for the men to find trees to get behind and get ready.

Bringing his rifle up to his shoulder, in the distance, he saw a quick flash of metal as the sun reflected off of something shiny. Then, a line of redcoats could be seen coming through the woods. Jacob knew they had lost the advantage, the British had the woods, and the militia would have to fight out in the open, which would place them at a disadvantage unless he could buy some time.

While holding his rifle into his shoulder, Jacob motioned with his right hand a "finger in the trigger" motion, which Samuel understood. He whispered, "get ready; we shoot when we see them!" It was passed down the line; the men were now anxiously waiting. They wouldn't have to wait long.

Jacob waited until he could see the white leather straps of their cartridge boxes and their faces before pulling the trigger on his rifle. Immediately after he fired, the rest of the company opened fire and caught the advancing British light infantry by surprise. As the woods filled with the grey smoke of the volley, Jacob led the company out of the woods while the British retreated from the unknown contact.

Having heard the fire, the line had held its position. The two 6-pound cannons in the center and the 2-pound brass gun on the right were in support. Jacob led them out of the woods, and they ran across the front and rejoined General Bull's line while Jacob went to report on what they had seen.

"Sir, the British were already in the woods and had the advantage, so we welcomed them for you," Jacob explained. Moultrie nodded and smiled.

"Thank you, Captain Clarke; let's see what happens next."

After a short while, the British appeared. They were advancing through the woods in open order and stopping on the opposite side of the field. A small howitzer rolled out and was placed in their center. General Moultrie watched and waited to see what the next move would be, as the British stopped moving once they were deployed.

Jacob, Samuel, and Jean stood behind the 6-pounders, having checked on their horses. Captain Heyward had assumed command of the battery, with Edward Rutledge on one of the guns. Heyward turned and looked at Jacob, "Do you know how to be a gun captain?"

Jacob smiled, "Yes, sir, I have done it on a few occasions."

Heyward pointed to the other 6-pounder, "She's yours then; make your shots count."

Nodding, they went over and joined the crew. The linstock was lit and glowing. Samuel and Jean went to the ammunition box and counted the number of rounds they had.

"Jacob, we have only 20 rounds!" Samuel called, and Jacob nodded. There was some commotion, and Jacob walked up to the gun and, taking out his telescope, saw a British officer advancing under a white handkerchief. One of the militia officers rode out.

The two met in the middle and discussed; having said whatever was to be said, the two officers returned to their lines. "What do you think that was all about?" Samuel asked.

"A parlay, we probably demanded their surrender; they refused and demanded our surrender," Jacob explained.

"How do you know it was refused?" That was answered by the British howitzer booming. The ball came screeching over and bounced just before the 6-pounders, rolling between them. Unfortunately, a lieutenant was standing up after getting a round ready and was promptly cut in half by the bouncing shot.

"Load solid shot!" Jacob commanded, then turned to Jean, "Take that lieutenant's place." As the gun crew went through the loading procedures, the order for the entire line to advance was given. Accordingly, both Bull's and Rutledge's lines advanced toward the British.

As the lines were going forward, Jacob looked over the top of the gun, aiming at the British howitzer. "Samuel, make sure the line doesn't mask us!" Samuel nodded and kept an eye on the lines moving forward, keeping their line of fire clear.

Satisfied the gun was ready, Jacob raised his sword, followed by Edward, who raised his sword. Nodding, Heyward gave the command of "Give, fire!" Jacob dropped his sword, and the cannon boomed with a thunderous roar. Watching intently, their shot flew high and tore through a tree behind the howitzer.

"Load solid shot" was given by Jacob, then as he looked over the barrel. He adjusted the elevation of the gun tube, so it was lower. He was looking at the howitzer, making it his target. Once the gun was ready, Jacob raised his sword and looked at Heyward. Once both guns were ready, Heyward gave the command, and both guns went off nearly simultaneously.

The sound was deafening as both cannons roared. They were rewarded when their round struck the howitzer near one of the wheels, disabling the gun and killing two gunners. Finally, they could see what appeared to be a sailor running away, carrying the linstock with him.

The gun crew cheered, with Heyward yelling, "Great Shot!" Jacob took it in stride, knowing the battle wasn't over yet. The men went back to loading the gun for the next shot.

"I don't think this is a raid for oxen, no?" Jean asked, and Samuel yelled back, "No, it sure doesn't look like a simple raid!"

The two lines of infantry began exchanging fire with one another. The British advanced to the edge of the woodline, and Moultrie moved their line closer now that the howitzer had been put out of action.

Jacob looked over the barrel once more, now elevating it for the shot to hit the trees and cause the deadly splinters to fly and the ball to bounce as he had seen in naval action. Both 6-pounders continued to bark, and even the small 2-pounder on their right could be heard firing in anger.

The battle see-sawed across the field, each line attempting to turn the flank of the other. Then, as Jacob looked over the gun barrel, he saw British forming to charge the battery.

"Load with grape!" Jacob commanded, and one of the gunners replied, "She already has a ball, sir!"

"Load grape on top; we'll give them a double charge!" Jacob spun the elevation to lower the tube just as the British charged from the trees and began running at the battery. Heyward spotted the charge, "Prepare to repel assault!" he commanded, pointing with his sword.

The infantry on either side of the battery took up supporting fire, blasting volleys into the British column as they charged forward, gleaming bayonets leading them into the fray. Jacob watched and waited for the right opportunity to make the shot count, knowing it could break their charge if done right.

"Easy lads, hold. Wait for the command," Jacob instructed. Heyward saw what Jacob was doing and did the same. Both 6-pounders were loaded and ready, allowing the British to close the distance. They were not firing, relying on the bayonet to win. The space closed, fifty; forty; thirty yards. The British yelled as they approached, becoming louder and louder. Finally, they were close enough to pick out details on their red uniforms.

"Fire!"

The command was barked, and both 6-pounders once again nearly fired at the same time. The fact that Jacob had loaded both grape and ball had a very telling effect as the British fell like bowling pins before they fell. A good numbered of the British lay in a heap; some were stagging, holding their wounds, and then falling. In either case, their charge was broken, and they returned to their lines.

The fighting was starting to slow, as both sides could not take advantage of the other, and ammunition was beginning to get low. Fearing that due to the low shot, Moultrie came riding over and ordered the 6-pounders off the field. But, as the oxen wouldn't come onto the field. So Jacob, along with the gun crews and some of the infantry who had run out of cartridges, pulled the guns behind the line and backed up the road.

The infantry covered the guns as they were pulled off, and it seemed the British were holding their line and not advancing. The sun was sinking, and that could have played a role in why the fighting was coming to an end.

"They must be short on cartridges as well," Jean commented, listening to the eerie silence of the battlefield, "or they would be taking advantage of us pulling these guns off."

"I think you're right, Jean; we both must be low on cartridges or even out," Jacob commented. Then he snickered. "We held them to a stalemate. We can't push them off the field, and they can't push us off. So neither can spend the night to start the fight the next day."

"Over what?" Samuel asked as he looked over his shoulder, "Continue the fight over Port Royal?"

Jacob shrugged. "We know it's good for shipping; it could be a base of operations for campaigns down here."

"Maybe the commander underestimated us," Jean added, "As you say, bit off more than he could chew, no?"

In the distance, they could hear the British give three cheers as they continued to pull the guns to where the oxen waited. The three turned to look back down the road where the battle took place and could see the head of the column marching their way.

Jacob thought as he helped hitch the gun to a cassion, then stood to look as General Bull led his column up to the guns.

"This is not the end, but only the beginning," Jacob replied, "I fear this is but a taste of yet to come."

CHAPTER 4

HOLD THE LINE

General Moultrie led the column back to Charles Town, and the men headed off to their respective barracks. News arrived that Augusta in Georgia had fallen, and now the colony was entirely under British control.

The militia units watching the British reported that they were still taking positions along the Savannah River but not moving. Then, finally, the threat of the British crossing into South Carolina seemed to have inspired some of the men and volunteers to join up, and local militia units began arriving. After Howard's disastrous expeditions, the Third and Fifth Regiments needed to fill their decimated ranks.

General Lincoln desired to deploy forces along their side of the river to observe what the British were doing and, if possible, prevent them from crossing into South Carolina. Disgusted that Howard wasted a good third of his army, Lincoln was pressed to get his ranks filled and ready if they had to meet the British on the field. To do so, he needed to see what caliber of men he had in his army.

Word was sent to the barracks that General Lincoln was coming to inspect the regiment, and the men and officers were forming in preparation. General Lincoln and his staff rode up, the general dismounted as the fifes and drums rendered honors, and the regiment was given the command to present arms. Their battle-won red and blue silken colors were dipped in salute, and the general returned Marion's salute.

After the command of order arms, Marion escorted Lincoln along the line of men; Lincoln asked Marion about the regiment's disposition of working muskets, how many of the men were in the hospital, and the overall condition of the unit. As Lincoln turned the corner of the middle company, he spotted Jacob, Jean, and Samuel standing with the staff behind the regiment. There was recognition in Lincoln's eyes, and he approached Jacob.

As General Lincoln approached, the staff came to attention. He stopped in front of Jacob and looked at Jacob intently.

"Do we know one another, sir?" General Lincoln asked as he stopped in front of Jacob.

"Yes, sir," Jacob answered, "Sergeant Penny here, along with myself and my Rangers, saved your life in Massachusetts."

General Lincoln paused, recalling the event, his eyes growing wide when he recognized Jacob, then reached out to shake Jacob's hand.

"My word, what a small world! It is nice to see you again, and down here, no less. We must get together and get caught up when time permits," rambled Lincoln, who then turned to Marion.

"You have a good man here; I can attest to that," commented General Lincoln, to which Marion nodded his head in agreement.

"Yes, sir, I can vouch for Captain Clarke here as one of my most trustworthy men of the regiment. You need something done; you call on Captain Clarke."

General Lincoln nodded his understanding and patted Jacob on the arm before moving on down the line of assembled men. After the regiment had been dismissed and General Lincoln moved off, Samuel turned to Jacob and asked, "Is that who I think it was, that jackass Lieutenant from Massachusetts that nearly had his head blown off had it not been for you?"

Jacob nodded and replied, "The very same, except now he is our commanding general."

Samuel shook his head, "This doesn't bode well for us."

After the inspection, many of the regiment's men asked Jacob where he knew the general from, to which he gave them the story of how a young Lieutenant Lincoln had tried to stop a bandit and his men in Massachusetts when he was a Ranger. His Rangers saved his life when the bandit turned on Lincoln, shooting his horse which pinned Lincoln's leg under its dead body.

Jacob and his Rangers had arrived just in time to stop the bandits from shooting the young lieutenant and saving his life, along with bringing the bandit to justice. Soon this tale began to spread around the regiment's company concerning Jacob and his personal experience with their new commanding general.

The neck was cleared, and a line of breastworks, gabions, and fascines was built across the entire width of land north of the city. Redoubts with gun positions were constructed into the breastwork in the line's three locations, left, center and right. In addition, a second redoubt was started behind the line as the initial base for the second line of defense.

Jacob, Jean, and Samuel walked the defenses, providing pointers or helping out where they could.

"Well, at least we're doing this when it's cooler," Samuel replied as they viewed out into the open killing ground before the defenses, "and the mosquitoes haven't come out yet."

More bad news arrived, the Georgia Continentals and Militia, having reconstituted in South Carolina, had tried to retake the City of Augusta. Instead, the Georgia Continentals had been lured into a well-planned, well-placed ambush and destroyed as a force. Survivors trickled back into South Carolina and limped to Charles Town.

As they worked on the defenses, the men dug harder and worked faster, and the defenses were forming well. Jacob assumed that fear must be motivating them, perhaps the fear for their families; if they didn't stop the British, their families were in danger. The Loyalists would seek vengeance and, with the British backing them, go after everyone who supported the cause of Liberty.

***

Maclane sat in the tavern's back room in the corner, waiting for his brigands and bandits to arrive so he could give them their new instructions. He also made contact with his real Loyalsist that did their duty more for King and country than coin and country.

Two of these Loyalists, George Fuller and Nathanial Harrison, had arrived and sat at a table, speaking quietly to each other. Mary Frith sat in the opposite corner, dressed in man's clothing as she always does.

The door opened, and both Edmond Ellis and David Friday entered, Maclane smiling as they nodded to him and joined George and Nathanial at their table. Then there was loud talking and laughing, and soon the door opened, and Big Harpe and his brother Little Harpe entered, with Big Harpe's women Susan and Betty.

"What are they doing here?" Maclane asked, and Big Harpe looked at the girls and back at Maclane.

"They're joining the family business," he replied in a rumbling voice, "and from what we have heard, business is going to be booming soon."

Maclane shrugged and knew it was pointless to argue with Big Harpe, as it was like arguing with a stump.

The Harpes sat at their table, the girls on either side of Big Harpe, and he bellowed for "Ale!" through the closed door. After a short wait, serving girls arrived with mugs of ale.

"I had them prepared for this meeting," Big Harpe answered with a smirk, "thought some celebrating was in order."

***

As the warm spring sun bathed the countryside of South Carolina, it also saw the return of hostile activities in the upcountry and along the Georgia Border. But, as Jacob and the other men sat in their barracks room, going over the news filtering down meant only one thing. The next phase of what Jacob believed was England's grand strategy focused on them. Charles Town must be the next objective of their campaign, having secured Georgia.

"What is on your mind Jacob," Samuel asked, "it seems you are looking into the future."

The conversations stopped, and they all looked to Jacob, for what he said was true.

Jacob shrugged, then looked at them all. "To be honest, I think we're next. All of these stories we hear from upcountry and along the border. I believe it is intended to draw our attention away from the city."

The men thought on it and nodded their heads. "Do you think General Lincoln will fall for it, take the army to go chase ghosts?" Shubrick asked.

Letting out a sigh, Jacob nodded his head. "He is headstrong enough, and I hope he takes a small force to the upcountry, and not all of us. That would leave the city unprotected."

"What about from the sea," Jean asked, "They were looking at Port Royal, and they have done it before; why not?"

The men thought on it for a few moments, neither coming up with a good answer. "Perhaps they had failed before and didn't want to repeat a mistake," answered Shubrick.

Jacob started to shake his head. "No, I think it will be a combined operation, splitting our attention in different directions, preying on the people's fear."

"Why do you say that?" Samuel asked.

Jacob smiled quickly as some of the pieces started falling into place.

"Look at what we just saw down near Port Royal. Why burn all those plantations and homes, other than drawing our attention to them, especially the rich land owners whose homes just went up in smoke."

Jacob held his left arm out, waving his hands. "So look here, look here! I am burning your homes on the coast."

Then he held his right arm up, waving that hand. "Look here, look here! We are running wild, causing chaos, killing, and looting."

Then Jacob looked at the men staring back at him. "So, what do we have?"

Samuel thought about it before looking up, "if we send out troops to these areas, we're splitting and dividing the army."

Jacob nodded, then Jean followed up, "Divide and conquer."

Smiling, Jacob nodded. "Divide and conquer. Together we can stand and fight, hold the line. If we're divided, we'll fall due to their numbers. Basic military strategy."

***

General Lincoln disliked waiting to be shown into the assembly hall, where he had to explain his plan to the Governor. "*Doesn't this man realize we have a crisis here,"* he fumed as he paced before the closed door. His three staff officers sat quietly by, waiting. Soon the door opened, and the officers were shown in.

Governor Rutledge was there, discussing some issues with a small group of the assemblymen, when General Lincoln approached.

"Ah, general, so good to see you," Rutledge bowed to Lincoln, "I was told you are here to present an idea for a campaign?"

Lincoln nodded, "Yes, governor, I would like to lead an expedition to retake Augusta in Georgia, then once secured, head south to invest in Savannah."

Sitting in his corner, not drawing any attention, the scribe Richard Pearis listened more intently to gather as much information he could to pass on to the British.

"Why Augusta," Rutledges asked, "Have you learned any specific details that would support a military operation? Last reports we had that it was firmly under British control."

"As you may not be much of a military man, I have learned that small Georgia Continental and Militia groups are striking against British outposts around Augusta. In addition, most of our border watchers report a good number of British units on the border and not in garrison at Augusta."

Rutledge bristled when Lincoln remarked on "not being much of a military man."

"General Lincoln," Rutledge replied with a cold, flat voice, "while I don't question your military experience, be well advised that here in South Carolina, I served with distinction as the second-in-command of Middleton's Regiment during our war with the Cherokee. So I have seen my fair share of war."

General Lincoln bowed in apology, "No insult intended; most governors I have met with before had no experience."

Rutledge waved his hand, "What do you want for your expedition?"

"I will take the army and march to Augusta and, in cooperation with the Georgia troops, retake it from the British."

"How much of the army?" Rutledge asked.

"Why, the entire army," Lincoln answered.

"No, you won't take the entire army with the British threat still out there to the south." Rutledge directed.

"What threat?" Lincoln questioned. "That small raiding force that came up the coast. I don't believe so."

Again, Rutledge shook his head in the negative.

"Governor, as the commander of the Southern Department, I can take what regiments I need to meet the enemy on the field." Lincoln challenged.

Again, Rutledge shook his head.

"You are incorrect, general; this is my army. These men are South Carolina State troops, whether militia or continental; they belong to me."

Lincoln shot back, trying to control his anger, "Governor, I was appointed by his excellency General George Washington, overall commander of the army, who speaks with the authority of the Continental Congress. These continental regiments are under my command."

Rutledge never changed his expression, just stared directly at Lincoln. Pearis, from his perch, smiled to himself; just like with the last general, there was no unity of command. Instead, he listened intently as the verbal duel continued.

"General Lincoln, neither your General Washington or the Continental Congress is here. But, with that said, I will allow a portion of the army to march with you on your little expedition, but I will not allow the city to be left defenseless. We still have defensive works to complete across the neck."

Knowing that was the best he would do, Lincoln nodded before turning and departing with his staff officers to issue orders for the coming expedition. Rutledge watched them leave and simply shook his head.

"Jack Ass."

***

Orders quickly were sent, and the Southern Army formed and marched out of the city. Like before, the 2nd Regiment and Jacob were selected to remain behind to defend the city. Jacob and the others watched the other regiments march past and out of the north gate, General Lincoln riding in front of the column, almost sitting with an arrogance that made Jacob shake his head.

"His hasn't changed since we saved them those years back," Jacob growled as he watched him ride by.

"Did you think he would?" Jean asked, and even Samuel snorted and shook his head.

"No, not him. It's something to do with how they raise them there, I guess," commented Samuel, "They all act like that."

Later in the afternoon, Jacob was called for by Marion. As Jacob expected, General Moultrie was waiting in the orderly room when he entered. However, Moultrie had a very perplexed look on his face. As Jacob entered, he looked at Jacob with a seriousness that he hadn't seen for a while.

"By your look, sir," Jacob began, "How may we be of service?"

"I am very concerned, having just come from speaking with the governor," Moultrie explained. "Lincoln wanted to march the entire army on his expedition to retake Augusta, by the governor wanted to make sure there was enough to work at least the defense and if required, defend the city."

Jacob nodded as Moultrie continued.

"Right now, all we have is the 2nd and the 5th, plus the Charles Town Militia to defend and work on the defenses across the neck."

Moultrie paused and paced for a moment as he gathered his thoughts. "Gentlemen, I have a bad feeling that there is more behind these operations up in Augusta. I think our British friends have learned some tricks or two, and we're being set up for an attack."

Moultrie turned and faced Jacob. "Francis, with your permission, I need Jacob and his uncanny gut. He and his men are to scout the border of Georgia and see what is going on. Then, Jacob grabs some extra men and horses and go find out the truth. I don't think the British would just sit on the border without having a plan."

"I agree, sir," Marion stated, "If someone could find out what's going on, it would be Jacob."

"Captain Clarke, gather your men, make haste to the border, root out what is going on, and report back as soon as possible."

Jacob nodded, "We'll leave immediately, along with some of our old friends in Shubricks company. We'll find out what is going on."

Jacob turned and left the orderly room, and Moultrie watched, his face set with a determined look.

"I hope he finds nothing, that I am overthinking this," Moultrie stated, "But I have a feeling that all that Captain Clarke will do, is confirm my fears."

***

General Prevost read the letter from the British intelligence agent in Charles Town, describing the current situation in the city. He was sitting next to a window, looking at the city's bright, sunny spring day.

"Oh, how I want this to be over and back in England," he whispered. He had not received an answer to his request to retire. Finally, the door opened, and the officers of the regiments began filing in for the next phase of their operation.

Once the officers were assembled, General Prevost joined them with the intelligence letter in hand.

"Gentlemen, I have received the latest information on our rebel friends from Charles Town," General Prevost Stated, holding the letter up. "Just as before, there is a rift between the governor and the army commander. We can use it to our advantage. We also just learned that a good portion of the army has marched, heading to retake Augusta."

The officers talked amongst themselves. General Prevost paused until the voices quieted.

"Gentlemen, we know our supply situation is still desperate, even with what we have secured from the local countryside. Keeping our men fed is still insufficient because these bloody privateers intercepted our ships."

Again the officers murmured their agreement, nodding their heads.

"Therefore, I have decided that seeing the rebel army marching north, I will lead an expedition again up the coast to secure as many supplies and livestock as we can. If we can draw the attention of this General Lincoln, then the better as we don't have enough men to defend Augusta if this rebel army intends to invest it."

General Prevost looked at his assembled officers as they waited for their assignments. They nodded their heads in agreement with smiles, looking ready for action.

"We will place the rebels and their general Lincoln in a tough position. First, he will have to move against us to stop our advance, or if he waits too long, we'll be between him and their precious Charles Town. After that, he will have no choice but to fight on our chosen ground. We will land near this Purisburg on the 28th of April to start this off."

"The 71st, 16th, and 60th will march, along with our Hessian Grenadiers, provincials, and Loyalist contingents. Captain Johnstone, assign two artillery batteries to accompany us on this expedition if we successfully draw the rebels away from Augusta. See to your men; you have three days to secure what rations are available and issue cartridges. The rest are to remain here as a reserve."

The officers departed as Prevost went through the details in his head. They were very low on supplies, so they had to live off the land, gathering as they went. Then, taking a deep breath and letting it out, he mumbled, "As long as the rebels don't know how desperate we are for supplies, the better." Prevost knew it was the role of the dice. To be victorious over these rebels or defeated by them was very close.

***

With eight chosen men they had known since the Middleton days, Jacob, Jean, and Samuel rode along the coastal road, speeding towards the border area. Riding across the Coosawhatchie River, they came across three militiamen riding towards them. The two stopped in the middle of the bridge

"Begging your pardon, sir," one of the militiamen reported, "We just learned of an engagement with Cherokee down on the Black Swamp. We're riding to report this to the city."

"Thanks for the information," Jacob replied with a nod, "Continue; we'll see if we can find these Cherokees."

The militiamen nodded and galloped off towards the city.

"Cherokee down here, I don't think so," Samuel responded, shaking his head. "They haven't been this far east and south as far as I know."

Jacob nodded in agreement, "Let's go find out what happened at Black Swamp."

They kicked their horses and started again at a trot towards Back Swamp. From what Jacob recalled, Black Swamp was considered a strategic position twenty-five miles from Purisburg. Usually, a small garrison was kept there from the 6th Regiment.

It was just past midday when they arrived at Black Swamp, where a small detail of local militiamen and some members of the 6th were putting out small fires on a farm. A sergeant from the 6th walked up and reported to Jacob.

"Sir, any word on our reinforcements?" he asked.

Jacob shook his head, "I don't know what to tell you, sergeant; we're here to see what is happening. We haven't heard any call for reinforcements. So what happened here, sergeant?"

"Well, sir," the sergeant began, "Our company was standing guard as part of our rotation when a good number of Cherokee attacked us in the night. First, drove us out of position, then went on a rampage, even burning good ole Captain Hartstone's farm here."

Jacob nodded, "How did you know they were Cherokee in the dark?"

"Well, sir," the sergeant continued, "they all wore that dark warpaint, attacking silently with bayonets, caught us by surprise. They never fired their muskets, just used the bayonets."

All of them gave the sergeant an odd look.

"Did you say bayonets?" Samuel asked, and the sergeant nodded.

"Yes, sir, they were very good with them. They were quick and quiet, took out our guards, and before we knew it, they were amongst the men sleeping, stabbing and striking with their muskets."

Jacob nodded, "Thanks for the information," The sergeant turned and returned to cleaning up the farm and putting out the fires. Then, they all came together in a circle to discuss what they just learned."

"The Cherokee don't use bayonets, no?" Jean asked, and everyone shook their heads.

"No, the British wouldn't give them, let alone train them on the use of the bayonet," Jacob stated, "Did you ever train the Huron or Ottowa?"

Jean shook his head no.

Jacob thought about it for a few moments. "We have Loyalists here, as their clothing could almost be considered like Cherokee in the dark. They would use the bayonet, and it wouldn't be hard to use some black powder and water to darken your face. I did it on a few occasions."

They all nodded their heads in agreement. Jacob continued, "If Loyalists are trying to take out this key position, then something is afoot. Let's camp and see what we can find in the morning."

They went off to the far side of the farm area, away from the militia and remnants of the 6th, to make their camp. After ensuring their horses were cared for, they set up their small camp. They kept a small fire to warm their rations and to have a little light. Leaning back against some logs, they smoked their pipes but kept their eyes and ears open.

"You think they're coming, don't you, Jacob," Samuel asked, "Your gut is telling you something."

Jacob nodded, smoking his pipe before blowing out a smoke stream.

"They're being sneaky, which is not normal for the British, as you know. I think they are removing anything that could spot an approaching army and warn the city. The fact they painted their faces and acted like Cherokee was brilliant."

"Brilliant? You think that was brilliant?" Samuel asked, and Jacob nodded.

"I do. Think about it. The Loyalists and British know the locals fear the Cherokee, and if the British can use that fear, they open up this corridor straight to the city. So Lincoln had no choice but to bring the army back if they thought the Cherokee were over here. A good plan."

They thought about it, and it did start to make sense. The rest of the evening was quiet, and the men went to sleep but kept one up as a sentry, even though the locals were nearby. It could happen again if they were already attacked once in the night.

No attacks occurred, and after they had finished their breakfast and prepared to mount up, Lieutenant Colonel McIntosh arrived with a 100-man detachment from the 5th Regiment. Jacob went over to speak to McIntosh. He explained what they had learned and suspected it had been Loyalists and not Cherokee due to the bayonet use.

McIntosh nodded. "Makes sense to me. The riders went to the governor, and General Moultrie has already sent for some Catawba riflemen to head this way."

Jacob headed back and rejoined their men. "Let's see if we can find some sign of these attackers."

They mounted up and spoke with the sergeant from the day before. He directed Jacob in the direction that the attack came from. They arrived at the edge of the woods, dismounted, and tied their horses to the trees. One man stayed behind while the rest headed into the woods to see if they could find some sign.

It didn't take them very long to find the attackers' tracks, and they followed them to what appeared to have been their camp before the attack. Jacob knelt and looked across the ground for clues, just as the other men did. He could see where they had slept and had a small fire. Searching slowly across the ground, Jacob's eyes looked for anything that stood out.

He found a dark spot, and when he touched it, he brought it up and tasted it. As he suspected, gunpowder. Someone had crushed some gunpowder and added water to it to smear on their face. Jacob continued to move, looking for more clues. He then spotted something shiny; when he retrieved it, it was a button.

Jacob stood, and wiped off the dirt as it seemed the button must have fallen off, then someone had stepped on it. Once the button was cleaned, a very obvious "60" could be seen on it. "60th Regiment," Jacob stated, and Samuel asked, "What did you say?"

Jacob held up his hand, the button being held by two fingers. "A regimental button from the 60th."

"Do Cherokee wear shoes?" Jean asked; Jacob turned to see Jean holding up a leather shoe that a good portion of the bottom was coming off.

"No, they don't," Jacob answered. "Well, I think this answers our questions; they weren't Cherokee but rather British. I believe it is what we feared; they are scaring people or hiding their activities in preparation for an expedition."

They all nodded, then Jean asked, "An expedition or an attack?"

Jacob shook his head. "We better get back and report to Moultrie about this."

***

General Prevost walked out of the decent house they had procured the night before, having been told the soldiers that had attacked the rebel position were waiting. When he came out, the three men were standing; their faces still had some black from the gunpowder smeared and streaked across their faces.

"Sir, we would like to report our attack against the rebel position went smoothly, driving the picket away and burning the farm they were using as barracks. We were able to move up along the coast more and learned there is nothing between us and the city."

Major Prevost joined his father as he spoke with the Soldier. "Are you saying there are no defenses to prevent us from marching on Charles Town?"

"None, sir, all of the bridges are still intact, no patrols for the exception of maybe some small rebel militiamen. We could speak to other Loyalists in the area, who were good loyal kingsmen. Most of the army is up north, nothing along the coast."

General Prevost nodded his thanks and turned, thinking of what opportunity had just landed in his lap. The rebels hadn't taken the bait to come after him, to meet him on the battlefield. Instead, they either must think he is no threat to them or doesn't know or care they are getting between them and their city.

"Your thoughts, father?" Major Prevost asked as the general finally smiled for once.

"I have them; bloody hell, I got them!" General Prevost said with glee as he rubbed his hands together. "I could bloody do it; take the city!"

"Sir?" Major Prevost asked.

"Change of plans," the general stated, "we will march directly to the city and demand their surrender as there is no one between us and the city to stop us. An easy victory!"

***

Jacob and his men rode back to Charles Town and informed General Moultrie that they suspected the British were clearing the area through force or scare tactics. Agreeing with Jacob's assessment, Moultrie went over to see the governor, and soon the word was passed to prepare to march.

It wasn't a large force being readied, but Jacob and his men were sent forward to scout for Moultrie while he brought a force up to the Black Swamp. Then, finally, the governor departed to head to Orangeburg to get more men and artillery.

As they rode, Jacob's mind wrestled with the situation. They were severely outnumbered. Even with the 2nd, 5th, and some of the 6th Regiments available, they were not the seasoned veterans they had back in 76. Most were not better than the militia; even some were better as they had the first veterans who had done their time and gone home.

What bothered him the most, Lincoln had been informed of their situation, and there had been no word or indications he was returning or sending more troops. Shaking his head, Jacob focused on the task at hand, to be the eyes and ears again for the army. Finally, they arrived at Black Swamp, where the company from the 5th still maintained watch.

"No, we haven't heard or seen anything in the area," one of the captains replied when Jacob asked.

"We're heading out and see if we can find anything," Jacob explained, "if we find or hear anything, we'll be heading this way quickly.

Leading the group down the road through the Black Swamp, they angled over to near the Savannah River and began to slowly ride along the bank, keeping inside of the woods. Jacob wanted to remain as much in the shadows as possible if the British were on the other side.

They covered some of the known crossing areas, and there were no signs of any British soldiers in the area. The river gurgled and rolled by; the only sound was the breeze in the trees. Jacob looked around, trying to determine what the British were up to.

Then there was a snap of fingers, and Jacob turned to see that Robert Clive, one of the chosen men, just had an idea.

"The old Baker's Ford," he said, "I only remember it as a child, but my father took me across there once heading to Savannah. After the King's Road became the main road to the city, no one used the ford, and it fell into ruin. Not sure anything is left there."

Jacob thought about it and decided to check it as there were no signs or indications on the main crossings. "If they are trying to stay out of sight," Jacob explained as they trotted behind the one scout who was leading them towards the ford, "then they may also know of old fords from locals."

Jacob and the scouts moved along an old trail, and it could be seen that there was little traffic through the area, except for animals. Robert stopped a few times to get his bearings, looking for landmarks, then led them down a few more trails before halting and indicating they should dismount.

It was a large old, gnarled oak tree, limbs full of Spanish moss waving in the breeze. "Ah, I remember this tree, the old man my father used to call it. The ford is just over on the other side," Robert explained.

Jacob nodded; after leaving two men behind to hold their horses and watch their backs, Robert led Jacob and the others into the brush and towards the ford. As they were getting close, Jaco heard unique sounds of splashing and jingling of equipment. Holding his hand to halt, he lowered his hand, and everyone crouched and moved slowly forward.

The closer they suspected the ford was, the louder the sound of splashing, tin cups, or metal canteens clanking together. Finally, they came to the edge of the vegetation, and Jacob signaled for everyone prone, and they slowly crawled forward. When they reached the edge, they were on a finger of land, pointing into the river.

Before them was what must have been the old ford, as it had been carved deep between two fingers of land jutting into the river. A long line of British infantry was in their red coats, holding their muskets and cartridge boxes over their heads.

Samuel softly whistled at the site, and Jacob pulled out his telescope to get a closer look. The line of soldiers stretched across the entire river, the men about chest deep in some areas. Jacob also saw horsemen coming across, wearing civilian/militia clothing.

"Could it be another raid for supplies or plunder?" Samuel asked. Jacob paused to focus on an item before handing the scope to Samuel.

Samuel focused on it, "What am I looking for?" he asked.

"Follow the line about halfway across, and you'll see it," Jacob replied.

Samuel followed the line, then stopped and focused. "Ah, I see what you mean," he stated. Being pulled along by at least four oxen was a 6-pound cannon, followed by a second one. The men walking with it and helping to push it wore the uniform of the British Royal Artillery.

Samuel looked for a short while longer before freezing at another spot. "Who are they? I have never seen that uniform before?"

"What do they look like?" Jacob asked, and Samuel explained.

"A dark blue, almost like ours, with a lighter color red cuffs and facings. They have really big, shiny metal helmets, though."

Jean perked up, "Metal helmets, can I see?" Samuel handed him the telescope and talked to where he saw them in the line. Jean focused, looking for a short moment, before lowering the telescope and handing it back to Jacob.

"Grenadiers, real grenadiers from over there. If I recall, they are either Hessens or Prussians. France had fought them before; they were allies with England."

"Why would they be over here?" Samuel asked.

"Didn't you know that the English King is also a Hanovarian Prince?" Jean explained.

"Whats a Hanovarian?" Samuel asked back.

Jean chuckled, "To be more precise, a state within the Holy Roman Empire called the Electorate of Brunswick-Lüneburg. It was explained to me that they called it Hanover, ruled jointly by England and Ireland. So he is the King and prince of all three."

Samuel still had a perplexed look on his face, "What's the Holy Roman Empire?"

Jean shook his head, and Jacob gave them a stern look.

"If we could concentrate on this problem before going to school?" Jacob chastised before looking out once more before making up his mind.

"My gut is telling me this is no raid, too many infantry, cavalry, and artillery. This could be a supporting force or the main one, but I think they are coming for the city because they know Lincoln and the army is gone. We are vulnerable."

"Why do you think this?" Jean asked, and Jacob simply nodded his head.

"Because if I was in command, and learned most of my enemy's army is away, now is the time to attack."

Everyone nodded in agreement, and Jacob motioned for them to slowly back away before turning and making their way to their horses. Then, quickly mounting, Jacob led them out at a good pace; they had to warn General Moultrie about this force. It was late afternoon when they arrived at Black Swamp, and Jacob quickly rode up to the picket.

"Where's your commander," Jacob ordered of the sergeant of the guard, "I need to speak to him right now!"

The sergeant ran over to the house still used as a barracks and returned with Lieutenant Colonel McIntosh.

Jacob quickly saluted, "Sir, there is a major force of British, Hanoverians, and Loyalists with infantry, cavalry, and artillery heading this way."

McIntosh's face became very concerned, "How long before they arrive?"

"We just got ahead of them, and we're on horses, and they were still crossing the river. If my guess is correct, they will wait until their force is completely across, rest then press on. They may be here in about two days."

McIntosh nodded, "Thank you for the warning, captain," then he looked at how the horses were hanging their heads. "Your horses are nearly spent. I can send a rider with a fresh horse to warn General Moultrie. Could you write a dispatch as I go get my rider ?"

Jacob dismounted and nodded he would. The rest of the men dismounted and stretched their backs and legs from the pounding ride. McIntosh called for parchment and a pen, and Jacob wrote what they had seen, the type of men and their estimation of about three thousand marching towards the city. After finishing it, he handed it to McIntosh, who passed it to a young man with a horse.

"Take this message to general Moultrie," McIntosh instructed as he handed it to the rider, "ride like the wind!"

The rider jumped up on his horse and took off in a gallop, throwing up dust and leaves as he pounded down the road towards Charles Town. Jacob with McIntosh watched the rider go, then McIntosh turned to Jacob.

"I have a company of a hundred men, full cartridge boxes plus a little extra. Do you think we could buy some time for the general?"

Jacob looked at the terrain before them. Mainly swampy terrain, large cypress trees with the ever-present Spanish moss, and only one road. They were on an elevated position, overlooking the road, but no defenses were erected.

"I think with a determined enough force, and if the enemy stays channelized down this one road, we may be able to hold them for a short time," Jacob stated as he rubbed his chin, looking over the ground. "Or until they roll their artillery up and blast us to pieces."

McIntosh gave Jacob a scathing look, and Jacob returned with a shrug.

"Just an observation, sir," Jacob explained, "They have 6-pounders that can fire on us that are beyond the range even of our rifles. So they can sit back and lob shot at us, and there is nothing we can do about it."

McIntosh saw Jacob's point, "Then I guess we better get started on building some defenses."

Jacob nodded, and McIntosh called for his officers and ordered them to build hasty earthworks with anything they could find. He sent a section forward to watch the road for any approaching British while the rest of the men worked on piling logs and whatever they could find into a wall.

Jacob looked down the road and was trying to estimate how much time they honestly had. He was also trying to estimate how fast that messenger could get to Charles Town and how quickly can Moultrie mobilize the rest of the army and get here to stop the British.

"This is going to be a race too close to call," Jacob said aloud before heading over to organize his scouts and how they can help.

***

General Prevost and his staff watched as the expedition crossed the river and marched into South Carolina. He was pleased they could learn from a local about this old ford, unused after so many years. It would have been difficult to force a crossing had the rebels been entrenched here.

The men came marching out of the river. They were being directed to assembly areas where they were to change their stockings as they waited for the entire expedition to be across before moving. As he watched, one of his orderlies brought the Loyalist Cavalry commander McGirtt to him.

"You asked for me, your lordship?" McGirtt asked.

Prevost nodded. "I need you to screen this expedition; make sure none of these rebels spot us until it's too late."

McGirtt nodded, "Any specific orders concerning the rebels and how I prevent them from discovering this expedition?"

Prevost shook his head. "You know these people better than I; you may use every means at your disposal to keep my expedition from being discovered until it's too late for those rebel commanders."

McGirtt gave a harsh, evil smile that even made Prevost shutter. Then, nodding instead of saluting, McGirtt turned and headed off to where the cavalry was resting. He was watching McGirtt going to gather his cavalry when his son joined him.

"Is there a problem, father?" he asked, looking in the same direction as his father, and the general only shook his head. "For the rebels maybe, if I read that man correctly. He is set on the vengeance of some kind, and only blood will satisfy his feeling."

***

With the sound of axes chopping, men were dragging trees to form a wall, with Jean showing them how to sharpen the limbs into an abatis. Jacob and Samuel, with a section, made gabion baskets filled in with dirt along with the logs, and fence posts were torn out. While not exactly pretty, it would be functional if they had to fight a rear guard action to buy time.

The men were on edge, not knowing when the British would arrive. The forward picket was rotated, so the men were fresh though stressed from the looming action. All men had their muskets and rifles close at hand if they had to man their defenses quickly. The first full day of construction ended with the sun setting, and the men settled down for a restless night.

Jacob with McIntosh walked amongst the men, checking on them and reassuring them. A good number of them have heard of Jacob, though mainly as a legendary story of the Ranger who could not die, to walk through a gauntlet and come out without a scratch. Jacob had heard these stories around the barracks but said nothing. Because it could give these men hope and determination, he would let the stories go.

When they overheard a conversation about the gauntlet as the men were talking about it and pointing at Jacob, McIntosh turned to Jacob.

"Did you walk through a Cherokee gauntlet without injury?"

"Not really, sir," Jacob explained, "While I did walk through one and not run, I was definitely injured. It took me weeks to recover and the bruising to fade away." Both men chuckled and continued their walk around the camp.

The second day came and went, and to Jacob's surprise, no British arrived. The men continued to work feverishly on their hast defenses while the pickets maintained watch on the main road. Jacob walked along the line of defenses when he spotted movement off to the side in the swamp and pulled out his telescope.

As he focused, he saw brown moving through the trees until three men appeared on horseback. Jacob focused in, and they wore the same clothing he had spotted at the ford. The Loyalist cavalry had arrived.

"McIntosh, sir!" Jacob called out, "we have company!"

McIntosh came over, and Jacob handed him his telescope and pointed to where he saw the cavalrymen. "Well, I be," McIntosh stated, "About bloody time you showed up. Wondering if you got lost or something."

He closed the telescope and handed it back to Jacob. "They must be using a side trail off the main road, perhaps scouting for the British expedition. Jacob nodded in agreement and looked closer to the front and down the road. Still no sign of advancing British.

"Well, they found us," McIntosh simply stated, "better get ready to receive them. It would be considered improper if we didn't have an appropriate reception for our guests. McIntosh quickly moved off and started directing his men to take up positions without using the long roll. He returned to Jacob.

"While I could use your assistance Captain Clarke, I need you and your men to ride on and find General Moultrie. Let him know we'll hold as long as we can, but as you said, if they roll up their cannon and pound us to pieces, we won't be very effective."

Then McIntosh came close and gripped Jacob's arm. "Please ask the general to move with all haste if possible." He smiled, turned, and headed back to his men. Jacob watched him go, having a strong appreciation of his leadership, before heading to gather his.

"Let's go and mount up," Jacob directed, "We need to go find the general and tell them the British are close, and we have to get here quickly!" They all nodded, went over to their horses, mounted up, and followed Jacob as he led them out at a trot. Jacob saluted with his helmet to McIntosh, who smiled and raised his sword in return.

McIntosh watched them ride down the road, the dust following close behind, before turning again and looking over their position. Then, taking a deep breath, he let it out slowly and shook his head.

"Unless we're fortunate, it will be a hard fight even to slow them down," McIntosh said out loud, "we will have to hold the line to the last man if need be, to buy time."

***

Jacob and the others rode hard, knowing that time was of the essence. Trees were whipping past, the Spanish Moss waving at them as they passed. The shadows were beginning to grow as the sunset, and Jacob could feel the horses were tired. As they approached the bridge over the Tuliffiny, Jacob spotted a picket and, as luck would have it, were men from the 2nd Regiment.

Jacob held his hand up, and one of the pickets called out, "Captain Clarke, is that you?"

"Aye, it is. May we cross?" Jacob responded, and the picket sergeant waved them across. Jacob led them at a walk, and the picket called out to Samuel and the others as they rode past. "Are they coming?" one asked, "Did you see the British?" asked another.

Jacob nodded and rode on; the pickets began chatting, having confirmed the British were marching. Jacob asked another regiment member where he could find the commander, and he was directed to where General Moultrie had his command established.

They dismounted and tied their horses to trees, "Samuel, see to the horses, get them water and feed if possible," Jacob instructed before speaking with the general. Samuel nodded and got the others working on getting water as Jacob walked to the command.

General Moultrie spoke with a few militia officers when Jacob approached and waited. When he was finished, Moultrie's face lit up, and he waved Jacob over. "Captain Clarke, what news do you bring? Have you confirmed the British expedition?"

Jacob nodded, "Yes, sir, we saw the column crossing the Savannah and sir, we believe this is not a raiding force for forage and cattle."

Moultrie nodded with a serious look, "Based on?"

"They had 6-pound artillery pieces being hauled, along with 3-pounders. You don't drag those guns on a raid. They are heading down this road, so the only place they can be heading for is Charles Town."

Moultrie went over to a field table and looked at his map. "Yes, and nothing to stop them between here and there is just us."

"Colonel McIntosh and a company of his men are at Black Swamp." Moultrie looked at his map, nodded, and called for an orderly. "Get a message to McIntosh and his company, tell them to fall back to the Coosawhatchie and cover the crossing. They are too far forward for us to support!"

The orderly nodded and took off at a trot to get a messenger. "Do we have any other reinforcements?" Jacob asked, and Moultrie snorted and shook his head, spreading his arms out.

"This is all we have, other than those working on the defenses at the neck. I've sent messengers to General Lincoln, advising him of our dire situation, and his latest message back was he felt its only a feint to distract him from capturing Augusta."

Moultrie frowned and looked at the map before continuing. "I've also reached out to the governor, asking for more artillery or cavalry, and have not received anything. So I have all these crossings to cover, and with only a hundred men at these points, we're as severely stretched thin as we are now."

Jacob looked at the different crossing points Moultrie had pointed out on the map and, while in a line, did stretch their line that, if the British concentrated their attack at one point, would easily break through. However, with artillery, it may make no difference as they had no guns to support their lines.

"Unless you need me, sir, I would like to see to my men." Moultrie nodded, "Thanks for confirming the British are coming and in force. We'll see what the morning brings."

Jacob returned to where Samuel, Jean, and the others were and told them to make camp. They removed the saddles and bags, rubbed them dry, watered them, and gave them feed bags. Once finished, they resaddled their horses just case they had to mount them quickly.

They built a small fire and rested on their gear. Jacob leaned against his gear, smoking his pipe as they talked. He watched the different militiamen moving across their position, heading towards a hill that overlooked the river.

"We're in for a fight, aren't we?" Samuel asked, and Jacob nodded.

Samuel and the others looked around, assessing their potential battlefield.

"We could hold the hill," Samuel pointed out, and they all looked over and thought about it. "Tear up the bridge; that should keep them from crossing while we take shots at them."

"If we were to cut trees and build an abatis," Jean pointed out, "at the base of the hill, could hold them back."

Jacob looked, puffing on his pipe, "All they would have to do is roll up their artillery and blast us, or with their cavalry, find a way to get around us and then encircle the position. So we're in a bad spot."

It wasn't a good way to go to sleep; many of them had difficulty as they thought about the coming fight. But, Jacob knew he was right, they were not in a good position, and the British had strength and mobility on their side.

In the morning, Samuel had their little fire up and was warming water and some of their rationed biscuits. Jacob walked over to speak with General Moultrie. He had moved his headquarters to the top of the hill and was directing the development of defenses.

"It would be a good idea to cut up some trees as abatis and set them at the bottom," Jacob advised, "if you intend to hold this ground."

Moultrie looked at what Jacob had suggested, nodded, and then looked at Jacob.

"Captain Clarke, in your honest opinion, can we hold here?"

Jacob looked at General Moultrie and bluntly told him, "No, sir, I don't think we can."

Moultrie nodded his head in agreement but pressed Jacob to explain.

"It's a matter of numbers. We have no cavalry to scout and learn of their movement; they do. They have freedom of movement and action and can find a crossing point to avoid our pickets and try to encircle your hill. Once they pin you in place, they will roll up their guns, and we have nothing to stop them other than riflemen, and they blast you to pieces."

Moultrie took a deep breath and sighed, then smiled. "Captain Clarke, though I hate to admit it, I see your point."

"Soldiers approaching from the rear!" was called out by a sentry, and everyone turned to see who was approaching. Was it reinforcements, or had the British maneuvered behind them? They waited to see, and it was reinforcements, but only about the size of a company.

Jacob recognized their leader, John Laurens, who had served with his father during the Anglo-Cherokee War and had met when he was younger in Charles Town.

"That's Lauren's son," Jacob commented, and Moultrie looked and nodded.

"Why I'll be; I believe you are correct, Captain Clarke."

The officer approached and, in proper military style, saluted.

"Sir, Colonel Laurens reports with his hand-picked North Carolina Light Infantry company." He looked over and, recognizing Jacob, nodded in acknowledgment.

General Moultrie nodded, "Are there any other reinforcements on the way?"

Colonel Laurens shook his head, "No sir, we were the only ones General Lincoln detached as we could make haste to here."

Moultrie nodded, "Is the general on his way?"

"Yes, sir," Laurens continued, "he was finishing crossing the Savannah when we were dispatched, and he was marching the army here at all haste."

Moultrie thought about, turned, and looked out over their defenses. "How long do you believe the army will take to get here?"

"It will be hard to say, sir," Laurens explained, "depending on the roads and the weather, it may be a couple of days before he can bring the army to bear on the British."

"Well, we will buy time to hold them here until General Lincoln can bring his army to bear."

Moultrie turned and looked directly at Laurens. "Are your men still able to march?"

"Yes, sir," Laurens replied enthusiastically, "my men are ready for action."

"I want you to take your company, and I will send another company of riflemen with you, and I want you to recover a company of the 5th Regiment that is serving as a picket on the Coosawhatchie River and bring them here so we can consolidate. I will start pulling in my command to build a defensive line here."

Laurens nodded, "Yes, sir, if you give my men and me a moment to refill our canteens and get some supplies, we'll be ready to march."

Moultrie nodded; Laurens saluted, turned, and jogged back to his company. Moultrie watched him head down the hill before coming over to Jacob.

"What do you think, Jacob, on our colonel here?"

Jacob looked critically, "He wants to be a hero, and I'm afraid he will get either his men killed or someone else's."

Moultrie nodded, "Captain Clarke, you and your detachment will accompany Colonel Laurens as my advisor. I will go get Captain John James, and he'll send some of his best riflemen just in case they make contact, and we have to deal with the cannons as you said."

Jacob nodded and saluted.

"Be careful out there, Captain Clarke; advise our new colonel if the situation warrants a withdraw, even if it means we lose that company from the 5th."

Once again, Jacob nodded before turning and heading down the hill to get Samuel and the others ready to march. He told them their task to advise Colonel Laurens and support the company's evacuation.

Once, they had put out their fire, shouldered their bags, and left their horses with the quartermaster until they returned. Then, they went over to where the Light Infantry were resting, and Captain James with his riflemen were arriving. Once all had gathered, Colonel Laurens got their attention.

"Men, we march to relieve the company serving as a forward picket. We must be on our guard as the enemy is before us and may be engaged as we arrive. We will prime and load before departing; sergeants see the men, captains, and lieutenants to your elements!"

Jacob and his detachment primed and loaded their rifles, as the light infantry and the rifle company did the same. Then, vaunting up into his saddle and with a dramatic flurry, Laurens drew his sword and waved the men forward. Leading the way, the column began trekking down the road, the leading element muskets at the ready.

"Is it me, or is our young colonel showing off?" Samuel asked.

Jacob nodded, "He has a lot of his father in him, dedicated to a fault. Middleton's Regiment would have fallen apart if it hadn't been for his father. The difference is that his father had experience; our young colonel here does not. So I think he is making up for it by using more flair and being showy."

"That's not a good way to be a leader," Samuel commented, "it's a good way of getting his men killed."

"Or us," Jean added.

They nodded, Jacob, watching the head of the column moving down the road. When the riflemen started to pass, Jacob and the others fell in behind them. Somewhere close by, the British were approaching, and there was a good chance they would bump into them out in the swamp.

CHAPTER 5

THE RACE IS ON

The column snaked along the road through the woods, the 0sunlight filtering through the waving Spanish Moss. The summer's essence was in the air for an early May, with warmer temperatures and humidity buzzing insects from the swamp. The sound of the column on the march must have been the same since time immortal. The clank of tine cups and canteens, the small talk and laughter of the men, puffs of dust as their feet plodded along.

Except for the leading element, the men carried their muskets and rifles in the crook of their arms, chatting lightly amongst themselves. Jacob and the others spoke with Captain James and his riflemen, wondering if this would be their first action against the British. Jacob thought about what he saw crossing the river and how the riflemen may play an essential part.

A short time later, the column came to a halt, and the men took a step off to the side of the road and sat down. Looking down the road, Jacob could see McIntosh speaking with Laurens. Then, as he was too far back to hear what was being said, he saw hand gestures and head nodding before Laurens yelled, "Prepare to march!"

The men stood up and reformed the column, and with a tip of his hat to McIntosh, Laurens led the column down the road. When Jacob approached McIntosh, he waved Jacob over.

"Captain Clarke, the British haven't arrived so far, but I think you may have a hot afternoon if they get there before you do."

Jacob nodded, "We'll get there and see to your men, sir."

McIntosh nodded his head and smiled. "So the general is going to make a stand of it at the Tulliffinny?"

"Yes, sir, he has recalled all the companies except for the few covering crossings in the immediate area."

McIntosh nodded. "Reinforcements, surely General Lincoln and the governor are making haste?"

Jacob shook his head, and McIntosh's face took a concerned look. Then, pointing down the road towards the head of the column, "Sir, that is our reinforcements sent from General Lincoln, Lieutenant Colonel Laurens, and his North Carolina Light Infantry."

"Surely not," McIntosh stated in shock, "Don't they realize there is nothing between the advancing British and Charles Town but us?"

Again, Jacob shook his head. "They still believe this is only a feint, but Laurens indicated that General Lincoln is marching from Augusta, but we don't know when they will arrive."

McIntosh shook his head with still a shocked look on his face before looking at Jacob.

"Please, see to my men, make sure they get back to me with the rest at the Tullifinny," then he turned and looked at the diminishing back of Laurens, "make sure they are not needlessly thrown away and lose their lives for nothing."

Jacob pursed his lips, "I'll see what I can do," McIntosh extended his hand, and Jacob shook it. Then, nodding, Jacob rejoined the others with the riflemen. Captain James nodded, and Samuel with Jean caught up to walk next to Jacob.

"What did McIntosh have to say," Samuel asked, and Jacob relayed to them what he had told McIntosh about their situation and his concern. Captain James nodded his head.

"I see his point," he commented, "I have concerns as well that we are getting into a fur-ball that might doom us all." The men around them nodded and voiced their agreements. Jacob nodded but kept his thoughts to himself.

After an hour of marching, the men no longer were talking and no longer carried their muskets and rifles at ease. Jacob guessed they must be approaching the Coosawhatchie River. The men scanned the woods and swamp to their left and right, including Jacob and his detachment. A short time later, the column arrived and started to bend around to the left.

Jacob became concerned as the column wasn't halting. They should be covered while the company from the 5th was organized to march. Jacob, with Captain James, moved to the front of the column and found Captain Shubrick, the company commander, and Laurens in a heated discussion.

"With all due respect, sir, are you daft!"

On the contrary, Shubrick stated, "there is not a very defensible position to take on the British. So our role was to hold and report, falling back to the main line."

"We will do no such thing, captain," Laurens shot back, "we will not only hold this line, but we shall engage the British, and not only stop them, but we'll also throw them back into Georgia!"

Captain James looked at Jacob, and then they looked at Laurens. Jacob could see a feverish look in his eyes, caught up in the moment leading to battle. He didn't see reason.

"Sir," Jacob began, "General Moultrie's orders were to advance and make contact with the company, then escort them back to the main line. Well, sir, here they are. Let us grab them and get back to the Tullifinny."

Laurens shook his head. "Don't you see, we have the advantage of the river before us and our flanks secured by the swamp. We can hold them and throw those invaders back across the Savannah by our aggressive tactics and engagement!"

Jacob stared in disbelief at Laurens, who was making no sense. "Sir, I have seen their expedition. They have artillery where we have none. They have cavalry that can scout and come from behind, and we have none. They have more men, and we're outnumbered. But, on the other hand, they have the freedom of action and movement, where we'll be pinned in place. They will shoot us to pieces if we stay here in simple, military terms!"

Laurens gave Jacob a stern look. "Don't tell me you have lost your stomach to fight, Captain Clarke. My father spoke highly of you, your determination and bravery, as time took its toll?"

Jacob could feel a rage boil up from within him and looked at Laurens with an icy, cold stare.

"I've seen and experienced battle twice as much than you have been alive; my role is to advise you on behalf of General Moultrie. This is a bad decision, and we should withdraw."

Laurens shook his head, his eyes showing fervent stubbornness when reality slipped someone's mind.

"I am the commanding officer here, and this is my mission. I am making a tactical decision, and we will make our stand here. If you do not follow my orders, I will bring you up on insubordination charges, and you will face a court-martial."

All three captains gave Laurens a hard look, one of disbelief he would say such a thing. Then, finally, Jacob spoke again in a low, cold voice.

"Sir, we are only attached to you; we don't fall under your command as you are not part of South Carolina. However, as General Moultrie's representative, I must advise you that you are disobeying a general's order and may be subject to a court-martial."

Laurens waved his hand in dismissal as he drew out his telescope. "The righteous will prevail when freedom and liberty call; there is no higher power than that! That is how I will be judged!"

Jacob and the other captains could see there was no getting through to him, nodded, and headed back to their companies.

"Captain Clarke, he is going to get us slaughtered if we make a fight of it here!" Shubrick whispered in earnest.

"I agree," Captain James said, "there is no advantage of terrain or height; just the river will slow them down."

Jacob shook his head. "They won't cross the river. If their commander is smart, and from what I saw with their artillery, all they have to do is roll them up outside of rifle range and start blasting us with shot."

The three stopped, ensuring they were well away from Laurens, who sat on his horse and looked at the far side through his telescope. Jacob turned to the other two, "Shubrick, take your company and anchor the right; James, take yours and anchor the left. I'll take my boys and stay near Laurens if something happens."

Shubrick looked at Jacob and nodded, "In case something happens to our illustrious, glory-seeking leader, you mean?"

Jacob nodded, "Somehow, fate always knows where to send the shot; I will be ready to assume command and get us out of here if that happens."

The two nodded, "Go get your men in place, and perhaps we make contact with the British; Laurens will see reason. Have your men find suitable covering and shooting positions; limit their exposure as much as possible."

Jacob looked at the two captains, who nodded back. "Good luck," he stated before turning to bring up Samuel and the others and find suitable firing positions.

***

McGirtt chuckled to himself, looking through his telescope.

"What do you see over there?" John Twiggs asked. McGirtt lowered and closed his telescope with a click.

"Finally, some action," he replied, "Some bloody fool of an officer has deployed his men across the Coosawhatchie River crossing, with no defenses, artillery, or cavalry. He is going to put up a fight in a bad position. We're going to have some fun!"

Walking back, McGirtt and Twiggs mounted their horses, which the other members of the scouting party were holding. Then, looking across the river once more, McGirtt turned his horse and trotted back down the road towards the advance guard of the expedition.

It wasn't a long ride when the pickets heard them approach and waved him through after seeing it was McGirtt. So he continued on the road, passing the different infantry regiments stretched along the length, until he came upon General Prevost and his son, resting under a shade tree.

Dismounting and handing his reins to Twiggs, he approached the general, who looked up expectantly.

"Sir, we have found rebels making a stand a little way up the road, facing the Coosawhatchie River crossing," McGirtt stated.

The general's face lit up. "How are they deployed?"

McGirtt snorted and shook his head. "Only in a line of battle. No artillery, no breastworks, and no cavalry scouting. They are just sitting there, waiting."

General Prevost bounded to his feet. "Bloody excellent, just standing there with no defenses?"

McGirtt nodded in the affirmative.

Prevost clapped his hands in excitement. "About bloody time, I thought this expedition was for naught. But, runner, get Colonel Maitland and Captain Johnstone and have them report to me immediately!"

A runner took off to get the two officers, and Prevost began to pace with a wide grin.

"What is on your mind, sir," Colonel Prevost asked.

"A great opportunity to teach these rebels a lesson! We'll break through their line and chase them down, punishing them."

A short time later, Lieutenant Colonel Maitland, commander of the 71st Highlanders, followed by Captain Johnstone, commander of the Royal Artillery, arrived. General Prevost turned and faced the two officers who reported in.

"Gentlemen, we have a wonderful opportunity that our scouts here have found for us. The rebels are standing at the crossing ahead, with no real defenses. Maitland and Johnstone, follow McGirtt here, and he'll show you where they are. Then, develop a plan; Maitland, you will attack, Johnstone your guns in support."

Then Prevost turned to McGirtt. "Bring all your cavalry; once the infantry and the artillery have broken them, ride them down and exploit the line. I'll bring the rest of the expedition forward to follow up on our success. Go see to your task!"

Maitland and Johnstone bowed to Prevost before trotting off to get their horses; McGirtt waited for their return.

"You brought us excellent news, McGirtt," Prevost stated, nodding at McGirtt, "I'll see to it you get a bottle from my personal stock, and your men get a double ration of rum."

McGirtt bowed his head in acceptance. "They will greatly appreciate it, sir."

When Maitland and Johnstone returned on their horses, McGirtt moved the horse and led them back to the crossing with his scouts. Once they arrived back, they dismounted and moved to a concealed position to observe while crouching. Then, all three pulled out their telescopes to scan their respective areas.

There had been no change. McGirtt saw the blue-uniformed men, and the leader who had been on his horse scanning was now walking along the front of the line. He could see some men positioned behind trees and logs off to either side. No earthworks, nothing to slow their attack other than the river.

"My God, this is beautiful," remarked Johnstone as he lowered his telescope. I can bring my guns up, take that line under fire, and drive them off that far bank. Then, your men would be able to cross with ease."

Maitland nodded and smiled, "Between your guns and our bayonets, we'll drive them off without much effort."

The three backed off slowly before turning to get their men. Then, they mounted and began trotting back to the expedition to prepare for action.

McGirtt had an evil grin on his face. "What is it?" Twiggs asked.

"We are about to get back at those who have done us wrong finally. We will make them pay for the insults and slanders against our families; our time for revenge has arrived. We are going to make them pay in rivers of blood!"

***

Jacob, Jean, and Samuel had found a thick cypress tree that had fallen to take position behind. Looking over, Jacob could see Laurens pacing in front of his horse tied to a branch, his light infantry sitting in the shade but with their muskets. Looking to his left, the riflemen were concealed behind trees and logs.

A sound of hooves could be heard from behind; Jacob and his men quickly turned and brought their rifles up, not knowing who was approaching. The three horsemen who rode up were from General Moultrie and rode to Laurens.

"Sir, the general is wondering why you have not departed to return to his position." The messenger stated, and Laurens shook his head.

"We are not abandoning this position; we must hold to give our defenses more developed," Lauren replied.

"Seem our illustrious leader over there just gave the messenger a different reason than he gave us," Samuel commented with a shake of his head. "He is becoming a bigger jackass every day."

"They're here!" A soldier in the light infantry called out as they scrambled to their feet and formed their ranks. Jacob, his men, and Laurens looked across the river and saw redcoats through the brush. Then they saw blue and red coats pulling ropes, and from around a bend, the first 6-pounder appeared.

When the British arrived, Laurens grabbed his horse's reins and leaped into the saddle. Up and down the line, the men prepared for action, taking up shooting positions, and those who had covered tried to shrink down for more protection as the second 6-pounder was pulled into view.

"Form the men in open order!" Laurens commanded his light infantry, which opened the spaces between the men in the ranks.

Jacob watched the deployment of the British as the third 6-pounder gun was pulled and wheeled next to the other two. Then, judging the range, the gun crews went up the activity to prepare the guns for firing. Finally, it was Jacob who had predicted and feared they would pound their position without risking a frontal assault.

Across the way, the ropes had been piled near the wheels of the guns. The gunners were taking up their implements, the ammunition boxes being carried behind the guns. Jacob looked over at Laurens, walking his horse up and down the line, giving patriotic speeches and encouragement to his men.

"Jackass," Samuel growled as he looked over his rifle. "Oui, my friend," Jean supported, "You are correct. I have never seen an officer who refuses to see reality."

Jacob nodded his head in agreement. "Be ready to move quickly; we may be pulling out of here on short notice."

"Take care, make ready!" Laurens commanded, drawing his sword. "Aim!"

"What is he bloody shooting at?" Samuel asked, "he has to know his men are out of range!"

"Fire!"

The muskets of the light infantry fired, while a good volley fell harmlessly short into the river. They began their reloading procedures.

"*Boom…boom…boom!*"

The three six-pounders barked, and the three cannon balls screeched over them. Jacob watched the gun crews begin reloading while the gunners looked over the barrels, lowering them.

Once again, the light infantry fired a volley, aiming higher but falling short. There were a few cracks from their left. The riflemen, but they didn't hit anything or anyone. Laurens continued to shout patriotic slogans and encouragement to his men.

Jacob shook his head and looked back at the British guns, which were about to be fired again.

Boom…boom…boom!

The balls struck the water just before their line and skipped into the defensive line this time. One ball bounced over the heads of Shubrick's company, one missed over Jacob's position with a loud cracking sound, but the third found the light infantry, tearing into the line and killing a few of the men.

"They have the range; now they are going to start pounding us," Jacob stated, looking back over at the mounted Laurens, a very identifiable target. "This insanity has to end!"

Jacob jumped out of their position and began trotting towards Laurens when the three cannons fired again. Instinctively, Jacob dove for cover as the balls came screeching over, another one striking the light infantry, and as fate or luck would have it, gun-fired grapeshot and struck Laurens and his horse.

The horse took a mortal wound, screaming as it fell and pinning a wounded Laurens under it. Jacob scrambled to his feet and ran over to the injured Laurens. Jacob grabbed him by the shoulders and pulled him out from under the dead horse. Laurens' arm was bleeding, and he was in shock by the injury.

Pulling the handkerchief from his regimental coat arm, Jacob tied it over the wound to stop the bleeding. He looked around for help and saw the messengers with their horses just behind them, using trees for protection. Jacob waved them over, grabbed their horses, and came to Jacob.

"Take the colonel here back to the Tullifinny, I'll get the men out of here, and we'll be right behind you!" Jacob ordered, and the men nodded. Laurens was placed on a horse in front of a rider. The other two mounted, then the three rode out and headed back down the road.

The three cannons boomed again, and the balls came screeching, though they did not hit anyone. Jacob could see that along with the guns being reloaded; he could see infantry forming to begin the crossing.

"Fall back! Fall back! Rifles cover, right flank fall back to the Tullifinny!" Jacob ordered, and the light infantry company reformed and began to move back to the road, some of them helping their wounded. Jacob saw they were trying to pick up their dead.

"Leave them! The British will see to their burial; get out of here!" Jacob ordered, and the reluctant men jogged after to rejoin their company. The guns fired, and the balls came bouncing and screeching, though now had little targets to hit.

Shubrick was leading his company at a trot, and Jacob nodded as they moved past and continued down the road. Jacob moved over to get ready to have the riflemen and his men fall back. Then, looking across the river, he could see the leading company of the British began their crossing of the river.

Jacob could recognize from their uniforms it was a Highlander regiment. They were walking through the water, and the guns had gone silent as their infantry masked them. Back behind the log, Jacob estimated the distance the Highlanders advanced had come within range of the rifles.

"As they come into range, fire by sections and fall back!" Jacob ordered, and Captain James replied they would. Then, nodding, Jacob took up a good firing position and looked over his sights. "Get ready," Jacob warned, "we'll fire when they get a little closer. We'll be the last one out."

When the British were about halfway across the river, the rifles on the right began to fire by sections, then took off jogging down the road. A few of the advancing British spun and fell into the river. After another section fired, they stopped moving. Now they had the upper hand, the British muskets couldn't reach them, and the cannons were blocked. A third section fired, and four more British fell.

The British column turned, heading back to the far shore. Jacob knew it was time for them to go, as the guns would be unmasked and take them under fire.

"Go, let's move before the guns fire!" Jacob ordered and leaped up and began trotting back, followed by Samuel, Jean, and the rest of their detachment. They were right behind the last of the riflemen. Then, after only trotting about thirty yards, the three cannons fired again, and the balls slammed into the trees and logs of where Jacob and the riflemen had just been.

***

McGirtt and his men waited patiently on their horses for the bombardment to begin. Unfortunately, they were not positioned to see the actual fighting, just around the bend that led to the crossing. The first shots boomed out, causing the horses to jump and skittish. The men reined their horses, getting them back under control.

"It would be nice if they could let us know when they do that," Twiggs commented. Finally, McGirtt dismounted and made his way through the waiting men of the 71st until he could see the cannons and the far side of the river.

With his sword raised, the battery commander looked to the left and right at the guns, whose gunners were standing ready. "Give fire!" was commanded, and the three guns fired, their booms cracking the air, the guns recoiling back. The other men helping took their position at the wheels and pushed the guns back into their firing positions.

McGirtt took out his telescope to look across the river and saw that the commander he had seen earlier had been hit with his dead horses pinning him. He watched a man run across, pull the injured officer out, and hand him to three horsemen who rode off with the wounded officer.

"*Won't be long now,*" McGirtt thought as he continued to look through his telescope. The uniformed light infantry began to reform and trot away when the battery commander again raised his sword to prepare to fire. Lowering his telescope, McGirtt covered his ears as the guns fired again.

Resuming his scanning, he saw another company of men trot across and head away from them. McGirtt lowered his telescope and closed it, and nodded his head. The rebels were beginning to fall back; time for him to get his horsemen ready.

As he started back to his men, the 71st formed its first company to begin their advance across the river. Mounting his horse, he motioned his men forward at the walk and took up their positions behind the column. Then he heard the sound of the rebels firing rifles at them, sounding like they were firing by sections.

The fire must have been effective as the advance stalled, then stopped. Another set of rifles fired, and McGirtt watched the few Highlanders fall into the river wounded or dead. Finally, the advancing company turned and fell back.

"No, no, keep going!" McGirtt growled as the British flowed back into their line, uncovering the guns and preparing to fire. Then, anger boiling up, facing the fact he won't get his revenge, McGirtt yelled back to his men.

"Prepare to ride! As soon as these guns fire, we charge across the river!"

Pulling his pistol, McGirtt waited, watching for the battery commander to give the command. When the commander raised his sword, McGirtt raised his hand and pistol. The commander dropped his sword, the gunners fired their cannon, and McGirtt charged his men forward, riding through the smoke and splashing into the river.

***

Jacob and his men were trotting down the road, where they ran into a section of Captain James' Company. "We're covering our withdraw!" the section sergeant yelled, and Jacob nodded, falling in with them. Jacob looked down the road, his gut telling him trouble was coming.

"Oh, no, trouble is coming," Samuel stated, "Jacob has that look again; his gut is warning him."

The sound of pounding hooves and horses coming down the road could be heard. The riflemen aimed down the road, and soon the Loyalist cavalry came into view.

"Fire!" Jacob commanded, and all the rifles fired, knocking five riders from their saddles and confusing the rest. Then, as their smoke rolled towards the disorganized cavalry, Jacob and the riflemen turned and ran down the road. Another section was in a covering position, and as they ran past, they yelled, "Cavalry right behind us!"

Jacob and the riflemen kept moving down the road, and after a quick moment, another sound of rifles firing could be heard behind them. They stopped, loaded their rifles, and waited to see if the cavalry came after them. But, instead, the riflemen who they had passed came trotting by.

"We broke their spirit," they called out with smiles, "They couldn't stomach our rifles and beat a hasty retreat towards the river. Jacob and the riflemen with him smiled and cheered before trotting down the road to catch up with the column, which they did a short time later.

There was no pursuit, and the column clumped across the wooden bridge crossing the Tullifinny and into the defensive line. After telling his detachment to head over to their campsite, Jacob went to speak with Moultrie. When he arrived on top of the hill, it was a rather angry and fuming Moultrie pacing like a caged wolf.

When Jacob reported, Moultrie acknowledged and asked, "Did that idiot think he could hold that line against the British, even after you explained the British numbers and guns?"

"Yes, sir," Jacob replied, "Even after I advised him he was violating your orders."

"Bloody young fool!" Moultrie growled, "While he may be brave to a fault, he is rash and reckless that will get his men killed! Then he shook his head before looking at Jacob.

"When the scouts brought him here, he stated we could not hold them. Is that true?"

Jacob nodded his head. "I afraid he was right, sir, even in this position, the British can sit back and fire their guns on us, and we can't hit them from here. It would be a matter of time they would grind us into meal, even if these militiamen stand when the shot comes pouring in."

Moultrie thought about it, sighed, and nodded. "I see your point Captain Clarke, and we have no choice but to abandon this position and consolidate what we have at the defenses oat the neck."

He then went to his field table, looked at the map, went over to the lip of the hill, and looked down at the wooden bridge.

"Captain Clarke, I have a special assignment for you. I want you and the detachment of Catawbas to destroy the bridge and use those special tactics to slow the advance. Hit and run tactics, block the road, just buy us some more time."

Jacob nodded his head that he understood his mission. Moultrie smiled, "I'll have the men prepared to move, and I'll get the Catawbas over to you so you can start work on the bridge. Get whatever supplies you need from the quartermaster before we move."

Jacob went to gather his men, then led them over to where the Catawbas had their small camp. There he went over to Captain Allston, who commanded the company. Allston smiled when he saw Jacob and his men join them, knowing full well what it meant.

"I take it you bring news from the general," Allston asked, and the rest of the Catawbas came over to listen in.

"The general has directed that my men and I, along with your Racoon Company, are to destroy the bridge and make the lives extremely miserable for the approaching British. Therefore, we are ordered to destroy every bridge, block the roads, and take a few shots at them repeatedly to keep them on their toes."

The Catawbas smiled and nodded their heads; they liked this type of operation. All around them, the rest of the men were preparing to march, packing their gear, and shouldering their packs. Jacob stripped down to his shirt and motioned for the rest to do the same.

"Let's get to work then."

Jacob and his men went over to the quartermaster. While packing, Jacob secured as many axes and tools as possible for defense construction to use against the bridges. Once they had their tools, they moved out onto the bridge over the Tullifinny. They posted four men armed with their rifles to watch the road as they began to tear up the planks of the bridge. Once torn up or chopped, the spans were dropped into the river to float away.

They moved down the bridge, carefully balancing on the beams while crossing. Except for one who fell to the delight of the others. The Catawba came out of the river spitting and sputtering. Even Jacob laughed at the poor soul's misfortune, but the Catawba also joined in.

Dripping on the plank, his rifle now useless, he had an embarrassed look.

"Go back to camp, change out of your clothes and dry out your rifle; the other three can cover us," Jacob instructed, and the Catawba nodded. Then, as he shuffled past Allton, he patted him on the shoulder, letting him know it was alright. Then, once a good section of the spans had been pulled up, they started fires on top of the beams. They caught and began to burn through.

Moultrie approached Jacob and Allton and nodded his approval.

"I know this is a tough one for both of you," he said simply, "but we have no choice. Buy us time, but don't sacrifice yourselves."

Both Jacob and Allston nodded their understanding. Moultrie smiled, shook their hands, and as he turned, called out to the company, "Good Luck!", then returned to the shore and joined the column as they were marching out.

They worked on dismantling the spans, floating them away, building a bonfire with them, and burning the beams and posts for the rest of the morning until just afternoon. Jacob looked out over what was left, and it was a blackened, smoldering mess of what used to be a bridge. It would take a reasonable amount of time for the British to repair or rebuild to get their men and guns across.

They returned to camp, packed their belongings, shouldered their bags, and cradled their rifles. Allston checked the Catawbas, and Jacob checked his. Then, satisfied, the Racoon Company and Jacob's detachment headed down the road towards Charles Town to find the next place for some mischief. This spot was found about a mile further down the road. The ford crossed where it became marshy, and the trees were close to the road.

They moved past the ford, dropped their gear, and Jacob's men secured their horses. Then, they grabbed their axes and began to chop down the trees. They made sure as they fell, they fell at an angle into the road but were still attached to their stumps. Then they cut the next set of trees, weaving them into the first. After a few hours, a thirty-foot section of the road was blocked by fallen and intertwined trees that the British would have to deal with.

Satisfied with their handiwork, they took up their rifles and gear and moved down the road. They would find a suitable place to camp for the night, and that spot should be near another small bridge over a waterway that they would destroy in the morning.

***

Prevost wasn't satisfied with their progress and was very disappointed that no military action occurred, except for the cannonading of the rebels at the Cooswhatchie. When they arrived at the Tullifinny, they had found the bridge destroyed and the beams nearly impossible to use as they had been burned. So they had to stop and build rafts to get the guns across, the infantry waded holding their muskets and cartridge boxes above them, and the horses waded through.

Then there had been those damnable trees cut down in their way that once more delayed their advance until they could chop through. Finally, it was their time to get even with the rebels interfering with his campaign plan. They had come out in open terrain between rivers, and the column began looting all of the farms and plantations along the way.

Prevost had no qualms about it, and he needed to feed his army and get supplies back to Savannah. He determined that these plantations must be supporting the rebels and had to pay for their support. So his men went in, drove the families out, and herded the cattle and pigs while securing grain and flour.

He found numerous wagons and, after filling them with the looted supplies, would detach some of his infantry to escort the supplies back to Savannah. He also happened to secure anything that looked of value and also sent it to Savannah to his personal quarters. To keep his men's morale up, all of the rum, port, and other spirits were given to them while he and the officers received their rightful share.

Then there were all of the slaves that had been left behind. Some stayed while others ran off along with the plantation owners. Prevost offered them their freedom from these rebels if they would support the King and the colors. Some of them took his offer, mostly single black men. Those with families shook their heads. As he had no means to take care of them, he left them on the burned-out or looted plantations to fend for themselves. For those who joined his column, well, he needed laborers to conserve his fighting strength.

McGirtt and his cavalry roamed well out in advance of the column, looking to find any rebels who were destroying the bridges or cutting down the trees to block the roads. While they were between the waterways, he and his men sought the vengeance he desired and attacked farmsteads, driving out the people and burning them to the ground.

He had to admit, and he enjoyed this, the thrill of finally getting the revenge he wanted after waiting years for it to come. The tide had turned, and the British had the advantage over the rebels. In service to the Crown, he could get away with what would usually get him in jail for thievery and brigandage. Now he did it with the blessing of General Prevost and the King.

McGirtt was leading his detachment down the wooded road again towards Charles Town, as a river stood between them and their goal. He was looking for a fordable area, away from any bridges he assumed would be destroyed. They were using a small side trail off the road, and he could hear the gurgle of the river to their front.

A gurgle meant that the water should be low enough to tumble over rocks, so it must be a ford. He could see to the other side of the trail the black swampy ground with cypress trees and Palmetto bushes and the rank smell that comes with a swamp. The horses' hoves were sloshing through some mud. Soon, they broke out of the vegetation, and before them was a ford.

It wasn't vast though the water was moving very quickly. The depth he guessed was about knee level on the infantry, they would be fine on their horses, and the guns should be able to make it. As he bent down to look closer at the bottom to see if it was muddy or sandy, there were barks of rifles from across the water.

Startled, McGirtt looked up and had to control his horse as the three horsemen next to him spun and tumbled off their horses, and one horse fell dead onto the ground.

"Back, back!" McGirtt yelled as he spun his horse around, "While they are reloading!" The horsemen turned and galloped out of sight and away from the unseen riflemen across the water.

The Catawbas, who had been sent to watch the ford, looked up from their concealed position, smiled, and reloaded. They would wait to see if anyone would come back for the dead and if so, they would be waiting for them. If not, they'll go over and see what they could find on the bodies.

***

Jacob and the Catawbas broke through the early morning mist and onto the neck above Charles Town. As they moved down the road, the shape of the defense line began to appear across the neck, with the profiles of men working in the thick morning mist.

Before them appeared an outer work, a triangle-shaped redoubt, the point was facing to the north of the neck, at the approach. The dirt walls were about five feet high, with a moat and abatis before it.

"Friendlies are coming in!" Jacob yelled as they halted just before the advance redoubt. A sentry moved forward to better see in the mist, and when he observed, Jacob and the Catawbas waved them in.

"Come on in, friends!" the sentry yelled back.

As Jacob passed by, he asked where he could find General Moultrie, and the sentry directed him towards the second line of redoubts being built behind the main line. Thanking the sentry, Jacob led the Catawbas passed the advance redoubt and into the sally port of the main defensive line, where men were moving about, working on strengthening the defenses.

There was another redoubt just behind the main defensive line; it will likely be used for the reserve in case they are needed on the line. Jacob found General Moultrie, along with Lieutenant Colonel Marion, at this new redoubt and a new officer Jacob did not recognize.

After releasing the Catawbas and having his men move off to the side, Jacob reported to Moultrie and Marion. The new officer, the general, was talking to stood out amongst Moultrie and Marion. He wore a light blue uniform with a lot of white lace and gold trim. A large cavalry saber hung from his waist.

Jacob waited until Moultrie saw him.

"Ah, just the man we're speaking of," Moultrie started, "Captain Clarke, may I present General Kazimierez Pulaski, whose legion has finally arrived to reinforce our situation here."

Jacob gave a slight bow and nodded to Pulaski, who returned in kind.

"As I don't see the British in hot pursuit of you and your men, I take it your mission was successful?" Moultrie asked.

"It was sir," Jacob explained, "we destroyed the bridges between the Tullifinny and here, plus knocked down a bunch of trees in the swampy regions that forced them to slow down. My scouts also reported seeing small sections of the British leading cattle, livestock, and other looted items southward."

The three listening officers nodded their heads. "So we have some time then," Moultrie asked, and Jacob nodded.

"A few days at least, maybe more based on what we did to the roads and what we saw, but they will be here soon. So how are we set for defenses?"

Moultrie turned and pointed out to the defensive line. "The general is finally marching here, and the governor accepted that this was more than just a simple raid or feint, that the British are moving and a great threat to the city. So the governor is marching here from Orangesburg with a large militia force. The call went out, and more militia companies are on their way here as we speak."

Jacob nodded, "What are my orders, sir?"

Moultrie smiled, "You have done great service to myself and the army; you and your men may return to Marion and the regiment."

Nodding, Jacob rendered the general a salute, then followed Marion as he led them to their position in the line. Jacob motioned for his men to fall in and follow Marion. But, instead, he led them to the left-most redoubt in the main line, and half of the regiment and the Charles Town Militia were assigned there.

After finding a place to drop their gear, Jacob followed Marion, who led him to the firing step of the redoubt to look out over the potential battlefield.

"The Charles Town Militia and we will hold the left side; Colonel McIntosh and the 5th Regiment are holding the right with the Upcountry Militia. In the advance works is Colonel Haris and the Pine Tree Hill Militia."

Jacob nodded as Marion pointed out the units on the line and followed Marion's direction as he pointed behind them.

"The rest of our men are in the reserves, in the half-moon-shaped redoubt along with the infantry of General Pulaski's Legion. We have artillery being moved into supporting positions and gunboats placed in the river to provide fire against the British as they advance down the neck."

Jacob turned to look over the defensive works and nodded with approval. All the time spent constructing the defenses appeared to have paid off. Jacob appreciated the effectiveness of the abatis. Jacob hoped they, too, could use the abatis to slow or stop the British here, just like back in New York.

Jacob watched two South Carolina Navy warships sail up and then drop anchor to cover the flank with cannons. The forty-four gun frigate Bricole and the sixteen gun brig Notre Dame were the two ships. Jacob looked at the gunports, with their cannons snouts sticking out, and nodded in approval; this should protect the flank from an enemy attack.

The men felt confident as they looked at the warships ride their anchor ropes, the ships having set their anchor lines in the stern of the ships along with the bow anchors so the guns were orientated towards the neck and the approach the British would have to take. Then, if need be, the naval guns could turn and fire down the front of the defensive line to support the infantry in the trenches and redoubts.

Jacob admired the hundreds of sharpened stakes serving as a giant porcupine and covered by the guns of the warships, which almost made him feel sorry for the approaching British. But, having participated in sieges of this scale, Jacob knew it could go in any direction and not get overconfident. Luck was an unplanned element in any battle, for good and bad. Still, though, they would have to cross open killing ground before the works before the British could charge.

He knew they only had the three 6-pound cannons and the three 3-pound cannons with the expedition, which meant they had the British heavily outgunned. So Jacob's only concern was if the British had warships they didn't know about that could try another run on the city as they did back in June of 1776.

The men sat around their small campfire at night, eating their rations and smoking their pipes. Finally, they asked Jacob if he could tell the story of the Battle at Fort Carillon. Jacob, leaning against his bags, pipe in the corner of his mouth, recalled that bloody day.

"We outnumbered them almost four or five to one, and the British were confident we could break through and take the fort from the French. We never made it to the fort; we never made it passed the outer defensive line like this one; we were cut to pieces."

The men listened intently; for some, this was their first taste of combat. Jacob could see in their eyes both the inexperience and overconfidence. The cockiness in their boasts.

"Lads, I'll tell you truly, we were the same, thought we had them bagged up tight on that spit of land called Ticonderoga. They proved us very wrong, horribly wrong, when they butchered our men stuck in the abatis. The most horrifying sound was the wounded caught in the abatis that caught on fire, and we were helpless to do anything. Think about that."

Jacob's hard eyes, the eyes that have seen more action than most of the new men put together, pierced into the latest men's soul, who nodded in understanding. Then Jacob smiled, not wanting to lower the morale of the men but just to give them a dose of the reality of battle.

"You will all do well," he intoned, "follow your instructions, keep with your officers and sergeants, and you too can tell your story of how you beat the British at the neck."

The following morning, fresh barrels of water were delivered as none were out there in the defenses on the neck. Jacob's men helped push and pull the six-pound cannons into position, and a battery of four guns was emplaced in their redoubt. Under the direction of the gunners, Jacob helped his men push the heavy field piece into position, pushing on the large wheels to get the gun into its position.

Once in position, Jacob wiped the sweat from his forehead with his shirt sleeve; he helped the gunners place their equipment near the gun. Samuel directed the men lugging the ammunition boxes, extra cannon shot, and grapeshot to where the men stacked them behind the gun. All four guns were emplaced and readied for the coming action.

Later in the day, Jacob ran his men through gun drills in case the artillerymen were injured or killed. The gun captains were happy to know that the regimental men could fill in if needed. It didn't take long for the infantrymen to get the hang of their positions on the guns under the watchful eyes of Jacob and Samuel.

As the British drew closer, the number of militiamen streaming through the lines steadily increased. Jacob was ordered to keep his men at the ready, to man the redoubt as quick as possible. Accordingly, Jacob's men carried their cartridge boxes and bayonets on them at all times; their muskets leaned up against the redoubt's wall.

Jacob saw Pulaski and his legion, including the infantry and his cavalry, head out and march outward. Then, a short while later, Jacob saw the Racoon Company of the Catawbas also march northward just behind the legion.

"Think something is afoot?" Samuel asked as he watched the catawbas trot out on the dusty road heading up the neck. "What's your famous gut telling you?"

Jacob stared intently to the north, trying to divine what would happen. He did have that feeling in his gut; that action was close at hand.

"My gut says the men should keep their muskets and rifle close, and I fear we may be seeing action real soon."

That was enough for Samuel, who turned to spread the word amongst the men in the redoubt, to be ready and stay close. Jacob continued to look out on the field, and Jean joined Jacob on the firing platform.

"What do you think?" Jean asked, looking out over the field, "How would you attack if you were in command?"

Jacob scratched his chin, thinking about it.

"I wouldn't. Granted, we know where Lincoln is, and he is marching here, and hopefully, he gets here to pin the British against us. But, from what we saw in the field, they don't have enough men to lay siege to us."

He turned and looked at Jean, "You should know you have been involved in sieges just like I was. What do you think?"

Jean nodded, "You are right, my friend; they don't have enough men or heavy guns to make a difference. We can hold."

***

McGirtt was riding next to Major Moncrieff, Prevost's engineer. McGirtt and his cavalry were escorting Moncrieff so he could look at the defenses of Charles Town and assess the possibility of action.

Scanning the woods around him, McGirtt kept a watchful eye. He had been already ambushed and shot at during their march towards the city. He was cautious. He knew they were close, approaching the old race track that, back in friendlier times, he had bet on the horses.

"We're getting close," McGirtt told Moncrieff, who nodded in response. Then, looking over his shoulder, McGirtt shouted, "Be on guard, watch out for ambushes!"

The cavalrymen cocked their pistols in their holsters and began watching the trees. They were edgy, having lost several men to these damn rebels and their ambushes. Everyone was wound tight like springs, anticipating another rifle firing on them from the trees.

As they rounded a bend in the road, McGirtt saw cavalry approaching wearing light blue uniforms before them. Their finally dressed leader seemed startled seeing them on the road. McGirtt quickly drew his saber and gave the command to "Charge!"

The ringing of blades drawn from their scabbards rang out as the Georgian cavalrymen spurred their horses into a charge.

McGirtt leading the column, charged forward as the rebels drew their sabers but did not have time to counter-charge.

Rising in his stirrups, McGirtt brought his saber down at a rebel horseman, who met it with his blade with a loud "clang!" He whirled his horse about and once more slashed at the rebel, who counter-stroked, then kicked his horse and fled down the road back towards the city.

Looking around, McGirtt spotted Moncrieff to ensure he was safe and saw that the rebels were falling back. Wheeling his horse about and waving his sword forward, McGirtt yelled, "Let's go get them, boys!"

The Georgians kicked their horses and, in a cloud of dust, charged off in pursuit of the fleeing cavalry. "They sure looked pretty but can't fight!" yelled McGirtt, and Captain Tawse, who was riding next to him, smiled and yelled back, "Aye, that's a shame!"

McGirtt and his men quickly closed on the fleeing rebels, riding through their dust cloud. Then, coming around another bend, the road left the woods and into a large open area of the old horse race track. The Georgians began to spread out as they cleared the confines of the road and onto the open field.

When McGirtt noticed the concealed infantry rise and brought their muskets to their shoulders, the rebel horsemen were beginning to turn. Kicking his horse harder, McGirtt yelled, "Ambush, get into them!"

The Georgians split; half charged after the forming rebel cavalry, and the other half near the infantry turned to charge into them, closing the distance rapidly. McGirtt led the section against the rebel cavalry, while Captain Tawse led the other section against the infantry.

The muskets went off; however, because McGirtt had ordered them to close the distance, their volley was not as effective as it could have been. Focusing on the enemy cavalry, McGirtt only heard the muskets go off as he closed on the rebel horsemen.

Charging once more into the enemy cavalry, McGirtt slammed into an enemy horseman, sabers clanging once more. There was a sound of pistols going off as the Georgians had drawn their pistols, firing at close range.

This time, rebel horsemen fell from the horses, hit by the pistol balls at very close range. The horses whirled and clashed, stirring up dust and the grey smoke of the pistols into a vortex. The sabers flashed and clang, the Georgians and the rebels fighting fiercely and with determination. To McGirtt, they had the upper hand as more rebel riders fell from their horses than his.

The rebel riders turned, and their leader began yelling, "Fall back! Fall back to the city!" Finally, the rebels turned their horses, significantly reduced numbers, and rode in the direction of Charles Town.

McGirtt turned and saw that Tawse had smashed into the ambush line, blades swinging down and causing havoc amongst the infantry who had unloaded muskets. McGirtt reined up his horse, feeling it was tired from the constant charging and was winded. Although his section held up, their horses were also winded.

"Hold boys, don't follow them," McGirtt ordered. Tawse had the infantry on the run, they were scattering like rabbits, and the Georgians were hunting them down like wolves. Finally, the rebels broke into small groups or individuals and headed for the safety of the woods. Eventually, Tawse halted his pursuit and led his section over to McGirtt.

Most of his men had dismounted and were going through the pockets of the dead and checking the wounded. McGirtt dismounted, handing his reins to one of his troopers, then went out and looked at the few wounded prisoners they had captured.

They had four rebel cavalrymen; McGirtt noticed they wore a light blue uniform and were well equipped. These were not ordinary rebels; they appeared to be a professional cavalry unit, maybe even one of these continentals he had heard of.

McGirtt stood over the prisoners, his mind binding their wounds. "What unit are you?" he asked one of the prisoners.

"Pulaski's Legion," was the reply he got from the prisoner.

"Never heard of you," commented McGirtt, "you're not from around here, are you?"

The prisoner sighed and shook his head. "No, we were sent down here by General Washington. I'm from Baltimore."

McGirtt nodded, "Who is this, General Washington, never heard of him."

The prisoner seemed shocked that McGirtt didn't know who Washington was. "He is our commander of all of the Continentals in the army. He gives the orders, and we follow them."

Shrugging his shoulder, McGirtt stated, "Well, in either case, you're done. We'll take you back and give you to the British. They'll see to your wounds."

The prisoner nodded and stood up along with the other prisoners. Their hands were tired and mounted on the few captured horses. McGirtt's men had been comprehensive, going through the dead and securing all of the weapons and loot they could find. Then, they used a few more of the captured horses to carry the loot.

McGirtt went over to Tawse, "how did we fare?"

"We have three dead; they lost fifteen." Tawse answered, "plus three of ours wounded."

McGirtt smiled and gave a curt nod. "We hurt them; we hurt them real good!" Tawse returned the smile and nodded in agreement.

"Let's take our engineer forward and let him look at the defenses. Then we'll inform his lordship of our little fight here."

***

Jacob and his men lined the wall of the redoubt, looking out over the field before them. They had heard the sound of battle, and the long roll of the drums was sounded. Then, after a while, the sound of fighting faded in the distance. Now only the sound of the breeze and men moving around in the redoubt.

Pulling his telescope out, Jacob focused on where the road exited the woods. A short time later, he spotted movement in the woods, focused closer, and saw the first of Pulaski's horsemen come out of the woods. Then the infantry began to trot out of the woods in small groups or individuals.

"This is not good," Jacob commented before lowering his telescope.

"What do you see?" Jean asked, and Samuel nodded.

"Looks like our Legion took a beating, there is a lot of them missing, and they're coming back in small groups."

"Like they had been running from an enemy, no?" Jean asked, and Jacob nodded.

"I'm afraid so; it looks much less than the number I saw marching out."

The legion men passed the word to the men in the trenches that the British were coming and were right behind them. After the legion came through, the Racoon Company appeared jogging out of the woods and entered the defensive lines, yelling, "We're the last ones, the British are coming, and they're right behind us!"

The long roll was played, and the army jumped into their positions in the trench or the redoubts. Jacob, Samuel, and Jean, along with the men of the 2nd Regiment, took up their muskets. The men manned their section of the redoubt next to one of the cannons that the crew had readied.

The gun captain ordered his men to their places, looking over the barrel to check the angle while the linstock man blew on his glowing linstock. Then, across the open space of the neck and before the advance redoubt held by the Camden Militia, flashes of red and the glint of metal could be seen in the woods before they broke out and began to form into the traditional British lines of attack.

General Moultrie, who was in the defenses, observed the British beginning to form their lines and ordered the cannons to open fire to break up the formations and prevent the British from getting their position set. The gun captains strained to see what the results of their shots were doing, but the distance made it difficult. They could not decern if they were on the mark or going over their heads.

The cannons up and down the defensive line boomed and barked. They threw their shot out towards the British, bouncing and skipping towards them. A wall of grey smoke from the cannon muzzles began to fill the space before the redoubts, the humidity keeping it low to the ground. The 6-pounders with Jacob's redoubt added their roar to the symphony of carnage.

The Camden Militia also began firing at the British, adding fire to the guns' chaos.

"What are those bloody fools doing?" Samuel shouted over the bombardment, "they are way out of range of hitting anything!"

Jacob nodded his head in agreement, and as if Moultrie had heard the comment, a runner was seen heading to the forward position, and their firing stopped. Their musketry had no effect other than releasing the building stress in the militiamen.

The guns continued a sustained pounding of the British, who seemed to be holding their position in the woodline. General

Moultrie continued to observe from the main line, waiting to see what the British would do. Jacob and his men were watching from the redoubt. The British cooly went about their business of forming for battle, sheltered in the trees.

The cannonade continued until night and was ordered to cease fire once the gunners could no longer see their targets due to the darkness. However, Jacob, Jean, and Samuel kept an eye on the firing step, looking over the field.

"Ah, my ears are still ringing," Samuel commented, shaking his head to try and clear the ringing away. Jean nodded, also trying to get the ringing to stop.

The sun had sunk away, the stars came out, and the nightly sound of the neck began with insects and birds doing their evening calls. The moon had not risen yet, the darkness of sundown blanketing men and the redoubts alike.

Marion joined them on the firing step. "Set up a rotation, keep a watch on the firing step while the rest of the regiment eat and sleep. Have the duty drummers ready to beat the long roll if the British make a night push."

Jacob nodded his head. "Prudent thinking, we'll keep the men at the ready. Where will you be, sir?"

"I'll be over with the general," Marion explained, "if something happens, send a runner to get me."

The three nodded; Marion returned the nod, jumped down from the firing step, and headed off toward the center redoubt where General Moultrie was commanding.

"Let's see to the men," Jacob commented, and Jean with Samuel went over to the different companies. Jean spoke with the company commanders while Samuel spoke with their first sergeants. Jacob walked inside the redoubt, observing as a company gathered their men and headed to the firing steps.

The rest of the regiment settled in, each company claiming an area within the redoubt to lay out their gear, no tents but sleeping under the stars. Soon small fires began to pop up as men started to prepare to cook rations. Their voices were low, a soft murmur in the redoubt as the men discussed the possibilities of the looming siege. Jacob silently walked amongst the redoubt, acknowledging calls and hellos from the men or answering questions about the future action.

Jacob returned to the shooting step, looking once more out over the dark open area before the redoubt. The odd sense of Deja Vu swept over him; how many times had he seen this, felt this, or experienced this. Then, turning, he looked over the inside of the redoubt, and before him swam the faces of his fallen friends. Shaking his head, Jacob acknowledged that too many of his friends had gone on before him.

Suddenly, a sound of musketry was heard, first a tiny sputtering of muskets; then it grew into a louder sound as more muskets joined in. Spinning, Jacob looked out over the field and saw the muskets were coming from one of the militia-held areas. Quickly scanning, Jacob looked for any sign of British, then shook his head. The militia was shooting at ghosts, all wired tightly from the cannonade, and the approaching British made them jumpy.

Soon, the sound of "Cease Fire, Cease Fire!" was heard along with the drum command being beat, and the firing ceased. Taking a deep breath, Jacob again shook his head, concerned about the level of experience and training with these militiamen. Jacob walked along the firing step, giving reassuring words to the men on watch.

"What do you think, Captain Clarke," one of the men asked as Jacob was making his rounds, "you think them British are actually going to try and take the city? My wife and children are in there."

Jacob paused, "To be honest, no, I don't. We have a superior position and a heavier number of guns than they do. If they are foolish enough to attack, we'll throw them back. Your family is safe."

In the darkness, Jacob could see the man smile and nod his head. "Thank you, sir. It makes me feel better if I hear it from you."

Jacob gave him a reassuring pat on the shoulder before continuing his rounds. Finally, a runner came up to Jacob, "Sir, a runner just arrived from the colonel." Jacob nodded and followed the man back to the runner.

"Sir, Lieutenant Colonel Marion sends word that the general is sending a lighting party under General Huger, and all are to hold their fire."

Jacob nodded, "Thank you for this information; return to the colonel and let him know we understand."

As the runner returned to the central redoubt, Jacob made his way back to the firing step and began passing the word, "hold your fire; the lighting party is heading out!" Once he alerted everyone, Jacob remained on the firing step as he had a bad feeling that began to swell in his stomach.

"What's going on?" Samuel asked as he and Jean joined Jacob on the wall.

"The general is sending out a lighting party, probably to chase those damn ghosts away that the militia is shooting at," Jacob explained, then turned, and as if on cue, a barrel of pitch began to burn in the moat before the redoubt on the right, illuminating it and the open space before it.

Once again, the crack of muskets was heard, then a few more popping before other muskets joined in. As before, the firing came from the right; Governor Rutledge, either not receiving the word or ignoring it, had the Upcountry Militia had opened fire on the movement near the line.

"No, you idiots, hold your fire!" Jacob yelled, but it was too late, and what he had come to fear occurred. Even the units who had heard the order to hold fire got caught up in the frenzy of firing. Then, starting from the right, more muskets joined in, thinking they were under attack.

"Hold your fire, you fools!" Samuel and the other men of the regiment began to yell down the line, but the firing continued. Then, growling, Jacob took off in a sprint, headed down the line, followed by Jean and Samuel, and began knocking down muskets and physically pushing the men to stop firing at their own. Sometimes, they physically grab their men's muskets or knock them up.

To add to the ever-growing confusion, the ships and barges in the river saw and heard the firing and opened fire with their cannons, thinking the British were conducting a night attack against the line. It took some effort, but order was restored, and the line stopped firing, but the damage was done. Jacob learned that General Huger was seriously wounded, and twelve men were killed by friendly fire before order was finally restored along the line.

Jacob was seething with anger. He and some of his men went over the top of the redoubt to help carry the wounded and dead back into their lines. It sickened him at the needless sight of the dead and wounded, having been hit by the telling cross-fire of the defensive line and supporting artillery from the line and the warships.

Men laid crumpled where they fell, a few missing limbs from the artillery. Jacob, anger coursing through him, helped to gather the wounded and carry the moaning men to help. As they carried the wounded back behind the line to where the surgeons had established a field hospital, Jacob could see a livid General Moultrie yelling at Governor Rutledge.

"What in the bloody hell were you thinking!" Moultrie yelled at Rutledge, who stood defiantly before Moultrie.

"Don't take the tone with me, general," Rutledge warned, "You're under my command!"

Having passed the wounded to the surgeon, Jacob moved over to the confrontation between Moultrie and Rutledge. Jean and Samuel followed and stood with Jacob.

"Did you not receive my orders to hold fire as General Huger was leading a lighting detail so we could see if the British were attacking us," shouted Moultrie, "rather than Blackbeard's ghost!"

Rutledge paused for a few seconds before firing back. "Yes. Yes, I did. We received the warning, but my men were confident it was a British attack." Pausing, Rutledge continued, "I had no choice; I will not be accused of crying wolf in this matter. I treated like it was a sneak attack, and my men had stated it was!"

Moultrie's face hardened, "You bloody well know what a chain of command is if you recall from our Anglo-Cherokee years? We can't have two leaders, as this is a military matter; I am in command!"

"Pish," growled Rutledge, "I am the President of South Carolina, and you are under my command! Therefore, I can rescind any order."

Moultrie's hardened face turned into a frown, and he stepped closer. Jacob saw that Rutledge did involuntarily twitch.

"Even if it means you kill your men then, the fact your disobeying of orders seriously wounded a good man, General Huger?"

There was a pregnant pause when Jacob decided to head back to their redoubt, shaking his head in disbelief.

"Bloody fool, bloody irresponsible fool," Samuel growled as they left General Moultrie and the governor still arguing with one another. They both felt the governor was wrong and should not have been leading men anyways. Leave the fighting to the soldiers; the governor should be taking care of the people.

Both men were still gesturing with their arms, Moultrie dressing down the governor while the governor argued he was in the right. Jacob hoped this wasn't the thing to come with the war, recalling how dysfunctional the chain of command was during the French and Indian War between the military and civilian governments. It would lead to nothing but disaster.

Shaking his head, Jacob, Jean, and Samuel continued into the trenches and returned to camp. The men were waiting, and Jacob explained what had happened, some adding their colorful comments about the stupidity of the twelve men's needless loss to friendly fire.

"What was he thinking, sir?" one man asked, another "Damn, twelve good men, dying not in battle but lighting fire barrels?"

Jacob knew how the men felt, especially after something tragic yet easily avoidable, but the fog and confusion of war can make mistakes. However, Jacob recalled when some of these mistakes were on purpose, when the hated Captain Reynolds fired on Jacob, claiming it had been a mistake but had been very intentional.

Sighing, it had been a waste; any loss at this moment is too significant. The army lost one of their better generals due to dueling commanders and fighting over who was in command. Jacob had seen every fight, every conflict; why should he suspect it would be any different this time, though he had hoped it would be.

CHAPTER 6

STONO FERRY

Jacob was taking his turn on guard, taking the late graveyard shift, the tough one just before the sunrise. Standing on the firing step, looking out over the open field at the flickering light in the distance of the British fires. Breathing in the fresh air, mixed with the smell of turned earth of the freshly built redoubt, Jacob thought of the coming battle. The British had been quiet so far, and siege lines and entrenchments were not digging on their side. This bothered Jacob; it wasn't making any sense. Jacob turned to see Samuel with two tin cups in his hands at the sound of approaching feet.

"Morning, Captain," Samuel greeted Jacob as he handed him a steaming cup of tea, then stood next to Jacob and looked out over the field. Taking a sip, Jacob continued to look out over the area.

"The men have the fires stoked up in the field kitchen, so they can at least have a warm breakfast or tea," said Samuel and Jacob. Then, looking to the growing pink sky of the coming dawn and the wispy clouds over them, Jacob responded, "I think we're not going to be hoping for warm anything soon. Summer is coming."

Samuel nodded in understanding and replied with an "Umm..hmm."

Swallowing a sip of tea, Samuel looked over at Jacob and asked, "What's on your mind? Something has you troubled?" Jacob pursed his lips and then nodded his head.

"Does this seem strange to you?" Jacob asked, and Samuel looked out over the field and thought about it for a moment.

"No, nothing seems strange; they are over there, and we are here. Nothing is going on," Samuel responded, then stopped and thought about it, mumbling, "nothing is happening."

Then he looked out over the field, then back at Jacob. "Nothing is occurring."

"It doesn't seem right to me unless they have changed tactics from the last war. They should be digging siege lines, bringing up heavy artillery, and preparing their lines. Instead, nothing is happening; it's too quiet."

Samuel looked out over the field and nodded his head in agreement. "Don't think they'll try a surprise attack after what happened last night and with all of these itchy trigger fingers facing them."

The two men stood there, looking out over the redoubt's wall as the sun rose, bringing light to the field and trees beyond.

Pulling his telescope out of his haversack, Jacob brought it up to his eyes and focused on the far tree line. Adjusting the focus, he could look into the woods in a limited fashion and look for any sign of British activity. He spotted none.

"I think either they are waiting for the rest of the army to arrive, or perhaps they are trying a feint," Jacob replied as he lowered his telescope and closed it with a click. Then, taking a deep breath and letting it out slowly, Jacob murmured, "We'll have to wait and see."

Samuel nodded, "I hate waiting," to which Jacob agreed.

As the sun rose higher, Jacob was joined by Jean while Samuel returned to check on the men and the sergeants. Samuel yelled and kicked the men to roll out of their blankets and organized the camp, packing their haversacks and backpacks.

"Let's go; you never know when those Bloody French and Indians will attack!"

Jean looked over at Jacob, who was chuckling lightly.

"French and Indians attack?" Jean asked, and Jacob nodded.

"Left over from our Ranger days, it is burned into his brain for stand-to we had to do every morning when we were with Rogers."

Jean nodded and smiled slightly, "He is not wrong, my friend; a good practice." Jean winked and headed down into the redoubt to check on the officers. After the regiment was awake and moving, Marion had the men keep their muskets nearby but carry cartridge boxes, haversack, and canteens. Jacob went about; spot-checking the men to ensure their muskets were cleaned and ready.

***

Meanwhile, in the city, General Moultrie had rode into the city and entered the assembly building to speak directly with the city officials, still angered over the senseless loss of life during the night.

Standing before the city council and staring directly at the governor, Moultrie spoke his mind in a loud and commanding voice.

"There must be a designation of authority, one person in command. Last night will not do! We shall and must decide on one commander, or everything will be ruined and destroyed. If you allow me to command everything militarily, I will not interfere in your business of civil rule if you do not interfere with my command. If you select to deal with the enemy through negotiations or civil matters, I will not interfere. I will run the military and meet the enemy on the battlefield."

A chorus of voices joined in, discussing the merits of what General Moultrie had just stated. However, he could see a division in the government, which made him concerned. On one side, he could hear assembly members argue that having a military officer in command made military sense. Then there were the others who appeared to shudder at the idea of a military man in charge; these were state troops and the state commands.

Moultrie tried to wait patiently, but listening to the bickering between the two sides of the assembly was starting to get him mad. These fools do not see the big picture of being at war with England and clearly a military matter, and not for some wealthy bumbling assembly members who were probably afraid of his own shadow.

Over time, and with great patience on Moultrie's part, Governor Rutledge grudgingly acknowledged he had made a tactical mistake and stopped the debate. General Moultrie would command the state troops and the city council while handling the civil aspects of the fight.

"Then gentlemen," Moultrie stated, "I will depart to not interfere with your efforts, and I will command our soldiers in the field."

Bowing to Rutledge, who nodded in return, Moultrie turned and headed out of the assembly building, hearing the voices rise again in debate about whether to fight the British or negotiate. He even heard the word surrender be thrown around.

Shaking his head, Moultrie grumbled, "Politicians, what do they know about war?"

***

"Captain Clarke, British party approaching!" a sentry called out, and Jacob moved up to the firing step to the sentry, who pointed at the small party coming towards them. A British officer with a man carrying the white flag and two escorts approached the line, and the regiment's men climbed up onto the firing step along the redoubts wall to see what was going on.

"Hold your fire; pass down the line to hold your fire!" Jacob yelled, "And I bloody well mean it!"

The command was echoed up and down the line. Jacob went looking for Marion, but he was not there but over at the general's redoubt.

"Well, let's see what this is about," Jacob grunted as he pulled himself into the artillery opening and approached the British party. "Ah, hell," Samuel grunted and followed Jacob with Jean right behind out into the field.

The British party stopped a hundred paces from the line and waited for Jacob, Jean, and Samuel to approach. As they approached, a single officer stepped out, took off his hat, and bowed toward Jacob. "This is going to be a formal meeting, I see," Jacob whispered to Samuel as he stopped in front of the officer.

Following suit and protocol to the best he could remember, Jacob also removed his helmet and bowed in the direction of the British officer.

"Lieutenant Colonel James Prevost, at your service, I bring a message for your city leaders that should avoid any unnecessary bloodshed."

Nodding, Jacob returned. "Sir, I am Captain Clarke; I will escort you to my commanding general so he may decide on your proper disposition."

The British officer straightened up and returned his hat to his head, nodding in understanding.

"Sir, you understand that before I am to lead you to my commanding general, I must blindfold you for the security of our position." Lieutenant Colonel Prevost nodded his head in understanding. "I place my safety into your hands, captain."

Pulling a pair of stockings from his haversack and using one of them, he tied it as a blindfold around the eyes of the British officer.

"Sir, if you place your hands on my shoulder, I will lead you to my commander; my lieutenant and sergeant-major here will see to your safety. Your men must remain here where we will return you once the meeting is concluded." Jacob instructed, and Prevost replied he understood.

As they walked slowly towards the lines, both of Prevost's hands on Jacob's shoulder, Prevost commented, "I am surprised that a provincial understands the rules of war. Have you served in his majesty's forces before?" Jacob knew the officer was just making small talk to calm the situation, so he answered.

"I served with Major Robert Rogers Independent Battalion of Rangers at Fort Edward during the last war, sir." From behind, Jacob heard the officers remark with an "Ah" before he warned him they were climbing through the artillery opening, which Jacob, Jean, and Samuel helped him through.

As they walked to the command position, Prevost remained quiet. When they arrived, Jacob untied his sock from around Prevost's eyes, in which he thanked Jacob for the safe journey; he blinked his eyes as they got used to normal light. While he thanked Jacob and Jean, Prevost seemed to ignore Samuel, who shrugged his shoulders and waited off to the side.

General Moultrie had been warned that Jacob was bringing an officer forward, in which Jacob saluted General Moultrie and, in a proper manner, introduced Lieutenant Colonel Prevost to him. Marion was there and nodded his appreciation to Jacob.

Once the general began to speak with Prevost, Jacob and Samuel backed away and stood in the background. Samuel whispered to Jacob, "So what do you think his proposal is that will spare us from bloodshed?" Jacob thought about it and then simply shrugged his shoulders and whispered back.

"You know the British as well as I do; do you think they would show compassion?" Samuel shook his head, "No, they don't seem very compassionate, especially during war."

Concerned, Jacob decided to listen closely to the conversation. "Seems we repeat ourselves, no?" Jean asked as he listened to the discussion, "how many times have you seen this in the last war?"

Jacob thought about how many he had seen or even participated in it. Jacob began to chuckle, recalling an incident right after Fort William Henry had been attacked, the people massacred, and the fort burned. A negotiating party arrived at Fort Edward, and the Rangers had gone out with sole intent to antagonize the French.

"I take it you recall a good one?" Jean asked, and Jacob nodded. He explained about the French party that had arrived at Fort Edward. "We also made sure to rub it in that we wanted to thank Montcalm for the beef they had during the raid where they had captured a good number of French oxen and had cooked them near Fort Carillon."

Jean started to laugh but controlled himself not to be loud. "Oh yes, my friend, the marquis heard of your insult and infuriated him. However, I was very impressed you had gotten away with it, and I decided to see if I could capture you or Rogers, or at least do better."

They stopped talking and listened in to the conversation as Prevost made his demand. "You will surrender unconditionally; all inhabitants of this city who fail to accept royal authority will be treated as prisoners of war, civilian and military alike."

General Moultrie stood there with no expression as Prevost gave his demands. "No," Moultrie simply replied to the demand, "That will not do. We will not surrender the city and defend it to the last man if necessary."

Nodding his head in acceptance, Prevost indicated their meeting was over. "Captain Clarke, please see the lieutenant colonel safely back through the lines," General Moultrie instructed, in which Jacob went through the process of blindfolding Prevost before leading through their lines.

***

Returning to the city, Moultrie presented what Prevost had demanded before the governor, as the city council members murmured and debated just like before over the demand for unconditional surrender.

"What do you think, general, can we stop them?" Governor Rutledge asked, and Moultrie responded he believed they could hold. The lines were manned and ready.

The governor turned to Colonel Senf, who disagreed with General Moultrie. "Your honor, the line won't stop those eight thousand British soldiers out there," remarked Colonel Senf.

Moultrie gave Senf a confused look. "Eight thousand, where do you get eight thousand from?" demanded Moultrie.

"I have my sources," Senf shot back; they say the British have over eight thousand men facing us."

General Moultrie shook his head in disbelief; his scouts had maybe three thousand British facing them, the same amount of men he had. Defense was in their favor; the British did not have enough men or artillery to break their lines. What frustrated Moultrie was the governor appeared to be listening and believing Colonel Senf, one of the governor's engineers and aides.

The city leaders who had been standing off to the side, having heard that Moultrie had arrived with news from the British, approached and spoke with the governor Rutledge as Moultrie waited.

"Based on what Colonel Senf has told me, I propose that we send a message to the British to see if we surrender, will they guarantee the neutrality of the harbor for the rest of this conflict."

As the city leaders applauded and cheered, Moultrie noticed it was primarily men with ties to the mercantile industry. Moultrie's stomach churned; even as a plantation owner who understood the importance of business, this was disgusting that the merchants were seeing to their welfare and nothing about loyalty to the cause or support to the army.

They would not accept royal authority and become prisoners of war, and these men would sit comfortably by while trade continued through the harbor. Finally, Moultrie was pulled back into the meeting with the governor called his name.

"General Moultrie, will you see our proposal is passed to the British?"

Moultrie looked up as Governor Rutledge handed him a rolled parchment, which he assumed was this ridiculous proposal. "Is this your desire to see what the British will grant for neutrality?"

Rutledge looked at Moultrie and though he did have a disgusted look on his face, followed with, "As we agreed, we won't interfere with military matters, as long as you don't interfere with governmental matters. This portion is now governmental, so please see to getting our proposal to the British."

"If they agree to this," Moultrie warned, "you can expect a good portion of the army will fade away, wait, and rise to take the fight to the British. But, on the other hand, you many sit idly by; they will not."

Turning, Moultrie and his aids departed the assembly and headed outside. The thought of just giving up infuriated Moultrie, and he was sure as Hell would not be the one to deliver it. So instead, he thought of someone who could be rash enough to take the message.

Mounting his horse, followed by his aides, they rode to where Lieutenant Colonel Laurens was resting, still recovering from his wounds during the fight at the Tullifinny. Laurens was recovering, though his arm was still heavily bandaged. When he learned what the proposal contained, Laurens adamantly refused to carry it to the British.

While he was pleased with Lauren's response, Moultrie had to appease the governor and still deliver the message. He would have to find someone else and was thinking about it as he rode back to the defensive lines.

***

"Captain Clarke, the general, wants to see you, Lieutenant Langy, and Sergeant-Major Penny," indicated the messenger who came to the redoubt. As Jacob, Jean, and Samuel headed to the command post, Samuel asked, "What did we do this time?"

Jacob looked over at his friend, "What do you mean by us? What did you do?" Samuel, pointing to himself with innocent eyes, "Me, what did I do? We haven't had time for anything except work, so I am innocent." Jean chuckled to himself but did not say anything.

They could see General Moultrie and Lieutenant Colonel Marion waiting as they approached the command post. "Ah damn, it's not what we did," whispered Samuel, "It's what we're going to do!"

"Captain Clarke, I need you to carry this proposal over to the British line, see if you can speak with Lieutenant Colonel Prevost, who had opened these negotiations," instructed Moultrie.

Then Marion spoke, "While you three are there, observe and report everything you can on our enemy. The governor believes there are eight thousand men over there; see if our information is right or his."

Jacob understood his real mission and gather information while delivering the message. General Moultrie looked at Jacob, "My position remains, we will not surrender the city, and you can pass that to the British. We will make them pay heavily for it!"

The three nodded in understanding, and Moultrie returned and read the dispatch from Governor Rutledge. "Good luck," Marion threw in, and the three turned and headed back to the redoubt.

They could find a large enough piece of white cloth to use as a signal, then tie it to a spontoon. Samuel would carry the spontoon, and Jean would accompany Jacob. The men wished them luck; once more, the three crawled through the embrasure for the gun and began walking towards the British after taking a deep breath.

The three strode purposely forward from the position towards the British. "Did they teach you how to do this when you became a captain?" Samuel asked, and Jacob shook his head no.

"No different than negotiating business, right?" Jacob asked, and Samuel replied he was asking the wrong man. As the three approached the tree line, they could see some barricades and brush thrown up in front of the forward pickets, from where they could see British soldiers looking over their muskets.

"Halt you rebel scum and state your business!" a British soldier yelled.

"We have a message from the city for Lieutenant Colonel Prevost," Jacob yelled out then under his breath, "you lobster-backed whore bastard." Samuel snorted but kept their white flag high and visible.

"You men show proper due!" yelled an officer, and Jacob could see the muskets come off them and a captain come from around the barricade and approach Jacob. Following the procedures, Jacob and Jean took off their helmets and bowed to the approaching officer, who took off his hat and returned the bow.

"Sir, General Moultrie sends this message from the city leaders for Lieutenant Colonel Prevost, who had initiated this negotiation." Jacob held out the message and presented it to the British officer.

The British captain took the message and responded, "Please remain here while I take this message and will return with a response." Jacob bowed and watched as the captain took the message, disappeared behind the barricade, and headed into the trees. Another British soldier, a sergeant by his epaulet, came out to watch them from the barricade. He watched them with a sneer on his face; Jacob, Jean, and Samuel turned to talk to one another, ignoring him.

"Keep your eyes open, I'll look over your shoulder, and you look over mine, see what we can discover."

Jacob knew it would take time, so he carried a conversation between Jean and Samuel, who followed along, slowly turning from time to time so they could get different views of the wood line looking over each other's shoulders.

"Don't see much; no lines or trenches built, no abatis or fascines. There was nothing that indicates a battle to come," Samuel whispered, and Jacob nodded. "Same here," Jacob whispered back; from the other side, it doesn't appear there are eight thousand men here; it doesn't smell like there are eight thousand here." Although Samuel agreed, an encamped army has a peculiar smell and was not here.

"I agree," Jean injected, I see some movement like drill in the woods, but nothing close to eight thousand or any heavy artillery."

After waiting, the officer returned alone, without Lieutenant Colonel Prevost. "Please accept the colonel's apology that he could not see you in person. He asked for me to pass his response to you." Jacob nodded his head and waited for the captain to continue.

"The colonel still indicates there is no change, unconditional surrender. He does not care what the governor says or asks; this is a military manner and for military gentlemen only."

Jacob accepted what the captain said and returned with, "Our commander has directed me that we will not surrender; if you want the city, come and get it." With a nod, the British captain smiled and saluted Jacob, who returned the salute, turned, and began walking back towards their lines.

The three went directly to the command post and told General Moultrie and Lieutenant Colonel Marion what the British captain had responded with, plus what they observed.

"Sir, there is no indication that they do not have eight thousand men, nor do we think they are ready for a fight." General Moultrie nodded and asked how Jacob had come up with that assessment.

"Jean, I, and the sergeant-major looked over their front area and saw no indication of any preparations. No trenches, no siege lines or heavy artillery positions, nothing to indicate they were preparing to attack our line here. They do have barricades and pickets, but nothing else."

General Moultrie and Lieutenant Colonel Marion nodded in agreement, knowing they had the military experience to back their observations.

"What do you think they are up to?" Marion asked, and Jacob replied, "I think they are either waiting for the rest of the British Army to arrive, or they are trying to scare the city into surrendering."

Both Moultrie and Marion nodded with Jacob's assessment. "I think you are right, Captain Clarke," agreed Moultrie, "I think the British are getting information from Loyalists in the city and know the city leaders are more interested in their profit margins than fighting. The British are using that against us. Thank you, gentlemen; once again, you proved we can rely on you."

The three saluted, General Moultrie returned their salutes, and they headed back to the redoubt. The men from the regiment were waiting for them like children waiting on their parents and, as kids, began asking questions about what they saw.

"To be plain," he stated, "We didn't see anything that spoke of a siege or an attack. We have been watching the same force since they crossed the Savannah, if not maybe a bit smaller. Nothing that looked like an impending attack."

"So, what is it then if not an attack?" one of the soldiers asked.

"A big bluff," Samuel stated, "We think they are trying to scare the city leaders into surrendering."

"What does the general want to do?" another asked.

"Fight, never give up," Jacob replied, and the men murmured their approval.

The men broke up and returned to their camp areas or details around the redoubt. The day remained quiet, the companies rotating their shift up on the firing steps while the rest waited, ate their meals and sat around their small fires as the sun went down. Then, Jacob was finally up on the firing step, looking across the open ground again.

Jean joined him, looking across the field. "This does not feel right," he stated, "If they were going to attack, it would have been now. But instead, they sent a party to negotiate, and we responded, now we are supposed to be attacking one another. That's the way of things, no? Have the British forgotten the way to wage war?"

'No, my friend, you are right. However, seeing they will be getting low on supplies, I am guessing they would have no choice. We didn't see much of wagons or supplies other than heading back to Georgia."

Then Jacob turned and looked over the men inside of the redoubt.

"They can only take so much of hurrying into position, to only wait. It wears on a man, and we could have problems if they lose their patience. So we will have to see what they do in the morning.

***

General Prevost stood with his staff as the column of infantry moved past quietly. They had muffled their tin cups and canteens to remain quiet, only the soft sound of their shoes on the mix of sand and pine needles as they began their march back to Savannah.

A small detail, the rear guard, was stoking up the fires to keep the rebels thinking they were still encamped. Prevost watched as the fire's glow danced off his face. Then, he turned to look at McGirtt, standing next to his horse.

"Are you sure your men saw the rebel army marching this way?" Prevost asked, and McGirtt nodded it was.

"Yes, your lordship, General Lincoln and his army will be here in the next couple of days, and if you don't move, will pin your backs against those redoubts over there or the city walls."

Prevost nodded. "Yes, yes. You are correct, of course." Prevost sighed, "I took a gamble, and they called me on it. There is no possible way we could dislodge them now."

He looked off in the distance, the outline of the city in the dusk of the evening, the fading glow of the sun reflecting off the church steeples.

"I had expected these city leaders to give it up without a struggle," Prevost grumbled to McGirtt, "You told me these men were sheep and would fold as soon as we would arrive."

McGirtt stared back and simply shrugged. "Yes, sir, I stand by what I said. It was not the city leaders standing up to you but the military leaders. But, may I point out, General Lincoln is not here, so it has to be General Moultrie, the hero of Fort Sullivan."

Sighing again, Prevost nodded his head in understanding, mumbling "so close" before turning and mounting his horse.

"Have your men cover the rear guard in case these rebels come out in force," Prevost ordered, and McGirtt nodded in understanding. Then, he returned to staring across the field at the dark shape of the defenses before the city.

"We'll see you on the next trip," he growled before mounting up on his horse with a grunt. Settling himself in his saddle and then set his gear. McGirtt turned his horse and headed to where the rest of his men were waiting for them.

***

Jacob woke before the sun, as he has for years, his body attuned to the early rising of a Ranger. There were other stirring and waking, going to the latrine, or getting cook fires started. Jacob looked around the camping area within the redoubt before heading to his perch on the firing step.

"Morning, sir," one of the sentries said as Jacob mounted the firing step, pipe lit and a trail of grey smoke following him in the morning breeze.

"Quiet night again, nothing seen or heard," the sentry continued, even those fires across the way went out."

That peaked Jacob's attention, and he quickly pulled his telescope, and tried to look into the far wood line, made difficult by the early morning light. It took a short while, but the sun was finally high enough for Jacob to focus and see trees and other distinct objects. But, unfortunately, he didn't see any sign of the British.

The sentry looked concerned when Jacob lowered his telescope with a severe look on his face.

"What is it, sir?" he asked, and Jacob slowly closed his telescope with a "click."

"I think we may have been bluffed, and there is only one way to find out," Jacob explained. He turned, jumped down from the firing platform, and headed back to his camping area. Samuel was up and had started on ash cakes; Jean was smoking his pipe.

"Grab your gear," Jacob commanded, "we're going for a scout." Samuel and Jean instantly stopped what they were doing and went to grab their rifles and bags. Jacob turned and went over to the duty officer.

"Whose company is next to stand the watch? Jacob asked, and the duty officer responded, "Captain Horry, sir."

Jacob nodded, "Go get me, Captain Horry, tell him to form his company and meet me at the sally port." The duty officer nodded quickly and headed to get Captain Horry. Jacob went over to get his rifle and bags, Samuel and Jean waiting.

"So, what did you see this morning?" Jean asked.

"Nothing, and that's the problem," Jacob replied.

"Nothing?" Samuel asked, "As in no British, nothing?"

"That's what we're going to find out," Jacob replied as Captain Horry and his company approached.

"What if you're wrong," Samuel pointed out, "We could be facing the whole British force!"

Jacob shrugged. "Well then, we'll offer terms for their surrender."

"Not bloody likely!" Samuel retorted, and Jean covered his face with his hand to hide his smirk and giggle.

"Captain Horry reporting," he stated as he approached Jacob, "what would you require of us?"

"We will conduct a scout in force of the British lines across the way. I suspect they may have pulled out in the night, but we need to confirm." Then, Jacob explained, Horry nodded his understanding, and a grin came to his face.

"Finally, some action!"

Jacob nodded. "Have your men fix bayonets, prime and load, then follow us in a column. We'll deploy into skirmish order and advance until we make contact or locate their old camp."

Jacob turned and led the column out of the sally port and onto the field with Samuel and Jean. Along with the everyday guard detail on the firing steps, men from the regiment began to mount up to see what would happen during the scouting expedition.

Once the company was clear of the sally port, Jacob motioned for the line to deploy into open skirmish order. Two men in file with about six paces in between. Jacob, Samuel, and Jean were in the middle, Captain Horry and his officers controlling the flanks. All advanced with their muskets at the ready, bayonets glinting in the morning light.

Jacob listened for any sound of the enemy and only heard the sound of their footfalls on the crackling grass. The silence was deafening, Jacob visualizing cannons and the howitzers barking from the tree line, their shot and shell crashing into them. But instead, insects jump before the footfalls of the advancing infantry.

As the line entered the wood line, all eyes began scanning the trees for any sign of the enemy other than the barricades they had passed. Finally, after moving a short distance into the trees, they found where the British had encamped; some fire pits were still smoldering, thin tendrils of smoke rising into the sky.

Jacob had Captain Horry take a third of the men and sweep one side of the camp, Samuel with another third sweep the other side, while Jacob and the rest of the company looked for any other evidence of the British numbers. After the sweep, the company was reformed, and Jacob gathered what they saw from all the men.

The men spoke of what they observed, between old fire pits, places where men had made beds on the ground, and the number of latrines found. From all the information, there were no eight thousand men here; maybe between two and three thousand men had been there. Jacob's trained eyes saw the tracks and trails leading away towards the road back toward Savannah.

The men murmured relief that they had not made contact with the British yet had no action other than finding the sign the British had been there. Jacob nodded, confirming his suspicion that the British had pulled out.

"Captain Horry, have your men unfix bayonets and get ready to head back to our line," Jacob instructed. The clanking sound of removing the bayonets as they were twisted off and slid into their leather sheaths. Horry formed his company into a column and followed Jacob back to the sally point near the redoubt.

To his surprise, Marion and Moultrie were waiting at the sally port. "Captain Horry, return to your duties," Jacob instructed, "My thanks to you and your men!"

"Maybe next time," Horry returned and led his company back to their camping area to prepare for their guard duty. Jacob, Jean, and Samuel headed to report to Moultrie and Marion.

"I see you went for a morning walk, Captain Clarke?" Moultrie asked with a grin, "We had just arrived to task you to do a little scouting of the enemy. What did you find?"

"They're gone, sir," Jacob answered, leaning on his rifle. "They must have backed in the night, kept some of the fires burning until the last men were out. From what sign we found, there were no eight thousand men over there, maybe two or three thousand."

Both Moultrie and Marion nodded, "So he tried to hoodwink us?" Moultrie responded, and Jacob nodded.

"I believe that was their intent," Jacob followed.

Moultrie grunted as he looked across the field at the now vacant positions.

"Had we not been here, had marched with Lincoln, the city leaders would have surrendered the city without a fight to safeguard their homes and finances. Too bad General Huger was wounded, and those men killed for nothing."

Jacob did not respond, just allowing General Moultrie to express his frustration.

"We will have to see what happens next when Lincoln gets here with the army," Marion followed, "we can't leave the city undefended to chase after the British unless the army gets here soon."

Moultrie nodded, "Yes, now we have to wait and see."

As foretold, General Lincoln and the Southern Army marched into Charles Town, moving overland from Augusta, Georgia. The general went to find Moultrie to get updated while the different units were ordered to head back to their barracks areas. A runner came for Jacob, and he rode to the headquarters where both Lincoln and Moultrie were speaking.

When Jacob arrived, he overheard General Lincoln asking Moultrie about his assessment of the British. "You believe there are only about two to three thousand men," Lincoln asked, "they must be low on supplies for being in the field for so long. That is why they didn't dig in; they're out of supplies. So this is our opportunity to crush them and secure South Carolina!"

General Lincoln began looking at the map and started issuing orders. "Send out scouts to locate and keep eyes on the British." Lincoln began to look at his papers for which units were available.

"Order the army to prepare to march immediately, the men to be issued ammunition and rations for a week."

General Moultrie nodded and asked which units were marching with the army. "Sir, if I can remind you, you just arrived after a forced march. Are the men capable of leaving so soon?"

"We have no choice," Lincoln responded, "We can't let this opportunity slip away. Order Sumner's Continentals, Huger's Continentals, Colonel William's Militia Brigade, Pulaski's Legion, and artillery support from the Fourth South Carolina. The rest of the army is to remain at the ready."

As Lincoln's aide wrote down the orders, Lincoln looked over the map, scratching his chin with his right hand.

"Moultrie, I have a special task for you. Send a detachment of our armed galleys and move along the river. I want you to make the British think you're coming after them and draw their attention while I pin them, then destroy them."

Moultrie nodded; he understood his orders, and then, after Lincoln finished with him, Moultrie walked around the table and, seeing Jacob, motioned for him to follow him outside. The barracks were now a hive of activity, seeing the army had returned and required resupplying the different units. So Moultrie and Jacob headed that way as the Second Regiment was still out in the defenses.

"While I move the armed galleys, I want you to take a company as a scouting force. They are to find and follow the

British, sending runners to keep the army informed on their location. They are to observe only; they are not to engage the enemy, only report." Moultrie instructed, and Jacob nodded his understanding.

"Nothing against our commanding general, but seeing how well he did on this last expedition, let's make sure we can find the British before we march all over South Carolina again, leaving the city exposed."

Jacob could see the point Moultrie was making, and it made sense.

"I will explain it to Marion to release a company to you; the rest will remain here to watch over the city in my absence. I know I can trust Marion more than some of these militia commanders.

"I understand," Jacob replied, already formulating a plan in his head. "Lieutenant Langy and the Sergeant-Major can accompany me, correct?"

Moultrie snorted, "There is no way I would separate the three of you," he answered, "I truly believe if I would allow it, you three could win the war for us."

Moultrie stopped and offered his hand to Jacob, "Good hunting out there, make sure General Lincoln finds the British this time."

Jacob shook the general's hand, Moultrie headed off in one direction, and Jacob headed back to the redoubt. He headed straight to his gear, and as expected, Samuel and Jean were already kitted up, and Jacob's gear was waiting for him.

"You're packed," Samuel said smiling, "We added freshly baked ash cakes, rations, and jerked meat. Jean thought that as you headed off, we were getting a task from the commander. So where we're going?"

Looking over at Jean, who shrugged and shook his head, always caught up in the game between Samuel and Jacob kidding one another. Jacob already knew it had been Samuel; his sixth sense was knowing when tasks arrived, just like his gut told him of trouble."

"We're scouting for the army," Jacob explained as he placed his shooting bag and haversack over his shoulder. "We're taking a company, so who is currently the best company for moving in the field?"

"As you saw, I would say Horry's Company," answered Samuel, and Jean nodded his head in agreement.

"I have watched their drill," Jean explained, "They are very good, very crisp."

That was all Jacob needed, and after placing his backpack on and grabbing his rifle, he led them over to Captain Horry's area. Luckily, they had already stood down from their guard duty and relaxed on their gear. So when Captain Horry saw Jacob, Samuel, and Jean approach with all their equipment, he jumped up and came over.

"Not to press Jacob," Horry asked with an excited look on his face. "But as you have your go-to war gear, are we going somewhere?"

"Yes, Daniel," Jacob responded with a smile, "You and your company are to accompany us scouting for the army, to make sure they do, find the British, and give them battle. We're moving fast, so pack light. Only bring what you need, have a couple of days of rations."

Samuel took a detail of men and headed to where the quartermaster was located to draw more rations for the company. With Daniel, Jean and Jacob began checking muskets and equipment for serviceability. The men talked in excited voices, finally some real action other than sitting in the redoubt or marching out to the Tullifinny and back.

Samuel returned from the quartermaster with his detail carrying their rations, and the men got down to business in cooking their rations. As some of the men cooked, the rest checked the ammunition they had been carrying since they were issued before building the defensive works. Any cartridge found to be of poor quality was changed out.

Once everything was in order, Jacob had Horry order his men to their beds to try to get some sleep. He knew it would be challenging; the men were anxious and excited to see some action. Most of them sat around their section area or laid on their blankets, talking about the coming scout.

"Never changes, no? Jean asked, leaning on his gear, pipe in hand. "No matter what army, soldiers are soldiers, and they are always excited and can't sleep the night before."

Jacob nodded, pipe resting in his mouth, glow bathing only his eyes and nose. "After we begin our march, that will change; they will be tired."

As the company still murmured and spoke to one another, Jacob, Samuel, and Jean got comfortable and, with only a couple of deep breaths, could fall asleep quickly, no longer caught up in the excitement of the approaching action. Instead, it was just another night for them.

***

Maclane watched with interest as wagons and carts arrived and departed from the South Sea Mercantile warehouse, and he was watching what items were being loaded. While he was satisfied with the business, the one thing that bothered him was this new Continental Currency of paper money. When it was coin, he was able to get his cut and still kept the books clean. This paper currency, what was it truly worth?

Watching with a keen interest to make his following report to the British command, from what he observed, it appeared the army under Lincoln was preparing to march. To where was something he needed to find out. He headed over to the waiting wagons and made small talk with the waggoneers with a bottle of rum.

He approached the waggoneers with a smile and greeted them.

"Greetings, friends. Must be hard work on a warm day like today," Maclane began, then offered the bottle of rum. "On behalf of the mercantile, I want to thank you for your service to the cause."

The waggoneers' eyes lit up, and they licked their lips. "Why, thank you most kindly, sir," one of the waggoneers answered as he took the bottle, "it is a hard day when we have to get the army ready to march on a warm day like today."

The waggoneer pulled the cork with his teeth, then took a good swallow before handing it back to Maclane. Finally, he shook his hands and pointed it was for all of them to pass around.

"How much time do you have to get our great army together before they march?" Maclane asked, and the waggoneers chortled.

"Great army, are you serious?" another waggoneer answered, wiping his mouth with his shirtsleeve. "This General Lincoln leads them all over the place like a chicken with its head cut off, can't seem to make good decisions. Then after marching all of these poor souls up and down South Carolina, tells be ready to march immediately. He has no care for his men!"

Maclane nodded, showing concern outwardly, but smiling on the inside. This was the information he needed to pass on. "Sounds like you speak from experience," Maclane followed, and the waggoneer nodded.

"Aye, that be true. I followed the army up into Cherokee Land during the last one and saw the same issue between the British and our commanders. At least they knew where they were going."

Maclane nodded, "Do you know where the army is marching off to? I saw a good number of wagons come and go."

After taking a deep drink and passing the bottle along, a third waggoneer said, "I heard something about chasing that fellow who was camped out in front of the city, trying to make them surrender."

The waggoneers nodded and mumbled their agreements on the rumor. Maclane nodded and wished the waggoneers a much cooler day before heading back to his office to write a dispatch.

"So, they're going after Prevost for his gamble," Maclane whispered as he entered the main building and headed to his back office. "*He has a head start, but who knows how far this Lincoln will chase him and whether or not he'll catch Prevost.*"

Sitting at his desk, he pulled out a piece of parchment and ink quill and began writing about what he had just learned from the waggoneers.

***

The crackling noise of the girl's throat mixed with the last gasp of air as Big Harpe's strong fingers crushed the life out of her. Her dead eyes were fixed when she stopped breathing, and she looked at Harpe in an accusing manner. He snorted and shrugged his massive shoulders.

"Sorry, my girl," he explained in a low voice, "I had no choice. If I could be out there and going after these damn rebels, I wouldn't have to find my entertainment like I used to. You can blame those rebels, not me. I had to answer to my instincts, you understand, of course?"

The girl continued to stare back in silence, and Harpe laughed at his wit. He had found her as part of a group of travelers coming up from the low country. The travelers had stopped to rest. Harpe had been behaving himself, following Maclane's orders of doing nothing but watching.

"Bah!" Harpe grumbled, "I hate waiting and watching; I need action." Harpe picked up the girl's body and, having found a burnt-out farm with a well, dropped the body down the well. He listened for the faint sound of a splash to make sure the body hit bottom before turning and mounting his horse.

It was late when he arrived at the house they had been using for the moment; his brother Little Harpe was sitting near the glowing embers in the fireplace. He looked up when Big Harpe entered the house and closed the door.

"Out a little late aren't we?" he asked, and Big Harpe gave his brother a hard glare.

"Be careful what you say, little brother," Big Harpe warned.

Little Harpe waved his hand in dismissal and relit his pipe. Then, after blowing a plume of smoke, he looked over as Big Harpe sat across from him. As Big Harpe brought a bottle up to his mouth and drank noisily from it, he wiped his face with his sleeve. The way the glow of the embers made Big Harpe's facial scars stand out even made Little Harpe shutter.

Big Harpe lowered the bottle, his eyes boring into Little Harpe. "What's on your mind, little Brother? Out with it!"

"We have a good thing going here," Little Harpe shot back, "Don't risk it because you have to go out and find a plaything to satisfy your black urges."

Again, Big Harpe took a long drink, and his eyes turned vicious. "What bloody good thing?" he growled back at his brother, "This sitting around and watching, not getting out there and causing mayhem and getting fat on loot!"

"Yes," Little Harpe returned, "We're still getting coin from the British for sitting and information. But you're right; it's not as much when we go after these farmers and townspeople.

So Maclane said to be patient. Besides, you have Susan and Betty up there." He pointed up to where Big Harpe's room was located.

Big Harpe shook his head, "They don't satisfy my need."

Little Harpe gave him an odd look, "Oh, what need is that?"

Leaning forward and with an evil grin, he flexed his hands and fingers. "To kill, with these! To take someone's life and feel it leave their body. I can't do that with the girls; I promised I would be nice and won't kill them."

Big Harpe leaned back and took another drink. "Besides, I think Susan may be in a family way."

Little Harpe's eyebrows shot up. "She will have a baby, and you be a father?"

Big Harpe shot his brother a dirty look, took a drink, and then in surrender, nodded his head.

"I would have never thought you would become a father," Little Harpe regarded his brother, who looked less than thrilled at the prospect of being a father.

"Hopefully, soon we'll be back in action," replied Little Harpe, "The British will allow us to do our business, on behalf of the Crown, of course, and then you can satisfy your need."

Big Harpe smiled and raised his bottle, "Then to those happier times, may they get here quickly!"

***

Jacob, Samuel, and Jean were up early, packed gear, and ready for the march. The company was up, each man rolling up their blankets and slinging them over their shoulders using slings. Although the men were carrying their canteens, bulging haversacks, cartridge boxes, and bayonets, Jacob had ordered them to leave their regimental coats behind and only wear their split shirts for comfort. The men swam in their straps to set them in a comfortable position.

Jacob took his rifle in hand, followed by Samuel and Jean, and headed over to Captain Horry, speaking to his sergeants.

"All set to go?" Jacob asked, and Horry nodded they were. "Good, form the men in the column, and follow me!"

The sun had not fully risen as Jacob led the men across the field and into the old British camp to pick up their trail. Already the air was full of the buzzing of insects, indicating it was going to be a hot day ahead, even for the end of May. Nevertheless, Jacob kept a good pace, spreading his men into two columns.

Knowing the bridges had been burned, Jacob believed the British would be heading southwest towards the coast. As they moved through the woods, they could find the trail the British had made moving through the area. Granted, you didn't have to be a master tracker to see the sign of the British pulling cannons and thousands of men.

Jacob took breaks so the men could rest, though he always kept men out as security and rotated the men. Nevertheless, they were covering the distance well, and it appeared the men were grateful for being able to do something other than garrison activities finally.

Samuel and Jean, along with the sergeants, checked the men's feet and shoulders. Sitting took the edge off even in a defensive line and softened the feet. Jacob and Horry walked up and down the line, watching.

"Where do you think they're going?" Horry asked Jacob, who thought on it before answering.

"Either the coastal road or they could be heading back towards Port Royal to be picked up by the navy. But, as we destroyed a good number of the bridges, and I am sure their scouts have detected General Lincoln, and the army is back, they are making a beeline for the quickest way back to Savannah."

Horry thought about it and nodded his head in agreement. "Makes sense; they should expect that we'll pursue them, just have to find them."

Jacob nodded, "That's where we come in; the quicker we can find them, the quicker the general can go after them."

By nightfall, they had arrived at an area known as Thirteen-Mile House near the Stono River and inlet. Jacob moved his men a short distance away and climbed a slight rise where Jacob saw the glitter of fires in the distance. Then, ordering his men to the ground, Jacob pulled out his telescope and saw the British in the distance with the fading light. They had found them.

"We'll camp here; Captain Horry, find me two men who can take the message back to the army where the British are. Samuel, see to the camp. Make sure we're in enough brush to hide us from their eyes if they come looking."

Samuel and Jean organized their camp into three points: Sergeants Jenkins and Ball had two triangle points, and Samuel had the other. Jacob, Jean, and Captain Horry were in the middle with Corporals Stedman and Arnold. Jacob and Horry remained at the crest of the hill, looking at the British in the distance.

They counted the flickering fires as the sun had gone down to get estimated enemy numbers. "It's hard to see them all," Horry and Jacob agreed, "We'll see more in the morning. It will take time for General Lincoln to bring the army up."

Jean crawled up and joined them on the crest of the hill. Jacob handed the telescope to him so he could see the British camp. "We're all set down below," Jean commented as he focused on the base in the distance, "Samuel has everything in order. He is a good man, no?"

Jacob smiled and nodded, "A very good man, one of the best."

Jean grunted and looked through the telescope, commenting, "Don't see any fieldworks, though it does look like they have roving sentinels." He lowered the telescope and handed it back to Jacob, who closed it and returned it to his haversack.

"Just have to see in the morning," Jacob commented before crawling backward, then turned and, after standing up, headed down to the camp. The men had settled in, positioned in brush and behind trees and watching the area around the camp.

Throughout the night, each point of the triangular camp kept one man up; from time to time, Jacob, Samuel, or Jean would check on the men during the night. There was no activity other than the forest creatures moving through the trees. More humid than usual for the end of May, the air was filled with the sound of insects chittering and buzzing. A light breeze did whisper through the trees and brush. Before the morning, Jacob had the men stand to watch the forest around them, but no enemy activity was observed.

Jacob had the men rotate through security and eat their cooked rations. Then, Jacob asked for a small group of volunteers to move closer to the British camp, and Horry had to pick those few as just about everyone wanted to go with Jacob. Once the scouts were identified, they reported to Jacob, who explained what would occur.

"We'll rotate between the camp and the hilltop where we'll observe the British," Jacob briefed Captain Horry. "I will take a small scouting party and move around the British position to get a better look. If we contact the enemy, we'll fight back here before we fall back. If you get hit while we're out, head back to the other side of the thirteen-mile house at Brake's Ford."

Once everyone understood, Jacob gave one more instruction to Horry. "Have two more runners rested and ready when we return. We might find more details that we can't see from here."

Horry nodded his head in understanding, "Good luck out there!" Jacob nodded, then motioned for the scouts to follow him.

Jacob took Samuel and Jean, plus the four more experienced men Horry had selected and headed out towards the British camp. Horry watched them as they entered the woods before returning to the crest of the hill to watch the British base.

Jacob and the others moved quickly through the trees and brush quietly at a crouch. The four men Horry had selected had also been long hunters and knew how to move silently. Jacob felt refreshed, returning to his Ranger days hunting his enemy. Except for this time, it was the British and Loyalists, not the French. He looked over at Jean, his face intense, probably feeling the old nostalgia of the partisan way.

Jacob led them to the east of the British position before they began to creep towards them. Then, using the brush for concealment, Jacob led his men forward slowly and quietly. Then, using only his hands, he signaled the men to line up and stay crouched.

Stepping carefully to not step on any dead branches and slowly moving other limbs out of their way, Jacob continued to move forward until they heard the gurgling of moving water. They came out next to the Stono River, the six men lowering themselves to their bellies and crawling along into a thick clump of brush.

Carefully and quietly, the men wiggled to make a space in the brush as Jacob slowly moved some of the brush so they could look out without exposing their position. Then, once more, Jacob used his hands to signal the other men to watch their flanks and rear while he, Jean, and Samuel looked at the British position.

Jacob slowly brought it up to his eyes and ensured his telescope didn't make a lot of noise. Samuel had taken a small quill, inkpot, and piece of paper on a small board, ready to take notes. Then, adjusting the focus until the British position appeared clearly, Jacob began to whisper to Samuel what he observed.

"Looks like they are building a floating bridge from what looks like the ferry landing out to the island. They have built small redoubts covering the ferry, and their camps are behind the redoubts. We didn't see those from the hill."

Samuel's quill made scratching noises as he recorded what Jacob was seeing. Jacob refocused the telescope, both for clarity and depth into the camp. He continued in a hushed whisper.

"They are also moving men by small boats, but I can't see where they are going, but they are going to the other side of the island."

Jacob scanned slowly, adjusted the focus on his telescope, and continued reporting as Samuel wrote it down, frequently jabbing his quill into his inkpot and scratching out the information.

"It's the same uniforms we saw crossing the Savannah, and to our front at Charles Town, red and blue, plus Loyalists, I'm guessing wearing normal clothes. They have artillery covering the ford and their redoubts and an armed galley on the far side of the ford and the floating bridge."

Jacob handed his telescope to Jean and had him look, believing it is always good to have a second set of eyes, especially someone like Jean, whose experience is as vast as his own. Jean began to whisper, and Samuel recorded.

"I don't see any supplies, no casks or boxes. No animals, so they must have butchered all those animals for rations. They are low on food then based on when they departed. They appear to be much less than before, so they must have detached platoons to escort any supplies they acquired to Savannah before destroying the bridges."

Jean lowered the telescope and handed it back to Jacob. Once they had all the information they needed, they slowly worked their way out of their concealment and headed back to their camp on the other side of the hill. They crept and were on alert if they encountered any British patrols. None was spotted, but they remained vigilant until they entered their camp.

Once in the camp, Jacob went to find Horry, who was back on the hill. Jacob crawled, and Horry told him what they had observed.

"Once the fog cleared and we could see better, we spotted a British ship being loaded on the other side of the island. There is no change to the camps, other than they are rotating sentries, but it doesn't look like any scouts are out."

"So that's what they're up to," Jacob responded, nodding his head mostly to himself, "They are evacuating from the island, so move men by boats while they build a floating dock, not a bridge, to move the men out to it."

"We need to get this to headquarters as soon as possible. Are the other runners ready?" Jacob asked, and Horry nodded they were.

They took the information they had gathered, gave it to the waiting runners, and sent them out to take the information to the army.

"Get this to the general immediately," Jacob instructed, "It's paramount they get this if he wants to confront them before they leave the shore."

***

Lieutenant Colonel Maitland moved about the British camp, checking on what men from the expedition were left. They were sorely low on provisions, having used up most of their supplies on the march down. Moreover, due to rebel ships plying the waters off the coast, they had not been resupplied until recently, when the frigate *HMS Perseus* and the *HMS Rose* had arrived at John's Island. So while they had not brought any reinforcements, they did get some needed supplies.

General Prevost and all enslaved Black people who had agreed to leave their masters boarded the ships and about half of the expedition. Nearly half of their expedition boarded and returned to Savannah. Prevost charged Maitland to hold the position until the rest of the expedition could be evacuated.

Looking across their defensive line, Maitland took in the two square redoubts they had built and a battery of three guns positioned between them, aiming down the one road leading to the ferry. So a marsh and a deep creek with an elevated causeway secured their right that Major Moncrieff had directed a small round redoubt built to block it, supported by a single artillery piece.

Covering the river, a second redoubt had been built at an angle to it; in case they had to cover a river withdraw. The remaining two cannons were placed here. Maitland only had his 71st Highlanders, the German Hessians, and what Loyalist infantry remained. Moncrieff was directing the abatis before the redoubts were strengthened.

While this was only a short duration holding action, building sharpened stakes and improving the abatis occupied the men's time as they waited for the next transport ship to arrive. What bothered Maitland; he had no idea when that would occur. If he were attacked in strength, he would be forced to cross over onto John's island as a fighting withdrawal. So he had positioned several longboats on their shore just in case.

The other issue that bothered him was the morning reports on how many men had deserted in the night. While he would like to think they were tired of waiting and making their way back to Savannah on foot. The reality was that they had just deserted and were roaming around the countryside, ripe pickings for these rebels to capture them and get information out of them.

Not a good position to be in, Maitland shrugged his shoulders and continued on his inspection. This was the only thing he could control, leaving the rest to fate and time, hoping both were on his side.

***

Jacob, Samul, and Jean watched the British camp while Horry rested in the center of their perch on the hill's edge. As Jacob scanned, he detected movement off to their right and turned his telescope in that direction. Focusing, he saw flashes of red and shiny materials moving through the brush.

"We have British on the right," Jacob whispered, pointing in the direction he had spotted them, "not sure if they are scouting or not.

"If they detect us, they will warn the British," Jean whispered back, and Samuel nodded his head.

"We can't allow them to do that; we must stop them," Samuel added.

Jacob lowered and closed his telescope, a grin coming to his face. "Better yet, if we could take some prisoners, we could get some useful information out of them about areas we can't see from here."

The three returned from their perch and instructed another team to assume their duties. Finally, Jacob selected a group of men who were rested and ready to go.

"There is a British patrol we think out there, heading in this general direction," Jacob explained, "We're going out to determine what they are up to and, if the situation is right, take some prisoners. No shooting if possible; that will give our position away. Use the back of your tomahawks if you have to hit them."

The evil grins Jacob saw coming from the men made him grin like a wolf. Then, nodding, he turned and trotted out of their camp with Samuel and Jean, followed by the ten men from the company. They moved quickly and quietly, weaving in and around trees at a crouch. They had only gone a short distance when they heard approaching voices.

Jacob raised his hand to halt the men, and then they all slowly knelt behind trees and bushes, concealing themselves from the approaching men. The accents were mixed, Jacob assuming some to be British, and the others might be Loyalists.

"Where are we to bloody go now, Tom," one voice complained, "we're wanted men now that we deserted."

"We'll head up to the Cherokee Lands," the voice Jacob assumed was Tom's answered, "They are friends of ours and have no love for these Patriots and rebels."

"Sure, but where are we going to get food?" another asked, and the voice that had answered before replied, "Simple. We take what we want from the farmers along the way. Some are supporters of the King, the others, we will take them, and if they fight us, well, we'll kill them."

"That's bloody murder!" a new voice was heard.

"So, we're already deserters, and they'll hang us anyways. So we take what we want when we want. They can only hand me once!" Jacob heard some laughter, but the murderous intent of these deserters made Jacob's anger rise.

The sound of sand crunching was getting closer; these deserters were getting closer. Jacob looked around; the men were ready, like coiled springs.

"Try to take them, prisoners," he whispered, "If not, kill them silently."

In a matter of seconds, the deserters came into view; eight of them, five in red uniforms, the others in a mix of green and civilian. Only two had muskets with them; Jacob pointed to Jean, then pointed at himself, then to one of the musket men, then the same for Jean. After that, he would take the other one with the musket.

When the deserters were close enough, the men sprang from their hiding. Like a wolf leaping at his prey, Jacob snatched the musket as he brought the back end of his tomahawk around, hitting the deserter in the side of the head that dropped him to the ground. Jacob spun to see that Jean had his arm around the throat of the other musket man, though he was sliding to the ground unconscious while Jean held the musket.

Samuel and the other ten men jumped out and surrounded the other deserters, growling, "Hold there!" Then, seeing they had nowhere to run and eleven muskets pointing at them, they quickly threw their hands up.

"Easy governor, easy. We'll come peaceful like if you promise to give us something to eat." One of the British deserters stammered, the others nodding quickly as they kept their hands high. Jacob looked them over and saw he and Jean held the only muskets. So Jacob led them as they surrounded the prisoners and marched them to their camp.

The prisoners were surprised to see that they had a camp so close to theirs, and it had been undetected. Jacob kept them in a group in the center of the camp. He did share some of their food with them as promised. Jacob was amazed at how happily the prisoners accepted their ash cakes and jerked meat.

"Thank you, gov'nor," one of the prisoners mumbled with a mouthful of ashcake, "best I have had in a couple of days."

Jacob sat down and lit his pipe. Then, seeing a few prisoners eyeing his tobacco bag, he passed it to them. The prisoners reached into their haversacks, pulled out their pipes, and filled them.

"You're not going to kill us, are you gov'nor?" the man asked, and Jacob shook his head. "Unless you give me a reason to, what's your name?"

Coughing as a piece of hurriedly eaten ashcake was stuck in his throat, Jacob handed him his canteen. The prisoner took a long drink that cleared the dry ash cake from his throat.

"Robert Parker gov'nor, and thank you for the food. We haven't had anything to eat for about four days; no supplies are left. No supplies have been dropped off since those ships arrived and took the general and those blacks with them back to Savannah."

Jacob nodded, then motioned for Samuel to come over. "Go get the small bottle of rum; bring it here."

"But I was saving that for a celebration," Samuel complained, but Jacob gave him a stern look, "I'll get you another one later; now go get it!"

Grumbling, Samuel stalked off to his backpack, returned with the small ceramic bottle, handed it to Jacob, and then took a seat next to him. Jacob pulled the cork and gave it to Robert. He sniffed it, then, realizing it was rum, took a pull before handing it back.

"Share it with your mates," Jacob instructed, and Robert nodded with a smile and handed it to the man sitting next to him.

"So, why did you men desert?" Jacob asked, and Robert gave him a cautious look.

"You're an officer, aren't you?" Robert asked, "Or at least you seem to be in charge." Jacob looked back at him and nodded. "You promised not to kill us; you'll keep your promise, won't you?"

Jacob again nodded, and the men seemed to relax a little. "Well, it doesn't matter; we'll hang if we return to the British, and we may have a better chance with you." The man took a deep breath and then sighed.

"To be honest, we didn't have much of choice. We ran out of food and supplies; nothing was getting to us; your ships intercepted anything coming up from Savannah. So I think we've been left behind, to be sacrificed so the general can get back to Savannah."

Jacob motioned for the rum bottle and handed it to Robert to keep him talking. "You don't seem very confident; from our count, you had a few thousand men with you," Jacob pressed, and Robert snorted his laughter.

"Thousands, not bloody likely. If you attack us now, we might be able to face you with a couple of hundred men, that's all!" Robert complained.

"Don't you have defenses as we had in front of Charles Town?" Jacob asked, and Robert shrugged his shoulders.

"A few small ones, supported by those cannons. We have been dragging those all up and down this bloody, swampy coast. Just a small wall to stop you all from pushing through to that long island on the other side."

Jacob nodded, then asked, "If I can promise your safety, could you draw out what the defenses look like?"

Robert again shrugged, "Why not? Maybe I can get a better job in your army." Then, taking a stick, he scratched out a general layout of the British defenses for the ferry, Jacob watching intently, memorizing it.

"That should do it, gov'nor, from what I can remember," Robert said and leaned back against a tree. Jacob nodded his head and then gave him a stern look.

"I'll keep my promise not to kill you if you and your men promise to stay point and make no noise. After that, I will turn you over to our provost, but let them know you may be considering changing to our side. Understand?"

Robert nodded, "Hear that, lads, we just lay here and relax, and these good men won't kill us. May even offer us a better job if we behave."

The men nodded and settled into their small group, staying in the center. Jacob rose and saw Captain Horry was waiting.

"Did you get any good information?" he asked, and Jacob nodded.

"That we did, enough at least to plan an attack once the army gets here," Jacob advised, "keep at least three men to watch our guests here."

Horry nodded and saw to arranging the guard shift. Jacob walked off to the side, and Jean and Samuel joined him.

"What do you think," Samuel asked, "Can we win if we attack?"

Jacob shook his head, "If the army gets here soon, we'll outnumber them and have the advantage. If General Lincoln takes his sweet time of it, there will be no one here for him to attack and the British escape."

Both Jean and Samuel nodded in agreement, "Well, let's hope he is moving quickly then," Jean commented.

As they waited for the army, Jacob continued to take his turn in the rotation in keeping the British under observation. From their vantage point on the hill, he could not see the redoubts described to them, but the trees in the way could have masked them.

One of the men crawled up to Jacob, "Sir, we have spotted men behind us, heading this way!" he said in an excited whisper. Jacob nodded, crawled down to the camp, and was led to the edge, where the soldier pointed toward the approaching men.

Listening, Jacob could hear the sound of horses' hooves and the sound of footfalls of a large number of men. "Have a care, men!" Jacob ordered, and the men took up firing positions, the prisoners lying flat on the ground. Not knowing who was approaching, Jacob had to be ready for anything. Captain Horry joined him, kneeling at his side.

Soon, two runners they had sent earlier guided two officers towards their camp on horseback. One of them was General Isaac Huger, who must have recovered from the incident of being fired on, and by the fancy uniform, he recalled someone from the Pulaski Legion. Jacob stood up and presented himself, signaling them to halt.

"Captain Clarke, this is the army's advance guard; permission to enter?" the runner asked, and Jacob motioned them forward into the camp. The two officers dismounted and led their horses into the center. All the men stood up, including the prisoners who watched the officers enter, especially Pulaski Jacob had met back in Charles Town.

After securing his horse to a tree, General Huger approached Jacob, nodding at the sight of the prisoners. "I see you have been busy, Captain Clarke," Huger commented, still looking at the prisoners, "Did you get good information from them?"

"Yes, sir, handy information."

General Huger nodded, "Well then, let us see what we are up against."

"If you would follow me, I'll show you our present situation."

Jacob led them to the top of the hill and pointed out the British position to them, sketching on the ground what they had observed from their position, plus the information they received from the prisoners about the river.

Huger and Pulaski quietly discussed a strategy, scratching it out on the ground as they discussed possible tactics to take the British position. "Are you confident the British force's size of only a few hundred?"

Jacob shrugged his shoulders. "Only what the prisoners provided; we couldn't get close enough to get a good count. But from what we have seen, it's less than what we saw earlier when they crossed the Savannah."

"We may not have enough men, but if we could catch them by surprise, perhaps we can do some damage before the army arrives," Huger commented, and Pulaski was deep in thought.

"If we act quick enough and strike fast, we may achieve that," Pulaski remarked, then nodded in agreement.

"We'll take it from here, Captain Clarke," Huger commented as they turned and headed down the hill. "You and your men have done us a great service; remain here and rest; let us take the risk for a change." Huger smiled, mounted their horses with General Pulaski, and returned to their men.

Jacob looked at Samuel, Jean, and captain Horry, who all shrugged then looked back at Jacob. "Settle in, lads; we will have a good view to watch this fight," commented Jacob, and his men took up positions along the hill, leaving three men to watch the camp and the prisoners.

Jacob and his men watched as their comrades formed for battle. They recognized the units as they formed into their battle lines. The right side was Huger's light infantry, the center was the First and Sixth South Carolina Regiments and two cannons, and the left of the line was North Carolina militiamen.

General Pulaski led his cavalry forward, but all surprise was lost; the British were awake for a change and fired on the approaching horsemen. The British and Hessian cannons began to fire, along with an armed galley in the river they were unaware of, and shot was falling amongst the cavalrymen. Jacob didn't see any cavalrymen fall, but they turned their horses and rode for the safety of the woods.

They didn't attack, and Jacob's men returned to their camp, disappointed that they didn't see any action. Then, as night fell, there was no attack from their comrades, and Jacob shook his head in disbelief and returned to the camp as a new set of observers took their position on the hill to keep watch on the British through the night.

A runner arrived at their camp in the morning, looking for Captain Horry and Jacob. "Sit; General Lincoln is holding a council of war and needs you both to be present. So I am to lead you to his camp."

Jacob grabbed his gear, nodding, and when Captain Horry joined him, Jacob turned to Jean and Samuel. "Take charge here and keep an eye on our friends across the way, now that we stirred them up yesterday. We'll see what the general has for us."

Both Jean and Samuel nodded, "Have a good time!' Samuel called after them as they followed the runner to where the army was encamped a short distance away. It was only a short walk when they broke out of the trees, and the southern army appeared stretched out, the men camping on their arms.

General Lincoln was using a fallen tree as a temporary table; a map laid out. Brigadier General Summer, with his North Carolina Continentals, General Huger, General Pulaski, and Governor Rutledge were with him. Jacob did see other officers standing in the back, from their clothing, militia officers.

Governor Rutledge looked up and smiled when Jacob entered the area. He came over and shook Jacob's hand. "Good to see you again, Jacob; you have been busy and providing us some good information. We could use some right now."

Jacob noticed that General Lincoln shot the governor a dirty look before standing. "Now that we have our observers here let's discuss how we can engage the enemy." He paused, then looked at Jacob and Horry.

"Can you confirm the layout of their defenses?"

Horry deferred to Jacob, who described what they had observed and received from the deserters. "They have redoubts facing the main approach, with artillery in mutually supporting positions. Anchoring their flanks are either the river or a large marshy swamp. They have the advantage of position; you, sir, have the advantage of numbers. From what we assessed, they have only four to five hundred defending. Most of the expedition has already been evacuated."

Jacob wondered if Lincoln noticed his slight jab about moving slow, with a good portion of the expedition already evacuated. But, while some of the assembled officers, including Rutledge, did, it appeared that Lincoln did not.

"Then, gentlemen, we will use our superior numbers in a surprise attack. Have the quartermaster issue twenty rounds per man this afternoon. We will march at midnight; I have local guides that will take us to the ferry."

Lincoln looked at the assembled officers to ensure they followed his instructions before continuing. "We will use stealth, the light infantry leading, followed by the North Carolinians, then the militia. Once we are close to their camp, the lights will deploy to the left and right to protect the flanks. Then, finally, the continentals will form the main battle line, the South Carolinians on the left side of the line, the North Carolinians on the right."

He then turned and looked at Pulaski. "You, the rest of our cavalry, and the Virginians will be held in reserve. Once we break through their defensive line, you will lead the charge and exploit the opening, supported by the infantry. Our guns will support the attack against the redoubts. Any questions?"

Lincoln looked at the assembled officers; they stared back, having understood the general's instruction. "Good, see to your men, have them rest, for we'll form to march just before midnight."

Then he turned to Jacob and Horry. "Have your company rejoin the army, report to the reserve." The two nodded their understanding, turned, and headed back to the camp to bring up the men.

"Sounds like a reasonable plan," Horry stated as they walked back to their camp, "what do you think?"

"It does sound simple and easy," replied Jacob, "But what I have seen of the general, and he generally messes up anything easy."

Horry looked over at Jacob and gave him an odd look. "How would you know that? Have you been with the general before?"

Jacob chuckled and shook his head. "I saved his life when he was supposed to simply arrest a man as a sheriff and nearly lost his life."

Horry shook his head, Jacob's tale reinforcing his opinion of the general's performance.

Jean and Samuel were waiting, Samuel with his typical expecting grin. "Are we joining the main army?" he asked, and Jacob nodded.

"Have the men pack their gear, get ready to move back, and fall in with the 6th," Jacob instructed, and he smiled broadly and went to get his gear together, stating, "Finally, some action other than sitting on my backside!"

As Jean was packing his gear, he asked Jacob, "So, does he have a good plan of attack?"

"It is a sound plan," Jacob began, "But there are too many areas where it could go wrong."

"Jean returned. "Such as?"

Jacob chuckled. "Such as we are moving the army quietly in the dark to attempt a surprise attack on the British redoubts. Once secured, Pulaski and the horses will charge through and cause mayhem. Too many things can and have gone wrong in the dark."

Jean thought about it and nodded his head. "Unless, of course, we have good guides, no?"

Jacob shrugged as he picked up and placed his gear across his shoulders. "It all depends on these local guides he said he had. We'll have to wait and see."

Horry came over, said the company was formed, and Jacob motioned for him to lead out, and they would follow in the rear. Following the same path they had taken before, they returned to the army's location; Jacob was happy to see a picket challenging them before walking into the camp.

Asking the picket where the Legion was located, Horry and Jacob led the company through the men, relaxing and talking amongst themselves, sitting in small circles. Some were sleeping, trying to catch up on rest before they started marching in a few hours. Picking their way through the groups, they arrived where horses belonging to Pulaski's cavalry were tied.

From there, they were directed to Lieutenant Colonel Bedaulx, the infantry commander for the Legion. When the company arrived, Horry, Jacob, and Jean approached Bedaulx and reported. Jacob had asked Jean to come as he heard French being spoken amongst the cavalrymen. So Jean did the asking, in French, of where they were supposed to go.

Bedaulx looked at Jacob, Horry, and then over at the company before making his decision. Speaking in French, they were directed to where, much to the joy of Jacob, a company of Catawbas. There, Captain Boykin came over, and after finding out they would be fighting together, shook their hands and led them over to where the Catawbas were lounging, smoking their pipes.

Jacob heard "Okwaho" being passed around; his Mohawk name, which meant these Catawbas, knew him. Horry had the men settle down, and they too lit their pipes and took up small talk with the Catawbas. Boykin and some of the older Catawbas sat with Jacob, Horry, and Jean. As their tradition in the past occurs, Samuel had his hat off, and the Catawbas were rubbing his bald spot from where he survived his scalping for luck.

***

Maitland paced back and forth at his command position, anticipating the rebels to attack. Why would they send their cavalry forward as they did if it wasn't to probe and identify gaps in his defenses? Now, he wondered how many he faced and whether he positioned his forces to meet them in combat.

Looking off to his right was the redoubt manned by his highlanders from the 71st. They placed two companies forward of the main line to serve as an early warning in pickets. Turning, Maitland looked to the left at the Germans manning the other redoubt close to the river. All six cannons were manned and loaded with grapeshot.

Seeing the day was waning and the sun was sinking, he had ordered the men to rest on their arms but remain in position. Unsure what to do, Maitland wondered if the rebels would attack in the dark or not. Hearing nothing that an army would sound like closing on his position, other than the sound of the night insects and birds starting to sing, Maitland began to doubt the rebels would come.

Motioning to his runner, he gave his order. "To all commanders, have your men stand down but maintain a guard force. Implement an eating and rest plan, but remain in position or on their guns if the rebels attempt a surprise attack."

After the runner received the message, he took off in a jog to spread the word to stand down. Maitland scoured the land once more, not seeing and sight or sound of an approaching army. "Well, we'll see what we will in the morning."

***

"Jacob, wake up; time to go," Samuel stated as he gently touched Jacob's shoulder. Jacob looked up, seeing it was dark and the night sky filled with stars. The runner had come by to alert the commands to prepare to move. Groaning, his body stiff, Jacob shouldered his bag and lifted his rifle. The army was rising and shouldering their gear up and down the line.

The command to "prime and load" was whispered down the line, and the men loaded their muskets and rifles, preparing for battle. A light breeze helped move some of the humid air, Jacob appreciating the night's clear skies, releasing the heat from the ground. It was still warm, though, for a late spring night.

Captain Boykin joined Jacob, Samuel, and Jean as they waited for the orders to advance. Jacob turned to Captain Boykin, "Do you know who these guides are leading the army?"

Boykin shook his head, "None of them are from us; I don't know who is leading. At first thought it was your company, seeing you have been here for a while."

Jacob shook his head in return, "Not any of us; now I have concerns."

The word to advance was whispered down the line. Eventually, the rear of the column where the reserves were, began to march. The cavalry walked on one side, and the infantry in columns of two walked on the other side. With the moon, the line of dark silhouettes that marched forward made it easy to see without loose contact.

Jacob and Horry, along with the column, kept their senses on alert. They were listening and looking at the woods on either side of the trail. Jacob's concern was that they had made contact with the cavalry yesterday, so there would not be an element of surprise. But, on the other hand, Jacob suspected the British would be on alert; at well level, during the night, he was not sure. Perhaps they were asleep, and they could catch them in the dawn.

Jacob snorted and shook his head, and Jean looked over at Jacob, guessing he was thinking about the Ranger tradition to be prepared for surprise French and Indian attacks in the dawn when the men are at the most risk. Jacob looked back, knowing Jean had read his mind and nodded. They will have to wait and see from their position in the rear.

Unfortunately, Jacob's doubt about Lincoln began to rise as the column switched direction several times, appearing not to know where to go.

"We should have been there by now," Samuel grumbled, "we could see them from our position on the hill. Where is the general leading us, Savannah?"

Jacob shrugged his shoulders, "Good question," Jacob commented as he looked up at the pink color on the horizon. The sun was rising, yet they were wandering around in the woods.

"Seems we are lost, or whoever the guides are, they are lost."

The sun was up; dawn had arrived when the column finally stopped. The heat and humidity were beginning to rise as the sun rose. Looking to the front, they could see the army deploying into the line of battle. Once formed, the reserve moved up to take their position behind the line. Jacob could see General Lincoln and his command staff to their front. Once the line advanced, the reserved moved forward, Jacob shaking his head.

"What's wrong?" Captain Boykin asked, Horry, listening.

Jacob looked around the area for landmarks before making his answer.

"This is not where the British are," Jacob commented, "after looking at the area around the British defenses, I don't recognize any of this."

Frowning and making a distasteful look on his face, Jacob continued, "The general has deployed us well in advance of the British. Their pickets will hear us coming, and with this heat, the men will be tired by the time we reach the enemy."

"Oh bloody hell," Samuel growled, "here we go again!"

Jacob had to agree; this is not the first time the commander deployed poorly, recalling the bloody day before the French redoubts at Fort Carillon.

The army was advancing in line for what seemed like a good mile. Finally, the first sound of battle reached their ears in the reserve. Jacob wiped the sweat from his eyes and forehead with a handkerchief. "Well, the game is afoot,"

The initial sound of contact was some sporadic musket fire quickly picked up in volume. "They must have ran into the pickets," Jacob commented, looking to their left front. "Sounds like they are having a real go at it."

Soon the distinct sound of volley firing from both sides could be heard, that what must have started as a skirmish was now in a fully engaged action. Grey smoke from the firing began to filter up and out of the trees and vegetation. From the distinct sounds, Jacob could hear artillery mixed in with the musket volleys. Then the firing slowed down; the deafening silence took the field.

Jacob wiped his brow again, heavy with sweat. "If it's not their ammunition, it could be this damnable heat. Summer is coming early this year," responded Jacob. The day was hot and humid, and it could be one of the factors that would decide the outcome of this battle. Then, after a short respite, the sound of fighting could be heard again from their front. The sound of battle now encompassed the entire front, though Jacob and the company could see none of it, only listen to it.

The fire once more began to slacken until it was some pops of more minor actions. "What do you think, Jacob," Horry asked, looking in the direction of the fighting, "Are we advancing and driving the British away?"

"Good question," Jacob responded, pondering what he had heard so far. The fight hadn't lasted even an hour, so either they were pushing the British or being driven. Then another point popped up in his head.

"We could be running out of ammunition; the men were only issued twenty cartridges, which, even with a sustained rate of fire, would be running low by now."

A horseman came riding up to the cavalry, "The general wants to advance and cover the retreat!" he yelled, and Pulaski led his horsemen forward at the trot.

"Well, there is our answer," Jacob commented, then turned and faced Captain Boykin and Horry. "If we're retreating, we should place a covering line here in case the British are in pursuit. So, Boykin, take your riflemen and cover the left side. Horry, take your company and cover the right."

Both officers nodded and deployed their men into an open skirmish line, facing the direction of the battle. It was a pleasant surprise when they saw the first unit approach, and instead of running out of control, they marched in good order. Then another company approached, marching in good order.

Jacob, Jean, and Samuel stood in the center, watching for any sign of a British pursuit, but so far, the army was withdrawing under good order. Looking at the men's faces, Jacob saw more frustration than fear. Nevertheless, it was not a broken army.

Then the first section of artillery was rolling by, with a few carts holding wounded. Their comrades were helping some walking wounded. Some men had no blood on them, but Jacob surmised they were injured from the heat from the worn expression and wet clothes from sweating.

One of the artillery pieces from the 4th South Carolina rolled up and deposited one of their gunners, who had a severe wound and was placed under a tree. Looking over at the pale, pasty complexion of the wounded man, Jacob could tell he was not for this world. A younger man wearing the uniform of the 4th, who looked similar to the injured man, knelt beside him.

The wounded man pulled his sword from its carrier and handed it to the younger man. "Never let it be dishonored," Jacob overheard, and then the wounded man closed his eyes and died. The younger man, now Jacob suspected had been the man's son, bowed his head and placed his hand on the dead man's shoulder before rising and rejoining the column. Jacob shook his head, then returned to watching the road.

General Lincoln and his staff rode by, followed by some of the cavalry serving as his escorts. Then the rest of the light infantry and the militia marched by, with Pulaski and his cavalry being the last ones. As they trotted past, he yelled to Jacob, "That's all; we're the last ones!" Nodding, Jacob had the Catawbas and captain Boykin pull back, then Horry pulled his company, and they brought up the rear, watching their backs.

The march back was uneventful; Jacob and Horry's Company stayed with the slower-moving wounded. The British did not pursue, mainly because they had no cavalry left, so Jacob spoke with some of the wounded to pass the time.

"We advanced in the column," Thomas Henry from the 6th South Carolina commented, "until we finally broke out of the trees, and there was the first line of those British Highlanders before us. The boys opened fire on us, so the colonel had us deploy into line right there and then."

Jacob nodded his head as Thomas continued, wincing from his shoulder wound. "Well, sir, we fired volleys back and forth, then the colonel had us charge bayonets, and we poured right into those Highlanders, until from what I reckon, was only ten or so of them left that ran away. The rest were dead or wounded on the field."

Wincing once more, Thomas paused, and Jacob listened. "After we reformed, we advanced towards the main line, and there was a large, rather deep creek before it. Good ol' Robert Hill entered and sank right up to his neck; we had to pull him out. We could not cross to get at the rest of those British."

Thomas paused, shaking his head and reaching up to rub his wounded shoulder. "That's when they opened fire in a great volley; we were maybe only sixty yards away from what I guess. That damn ball tore through my shoulder, taking me out of action. Seeing we couldn't reach them, and they were pouring fire into us, the colonel ordered us back."

Jacob nodded, "Thanks for filling us in; we didn't see much from the rear in reserve."

Thomas smiled and nodded, "To be as it may, I would have much rather been back in the rear instead of having this here broke and bleeding shoulder."

By the end of the day, the army arrived before Charles Town. Once they passed through the walls, the regiments and companies returned to their barracks area. Jacob, Jean, and Samuel headed to the defensive lines and found the local militia had taken over. The 2nd was now out on the island at the fort.

As it was getting late, Jacob and the others headed to the barracks, where it was confirmed that the regiment was over at the newly renamed Fort Moultrie. The fort had been renamed after General Moultrie in honor of his defense of the city. They decided to go into town, pay for a good meal, and then return to the barracks to sleep.

They made their way out to Fort Moultrie in the morning, where a smiling Marion welcomed the men back to the regiment. "So, how did it go? Did we catch them?" he asked, and Jacob told them of their fight at Stono Ferry. Marion shook his head.

"So damn close," he remarked, "and the British got away, which means they are planning on heading back this way sometime in the future."

Jacob and the regiment remained the rest of the summer conducting garrison duty, rotating between Fort Moultrie, the defensive line on the Neck, or out at Dorchester. Then, finally, Captain Horry was sent up to Dorchester. Seeing an opportunity to give up, Jacob, along with Samuel and Jean, went along once again as advisors and trainers, and they needed to check on the fort's condition and the powder magazine.

Is that the sole purpose of this volunteering," Marion asked with a twinkle in his eye, fully knowing why they were heading up to Dorchester. Jacob kept as much of a straight face as he could.

"But of course, sir, we have too many new, and Dorchester has always been a good training field," Jacob explained, and Marion nodded.

"Well, if time permits, perhaps you should stop by and see your family and what news your long hunters may have picked up." Marion winked before heading off to the fort.

Jacob smiled and headed over to gather Samuel and Jean before heading back up to Dorchester and, when time permits, home.

First, they reported to Captain Horry and checked the condition of the small tabby fort and the powder magazine there. The stores of ball and powder, plus stands of muskets, were in good condition, but Captain Horry was having his men check and clean the muskets.

"We'll be busy at this for a few days, Jacob," Horry commented, "not much for you and your men to do, so why don't you go home and see your family. We'll be ready to train when you get back."

Nodding, Jacob went to grab both Samuel and Jean, and they headed to their home. The present wolves, now full size, parked and yapped at the sight of the three as they rode into the compound. Samuel and Jacob were amazed at how big their boys were and their girls working around the compound.

"Mama, Papa's home!" Richard called out, dropping the hoe, and raced to see Jacob. As soon as he was off his horse, Jacob was nearly knocked down by Richard, who crushed him in a bear hug, and his two wolves, Waya and Red, crashed into him from the other side. The only thing that prevented him from falling was his wife Maria joining the group and hugging Jacob.

"How long are you home for?" Maria asked, and Jacob replied for only a few days. Then, as the wolves finally untangled themselves from his legs and sat on their haunches, Maria looked at Jacob up and down.

"Samuel, he is not looking like he is eating enough!" Maria yelled. Samuel, like Jacob, was surrounded by his family and replied in a muffled shout, "Not my fault; blame the governor!"

Jean took it all in, standing off to the side, joined by Peter, who shook his hand and welcomed him back.

"Well, let's make you a good home-cooked meal to get some flesh on those bones!" Maria commanded, and everyone headed into Jacob's house, where the women got busy in the kitchen, while Jacob leaned his gear in the corner, looking at the scarring of the years his rifle had leaned in that corner over time.

Samuel and Jean joined them a short time later, stowing their gear. They joined Jacob sitting in a chair beside the fireplace with no fire. He was smoking his pipe, Samuel, and Jean joining and adding their smoke to Jacob's. Then Peter arrived with tankards of ale, and then they sat around, Peter bringing them up to date on the local activity.

"We are getting word from our Catawba friends that Loyalists were seen in the area near the Chickamauga Towns in the Tennessee," Peter explained as he puffed on his pipe, getting the bowel lit. "The Catawbas are concerned those Loyalists are stirring up trouble again. So our friends are keeping their eyes on them."

"We're also getting stories of the actions down your way," Peter continued as he took a long drink from his mug. "Heard it's like the old days once again, the commanders not know where to go, and allowed the British to run away, victory slipping through their fingers."

Samuel snorted, spilling some of his beer, "Bloody right you are!" Samuel commented, "That bloody slow-moving Lincoln not only allowed the British to escape when we had them pinned against the wall in Charles Town but once again at that stony ferry or what not!"

Jacob knew his friend was fired up over their commanding general and a little tipsy from not having beer for a while as they had been in the field. But Samuel was right; they had two good opportunities to defeat the British and perhaps impact the war here in South Carolina. But, unfortunately, fate being fickle as it was, the victory was not yet meant to be. Now Jacob wondered if this would come back to haunt them later.

The conversation ended as the big meal was set out, and they all gathered around the table. Having been living on field rations, even the meal they purchased in Charles Town could not compare to Maria's cooking. Roasted deer, German dumplings, and a thick gravy would again put flesh on Jacob's bones.

Later that evening, they gathered out under one of the great trees, circled by benches and a small fire burning in the center for light. Maria sat next to Jacob and snuggled against his shoulder, clinking her mug against his. She then looked up and traced the lines on Jacob's face with her fingers, from his scars to the new wrinkles.

"You're getting old, my love," she commented, tracing the new wrinkle lines, and Jacob scoffed.

"From being out in the sun too long, that's all," he commented, but he knew Maria was right. Although he was not as young as he wanted to be, time was moving forward and dragging him along.

They remained at the compound, Maria's parents, who had been away visiting, welcoming Jacob, Samuel, and Jean home and asking them for news. Jacob recounted the activity and actions they had and the close calls. They answered as many questions as they could. The rest days did them good; Jacob felt better and wasn't as sore in the morning as he was in the field.

Their time to return to Dorchester arrived, and once more, as they have on so many times, they said their goodbyes and headed back onto the road. "Ugh, your wife is a much better cook than mine," Samuel commented, rubbing his belly, "make sure she doesn't teach mine to cook better, or I would get fat before I am ready."

While at Dorchester, Horry's company enlistment ran out. Jacob, Samuel, and Jean went over as Captain Horry addressed the company about rejoining the army or would they go home. Jacob was pleasantly surprised to see most of his men remained. Only a few did not reenlist, though they did promise to return after they took a break, or if word reached them the British were going to attack them, they would return for a short while.

The orderly came out from the regiment to record in the orderly book how many men reenlisted, took their names, and issued pay. This was the norm for the rest of the summer;

Jacob didn't see any more action other than guard rotations. He, Samuel, and Jean focused on training the company and the different companies in the regiment as some had no recruits. Though they didn't know yet, they would soon miss the dull routine life of garrison duty, as the action would seek them out.

CHAPTER 7

1779: ON TO SAVANNAH

Big Harpe was in a foul mood as he sat in the corner of the Six Mile Wayfarer House, the thunderstorm outside mirroring his thoughts. Little Harpe and the others, having responded to the summons from Maclane, still gave him a wide berth. Even with a large tankard before him, Big Harpe leaned back on the back two legs of the chair against the wall, his large arms crossed on his massive chest.

"He looks like he could chew boulders," David Ross whispered, leaning over to Little Harpe, who nodded and took a long drink from his tankard, his eyes looking over the lip at his brother.

"Aye, if I was you, stay away and don't say anything rash," Little Harpe warned, "he is out of sorts at the moment. But, hopefully, Maclane brings good news."

Little Harpe did not want to bother his brother. Susan, Big Harpe's main woman, was pregnant and, at the moment, demanding to be around. Then there was his demonic need for murder that hadn't been satisfied in a while. This meant Big Harpe was a spring tightly wound and ready to go.

A short time later, Lavinia Trout opened the door, with Maclane following her in, his heavy cloak dripping with rainwater. He removed his cloak and hat, hanging them over the back of a chair, before sitting down. He saw everyone's eyes were upon him in expectation, including Big Harpe's hard, cold, evil eyes. Maclane smiled.

"You are all wondering why I called you here, seeing our last conversation stifled all of your activities," Maclane stated, and the gathered group of murderers and brigands murmured he had. He smiled once again at their response.

"I am here to inform you that you are to return and, if possible, increase your activities against these rebels and their supporters."

Everyone ones face lit up, Big Harpe's most of all. "About bloody time!" he roared.

"The crown is concerned these rebels are getting too bold and need to be taught a lesson that they don't control as much of their territory they think they do," Maclane stated, looking at the gathered ruffians.

"Spread your activities, have these rebels send their garrisons all over South Carolina, keep them running around and on the move. Never let them sit for a while; keep them off balance." Maclane amplified, and the ruffians nodded their heads in agreement.

"We can do what we want, correct?" Big Harpe asked, and Maclane nodded slowly.

"Murder, rape, burning, looting. All the good things in life?" Big Harpe followed up, and again Maclane nodded his head. The evil grin on Big Harpe's face brought a chill to Maclane, but he didn't show it outwardly.

He threw several bags of coins on the table, "Here is your pay; anything you take can be considered your bonus. Happy Hunting!"

Maclane raised his mug, and the gathered ruffians, including Lavinia, Mary Firth, the Harpe Brothers, and David Ross, raised their mugs in salute. Then, they started discussing dividing South

Carolina so they wouldn't compete with one another regarding raiding and booty.

Maclane sipped from his mug, satisfied. It was not his position to question why the Crown would use these dredges of society, but they had their purpose and were expendable. It will keep these rebels off balance. Who knows, maybe even drive some of these uncommitted locals into the welcoming arms of their King once again. He would have to look into that.

***

Jacob continued to serve as the regimental training as the different companies continued their drill routine, including returning to conducting cannon crew drills once again while in the garrison in Charles Town. While a good number of the original men from the regiment remained, there were a lot of recruits that needed training. Jacob advised that many returning veterans were promoted to sergeants and corporals.

While the regiments drilled, General Lincoln, his staff, and the senior officers, including Moultrie, focused on the City of Savannah. He desired to take the city, drive the southern British from his sector, and secure the southern colonies. Feeling encouraged from what he felt were his victories: stopping the British outside of the city, then forcing them to evacuate out of South Carolina, General Lincoln thought it should be an easy march and taking of the city.

"Sir, too many points must be worked out for the army to not only march on Savannah but take it." So Moultrie advised, and Lincoln gave him a tired look, already knowing where Moultrie was going with his advice. "Governor Rutledge will need to be included in this and give his consent."

Sighing, Lincoln nodded. "Yes, we'll see the governor, and I will explain our plan to him. He is a reasonable man; he will see I am right as it will take pressure off him from this British force to the south." Gathering his notes and a map, Lincoln went to see the governor; Moultrie and his staff accompanied him to brief their plan to the governor.

Not only was the governor there at the assembly, but so were some members who were very interested and seemed supportive of the military expedition. In the background, his ears peaked, was Richard Pearis, remaining but very attentive. All of this information would be greatly rewarded by the crown, and he had visions of what he could spend his coin on.

"As you see, governor," Lincoln was summarizing the plan after providing the details and the plan to Rutledge, "We already have superior numbers based on the amount we have been inflicting on the British, and the report from our navy that no resupply ships have gone through to Savannah. The British are in poor shape, with poor morale and poor logistics. This is the time to strike and be victorious!"

Rutledge didn't like giving up the control of the South Carolina Continentals, but he did see Lincoln's point. If the British were in that rough condition, it would be incredibly beneficial to him if the threat of the south was removed. Slowly nodding his head, Rutledge agreed.

"You make a good point, general," Rutledge commented, "if you feel confident that you can be successful without placing my men at unnecessary risk, then you have my blessing. Best of luck!"

As the assemblymembers voiced their approval and the other staff officers chimed in on support or other requirements, Richard Pearis slipped out of the assembly house. Then, unobserved as everyone was focused on the maps and notes, he made his way over to Maclane's office to pass what he heard.

***

Once he returned to his officer, Lincoln penned a letter to General Washington and the Continental Congress, explaining his desire to take Savannah. He worded it to show how their efforts in the south would support the strategic situation in the north, as their stalemate with the British appeared to be continuing. Then, in a coup to General Lincoln's plan, he received word from General Washington that not only did Congress approve of the taking of Savannah, but their new allies, the French, were going to commit a fleet and four thousand men to the campaign.

Lincoln nearly pranced around the office in jubilation, shouting, "I got it, I got it! Congress and his excellency approved it, and we're getting the French Fleet and men!" His staff just watched as Lincoln celebrated the approval of his plan until he finally stopped and took a deep breath with a big smile.

"Right, let's get down to business!" Lincoln stated and, with his staff, began to work on the details of the plan for the coming expedition.

The word trickled down to the men in the regiments, including Jacob and his men. They were heading to Savannah, but the French were going to help. Some of the men in the barracks whooped and hollered when they heard the news, clinking their tin cups in celebration, while Jacob and other French and Indian War veterans sat pensively while sipping from their cups.

Samuel looked over at Jacob, deep in thought, staring into his mug after hearing the news about France's support. "What's on your mind, Captain?" asked Norman Skelly, one of the recruits who had recently been assigned to the regiment. Then, after swallowing a gulp from his tun cup, Robert Baird pointed to Jacob, Samuel, and a few other men in the company with his cup and explained.

"The Captain, the Sergeant-Major, and those men over there all fought against the French in the last war. So I'm guessing the news about the French as our allies aren't sitting well with them."

Then realizing Jean was sitting there, not saying a word, Robert looked abashed from his comment. "Sorry, sir, meant no disrespect."

Jean snorted and smiled, looking at Robert. "No, no. I agree. You can't rely on those French regulars. I couldn't stomach them sometimes.

Robert, and some of the others who knew Jean had been on the other side during the last war, seemed confused.

"Jean is not French," Jacob commented, raising his cap to Jean, "He was the best Canadian Partisan Leader I ever fought against and the finest officer I have fought with!"

The men all raised their cups and cheered, the tension of the possible insult being released.

Samuel nodded, "You can bet on that," he returned, "but it is a good question. How can we rely on these French that not too long ago, we were fighting."

John Cameron chimed in, "I am sure they forgive and forget, no sore feelings from this last fight, right?" The comment received some chuckles from the gathered men, yet Jacob still sat and was deep in thought. Jacob smiled as the men chuckled, then added his views.

"Like you all, I have concerns about the coming campaign for Savannah. I am concerned that our leaders are overestimating our capabilities and underestimating the British. Too often, I have seen this and its terrible results. But, then our new allies, I have to admit, I hold in high respect."

This caused some startled looks from his gathered men, even Samuel, but Jacob explained, holding up his hands as his men gave him startled looks.

"Let me explain; I hold any of my enemies that shown great skills in high respect, whether they are British, French, or Cherokee. They earned my respect, and I respect their skills;

not doing so is foolish. So many times, I have seen leaders, ours or the British during the last war, fail to respect their enemies. They should have and were slaughtered instead." Jacob looked at Samuel, "You know exactly what I am talking about; you saw it with your own eyes."

Samuel nodded and knew which way Jacob was heading with his explanation. Jacob continued, "Fort William Henry, Fort Carillon; our leaders underestimated the enemy they did not hold in respect and overestimated their abilities. As a result, the French and their Canadians, especially their partisan leaders like Jean here, or even Langy who gave Rogers a run for his money, nearly destroyed us had not fate and luck smiled on us." Jacob looked to see if he had the gathered men's attention.

"If we don't respect our enemy, they will surprise and kill us, and I don't want that to happen. Seen it too many times before." Jacob's eyes took on a distant look, going back in time. Finally, the men began to nod and understand Jacob's point, respect your enemy, or face your doom in ignorance.

***

Maclane leaned against a shaded corner of the mercantile warehouse, smoking his pipe and watching the activity as wagons and carts came and went, loaded with supplies. Aslabie may have been a flop, but he finally grew up, and within that empty head, a mind for the business grew. As the primary and only actual mercantile in the city, this rebel army was buying all of their supplies from him.

He scoffed at the thought of "buying" now this bloody continental script of paper money came out. They still tried to force the use of coins, but when it came to push and shove, they relented and accepted this paper currency.

"You seem to be doing well for yourself," commented Bedlow, who had quietly approached and stood next to Maclane. Satisfied he did not flinch or jump at Bedlow's approach, Maclane nodded.

"Aye, we seem to be doing alright for ourselves," Maclane responded and turned sideways to look at Bedlow. He dressed in non-descript worker's clothes and a workman's hat. He offered his tobacco pouch, and Bedlow nodded his thanks, filled his pipe, then, using an ember from Maclane's, lit his.

"Any updates on this planned attack?" Bedlow asked. Maclane shook his head.

"My man reported as of this morning's meeting between General Lincoln and Governor Rutledge in the assembly that all is in order. Once supplied, the army will march around mid-summer to invest in Savannah."

Bedlow nodded, "What about this rumor of the French coming south to support?"

Maclane shrugged his shoulders. "All rumors from what I know, but my man at the assembly mentioned that this General Washington was brought up. The overall commander of the rebels is sending both a French fleet and a French Army to support the attack."

Bedlow, the master spy for the Southern Department of the Colonies for the British Empire, nodded in concern. But, unfortunately, the British fleet was away, and with the French reinforcements, Prevost may have his hands full, even with the information he would provide him."

"Have you activated your nefarious assets to the north?" Bedlow asked, and Maclane nodded.

"Aye, they are, and those bloody scoundrels will be making the rebels' lives more interesting very soon."

Bedlow despised using these ruffians and vagabonds, especially what he had learned about this Big Harpe person; he did not want the Crown associated with these murderers. So hopefully, in a way, these rebels can make short work and remove these liabilities from their service.

"What of the Cherokee and the other tribes," Bedlow asked, "What have you heard from Stuart?"

Maclane shuffled his feet as he thought about a response. "They're done; they won't take up the tomahawk anymore since the end of 1777. Stuart, trying to lead that attack back in 1776 against the rebels that not only failed but saw thirteen Cherokee towns burned, fled to somewhere in Florida."

Bledsoe puffed on his pipe, blowing out the smoke in a long, grey stream. "Cameron recently passed that the only tribe still fighting, the Chicamauga Cherokee struck against some rebel towns on the frontier, got stopped as well. Then the rebels marched on and burned some of their towns. So we have no more Cherokee support."

Bedlow frowned and nodded his head in understanding. "Then I guess we must go with the lesser of the two evils and release your ruffians and murders to scare these rebel supporters. Make them keep the rebels off balance."

Maclane nodded, Bedlow nodded in response, turned, and walked away. Maclane returned to watching the activity of the loading. Thinking, how was he going to incorporate his band of thieves and murderers to his advantage, and how he can achieve his goal and, if fate smiles, remove some of these ruffians from associating with the Crown or directly back to him.

***

By August, the army began to assemble, and orders were sent out, all men on leave to return to their regiments. The Second South Carolina was given orders to be prepared to move at a moment's notice, and Jacob made sure the men had all of their gear ready to go. Each man was issued sixty cartridges loaded into their cartridge boxes and haversacks, along with spare flints. The men also cooked four days of rations and packed them away in their haversacks and packs.

As Jacob, Samuel, and Jean met with the quartermaster in the middle of a sea of activity as numerous carts and wagons dropped off supplies or headed back into the city, they spotted an old friend limping through the crowd.

"Peter, what in the bloody hell are you doing here?" Jacob shouted at his old friend, who spun around when he heard his name, ever-present pipe clenched in his teeth, and gave a big smile when he saw it was three of them.

"Ah, my old friends, business is good for us!" Peter shouted as he hobbled over and shook all f their hands. "The Army needs food, we have food, and they need people to move it. So not only did they buy our smoked meats, they are paying us for moving it."

Jacob moved closer to his smiling friend and asked, "How much?"

Tapping out the ash from his pipe on his boot heel, Peter shrugged and replied, "All of it."

"All of it?" Jacob asked, and Peter clarified. "They paid for all of our vagons and carts, all die meat we could load, and they are paying for die men to drive them. We have been contracted to support the army and are paid very well."

Peter turned and gestured toward the mass of wagons and carts, and Jacob recognized the men from his business and home compound. Peter turned to light and puffed on his pipe. "If dis war keeps going, ve keep getting contracts, ve will be rich!"

Jacob smiled and patted his friend on the shoulder before asking about his family and how they were doing well.

"They're getting by, my friend, the boys," nodding at Samuel as well, "are stepping up and are turning into excellent hunters like their fathers, couldn't ask fer more. Die little girls are not so little. Helga is very much like her mother; she is very handy with a knife ven it comes to the skinning and even goes on hunts with the boys."

Peter paused for a moment before continuing. "We are doing well; it's been quiet, both good and bad."

Jacob looked at his friend, "good and bad?"

Peter nodded as he puffed on his pipe, "Yah, good that der is no trouble mit them, Loyalists. Bad because der is no trouble mit them, Loyalists. Mark my word, something is up."

Jacob nodded, "Keep them safe old friend; hopefully, we can end this business by getting back home soon. Honestly, I am starting to tire of war and being away."

Peter nodded and shook their hands in parting before turning to get on a cart to head back to their home compound.

They returned to the company and inspected the men; everything was in order. Jacob nodded his head in approval; all of their hard work and instilling discipline was paying off. The regiment was a professional and organized unit that trusted one another as comrades-in-arms. They worked together, took care of one another, and were ready.

Jacob's only concern was how the rest of the army would perform, seeing most of the units were local militia units. So, while they waited for the orders to march, the Second South Carolina was moved out to Sullivan's Island with the 3rd North Carolina, instructed by Jacob and his company on how to crew cannons.

**

"Are you sure your information is correct?" General Prevost asked Bedlow, who stood before him in his British uniform.

"Yes, sir," Bedlow answered, not liking being questioned on his accuracy. "We have several sources which all confirm that the rebels, supported by the French, are coming for you."

Prevost was refusing to see how he could be the attention of these rebels; this General Washington and the main Rebel Army was up north the last time I heard."

"They still are, sir," Bedlow answered, "however we have a very reliable source observing the French fleet has departed and is sailing south."

"How reliable?" Prevost asked irritably.

"Admiral Graves of the Royal Navy in New York sent a dispatch from Captain Symonds, who spotted the French fleet under sail heading south from Rhode Island mid-month. That means they will be arriving soon."

Prevost stood up from his seat and began to pace the room, deep in thought. In the room was Lieutenant Colonel Frederich von Porpeck of the Hessians, the Royal Engineer Major Moncrieff, Lieutenant Colonel Athomas Brown of the Provincials, Lieutenant Colonel Cruger of DeLancy's Loyalist Brigade, and Lieutenant Colonel Maitland.

'Right, guess we better get down to work." Prevost declared, then turned and faced his assembled staff. "Put everyone who can carry a shovel to work; I want the defenses around this city ready. To finish the defenses, I mean everyone, soldiers, townspeople, slaves free or not."

He stared directly at Maitland. "Pull your forces back, abandon your garrisons at Sunsburry and Beaufort as fast as possible, consolidate your command here."

Maitland nodded his head in understanding, and Prevost motioned him free to go and see to get his command to Savannah. He then turned to Moncrieff.

"Make sure the redoubts are strong, the abatis is in position and work with the artillery to get guns in positions. Then, if the French fleet is coming, sink vessels in the harbor and the river to block their passage."

Moncrieff nodded his head in understanding. Then, Prevost moved on to Brown. "Send out your cavalry. Scout all the approaches to the city, and be on the lookout for the French Fleet. I want to know as soon as their sails are spotted, and I want them tracked!"

Brown nodded his head in understanding. Then Prevost looked at the rest of his officers. "Make sure all is ready, muskets serviceable, and issue forty rounds to each man. Make sure guns are ready and crew them with navy personnel if needed. See to it, gentlemen, I will not lose to a bunch of backwoods rebels, and never to the French!"

***

In early September, General Lincoln finally ordered the army to march; their objective was Savannah. As the army marched out, Jacob was not very impressed with what they called an army when it was only twenty-eight hundred men, not the tens of thousands of men during the French and Indian War campaigns against Fort Carillon and Quebec.

The Second South Carolina was assigned to the Second Brigade under the command of Brigadier General Isaac Huger, which also had all of the light infantry companies converged into one light infantry battalion, along with some North Carolina Continentals. Jacob observed the North Carolinians under Lieutenant Colonel John Laurens was with the brigade, Laurens having healed from his injuries. His light infantry had been combined with the light companies from the first, third, and fifth of the North Carolina Continentals.

Samuel saw that Jacob was brooding as the regiment began to prepare for the march. So he went over to see what was bothering his friend.

"What seems to be on your mind, Jacob?" Samuel asked as he sat next to Jacob, who had been sitting on some crates, thinking. Blowing out his breath, Jacob replied

"Have a bad feeling about this one, Samuel, something is nagging me, and I can't place my finger on it. We may be in for a tight fight on this one, so I am thinking about the family. More worried about them than I am about myself." Samuel looked at his long friend and punched him in the shoulder.

"Don't worry about it, I promised your wife I'll take care of you, just like you will take care of me, or our wives will kill us. Still, I trust your instincts; they have been right so far. So what are you going to do?"

Jacob thought about it, then snorted and stood up. "I will start getting myself together and take care of these men. Whatever happens, will happen, and if I am dead, I guess I am not worrying about much. Still, I will find Peter and let him take some of my items home for safekeeping, just in case." Samuel nodded; it made sense, and he decided he would do the same.

Jacob, Jean, and Samuel brought their rifles and some gear from their barracks and found Peter in the wagon line forming behind the column as the column was being formed. "What's dis?" Peter asked as they placed their extra and personal gear in the wagon Peter sat on.

"Just in case, my old friend," Jacob replied and looked up at Peter, "I have a bad feeling about this. So we want you to hold on to our extra gear; we can always come home and get them." Nodding slowly, Peter understood and didn't question Jacob.

"Good luck, my friends," Peter said as he shook their hands and watched them move and join their men in the column.

He watched from his perch on the wagon, smoking his pipe, knowing from the past when Jacob showed concerns, then they should be listened to.

"Bah, nothing I can do about it!" Peter commented aloud, "It's up to fate and the almighty for this one."

With drums and fife playing, the column marched out of the city, General Lincoln leading the way to the roar and applause of the city dwellers as the army marched by. The soldiers marched in unison, their arms shouldered properly and smartly as the column wove its way through the streets.

Maclane with Daniel Claus stood and watched as part of the crowd as the column marched out. "Get your horse to Savannah, tell them they are on their way. If Lincoln is slow as he has been, Prevost should have time to get ready."

Claus nodded and looked at the snaking column before nodding. Then he turned, headed off to get on his horse, and headed to Savannah.

Once the army was through the walls and had passed the outer defenses, the command of "Arms at will" was given. So the soldiers began to carry their muskets the best way they could. The drummers slung their drums over their shoulders and carried them by their straps.

Jacob and the regiment were in the front of the column. The men carrying their muskets either slung over their shoulders with those who had slings or cradled in their arms. The men clanked as tin cups attached to their haversacks banged against their gear, the clanking becoming a steady and constant rhythm.

Dust rose and blanketed the warm air as their feet moved along the road. "At least it's not raining," commented one of the men, and Jacob had to agree. Rain would have turned the road into a churned mire of mud and muck after the army marched through.

Still, he felt for the men bringing up the rear of the five-mile-long column. General Lincoln had directed that a company of Continentals would march behind the column to secure any stragglers and keep them with the army. Along with breathing in all that dust, the men in the rear had to follow all of the wagons, horses, and livestock, including all the manure they left behind. Jacob did not envy those men and hoped they would be spared from that duty.

Every hour or so, the column will halt, allowing the men to rest for a short spell and drink. Then, finally, the column split in half, and one half went to one side of the road and the other half to the other. This allowed messengers on horses to ride up and down the column carrying their dispatches. The men found what shade they could or simply sat on the ground resting. For the moment, the men relaxed and bantered with one another. Jacob knew this would end when they would become exhausted from the march, in which many would sit in silence then, too tired to talk.

Jacob was proud of his men, their training and constantly marching had conditioned them, and they seemed to be in good shape, for now. But, of course, they still had days of marching, and time would tell. Still, Jacob sat with his men, talked with them, shared their misery, and strengthened their bond. The army marched until sundown before it would go into camp for the night. No tents were set up; the companies laid out their ground cloths, the air still warm enough for just blankets.

Some of the men built small fires, and they sat around the comfort of the dancing fire light, the men smoking pipes and passing the time. Jacob still set a watch and rotated the guards amongst the men to prevent at least their portion in the camped column from being surprised. While there had been no Loyalist attacks, it didn't mean they were not being watched. The men were not up too long before they laid out on their blankets, and soon the sound of talking was replaced by sounds of snoring.

Messengers moved up and down the column before sunrise, waking the men and getting them ready to march. Many men moaned as they packed their ground cloths and blankets and shouldered their packs. Many men swam in their straps, trying to settle the straps on less sore places on their shoulders. The column would repeat this for the next four days as they continued towards Savannah. Finally, as Jacob had predicted, the men settled into the routine of just placing their feet in front of the other and eating up the time and distance.

Even Jacob had to admit that this march was tiring him out, and he felt he was in better condition than most. Jacob recalled moving further and faster when he was a Ranger in New York. It had to be the restriction of marching in a column instead of spreading out, making him feel more sore and tired than when he moved on his own. His men were still hanging in there, better than the men from the other companies and the militiamen. They were starting to show some wear, but they were soldiering in good form.

General Lincoln learned on the twelfth of September that the French fleet had arrived off Savannah from messengers and scouts, so he ordered the army to press on faster to get to the city. When the messengers arrived to tell the regiments to pick up speed, the men groaned, but shouldered their gear, lowered their heads, and pressed on the march.

On the thirteenth, the army arrived at Cherokee Hill and prepared to cross the Savannah River. However, the British had burned all the bridges. It seemed they took all the boats from the river that could be used to transport the army across. The army went into camp as General Lincoln decided how they would cross this obstacle.

Having gathered his staff, who were all sitting on crates and boxes and using a large box as a table with a map, Lincoln planned their next step. Jacob, having been invited by Marion, the two standing next to Moultrie and Huger.

"General Pulaski, any reports from your scouts on a suitable crossing for your cavalry?" Lincoln asked the Polish commander, who shook his head no.

"My men found a single canoe, and we could use it to move across." General Lincoln looked up at General Pulaski, "How are you going to move your horses across with a canoe?"

General Pulaski replied matter of factly, "My men use the canoe while the horses swim alongside one at a time."

Lincoln nodded in understanding and returned to looking at his map of Savannah and the surrounding land. "I need to know what they are up to," sighed Lincoln, "General Moultrie, send out some of your lights which are experienced scouts, to gather information on our enemy, and report back to the army. They have two days to gather information about the enemy and their defenses. See to it."

General Moultrie nodded and turned to Marion and Jacob. "You heard the commander, Captain Clarke; go get him some information."

Jacob nodded, turned, and headed off at a trot to hand pick a team to head out on the scout. Once back at their camping area, as he typically does, Jacob called for Jean and Samuel and the men from Captain Daniel Horry's Company they have used as scouts.

Jacob explained to the assembled scouts. "Standard practice, get information so the leaders can make some decisions. General Lincoln needs details on the enemy defenses around Savannah. We will make our way if we can get to Savannah, gather the information, and return to the army in three days on the road to the city."

The scouts all nodded their heads in understanding as Jacob continued. "We must evaluate the defenses, their condition, and the strength of the opposing forces. The rub is, we are to attempt to avoid contact or detection with the enemy during the conduct of the scout, any questions?"

The assembled scouts shook their heads, chorusing, "Understood, Sir!"

The men gathered their equipment and gear; they were already marching light as it was, so all they had to do was shoulder their cartridge boxes, bayonets, canteens, haversacks, and packs. As they were forming up, Lieutenant Colonel Laurens stopped by.

"Colonel Marion told me you are heading out on a scout; I wanted to wish you luck out there." Jacob nodded as Laurens moved on through the camp. Jacob and Jean stared at Lauren's back as he moved along the line.

"What do you make of him?" Jean asked, nodding in the direction of Lauren. "He was not a good leader at the river, no?"

Jacob stared at the back of Laurens and shook his head. "I don't know yet, Jean, I don't know. He has great potential but very rash, I think."

The scouts returned, their gear shouldered and muskets ready. Jacob checked on the men and ensured they had all of their equipment and it was well secured. "We'll be moving fast and quietly, and we'll need to find a place to cross or ford the river. All set?"

The men nodded, then took up their muskets and followed Jacob out of the camp, Samuel taking the last position in the line and Jean in the center. They trotted out of the camp and moved towards, then along the river, looking for a place to cross.

Finding no bridges or boats, they found a place to the ford where the river was only chest deep. Holding their muskets, cartridge boxes, and bags over their heads, the men entered the river and slowly made their way across it. Each man carefully placed their feet, the water gurgling around them as they crossed.

The first two men out of the water on the other side quickly replaced their bags and took a knee behind some trees. They watched, covering the rest of the men as they made their way out of the river. Then, dripping from their chests down, the men quickly moved onto shore, replacing their bags and resuming their positions in the section.

Once Samuel had accounted for everyone, he nodded to Jacob, who motioned for the men to forward. From now on, they were going to limit talking and use their hands to communicate as they moved through enemy territory. Not having much time, Jacob decided they would dry as they moved towards Savannah.

Jacob led them along the river, using it to help navigate them towards the city. He kept the men in trees and shrubs as they moved, constantly looking for enemy patrols, especially cavalry. They moved cautiously but quickly as possible, knowing they only had two days to report before returning to the army. They covered a lot of ground, only spotting some farmers and even two fishermen from their concealed locations, but no sign of the enemy. Finally, as the sun set, Jacob directed the men into a thicket near the river, where they made tight camp.

After the men entered the thicket, they took a knee and listened to see if they had been followed before Jacob gave the motion for them to settle down and make their beds. Two men remained on watch as the others spread out their blankets, and two men took everyone's canteens to the river and drew water. After they returned, Samuel pulled out a flask and poured rum into the canteens, and the men swirled them around, the canteens making soft swishing sounds.

The men rotated, pulling watch, eating their cooked rations, and getting some rest. Jacob, Jean, and Samuel checked the men, their feet, and their equipment before they too settled down to eat and rest. Jacob looked up into trees as the darkness covered them, the Spanish Moss swaying in the evening breeze. The men remained quiet; if they had to talk, they crawled up to the person and spoke very softly in their ears so the sound wouldn't travel.

The night passed uneventfully; they could rest and restore some vigor before Jacob had them all awake for stand to. Listening, they heard no sound except for the gurgling river past. Everyone repacked their gear, kneeling and ready to go. Nodding, Jacob waved his men forward, Brewer and Nevel leading them out. It did not take them long, and before midday, they arrived outside Savannah city. In a crouch, all of them slowly climbed a short rise, stopped at the lip, and looked out towards the city.

They were on a short ridge overlooking a small creek that had branched off the river and a swamp that the stream ran through. The ground rose on the other side of the creek and marsh that went to the river. The city itself had its back to the river where it had been a bustling trading port. Jean and Samuel watched their backs, the others spreading out in a small circle, their muskets ready.

Jacob pulled out his telescope to look at the activity across from them. The British had been very active since they had taken the city, building a defensive work surrounding the city facing them, using the river as part of their defenses. Using the telescope's focus, Jacob viewed the earthworks, the integrated square redoubts, and abatis under construction.

"Samuel, you and half of the men remain here and collect on what you can see for activities. Then, if you can do it without being detected, move as close as possible and get details on this side of the works and the approaches." Samuel nodded his understanding.

"Jean and I will take the other half and try to see the city from the other side. Then, I will return to you and move back together. If we're hit, make your way back to the army. We'll make our way to the army if I hear you getting hit. If we have to run, head back to where we crossed the river."

Brewer, Nevel, and Corporal Stedman from Horry's Company stayed with Samuel as Jacob led Hansen, Baird, and Ballard. Making sure there was no one around, Jacob and his men made their way into the swamp and carefully made their way across. Their feet were sucked into the muck with soupy sucking sounds as they worked their way across the marsh. They only heard insects and birds, their feet sinking and making the sucking sound in the mud. Jacob shook his head; crossing the swamp would make the approach difficult for infantry and extremely difficult for cavalry or artillery.

When they reached the creek, they slowly lowered themselves into the stream, which only came up to their knees. Slow moving, the mud from their legs turned the creek brown as they crossed; Jacob and his men finished crossing and then continued across the rest of the swamp before climbing the rise to the top of the next ridge. Crouching low, they stopped at the lip of the hill and, finding some bushes for concealment, got a better look at the British defenses. Hansen, Ballard, and Baird pulled security while Jean recorded what Jacob observed as he pulled out his telescope.

The British had used the terrain to their advantage when they built their defenses around the city. Earthen solid walls were constructed, and Jacob could see cannon openings in the redoubts. Connecting the redoubts were earthen and log walls, creating a vast, slightly curving crescent whose ends were anchored on the river.

Through the telescope, Jacob could see men in shirts busy working on the walls and redoubts, building abatis and sharpened stakes angled out from the defenses.

"Well, we use the same book, so it's no surprise how they are setting up their defenses," commented Jacob, and Jean nodded as he wrote down what Jacob described. "Oui, sounds like Carrillon, no?

The area in front of the defenses had been cleared of trees and brush, making clear fields of fire. "Hopefully, we also follow the book and lay a siege instead of trying to march across this open area to storm those defenses," Jacob commented.

Once he had everything he could gather, they backed slowly down the ridge and moved to the west, using the rise to mask their movements. Jacob always made sure there was a brush for them to conceal before climbing to the top. Before cresting the ridge, they took their helmets off, not wanting their silver crescents flashing in the light and giving their position away.

Jacob probed along the ridge a few times, gathering information while Jean wrote it down as Hansen, Ballard, and Baid watched for any enemy. When the sun began to sink, they backed away from the ridge reasonably and, after crossing another stream, found a thick bushy area where they made camp. Seeing only four of them, Jacob decided just to sleep, hoping the brush would conceal them from any eyes looking for them. Jacob didn't sleep; he never truly slept while out on scouts. He more or less snoozed, resting lightly while listening for any sound of the enemy.

They quickly ate their cooked rations when the sun rose before returning to the ridge and continuing with their scout. Again, using the same tactics, they would slowly climb the bank and look. Using his telescope, Jacob looked at the different uniforms. He could identify British regulars by their red coats, dark blue coats of the Germans, green coats of Loyalist Provincials, and civilian clothes of the Loyalist militias, all mixed.

To get a better perspective, he would pass his telescope to Jean, who would look, then provide his assessment. From what Jacob could guess, about two thousand soldiers, Jean concurs.

"Hopefully, they will use the French Fleet and siege artillery to knock those defenses down," commented Jean. "They look very tough to me."

"I agree, Jean, I agree," Jacob commented. "How well will our Lincoln do with whoever the French command the ground force.

"My opinion," Jean commented, "not well."

"My thoughts as well," Jacob returned.

Having had crept as close as they could, and their luck had held, Jacob decided it was time to return to Samuel so they could make their way back to the army. But, first, review their notes with Jean, ensuring they covered everything they could before returning.

While luck may have held out for them during the scout, it left them as they crossed the swamp. Luckily, they had found some scrub brush when they heard men's voices approaching. Crouching in the bush, Jacob knew they would be spotted if the approaching men got close enough. Although they had nowhere to run because of the openness of the swamp, Jacob knew they had only one option. Slowly pulling his knife from its sheath, Jacob's men didn't need to be told what they must do and were prepared to rush the approaching men.

Getting his feet under him, ready to spring, Jacob saw the flash of red as the men came into view, four men in red uniforms with fishing poles on their shoulders but muskets in their hands. When the men were almost upon them, Jacob quickly sprang from his bush, knocking his target down, and his knife quickly flashed out, slicing his target's throat. Hansen quickly buried his bayonet that he held in his hand into the stomach of his target, riding him to the ground. Then, using his musket as a club, Ballard butt-stroked his mark with a hard crack and, as his target fell, used the butt again to smash the face of his fallen target.

As Baird moved out of his concealment, his foot found a deep mud patch, and he stumbled, missing his target. The British soldier, startled, turned and began to run back towards the city. Not hesitating, Jean hurled his tomahawk, which spun only twice before striking the running man's back. Then, moving quickly as the British soldier fell, Jacob promptly moved up and pinned him to the ground; using his free hand, he pulled the man's head up and slit his throat.

The men paused and listened, only hearing the creek gurgling. Then, wiping his knife blade on the uniform of the dead British soldier, Jacob resheathed it and handed the tomahawk to Jean. They pulled the bodies and sank them in the swamp near the creek, taking their muskets and sinking them.

Once complete, Jacob looked at the faces of his men, nodded, and led them across the swamp and back to Samuel's position.

"Hopefully, they'll think they deserted," Jacob and Jean nodded. Remaining cautious, they spotted no one and arrived safely back at Samuel's position as the sun began to sink.

"How did it go," Samuel asked, and Jacob returned with a shrug, "About normal."

Samuel gave him a stern look, "then that means you ran into someone or someone, right?"

Jacob gave him a shocked and hurt look, "Whatever do you mean?"

Samuel snorted. "If you say about normal, that means you had a run-in with our British friends."

Jacob shrugged, "There were only four of them; we made quick and quiet work of them."

"Hmm, mm," Samuel commented, then patted Jacob on the shoulder, "Let's go."

Not waiting, Jacob motioned for the men to move and began to make their way back to the army. As before, they used the river as a guide, moving at a good pace with the moon bathing them in a silvery glow and making it easier to see the ground around them.

Jacob expected the army to follow the river as they did, and they found the army just after midnight. Carefully approaching the pickets and using the password, they passed through the picket line and made their way to the army. Jacob thanked the scouts and returned to find their company, while Jean and Samuel accompanied Jacob as he sought out General Moultrie.

Moultrie's aid woke him, and he quickly rose from his sleeping cloth and welcomed them back. "Everything goes well?" he asked, and Jacob responded that they had the information General Lincoln requested.

"What is your opinion Captain Clarke, having seen their defenses," Moultrie asked as he pulled his regimental coat on.

"Sir, it's going to be tough, just like our defenses of the neck, except we're on the wrong side. They are well prepared and dug in with artillery looking over a clear killing ground. We won't be able to take it by storm, only by siege." Moultrie nodded with the news.

"I trust you were not spotted?" Moultrie asked, to which Jacob replied, "No, we were not spotted."

Samuel almost chuckled, but Jean punched the side, making him cough.

"Are you well, sergeant-major?" Moultrie asked.

"Just the night air," Samuel answered, I think I swallowed a bug."

General Lincoln was up when Moultrie led Jacob, Jean, and Samuel to give their report. Lincoln listened intently as they described the defenses, using a stick to draw out the defenses in the dirt. They told of the redoubts and walls, the clear fields of fire, and the number of men and cannons they observed.

"Well then, we have no choice; we will have to work with our French allies to lay siege." Lincoln accepted the notes and sketches from Jacob and responded, "You did well, just like I expected. You're a great asset to the army, Captain, Lieutenant, and Sergeant-Major; thank you for what you have done."

CHAPTER 8

THE SIEGE OF SAVANNAH

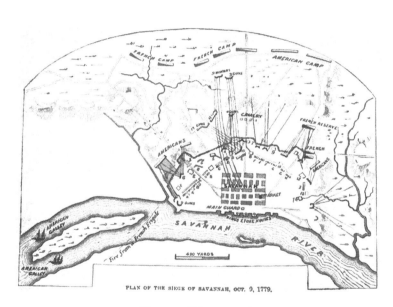

PLAN OF THE SIEGE OF SAVANNAH, OCT. 9, 1779.

Siege of Savannah

Major General Augustine Prevost was feeling his age. Looking at his map and rubbing the stubble on his chin, General Prevost sighed deeply and wished the younger commander had been sent down to replace him.

Instead, Brigadier General George Garth had been sent south from New York, but Prevost received word that his ship had been intercepted and captured. So the burden of command would remain heavily upon his shoulders. Prevost shook his head and bent over his map, trying to scry the future from it.

"What the bloody hell do you expect from me?" Prevost asked his map, "The French are blockading my ports, can't get supplies and reinforcements from the sea, and the Loyalists are no longer joining our ranks."

Rubbing the exhaustion from his eyes, Prevost stood up and picked up the dispatch from the scouts he had sent out. "French troops had landed thirteen miles away, and many ships anchored offshore. The scouts observed large artillery being offloaded and brought to shore." Then, taking a deep sigh, he dropped the report on the table, fluttering and landing on the map.

Prevost then picked up the dispatch the French commander, the Admiral Count Charles-Hector d'Estaing, had sent him.

"Commander, City of Savannah, I demand the surrender of your position immediately to the arms of his Majesty the King of France to avoid unnecessary bloodshed and loss of life. Know that I have personally taken the island of Grenada with a smaller force than what is about to invest in your position. Know that not surrendering will place the blood of your men and the city's innocents on your hands, and you would be personably responsible for their needless deaths."

"Orderly, bring parchment and quill." So Prevost ordered, and a short time later, the orderly arrived, sat at a smaller desk, and readied to write the dispatch for the general.

"My esteemed Admiral Count Charles-Hector d'Estaing. Sir, I humbly request a time of truce to confer with the city leaders and present them with your demand. Then, please allow time for us to confer and send our reply in conjunction with the City."

The orderly finished the dispatch, brought the general's seal, and warmed wax so he could affix his seal before the orderly folded the message.

"Send for my commanders," Prevost directed as the orderly bowed in understanding before turning to get a messenger.

As Prevost waited, he rubbed his chin and stared at the map. "Time, I don't have much bloody time!" he growled at the map. Then, with his finger, he traced the outline of the defenses on the city's outskirts. Prevost thought he had a strong defense, the river behind him anchored on the flanks by swamps and streams. This would force the attackers to attack only one side where he can build his strength, even for a short period.

Soon, the officers began arriving. Prevost looked at his assembled officers standing around the table that held his map. His younger brother, Lieutenant Colonel Mark Prevost, who had taken command of his old unit, the 60th Royal Americans, spoke with Lieutenant Colonel John Maitland of the 71st Highlanders. Captain Sir John Baird, who commanded all the light infantry, looked closely at the map while Lieutenant Colonel Frederick von Porbeck, who led the German contingent, stood off to the side puffing on a long stem pipe.

Also looking intently at the map was Captain Charleton, who commanded the artillery that would be critical in the city's defenses. Finally, standing in a group to another side of the room were the commanders of the different Loyalist units from Georgia, New York, New Jersey, North and South Carolina, the British Legion, and King's Rangers.

"Gentlemen, if I could have your attention," began General Prevost, and the assembled officers stopped their discussions, looked up, and moved closer to the table.

"I have feined a need for a truce to confer with the city leaders to buy us some more time, how little it is, to prepare our defenses. After that, we'll have to be ready to repel these rebels and the French. Are we ready?"

Prevost looked around the table, and it all seemed the men nodded their heads they were. "Captain Charleton, how are we set for artillery?" Charleton looked at his notes before responding.

"Sir, we have about a hundred pieces of artillery; all have been emplaced in redoubts, and strong points were they will be able to support across the front of the defenses. The naval guns and crews have been emplaced and integrated into the defenses, and the artillery is ready."

General Prevost nodded in approval, then asked, "How are we set for supplies, powder, and shot?"

The Quartermaster, Major Dunham, replied, "We have enough provisions to support the garrison for about a month, perhaps two months if we shorten rations. We have enough shot and powder for the garrison to hold a sustained defense for a couple of weeks."

General Prevost nodded and asked, "Morale, how is the morale?"

"The men are anxious to have at these rebels and give them British steel!" commented Maitland, supported by several "Huzzahs" from the assembled officers.

Prevost finally felt confident and not as old as he had been feeling. The exhaustion and weakness faded, and a new strength flowed into him by looking at his assembled officers.

"We will use what little time we have before I am supposed to respond to the French's demand to surrender. We shall not. Well then, I guess we now have to wait on the rebels; it seems we are ready for them!" stated Prevost, and the officers responded enthusiastically.

***

Before reaching Savannah, the army was camped around the Millings House, about three miles left. As he packed his backpack, Jacob recalled the day before, after the army arrived, how Lincoln still held court-martials for infractions. In addition, General Lincoln had posted severe penalties for anyone found destroying rail fences or property of the local plantations, misuse of their ammunition, and very harsh punishments for looting.

Jacob understood these orders, the same issues armies faced since the days of the Romans, curbing the dark side of human nature. The other orders that Lincoln put out were precise to their mission. No one was to leave the camp, no firing of muskets in the camp, and no one was allowed through the pickets without written orders. Security of their march was paramount, but Jacob was sure unfriendly eyes had already spotted them, and the British knew they were coming.

As Jacob was settling his pack on his back, the sound of the lash carried on the morning air. One of the guilty was receiving his punishment. A soldier was found guilty of desertion and was sentenced to one hundred lashes to be carried out before the march. The man was only receiving the first twenty-five today, the other three sessions for the next three days in the morning.

Jacob, along with Jean and Samuel, were to join the lead company and take them along the same route they had used during their scout. As they were settling their gear on their shoulders, reinforcements from the North marched into their camp. A column of Virginia Continental infantry marched along, the 1st Continental Light Dragoons trotted by, and we're heading to where General Lincoln was camped.

"Well, that's a sight for sore eyes," Samuel commented, watching the Virginians and the cavalry move past. "About time we received some help."

Jacob nodded but did not comment as he watched them move by. They looked well enough, but time will tell. He didn't know what experience these men had, whether they had seen battle or not. Jacob suspected they were in the same shape as they were, all the veterans of the first three years had left, and new men manned the regiments.

The word was passed down the line to prepare to march. They moved to the head of the column to join the advance guard. When they passed General Lincoln and his staff, he spoke to the newly arrived Continentals and Cavalry commanders. Moultrie saw them pass by and nodded to them.

The lead company of light infantry, who happened to be from the 2nd, was under the command of Captain Thomas Dunbar. When Jacob, Jean, and Samuel arrived, he welcomed them with a large smile.

"Heard you were going to lead us on a scenic jaunt through the woods and swamps?" he asked, and Jacob nodded.

"That's all right; I heard you were getting bored and wanted to go on a walkabout," Jacob answered with a grin. Dunbar nodded his head.

The company of only sixty-two men was mostly veterans who had stayed on or reenlisted to stay in the regiment. Jacob had served with them or trained them in one form or another. So the company was happy to see the "Old Three" that they refer to as Jacob, Jean, and Samuel from their years not only with the regiment but from their experiences.

Jacob called for the company to assemble around them and explained what they should see along the route. Then, using a stick, he drew a general course they would follow in the dirt and described the critical terrain they should be looking for.

"We are the eyes and ears for the army," Jacob explained. "We must ensure the army gets to where it is supposed to go and ensure it does not run into an ambush. I'm sure they know we're coming, but let's be safe and be the early warning if possible. Any questions?"

Jacob looked around the company; Dunbar and the rest shook their heads. They understood what they had to do. Jacob nodded and smiled. These men knew what to do, so he didn't have to spend as much time with them.

"See to your gear; sergeants do a final check before the order to move is sent."

It wasn't long until the messenger arrived, directing them to lead the army out. Jacob nodded to the messenger, who turned and rode back to General Lincoln.

"I'll take the lead platoon with Samuel, Thomas; you and Jean take the second and place out flankers. Let's get this army on the road."

Taking his position with the lead platoon, Jacob nodded and waved his hand forward, and the march began. The platoon spread out, covering both sides of the road, and spaced between the men, so they weren't right behind one another. Again, Jacob nodded and smiled; the training that he, along with Jean and Samuel, was evident. The men were automatically scanning the woods on either side, eyes, and muskets moving.

Following the same route as they did during their scout, Jacob and his company led the army to the area just before the swamps near Savannah. Sweat trickled down Jacob's face, it was a steamy day, even for a late September morning, and only a slight breeze moved the Spanish Moss. The woods echoed insects, which to Jacob was a good sign. Silence would have meant someone was close.

They were a good quarter mile ahead of the army; at least Lincoln had enough sense not to be playing martial music while they marched. So only the sounds from the woods and swamps were heard.

"Horses approaching!" the lead scout called out, and the men automatically jumped to the side of the road, sought shelter behind trees, and brought their rifles up, not knowing who was approaching.

As the sound of hooves approached, the men waited while looking over the barrels of their muskets. When the horsemen came into sight, Jacob recognized them as riders from Pulaski's Legion. Jacob stepped out into the road and held his hand up. The horsemen, spotting Jacob, raised his hand and halted the three other riders with him.

Then the rest of the advance guard came out, and the horsemen had surprised looks on their faces, seeing the number of rifles and muskets that had been leveled at them. Jacob approached the lead rider, who had raised his hand.

Looking down at Jacob, the lead rider spoke, "Captain, I am Lieutenant Grenier, from the 1st Troop of Lancers, Pulaski Legion. How far is the main body?"

"They are about a quarter mile behind us," Jacob stated, pointing over his shoulder, "What news?"

"We have contacted the lead elements from the French, Colonel de Noailles' division. They are marching and should be here by nightfall or tomorrow morning."

Jacob nodded, Dunbar with Jean and Samuel joining them on the road. "How big of a force did they bring?"

Lieutenant Grenier smiled, "A considerable force while the siege artillery they are dragging is slowing them down. They are using the naval guns from the warships, and the mud is slowing down their process. However, the rest of the army is moving ahead and will be joining us soon."

Jacob nodded, "Thank you for the info; follow the road, and it will take you to the general."

Lieutenant Grenier nodded thanks and led his horseman down the road towards the army. Jacob waved, and the company stepped out onto the road. Then, turning, he pointed up the road from where the horsemen came.

"The bend towards Savannah is up ahead, which will mean we are very close to the city. It would be there if there were an ambush or picket for early warning. So we must exercise caution." Jacob briefed, and Dunbar nodded.

"I'll lead the first platoon forward, and if we make contact, we'll hold them in place while you take the rest of the company and flank them," Jacob instructed, "That is if we do run into anyone."

Dunbar and Jean returned to their company while Samuel stood with Jacob. "You think they are up there, waiting for us?" Samuel asked.

Jacob looked up the road, pondering the questions. Then he shook his head slowly.

"I'm not sure, to be honest. A smart commander would have pickets watching every major road an army would march on if they know we're coming."

Samuel looked at Jacob, "Smart? You mean the same one we bluffed away from Charles Town, smart?"

Jacob looked at Samuel, "Maybe, or the same one who stopped us at Stono Ferry. Who knows, but we must be ready just in case."

Samuel nodded his head in agreement. "Well then, let's go find some trouble!"

Jacob laughed at Samuel's comment before motioning the platoon forward. Everyone moved at the ready, muskets held before them as they scanned the woods next to them. It was only a few moments when the turn in the road was spotted ahead. Jacob kept his eyes focused on the trees, expecting either a volley or a shout, but received only silence.

Waving his arms, the platoon deployed into a sweeping line and went through the curve, moving deeper into the woods to see if an ambush was waiting. The men only found thorns as the only enemy. When the edge of the woods came into view and the open plains towards Savannah appeared, Jacob halted the platoon.

Dunbar and Jean joined Jacob and Samuel, looking towards the City of Savannah in the distance.

"We checked down the other road, no contact either. So why wouldn't the British have a picket here? This is the road from Charles Town?" Dunbar asked.

"We were wondering the same thing," Jacob replied. "Either they are confident about their defenses or not very good at fighting in the field."

"Hopefully, they are not good fighting, then confident," remarked Dunbar, "though I suspect I am wrong."

The company remained in place until the lead company arrived for the main column and halted. Soon General Lincoln rode up and joined Jacob and Dunbar at the edge of the road after dismounting.

"So, there's the prize," Lincoln commented, looking at the city in the distance. "We beat the French at least; we will set our camp up here in the woods."

The word was passed, and the army moved into the woods to the best of their abilities amongst the trees. Following the prescribed procedures for company lines, the quartermasters with the first sergeants arranged the regiments and began building shelters for the duration. Jacob, Jean, and Samuel made a small camp near the 2nd Regiment, using their ground cloths as lean-tos, and built a small fire to cook their rations.

The next day, the lead French infantry and grenadiers in their tall black fur hats arrived and went into camp on the right side of the American camp. Unfortunately, their camp seemed to have drawn the British's attention, and seeing they were closer to the city than the American camp, the British welcomed the French by firing on them with the guns from the defenses. Luckily, the woods were thick enough to deflect the flying shot, but the opening salvos of the siege had begun.

Jacob and the other men looked up when the boom began from the British guns but was relieved to see that none of the shot was flying their way.

"Well, lads," commented Jacob, "now the fun begins!"

The army spent the next couple of days setting the camp, stockpiling the supplies that the wagons had brought, and moved their artillery to the front of the camp, facing the city on the rise a reasonable distance away. Following the standard siege tactics, they would have to dig trenches and approaches to get their guns close enough to fire but protected from the British artillery.

Jacob wrestled with old emotions as the French officers and soldiers moved around the camp. Having fought so long, so hard, and so bitterly against them, it felt odd that now they were friends. Some may forgive, and most have no idea seeing South Carolina only dealt with the Cherokees. Jacob lost many friends to the French and their Indian Allies in New York.

Jacob was leading a work detail when they observed the French commander with his staff give an overly flowery bow to General Lincoln and his staff.

"They love to show off," Jean stated as he stood next to Jacob, "Even with us in Montreal, they always wanted to make sure we were below them as colonists and not true French like they."

"You still fought for them," Jacob commented, and Jean shook his head.

"No, I fought for my people, not them." Then Jean looked at Jacob. "You fought for the British against us, yes?" Jacob sighed and nodded his head. "See, it's an upside-down world we live in, my friend; we were enemies once, now friends. So it seems the French will be our friends."

Jacob watched the French staff join Lincoln and his staff. "An old saying I heard, the enemy of my enemy is my friend. Strange times indeed."

Then Jacob turned and placed his hand on Jean's shoulder. "Sorry, my friend, I do not hold a grudge. But, seeing them after so many years is hard to handle sometimes."

Jean nodded, "Yes, I understand. I don't like continental French either, including back during the war. They treated us like the British treat you, as a subject, not a person. So I agree with you if that matters. We are still friends. Leave the past buried in the past."

Nodding his head, "Let's get to work; it will take my mind off of this mess." Jacob led a work detail assigned to help the artillerymen move their guns into position. The engineers and the artillery chief selected a slight rise where they would emplace a battery of guns to protect the crews working on the siege lines.

Jacob and his men helped the Fourth South Carolina push their seven guns into position. The biggest, an eighteen-pounder, was first moved into position, half of the company helping to push the gun while the other half worked on fascines and gabions to protect the guns.

Sweat pouring down his face, Jacob pushed with all his might to help move the monster gun up the rise and into the battery as his men pulled the ropes dragging the gun. He felt alive and good to be active, and his muscles worked instead of walking. When the gun was emplaced, all the men sank to the ground and breathed heavily, smiling from the exertion.

Samuel slumped down next to Jacob with a tired smile on his face. "I hate to admit it, but that felt good to be working again instead of walking or sitting around." Then he flopped down on his back, looking up to the sky.

"Are you feeling old?" Jacob asked, seeing Samuel always enjoyed rubbing the fact he was older than he was, but it wasn't by that much.

"Well, I am working for two, so I should be tired. However, I have to pick up the slack of those older than me, out of respect."

Jacob looked down at his friend while the rest chuckled, "Of course."

After catching their breaths, the men moved back down the rise to the six waiting guns, a single six-pounder, and the rest were four-pound cannons. Along with the men from the Fourth, Jacob and his men spent the rest of the day pushing the guns into position at the top of the rise. Once the guns were in position, Jacob and his men helped stack powder and shot as the crews placed the artillery equipment at their guns.

By nightfall, the battery was ready for action. Jacob and the men returned to camp, collapsing to the ground, giddy from exhaustion. As Jean and Samuel, along with the rest of the detail, lounged and stretched their sore bodies, Jacob went over to the quartermaster and secured their rum ration and a little more, which the men greatly accepted.

"Will help with the aches and pains," Jacob commented as he went about, pouring the rum into the tin cups of the men. In return, they smiled and raised their cups in salute before drinking them down.

Pulling their rations out, the men began creating their evening meal. Samuel was already at work, combining their rations into a stew that they would soak their hard bread in. Jacob sat down near his gear and pulled his wooden bowel and horn spoon out of his haversack. For as many years he had to know Samuel, he was one of the best field cooks he had met. Able to take any ration and make it to a good meal.

After taking a quick sample of the stew, Samuel nodded and then ladled the stew into their waiting bowels. Jacob, along with Jean and then Samuel, crumbled up the hard, dry bread so it could soak up the juices from the stew to be eatable.

"Brings back memories, doesn't it?" Samuel asked as he lit his pipe, waiting for his bread to soak a little more.

Jacob nodded, "That it does, both good and bad. It always seems the circle keeps coming back around. But here we are again, with good friends, around a fire. So let's leave it at that."

"Here, here!" Samuel replied, raising his pipe in salute. They began eating their stew, the crunching sound of the half-soaked bread. The camp sounded like the camps over time, the voices from the different camps mixing with the sound of the woods and the army's activity.

Though they may be tired, the men had to pull guard duty from the battery they had just completed. Jacob walked along the small wall built from the gabions and fascines; his men helped to build and from trees that were cut down when the camp was made. It was a pleasant night, a breeze blowing across the plain. The men stood easy with their muskets, murmuring. A good number were always looking towards the city. Jacob could see the flickering watch-fire lights in the distance from the British lines, dancing like fireflies in the night.

As the night continued, the weather changed, and soon a cool rain began to fall steadily. When Jacob returned to the camp following the guard shift, the rain had not let up, and puddles were forming around the camp. Jacob crawled under his lean-to and wrapped himself in his blanket so his body warmth would help dry his clothes. Jacob could see other men's faces looking out from under their lean-tos.

"Try to keep your locks dry, do the best you can," Jacob called out, and the men nodded.

The rain continued, and the puddles grew into small ponds and streams running through the camp. Finally, when the sun rose the following day, the rain stopped, and the sun came out. Although the quality of lean-to construction was observed during the morning formation, those who built good lean-tos were reasonably dry, and those who looked like drowned rats needed more training on building.

That would have to wait as orders were given to begin the construction of the siege lines. Jacob would accompany Dunbar, and his light infantry company, who would provide security for the digging details in incase the British sallied from their lines. The colonials were working alongside the French; they were working on the left as the French were digging their positions on the right.

Jacob and the light infantry deployed into a skirmish line, two ranks with two soldiers, one behind the other, spaced out five paces between groups across the front of the men working. The digging crews were building the initial trench line on the top of the slope from the swamp on their side of the open field, some fifteen hundred yards from the British line.

Jacob's line advanced to the front of the workers by a hundred yards, and Jacob was given the command for his men to kneel. Jacob and Samuel remained to stand, attaching themselves to the first platoon again; Dunbar with Jean was back with the second. Jacob walked along the line of men as they knelt, their muskets ready. Jacob removed his leather helmet and wiped his brow with a handkerchief.

From the British line, some muffled booms could be heard. Both Jacob and Samuel looked at Jacob, yelling out "In-coming!" as they searched the sky for the falling shots screeching through the air were black dots as the mortar rounds finished their arch and fell towards them. The shots impacted with wet thumps, the ground still wet from the days of rain. Jacob and his men waited in anticipation as the fuses ran down, then the ground erupted in explosions. The rounds had fallen short.

"Their gunners will be adjusting their aims," Samuel yelled out, "watch for the rounds."

Along with the muffled booms, there were louder booms, and smoke could be seen from the redoubts facing them.

"Ah damn, heavy artillery!" Samuel yelled, and the men again began scanning the sky for the rounds. Most of the artillery and mortars shot aimed at the French, though they were not spared from the British's attention.

"Here they come!" one of the men yelled, and Jacob, too, could see some falling shot. Looking out across the field, Jacob could also see the cannon balls from the heavy guns finishing their arches, crashing into the ground, then skipping along on their flat trajectory, kicking up clumps of dirt in green and brown clouds.

The black cannonball bounced a few times, the arch from the bounce getting smaller and smaller as the energy was expanded. Finally, the ball, an eighteen-pounder, rolled and stopped in front of Jacob. As they watched the British line, none of the British came out, though they did continue to fire their mortars and guns at them. No one was hurt, and their replacements came out and relieved them.

Dunbar reformed his company and marched them back to their camp as Captain Smith deployed his light infantry company from the Third Regiment. Marching in two files, Jacob followed the company back, and they returned to their camp, then stoked up their fires to cook their meals for the night.

The constant rain was affecting the condition of the army. While Jacob appreciates the regimental wool coat to help keep the rain off, most of the time, when they were on work details, the men wore shirts or frocks made from linen. Moreover, being out in the constant rain physically affected the men; some came down with the cough and other ailments. If any of the men appeared sick, they went to the surgeon immediately, knowing how fast sickness and disease could spread through the camp.

Jacob, Jean, and Samuel checked the men's feet; their wet and sodden stockings led to bleeding feet as the skin shriveled from the constant wetness. Jacob also checked the men's lean-tos so they could at least rest dry and store their equipment. The dampness was getting into the cartridges; some that Jacob checked were solid as the powder became wet and dried into a useless hardened tube. The wetness was also causing the muskets to become rusty, so Jacob had the men check and clean their muskets; they had to work. At least it gave them something to do.

In the following days, while Jacob once more protected the colonials and the French working on the siege lines, the British ventured out in the early morning of the 24th when three light infantry companies attacked two hundred French light infantry. Jacob, with Captain Warren's Company, was ready, though the British advanced on the French and not them.

Watching the ensuing skirmish, Jacob reminded the men to stay vigilant, as the British could be using it as a diversion to attack them. The fighting on their right was growing; the "whomp" as volleys fired between the British and the French skirmish lines. The sound of battle rose, the grey smoke settling on the field.

During the fight, the French grenadiers counterattacked, driving the British companies back into their lines. Caught up in the charge, Jacob observed the grenadiers chase the British as they ran to their lines, then up and over their defenses. Instead of holding, the grenadiers kept going.

"No, no, you stupid, arrogant bastards!" Jacob shouted as he watched the grenadiers, bayonets lowered, charge after the fleeing British. Then, as the French closed on the enemy defenses, the cannons in the redoubts opened fire on the grenadiers, their bodies crumpling to the ground.

Looking behind, Jacob could see men were massing, preparing to charge out to their rescue; even Captain Warren had drawn his sword, being caught up in the moment. Raising his hands, Jacob bellowed, "Hold your ground!"

Looking out at the fight, then sheepishly back at Jacob, Captain Warren and the rest of the men relaxed.

"I know you mean well," Jacob commented. "All you would do would end up like them, shot to pieces. Your hearts are in the right place, but it wouldn't matter."

Jacob would later learn from Marion that not only was it a careless and senseless attack but during the fight, the French's only chief engineer and artillerist who was planning and conducting the siege was killed.

"Well, that's bloody wonderful," Jacob commented, "and typical. Why would their engineer attack other than seeking glory? He only found death. So who is going to plan this siege?"

Marion shook his head, "I don't know, but I think they will just keep building, relying on their commanders."

This would become very evident in the following days when the French commander, Admiral D'Estaing, was not pleased with the progress and felt that the gun positions the French had built were wrong and had to be rebuilt closer to the British line. He ordered that the larger siege guns be brought forward, while the only gun position that Jacob and his men had helped build covered the French work crews, which must have infuriated the French.

The French repositioned their guns to new positions and fired a few rounds at the city. The British returned fires with some mortars and heavy shot but did no real damage. The siege returned to a quiet but busy event as colonials, and the French continued work on the siege lines. Jacob was on guard shift two nights after the French engagement with the British, looking out across the field towards the city. The visions of the grenadiers falling transported him back to the mountains and cold lakes of upper New York.

He recalled back to one of his first actual actions against the French. The same white uniformed French, and their Grenadiers in their tall black bearskin hats, charged across the field at Lake du Sacrament, later known as Lake George, against their hasty fortifications. Although at the same time, they had two artillery pieces, these charging men were shredded by grapeshot.

The vision of the white uniforms falling like shattered dolls was haunting his memories. Jacob recalled many similarities between this new engagement with their French allies and the last war where they were his enemies. Yet, he was still wrestling with how to accept these new allies, where the hatred he had felt towards them during the last war was rising to the surface.

The sights, sounds, and smells kept drawing him back into the past, the bloody fighting, old adversaries, and the losses. It drew out the faces of long-lost friends, of Konkapot, who he grew up with, buried under some tall pine trees near Fort Edward, along with his other ranger comrades fighting for the crown. Buried alongside them, his first love Maggie was killed by the sadistic Sergeant-Major Lovewell. While he did love his wife and family, Maggie's face was there from time to time, and Jacob believed she would have approved of him moving on.

Jacob was pulled back into reality quickly as the sound of fighting could be heard from the right. It seemed the British returned for another fight, and the Fench responded.

"Sound the long roll," ordered Colonel John White, the officer of the day. "Form companies!" Jacob, followed by Samuel and Jean, joined Dunbar's men, who quickly reacted to the drum sound and formed into their two ranks.

"Captain Duncan, lead us out towards the fighting!" White ordered, and Duncan drew his sword.

"Double files right, follow me!" Duncan yelled, swinging his sword forward, and his company followed. Jacob, with Samuel and Jean, trotted just behind the company as White's regiment followed suit.

It was dark as they marched towards the sound of musketry that flashed and flickered from the fight. Colonel White ordered Duncan to head at an angle to try and catch the British from the flank as they were concentrating on the French. Jacob looked to their front, and the French's white uniforms made it easy to see them as white blobs in the dark when they fired. Nevertheless, the sight and sound of battle were close enough that Colonel White ordered the column to halt. Then he gave the command to "display to the left with the right in front, left face. March!"

Duncan and the light infantry stayed on the right side as White's regiment began to form a line to the left. White's first platoon stood their ground while the rest of the column faced to the left, then marched forward, and the platoons stopped once they were cleared of the platoon next to them. They then reformed on the left side of the platoon and dressed their ranks.

This continued until all the men were in a long, two-rank line. Then, like Jacob, Colonel White looked into the dark at the fight before them to ensure they were not firing on their own.

"By platoons, fire by platoons!" Colonel White ordered, in which Dunbar gave the order for his first platoon to make ready, then aim. They could barely see what they think are red uniforms when Dunbar commanded fire. As a unit, the muskets cracked and boomed, then automatically started to load.

Jacob and Jean, and Samuel held their fire, watching and waiting.

"Can you see anything?" Samuel asked, "Do we know who we're shooting at?"

After a couple of volleys, Colonel White ordered the line forward. With their loaded muskets shouldered, the line advanced. A layer of musket smoke hung about eight feet off the ground, making a foggy grey sea of mist. Jacob scanned the area to their front, trying to see anything remotely like a uniform, afraid they may have fired on their allies.

As they advanced, the air in front of them exploded in flames as a line fired a volley. From their left, Jacob could hear the bullets smack with a wet sound, the men falling and screaming. Halting, Colonel White gave the order for a company volley. Following the orders, the first company presented took aim and fired, their forty muskets belching flame and thick grey smoke adding to the fog. As the first company loaded, the next company went through the firing process.

Jacob strained his eyes, trying to see who they were firing at, other than the dark shapes before them. The two lines fired back and forth; men were wounded and pulled out of line. Jacob was scanning through the smoke when they saw the silhouettes of the opposing line approach during one of the larger flashes from a volley.

Looking intently, he could see the uniforms as they fired were white! "Jean, tell them to cease fire!" Jacob yelled as he took up the call to cease fire. "*Cessez-le-feu! Cessez-le-feu!*" Jean yelled. It still took some time to get the firing to stop, too late for another six men who fell from a close volley. Jacob was angry as the French officers approached their line, gesturing and yelling at Colonel White, who screamed back just as loud.

"They're blaming one another, calling us bafoons and amateurs," translated Jean, who shook his head. Jacob fumed as he listened to the senior officers yell back and one another through translators. Jacob wandered over the area between them and followed the terrain. The British had been there but had withdrawn for some reason, perhaps trying to lure the French out again like before. Instead, they shot at each other, killing or wounding about fifty men between the French and their companies.

"Well, I'll be damned," grumbled Samuel, and Jacob asked why he would say that.

Samuel swept his arms before him, then pointed towards the British lines. "They played us against one another; we did the dirty work for them, shooting one another on their behalf. You have to admire their cunning."

Dunbar's company faired better than the other units, only six total wounded and none killed. It was angry looks that the men shot back at the French as they carried their dead back to the encampment. The officers were still arguing with one another, Jacob wondered why the British didn't attack then and there, but luckily they didn't.

Shaking his head over the lunacy of the situation, Jacob went back to their camp. He flopped on the ground near his lean-to. Jean and Samuel joined him, Samuel sitting with a long grunt.

"Well, that was a fouled-up action," Samuel commented, "it could have been a lot worse."

Having lit his pipe, Jacob nodded his head. "Aye, you're right. This bloody fog of war and not knowing. This is why armies don't fight at night."

Jacob learned a few days later that the French could get revenge on the British, having discovered they had captured a British man-o-war that had their pay, and the French flaunted their victory to the British defenders. Samuel gave a speculative look, "Hmm, piracy is still an option for afterward."

Jacob kept them busy with drill and work details, concerned that the men would become bored and look for trouble. His main concern was that the lack of activity would impact the men's morale, and with the coming battles, he knew their men must be in high spirits.

By September, the gun positions were completed, protected by a line of trenches and pickets. However, it still wasn't easy; the French once again fired in the darkness at movement, which turned out to be their workers. To add insult to injury, the Brtish could land accurate artillery and mortar fire on the French workers whose own men had just shot.

While not on duty, Jacob and his men watched as the big guns commenced firing on the city. Echoing "oohs and ahhs" from his men, even Jacob joined in. It helped to take the edge of the dull routine, and he knew his men needed to get it out of their systems.

"Sure is a fine show they are putting on for us," Samuel commented from around his pipe stem as he leaned back against a tree, "I hope they didn't go all out for just us."

Laughter could be heard from the other men watching the fireworks, and Jacob nodded. So far, it seems their morale was holding. However, he was still concerned if they decided to assault across that sizeable open field, and the British lines had not been softened enough so they wouldn't be slaughtered.

It took a few more days for the French to complete their preparations; then, on the night of October Fourth, fifty-three heavy guns and fourteen mortars began firing on the city, determined to blast it to rubble. The American and French warships who fired from the sea supported the barrage. Jacob and his men helped the guns by lugging the shot and powder to the crew; most of Jacob's men recalled their training on artillery. They took turns relieving some gunners to rest from the exhaustive work.

The first gun to fire was an American gun, waiting for the sound of reveille being played on the British side. When the music drifted across the field, Captain Gibbes fired the first shot of the bombardment and watched triumphantly as his shot hit the flagpole and knocked down the British colors. The crews erupted in cheers, taking it as a good omen.

Unfortunately, the tremendous barrage only lasted four hours due to the poor construction of the siege lines and not having a proper siege engineer anymore. The batteries on the left side of the siege lines collapsed due to poor construction. Even the galleys supporting the barrage from the river, having seen the barrage end, ceased fire.

The only gun they had could effectively reach the city was the large eighteen-pounder. Giving the crew from the Fourth a break, Jacob and some of his cross-trained men went through the slow, steady pace of loading and firing the gun. It still took a coordinated team to service the gun almost as big as the massive thirty-two pounders from the fort.

When Jacob gave the load command, it took two men to pass the powder bag, and the man using the rammer had to put effort into the twelve-foot-long rammer. It also took two to three men to load the sizeable eighteen-pound cannonball safely. Aiming was still challenging, looking over the barrel to get the ball to arch and land at a great distance.

Once loaded, Jacob had to try and calculate the angle of the gun, so he elevated the gun, but Jacob was just guessing. He wasn't sure he was hitting anything; just hoping he was either lobbing the ball over the walls into the city or bouncing it into the defenses.

After making sure the men were clear, Jacob gave one final look over the barrel before giving the command to fire. With a roar, crack, and boom, a long snout of flame and smoke shot out, the gun rolling back ten feet on a well-worn wheel groove, then gravity returning to its firing position.

The wet weather returned, rain falling on the bombardiers and defenders alike. The artillery was starting to take effect, as fires could be seen burning from the city. Orders were passed to continue firing and, in some cases, increase the tempo so the defenders could not put out the fire and the city would burn.

On the night of October 6th, the French tried to bombard the city into submission and even fired projectiles that were designed to set the buildings on fire. Jacob and the others watched as these sparkling shots arched up and over to land within the city. But minor damage could be seen due to the wet conditions from the constant rain, even with over a thousand shots fired. No fires illuminated the sky. The rain returned harder, making the situation wet, muddy, and miserable.

Jacob, Jean, and Samuel checked their lean-tos, then went about and studied the regiment's lean-tos. He showed them how to use branches to weave a better roof and sides. He also ensured the men kept their gear covered, especially their cartridge boxes and muskets.

Samuel sat under his lean-to, sad face, and even Jean looked miserable, wrapped in his rain cloth. The rain was dripping steadily from their roofs in small streams. As men walked through the camps, the company streets were flooding and becoming seas of mud. A few men lost their shoes in the muck, while some walked barefoot.

"Recall back on the island when the river rose from the melt and ran through the cabin?" Samuel asked, and Jacob nodded, recalling that winter thaw up in New York. "Seems we're heading in that direction, though no river."

As the rain continued to fall, Jacob had his men dig small trenches to move the water instead of pooling into large puddles. The available straw was placed around where the officers met while the men dug drainage ditches along the company streets, but sometimes to little avail.

Using a tarp from some of the wagons after they had dropped off supplies and returned, Jacob, Jean, and Samuel built a rain fly held up by twine and supported by a stripped limb that made a pointed top. Using logs and old crates to sit on, they had a semi-dry area to sit, eat their rations, and socialize.

It seemed that Mother Nature was trying to clean the stain of the siege away, but the guns continued to fire. Still, Jacob watched the men and was amazed at their resilience. This was reinforced when Jacob watched as men carved wooden boats, then had boat races on the growing streams winding through the camps.

The racers would take their boats to the top of a hill; then, the boats were dropped on command. Then, they rushed along with the stream to a finish point, the men cheering for boats they had wagered on. It was catching on, and soon other companies were building their own, and more competitions were created.

While Jacob knew that gambling was frowned upon by the higher staff officers, he also knew the men had to let off steam before the inactivity or dullness of siege work, combined with the rain, would cause tempers to flare and disciplinary problems would arise.

***

However, little to Jacob's knowledge, inactivity would not last long. Jean Baptiste Charles Henri Hector, Comte d'Estaing, and General Lincoln held a council of war to discuss their next course of action. The city had not capitulated, and D'Estaing wanted that city. He had lost his chance for fame and glory when tasked to take Rhode Island, but a storm defeated him, not the British.

D'Estaing needed to redeem himself for his honor and reputation to his King. The officers gathered inside the large and spacious command marquee tent of D'Estaing. All the French officers in their fine uniforms were to one side. While speaking to one another, they would look over their shoulders at the Americans, who were all gathered on the other side.

"Captain L'Enfant, what is your assessment of the British abatis and defenses? Had the artillery done its job?" Again, D'Estaing asked in French; the Americans had to rely on translators. Finally, Captain L'Enfant, an engineer, faced his commander and reported matter of factly, "It would take ten days to clear the abatis and take the defenses. This damned rain has made everything wet; nothing will burn."

D'Estaing did not like the answer. "No! This will not do! We will take this city, and we will take it now!" D'Esaing slammed his fist onto the table that held his maps, knocking over several empty wine glasses.

D'Estaing looked around the tent at his French and American commanders, "Are we not ready to take this city? Surely they just needed to be pushed over slightly; our artillery and this damned rain must have destroyed their will to fight!"

His commanders looked at one another, then Count d'Autichamp, the commander of D'Estaing's division, boldly stated, "We will lead the charge and take this city for you, my commander!" This was followed by the other French commanders shouting their men were ready. The only commanders not so keen on the attack were General Lincoln and the American commanders.

D'Estaing, smiling from his men's warm reception of his idea to attack, was shocked when he turned to the Americans that they were not caught up in the same fever, and his smile turned into a frown.

"What is this?" asked D'Estaing through his translator, "Do you Americans lack the courage for such a simple assault? What of your glorious revolution and desire for your freedom? Do you expect us French to do the dirty work for you?"

When General Lincoln heard what D'Estaing had asked through the translator, it took all his self-discipline to remain calm and collective while the other commanders looked at the French in distaste.

"Are you questioning our courage, our determination?" asked Lincoln. After it was translated, D'Estaing laughed and said they had misunderstood his joke; perhaps it had been lost in translation.

"Do you have concerns, General Lincoln? If so, I would like to hear them," replied D'Estaing. As General Lincoln explained his concerns, he could help but overhear the soft talking behind hands and laughter from the French commanders who looked at them in sidelong glances with disdain.

"My concerns Sir," explained General Lincoln, "is this is not a wise and prudent attack, that we would lose many men in the process. Moreover, I am concerned for the cost to my men."

D'Estaing shook his head, making a "tsk…tsk" sound before responding. "As you Americans are new at this, do not worry. We, the French, have been doing this style of fighting and have defeated the British many times. We will defeat them here and now, just like before!"

Once again, the French officers cheered and clinked wine glasses as they toasted their imminent victory. General Lincoln shook his head slowly, still not liking it.

"Sir, I would advise against it, but if you order the attack, we'll show you how well we can fight."

D'Estaing looked at General Lincoln, "It is so ordered; we attack tomorrow!" D'Estaing poured and offered a glass to General Lincoln, who refused, stating, "I must see to my men and issue orders." As General Lincoln and his staff left, D'Estaing drank the glass he had poured for Lincoln, muttering "Amateurs!" before joining his officers in a round of toasts to victory.

As General Lincoln and his staff made their way back to their camp, he could hear the mutterings from his officers, who also believed it was foolish to attack now. Still, the commander had issued orders, and he would follow them. "Make sure all men receive forty new rounds of ammunition, and this rain may have ruined most of their ammunition they have on hand and issue spare flints." Looking off in the distance at the glow from the city, fires burning inside as the heavy guns continued to fire. "The men are going to need everyone round they can get."

CHAPTER 9

THE SPRING HILL REDOUBT

Word trickled down to Jacob and the men of the 2nd Regiment of With D'Estaing's orders to attack. Marion sought out and found Jacob speaking with Samuel and Jean, "We have a council of war," Marion stated, "I believe it would be a good idea for you to come, as you are my military advisor."

Jacob turned to follow Marion, nodding his head, with Samuel shouted, "Best of luck, don't volunteer us for anything, and don't get us killed!" Jacob shrugged, "I can't promise anything, but I will try."

"That may be the tip of the day," Marion stated as they walked towards the siege lines where Lincoln was holding his council of war. "From what the general explained from the meeting with the French, he felt their plan is foolhardy, and they covered it by questioning our bravery."

Jacob shook his head. "Sounds about right; when you have a bad plan, challenge your allies' bravery, and they usually will do something rash to prove you wrong. Many men die that way, proving a point. I've seen it happen."

Marion nodded his head in understanding. "That's why I am having you come; bring that experience and common sense you have, and maybe Lincoln will listen to you."

Jacob snorted and shook his head. "I highly doubt it though he does owe me his life. It means nothing now."

Marion and Jacob arrived at the council, where Lincoln had set up a field table, and the various commanders from the army were there. General McIntosh commanded the first brigade; General Huger commanded the second brigade, the one where Marion and the 2nd Regiment fell under. Colonel White of the Georgia Brigade, Colonel Campbell of the North Carolina Continentals, Colonel Parker of the Virginia Continentals, and General Williamson of the South Carolina Militia.

Also present was Colonel Beeckman of the combined artillery, General Pulaski representing his Legion, and Lieutenant du Rumain of the South Carolina Navy. A few other regimental commanders were there; Colonel Thomas Sumter came over and shook Jacob's hand.

"It's been a while, my friend," Sumter whispered as he shook Jacob's hand "it's good to see you again!" Jacob smiled and nodded his head to Sumter.

General Lincoln looked up from his map that was laid out on his field table and then turned to face the assembled officers.

"Gentlemen, to the matter at hand. General D'Estaing has directed we will attack now, feeling between our artillery and the weather, the enemy has been softened up enough for the attack."

Lincoln paused as the assembled officers grumbled about the decision, which they all, for the most part, felt the situation did not support an attack. Lincoln waited for the murmur to settle before continuing.

"I support your views; I argued that this is a mistake;" Lincoln paused and frowned, then continued." "Our illustrious French allies challenged our bravery and honor, stating we don't know how to fight. Well, gentlemen, let's prove them wrong!"

Jacob looked over at Marion and slightly nodded his head, proving his point. Marion nodded in agreement and waited to see what the plan would be.

Looking across the field at the British defenses, Lincoln pointed across the open area at the British redoubts and fortifications line.

"We must find a weak point in their defenses, concentrate our artillery, then strike hard with the assault. Captain Lenfant, what are your thoughts on the matter."

Captain Lenfant, an engineer, joined Lincoln as he looked across the field.

"For the most part, the defenses are solid, except for the smaller redoubts on our left, which was designed to cover the British right. However, we have observed that the supporting wall had not been fully finished and did see some sign that the barrage had some effect on it."

General Lincoln nodded and motioned for the brigade commanders to join them, looking out across the field. "Of the weakest points, Captain Lenfant, where should we concentrate?"

Lenfant looked out across the field as he recalled their observations from the past few days. He then pointed to a small hill on their left.

"There, we learned its name is Spring Hill; we believe it is the weakest point and should be the focus of the attack."

The officers looked across the field at the small hill; Jacob looked and shook his head while walking off to the side, with Marion following.

"What are your thoughts?" Marion asked.

"It may be the weakest point, but we still have to get there. The attack will be under constant artillery fire as we cross the field. Even with all of our siege artillery, the closer we get to their lines, we will lose our artillery support and be under theirs."

Jacob frowned and shook his head. "It will be Carillon all over again unless they try to do something crazy like a night assault. Granted, if done right, could conceal us from their artillery, but controlling it would be a nightmare! It could still be a slaughter;

I have a bad feeling about this one being true and honest. A terrible feeling."

"Sir, the French are arriving!" an orderly yelled as D'Estaing, and his staff arrived. Lincoln and the brigade commanders stayed at the front, where the junior officers, including Marion and Jacob, stood off to the side. Lincoln properly saluted and gave a curt bow to the overall commander.

Joining Lincoln and pulling out his telescope, he looked across the field at the British lines. The translator joined them; Jacob wished he had brought Jean with him. Lincoln pointed out what he had discussed with the assembled officers, their objective being Spring Hill.

"Once we cracked the enemy defenses there, it would be a simple matter to exploit the breach and pour into the city," Lincoln explained; D'Estaing nodded, then, using his walking stick, drew out his attack plan on the ground. First, he drew their British lines, then five columns.

"I will combine all of my grenadiers into one column, and I will personally lead the attack to break open the defenses at this Spring Hill. Colonel de Steding and Colonel de Noailles, you will attack these British redoubts on our right to support my attack on the hill."

D'Estaing drew from the arrows of the column pointing to where they would attack. He then turned and, through the translator, spoke to General Lincoln.

"General Lincoln, your two columns will support our attack, and once we break through, join in exploiting the breach." Then, using his walking stick, he drew the arrows from the columns representing the Americans.

General Lincoln looked to his commanders, "Lieutenant Colonel Laurens and General McIntosh, you will command the two supporting columns. I will lead the reserve."

D'Estaing waited for Lincoln to assign the roles before moving on. "General, you will also dispatch men to draw the enemy's attention by conducting a feint against the city's eastern side."

Lincoln nodded, then turned and instructed, "General Huger, you will lead the feint." Satisfied, D'Estaing continued, "If successful, your men are to drive to the river, then join us in the city."

D'Estaing paused as he thought for a moment, tapping the ground with his walking stick as he visualized his plan drawn out in the dirt.

"Seeing we have had some problems in the past for night operations, I want every man to wear large white cockades in their hats," D'Estaing stated as he looked at both his staff and Lincoln's staff. He paused once again, rubbing his chin in thought as he looked at the sketch in the dirt.

D'Estaing turned towards the American officers, "General Lincoln, your men will wear your shirts over your regimental coats so we may identify them. We must take extra care to ensure we do not hamper ourselves so we may focus all our efforts on breaking the enemy. And gentlemen, they will break!"

After all the translators were finished, D'Estaing gave his last instructions.

"We'll attack with surprise at night. Both camps are to have men unable to make the attack to keep fires burning. There will be no artillery in preparation for the attack. Once we breach, the gunners who will follow the columns will take command of the captured artillery, then turn them on the enemy."

D'Estaing turned and looked at his cavalry commanders. "The cavalry detachments will support by following the columns in, then charge through the breach."

D'Estaing paused and looked at the assembled officers with a stern look. "This must be by surprise; I cannot express how important this is. No one, and I mean no one, is to fire until the command is given. Anyone found firing before orders will be put to death for failing to follow orders, understand?" It seemed D'Estaing was looking more at the Americans, and Jacob could see the rift continued to grow.

General Lincoln turned to the staff and the assembled officers.

"Lieutenant Colonel Laurens, along with your light infantry, will command the Second South Carolina and the Charles Town Militia. General McIntosh, you will have the First and Fifth Regiments. General Huger, you will have the First and Second Brigades of the South Carolina and Georgia Militia. I will bring up the reserves and plug holes where they are needed. General Pulaski, your legion will follow Lieutenant Colonel Laurens. See to your men, and be ready to form in a few hours."

As the Council of War broke up, the commanders headed back to the camp to prepare their men for the assault. Marion looked at Jacob in awe as they walked. Jacob looked down at Marion with a puzzled look.

"What's on your mind?" Jacob asked.

"How did you know?" Marion asked, "It's like you knew the worst case was going to be presented. A night assault with unloaded muskets, under pain of death no less! How did you know? Is this that gut thing that Sergeant Penny keeps going on about?"

Jacob chuckled and then shrugged his shoulders. "It's something from probably too many years of being shot at, I guess. I have learned to trust my instincts and my gut feelings. It has saved us more than once."

Marion stopped and looked at Jacob in seriousness. "So, your gut is saying this will end badly for us, isn't it?"

Jacob paused, looked back at the officers still at the meeting, Lincoln and his staff, and the arrogance of the French officers who were having difficulty not looking down their noses at the Americans. Jacob saw two main issues; no unity of command and a broken chain of command. D'Estaing was leading from the front in the main assault. Lincoln was leading from the rear in reserve.

Jacob recalled one of his earliest battles when he was a Ranger, the Battle at Lake Sacrament, when Sir William Johnson had formed a defensive line, and the French attacked. Leading the attack were grenadiers. Boldly charged down the road and right into the muzzles of their cannons, being shredded. Jacob shook his head; it seems history will once again repeat itself.

"We also need to worry that we're under Laurens again, seeing how well he did at the Coosawhatchie. While we need a bold and brash commander for this one, perhaps, it will do us no good if he is killed."

Jacob looked directly at Marion. "If that happens, you must be ready to assume command of the brigade."

Marion nodded, "As long as you are prepared to take command of the regiment if needed."

Jacob shook his head, "Not my place. Isn't that the responsibility of Major Dillent; he is your adjutant?"

Marion shrugged, "Jacob, it is time for you to use your talents for what they are meant for. You are a natural leader, and it's time to take command and lead men. It is your destiny."

Jacob shook his head, "We'll see, sir, but let's get through this fight and hope for the best."

***

The entire army was preparing for the assault, but Sergeant Major James Curry had enough. He had enough of rain, enough of marching; he had enough of it all! Curry had thought being a member of the Charles Town Grenadiers would give him prestige and that they would just stay in the city, be an honor guard at festivals and get free drinks.

Now they wanted him to be part of this foolish attack led by the French. He looked around as the men of the militia were getting their equipment ready or eating some tough biscuits. He shook his head as he watched the regular army wear their waistcoats outside their coats, having been ordered to do so.

"No, James, my boy, I think it's time we look for better things to do," he thought. While everyone was busy getting ready, no one noticed him slip away, and with the lengthening shadows of night, James made his way to the British. He left his musket and gear behind, only took his possessions with him. Finally, the sun had set, and he followed the low ground to stay concealed from any sentries on the siege line.

"At least it stopped raining, and they're no longer shooting those damn cannons. Loud enough to drive one crazy," James thought as he carefully moved through the high grass, trying to avoid any deep mud. Once he was sure he was far enough away, he moved to the raised causeway and made his way to Spring Hill.

He could see the sentries on the redoubt and slowly approach with his hands raised.

"Hello in the redoubt!" he called out, getting the sentries' attention. "I have had enough, and I want to give up!"

The sentries, which turned out to be South Carolina Loyalists, escorted Curry into the redoubt. Curry saw that it was smaller than he thought; inside the small rectangular redoubt were fifty South Carolina Loyalists, under Lieutenant Colonel Thomas Brown's command, whom the sentries turned him over to.

Inside, Curry saw twenty-eight dismounted troopers from the Captain Tawse's Georgian Dragoons, along with other twenty-eight men from the Royal American Regiment. Rounding out the support were naval volunteers operating the six cannons set along with the two triangular sides of the redoubt.

"Who do we have here?" Brown asked; Curry stood straight and responded with "Sergeant Major James Curry, formerly of the Charles Town Grenadiers."

Brown nodded, "I take it you have seen the errors of your ways and have come to ask for mercy from his Majesty's forces?" Brown looked at Curry up and down, taking in his uniform and personal bags. "Why should we not hang you for being a traitor?"

Curry was taken aback by the threat of hanging and had to think quickly. "Because I have information that you need. If you hang me, you can't get the information."

Brown looked at Curry, dead in his eyes. "What information?"

"About the attack that is getting ready to happen in a few hours."

Brown paused and thought about it, then nodded his head. "Alright, sergeant major, we will see how beneficial your information is. If it's good, then we'll not see you swing."

With that, Brown motioned for a couple of his men, and they escorted Curry into the city and General Prevost's office. Once they arrived, he was brought into a parlor where he sat in an oversized, comfortable chair next to a fire, and he sighed in comfort. Then, Brown departed but left the two guards to watch Curry, who had no intent to leave the comfort he was feeling.

Soon, black servants arrived carrying a small table that was placed before him, and another servant brought warm food and set it before Curry. Breathing in the pleasing aroma of the food, Curry shrugged his shoulders, took up his silverware, and began eating the meal. Finally, a third servant placed a glass before him and poured wine.

"Sir, please let us know if you need anything?" the servant asked, and Curry said while chewing on a mouthful of roast deer,

"Some bread would be nice." Curry watched the servant depart, and he chewed and enjoyed the meal. Then, in his first authentic meal in weeks, he nodded in agreement, "*James, me boy, you made the right choice*," he thought, then took another bite.

James liked all of the attention he was getting, sitting in a large home, warm and dry and with a glass of fine wine no less. So this was what life was supposed to be. The servants, leaving him the glass of wine, had cleared the table. General Prevost and Lieutenant Colonel Brown entered the room, and Curry stood up as the general approached him.

"So, my friend, what can you give us?" asked General Prevost, Brown watching intently to determine Curry's fate. Curry gave up everything. The entire assault plan. He explained that the focus of the attack was Spring Hill. The location of the feint and even the plan to wear their waistcoats outside of their regimental coats to prevent them from shooting at one another all were given to the British.

Prevost smiled and nodded his head. He looked at Brown, who shrugged and nodded in the affirmative.

"Right, thank you for your service to the King. You will be shown to a private room and your needs. All I ask is try not to run off; we'll be forced to shoot you then."

Curry nodded. He understood; Prevost turned and, with Brown, headed to another room where he had assembled his commanders in case the information they received would benefit them. He entered the room and greeted everyone with a large smile.

"Gentlemen, we have them!" General Prevost clapped and rubbed his hands together. "Lieutenant Colonel Maitland, you will personally take command of the Carolina Redoubt and reinforce them with your Highlanders. Then, we will shift our strength to support the three redoubts on the right and have your Loyalists place these large white cockades and white shirts outside their coats. But, then, it will all be too late when they realize they had been had!"

***

"Skreetch…skreetch…skreetch," Jacob passed the sharpening stone along the edge of his tomahawk. Jacob also tested the edge of his fighting knife, which was razor sharp. While Jacob carried his sword, he preferred to fight with a tomahawk and knife.

Finished, he placed the tomahawk into a sword hanger, generally for a sergeant major's sword and bayonet. But, instead of a bayonet, he carried the tomahawk in its place. The knife stayed in its sheath in the small of Jacob's back. The sun was falling, and Jacob sat on a log chewing on a biscuit, knowing he would need as much energy as possible.

He watched his men and their mixed emotions. Some were excited, joking, and talking with their comrades. Some of his men were quiet, sitting with their thoughts or saying silent prayers. A few did look scared, and Jacob could not blame them. Not many of his men were veterans of the fighting in 1776. Many of those veterans left or were sent to replace other men in the regiment. Samuel was making his way amongst the men, laughing and joking with them, keeping their morale up and not dwelling on the looming attack. Everything was ready, and muskets cleaned, cartridges dry and packed, bayonets gleaming.

Jean sat next to Jacob, completing his rounds of checking on the officers. Finally, he pulled out his pipe, filled it with tobacco, took a burning branch from their small fire, and lit it.

"How do they look?" Jacob asked, and Jean shook his head.

"In a word, scared. They try hiding their fear from their men, but it's still there."

Jacob nodded his head as he chewed on his biscuit. "Do you blame them?" he asked, and Jean shook his head.

"To be honest, I am slightly afraid of this coming attack."

Jacob looked at Jean in shock. "You, the great hunter of Rangers and the one who nearly bagged Rogers, scared?"

Jean nodded and smiled, "Oui, my old friend, I am the smarter one and see the danger that looms. It would be foolish not to be afraid."

Jacob snorted but nodded his head in agreement. "What does that make me?" he asked.

"The crazy one who laughs at danger and leads the way!" Samuel answered as he flopped down next to Jacob and Jean. "You are too brave for your own good; we'll stay near you."

Jean and Jacob joined Samuel, chuckling about his comment before he paused and looked thoughtfully into the fire.

"The men are ready, just like we've seen in the past. Some don't know what they are getting into; some do, and others are too scared to think about it. But, they have each other, and I think that will hold them tight when this bloody business begins."

As the reddish glow of the sunset started to fade, Colonel Laurens began assembling the men of his brigade quietly without using drums. As the companies formed, Laurens came to Jacob, Samuel, and Jean.

"Captain Clarke, you have scouted out this place, correct?"

Jacob nodded. He had, "Along with the Sergeant Major, Lieutenant Langy, and a few of my men, why?"

Laurens looked over at the guide who was speaking with General Lincoln. "I don't trust our guide, to be honest," Laurens explained, then moved closer in a voice so he would not be overheard.

"He is a Frenchman, said he worked on the defenses here, but it had been a while ago, and to be perfectly honest, I don't trust him. So I may need to call on your experience to lead us if this man fails."

Jacob looked over and saw the guide speaking with General Lincoln. His hands pointed toward the swamp, off to the causeway, and the defenses left.

"We'll stay to the front of the regiment if you need us," Jacob replied, and in the dark, could see Laurens nod before walking off to check on the rest of the brigade.

"At least he isn't on a horse this time," Samuel commented, "won't be such an easy target like last time."

It was about midnight when General Lincoln nodded, and the messengers ran to the columns and gave them the orders to move. Without much sound, Laurens had the column move. The men carried their muskets at the trail, carried easily along their side instead of their shoulders. As per D'Estaing's orders, none of the muskets were loaded. Jacob did not like the helpless feeling of having unloaded muskets.

The column wove its way through the dark, following the guide. Jacob looked around, re-orientated himself, and knew exactly where they were. It was confirmed when they started to descend; they were heading into the flat, open swamp below the ridge. While the men tried to be silent, it could be heard when they first sank into the mid.

The only sound in the night air were birds, insects, and the "thuck…thuck…thuck" as the men carefully and slowly pulled their feet out of the clinging muck and mud and placed their next step. The column moved slowly. Some of it out of necessity for silence, and the other was because the men were moving slowly because of the swamp.

Some men had to stop and quickly pull their shoes from the mud, having been stripped from their feet, and place them back on. It got so bad that some men took them off and carried them until they got to dry ground. The slow movement was consuming time, and Laurens was concerned they wouldn't be in position. The French columns had left, but they didn't have to traverse swampland.

Halfway across the large swamp, the guide stopped and started looking around, which forced Laurens to halt the column. With Jean in tow, Jacob didn't like it and

"What's the damned problem?" Laurens hissed, and the guide stood there, looking in different directions, scratching his head.

"Everything looks different from when I was here last." The guide commented, then Laurens asked, "when was the last time you were here?"

The guide shrugged and replied, "Back in '78 when the British first took the city. I think we're lost." It took all of Lauren's self-control from not blowing up looking at the sheepish guide. "Get Captain Clarke up here!"

Jacob made his way to the front of the column and joined Laurens and the guide. Even in the dark, Laurens had a smoldering look about him, both fists on his hips, staring at the guide whose head was hung low.

"Captain Clarke, our faithful guide here, is lost as a newborn babe. Would you please take the lead and get us back into the attack."

Looking around to confirm his bearings and recall from the scout, Jacob began leading the column by veering to the right, and the guide had led them too far to the left. They would have run into the river, not their position on that course. As they followed Jacob, he could hear the guide mumbling, "I think I know, oh wait, maybe it was over there...."

It was still slow movement and continued to eat up time, but Jacob could see the dark shape of the rise in the distance and knew they were on track. On the other hand, Laurens was becoming more agitated and stopped the column as it arrived at one of the creeks.

"I don't think your man knows where he is going," the guide commented, and Laurens called for Jacob.

"Captain Clarke, do you know where you are at?" Jacob walked up to Colonel Laurens and quietly replied, "Yes."

"How are you so sure?" Laurens returned, and Jacob moved a little way to the creek before stooping down.

After a moment, Colonel Laurens, the guide, and the lead men of the column watched Jacob lift from the creek the bloated and rotting corpse in a uniform that fell apart and dropped back into the water.

Washing off his hands before approaching Laurens, Jacob explained, "I am sure I know where I am because that's the man I killed during the scout and hid the body so his comrades couldn't find it. Our spot is right over there to the left, and it's dry solid ground. Luckily, the darkness hid Lauren's shocked face and reminded him to probably not question Jacob's ability again.

Jacob led the column out of the swamp and onto dry ground, just below the rise where it halted. Jacob led Laurens, and the other offers to the top of the ridge while the men either replaced their shoes or dumped water and muck from their shoes, then replaced them.

At the top of the slope, Jacob motioning them to get low and crawl up pointed out their objective, which was in front of them, though at a slight angle.

"There you are, sir, our objective." Jacob indicated as he pointed to the redoubt on the small hill, five hundred yards away and easily seen in the grey of predawn, which was growing from the east.

Laurens smiled but quickly faded as the sound of fifes and drums from their right caught their attention, all of the officers looking to the right. "What in the bloody damn blazes?" Lauren asked as he strained to see what was going on.

Unknown to Jacob and the men in the column, the French were having a demonstration of seniority. By French military tradition, the most senior company would lead the column, and a company commander had not allowed his place of honor.

After arguing and comparing seniority, the company commander was correct. But, instead of just moving to the front of the column, he did it with his fifes and drums playing their marital music as the commander strutted to the front, leading his company.

"Well, so much for the element of surprise," remarked Jacob, and Laurens replied, "You very correct there, Captain Clarke; what else could go wrong?"

Jacob shook his head, but that gut feeling was coming back, that feeling the assault was not going to go as planned.

In answer to his question, from across the opening in the vicinity of the Spring Hill redoubt came the eerie wailing of bagpipes. Colonel Laurens looked across the way from the direction of the pipes.

"Why are they coming from there? Our information didn't have Highlanders here; something's amiss." Laurens slowly raised himself, trying to see if the French were in position, but couldn't see anything.

"Have the men get ready; we will wait for the signal and follow orders, even though the French who made the orders can't seem to follow them!"

***

D'Estaing was incensed by the sound of the fife and drums. He paced back and forth in front of his grenadiers. He knew the element of surprise was lost, but he couldn't cancel the attack. After his failure at Rhode Island, this would doom his career and fame, and he couldn't live with that. He would wait for the rest of the assault columns to get into position and order the attack.

Perhaps he can snatch victory from the mouth of defeat, but he will see to this commander who had to play his fife and drums, contrary to his orders. What kind of example can the Americans show if they don't follow their orders. What would these amateurs think?

From the left, D'Estaing heard firing; the diversionary attack had begun. He sensed an opportunity; now that the British were looking towards the feint, he could salvage this assault and still win the day with his grenadiers. He moved quickly to brief his new plan to his supporting French columns.

General Huger's diversionary attack had done what it was supposed to do, draw the British attention. However, when the British returned fire, it tore through the ranks of the men who had been wading through rice fields for several hours, twenty-eight men fell dead, and the column broke and returned to the lines.

Having briefed the supporting columns, D'Estaing raised and waved his arm forward and launched his diversionary attack in the center. The supporting attack advanced, stopped just before the redoubt, quickly reformed and loaded, and fired their first volley. The balls smacked into the soft, spongy wood of their redoubts, having learned from the defenses of Fort Sullivan.

As soon as the French fired, the British stepped onto the firing platform, and the British returned fire, the French crumbling and reeling while in a tight column formation. Then, as the smoke of the British rolled over the French, they turned and began to head back across the open field towards their camp.

D'Estaing paced, not hearing the supporting gunfire from the river, unaware that the galleys had not departed nor would participate in the attack. Finally, drawing his sword, he couldn't wait any longer, the frustration and impatient with his men driving him to action.

Giving the command to "Charge Bayonets!" No longer worrying about secrecy, the drummers beat out the orders as the assembled grenadiers and infantry gave a shout and lowered their bayonet-tipped muskets. D'Estaing looked at his assembled men; muskets lowered, bayonets pointing the way, eyes determined.

He turned, raised his sword high, and swept it forward towards the redoubt.

"Charge!" D'Estaing shouted in which his men shouted "Vive le Roi!" and surged forward across the field. As the French charged at the redoubt, the British guns opened fire, shot and grapeshot screaming in and around the charging Frenchmen. Sword held high, pointing forward, D'Estaing's legs pumped and churned through the muddy field, his men charging right behind him.

The whistling and shrieking as cannon balls bounced along the muddy field, sometimes burying themselves deep and causing no harm, others tearing into the ranks of white-uniformed Frenchmen, covering their uniforms in red blood and gore. The charge continued with the bouncing grapeshot and solid shot crunching in and among the Frenchmen.

The British muskets were resting on the top of the redoubt's walls, waiting to add their deadly voice to the symphony of destruction. The artillery barked and boomed, the smoke billowing like angry clouds over the field. Then, as the French closed the distance towards the redoubt, the British and Loyalists inside the Spring Hill began to aim over the top of their muskets, waiting until they came closer to make their volley count.

The attacking Frenchmen stormed about the Spring Hill Redoubt's outer slopes, crashing against the moat's outer abatis and lip before the redoubt. In range, the British and the Loyalists fired volleys into the massed Frenchmen, tearing into their ranks. The Frenchmen leaned against the wooden abatis, trying to use it for cover, loading and firing up at the redoubt.

Fighting through a murderous crossfire from the supporting redoubts, D'Estaing and his grenadiers fought through the abatis and charged up the slope of the redoubt. Waving his sword in a circle over his head, a musket ball smashed into his arm. Grunting, pausing only for a moment, D'Estaing continued, blood splattering his fine white uniform. Finally, he made his way to the top of the parapet.

"Advance my brave grenadiers. Kill these wretches!"

His encouragement was answered by "Kill the rascal French dogs!" was shouted by the Loyalists, along with "God save the King!" It was an ugly fight on top of the redoubt, volleys at point-blank range, bayonets flashing. Finally, the white and gold French flag went up, and from their position, Jacob and Colonel Laurens thought grudgingly, perhaps this will work after all.

The sound of the fighting in and around the redoubt was intense. The smoke of the muskets and cannon boiling over and out like a volcano. The shooting was too much, and the French began to fall back, being pushed out by a determined charge by the South Carolina Loyalists, who drove them out by the tips of their bayonets, then fired at them at close range.

D'Estaing rallied his men, and the grenadiers charged again, climbing over their fallen comrades' bodies. Once again, they were caught in the bloody seesaw of fighting across the parapet. The British and Loyalist defenders dug their heels in and made a hard fight of it. Once again, the French were driven out, only to attack one more time.

Briefly, the Loyalists were wobbling, and it seemed the French would finally get a foothold. D'Estaing turned to look for the supporting columns of French troops, but they were nowhere to be seen. They couldn't hold, and D'Estaing, tears streaming down his face, had no choice but to order the retreat from the charnel house of the redoubt.

As the French withdrew, the Loyalists again pursued. They fired a volley at point-blank range from the top of the parapet. D'Estaing was wounded again, taking a ball in the thigh and going down. Almost left behind, had it not been for a Lieutenant who ordered some grenadiers back to recover the fallen D'Estaing.

The first two grenadiers were shredded by artillery fire and fell with D'Estaing before another set of grenadiers successfully recovered and carried him back to their lines. After that, the British poured artillery fire into the French, loading everything they could into the guns, silverware, knives, broken blades, scissors, and even chains that were just shredding bodies into reddish-pink mists whenever they hit.

Colonel Laurens could see the French were breaking and decided they had better get into action and see if they could save them from total destruction. "Fix Bayonets!"

In fluid motions, Laurens drew his sword, and the two South Carolina Continental Regiments fixed their bayonets with clicks and snapped the muskets into their shoulders. The militia was not as fluid, but those with bayonets set them and brought their muskets to the shoulder ahead of the command. "Shoulder, firelocks!"

Lauren took a deep breath, whispered a quick, silent prayer, brought his sword up, and then shouted, "To the front, march!" and slashed his sword down.

Leading the column up and over the ridge, Jacob was leading, still, the first in the column as they began to march across the five hundred yards of open field. Then, except now, the area was strewn with dead and wounded French soldiers, some either limping or crawling back towards their lines.

With the French withdrawing from the attack on Spring Hill, the British and Loyalists had time for a breather and to restock on ammunition. In the distance, they could see Lauren's column come onto the field and begin to angle towards them. The gunners resumed their positions on the cannons and shifted their aim to take the new column under fire.

The British began firing artillery at the column the first hundred yards, the balls skipping over the ground towards the column. The fire intensified as they closed another hundred yards, three hundred to go. As the cannons boomed, the men instinctively ducked but maintained their columns. Instinctively, Jacob began to crouch down, making himself a smaller target as the shot bounced by him on both sides, dirt, and mud flying up. A couple of the men next to Jacob were hit, blood spattering across Jacob's uniform.

They started running into the causalities two hundred yards from the redoubt. In small groups, Frenchmen supported the wounded, two men helping a limping, injured man to the rear. Sometimes, the soldiers limped, using their muskets as a crutch. A few reached up to grab the legs of the advancing men, pleading not to go into that maelstrom and to take them back to the rear.

Laurens began jogging forward, the men picking up their pace to keep up with him. Jacob's breath was coming deeper, faster, the adrenaline of the fight coursing through his veins. His focus was on the redoubt, and it seemed the carnage around him went silent or muffled, as his total focus was on his objective, his breathing loud in his ears. The ground erupted around him as the grapeshot crashed into and around Jacob's feet.

There were more bodies now; several dead Frenchman laid out with small pieces of metal lodged in them, the scrap metal the British fired from their cannons. Jacob nearly stepped on a man trying to push his entrails back into the open cavity of his abdomen, and it kept snaking out. Jacob shook his head and kept moving forward.

Another Frenchman was leaning on his musket and hopping towards the rear, having lost the bottom half of his left leg, which he was holding in his hand. He did not stand for long before toppling over from blood loss. Shaking his head, Jacob cleared the image and focused on reaching the redoubt. The dead French soldier's empty, lifeless eyes watched Jacob move past.

It was now or never, and Colonel Laurens gave the command of "Charge!" pointing forward with his sword. The muskets lowered and bobbed as the men began to run, the tips of their bayonets jumping up and down as they started a low, primal shout. Looking over his shoulder, the column was charging, and right behind his company was the lead company of the Second South Carolina, her red and blue flags leading from the front.

They reached the last hundred yards and began charging through the charnel house of broken and shattered Frenchmen, some nothing more than bloody, pulpy mounds from the artillery. The redoubt raised above them, the abatis before them, separated by the moat. Bodies were lying and stacked against the abatis or lined the bottom of the ditch.

D'Estaing, supported by the two grenadiers carrying him to the rear, looked up groggily from his wounds to witness the ferocious, lion-like roar of the Second South Carolina with flags flapping charged past. He admired their élan and wished his men had the same courage these amateur South Carolinians were showing.

"Bon Chance!" he whispered and did wish them luck in carrying the day where he could not. As he watched, the column's rear began to break away; the Charles Town Militia was already breaking and running towards the rear. They haven't even reached the hundred yards mark.

The charge also caught the attention of the British and the Loyalists, who were pouring more fire into the charging column, both musketry and flanking artillery fire. At this range, the brave men of the South Carolina regiments, in their distinct black leather helmets, began to crumble as the cannon shot began to crash through the ranks, knocking men down like ten pins. Nevertheless, the column didn't stop but kept charging forward, stepping over the falling men, the rear men pressing forward to fill the gaps.

The air filled with choking smoke, making it difficult to breathe. Jacob, who was yelling alongside the men, primarily out of the primal need to face fear screaming, legs were pumping as he charged forward. Muskets balls whizzed and snapped past, now that he could see the puffs of the enemy muskets firing at him and the darker, longer gouts of flame and smoke of the cannons.

The air buzzed as if they were in the middle of a giant swarm of angry wasps. Cannon boomed, and within seconds, Jacob felt a stinging sensation along his right side as tiny slivers of fragments hit his face, shoulder, and upper body, most of the pieces absorbed by the wool, but they did dig grooves across his face and nose.

Looming before them in the fog of musketry and cannonade smoke were the sharpened, angle logs of the abatis; they had dead Frenchmen leaning against them or laying down into the ditch. The French had tried to cut some of the abatis poles down, but only a few had been cut through. The axes that had been used lay about the ground near the abatis where they had been dropped.

"Grab the axes!" yelled Laurens, and some of the men grabbed the fallen axes from the dead Frenchman's hands and began to cut a few of the poles down to open some space between them.

As men started to chop, Jacob quickly formed a firing line and provided some covering fire to keep the enemy's heads down.

The men quickly came together as Jacob commanded, "load!" As the men went through the loading process, the balls and chunks of metal pinged and bounced, slapping off the abatis and throwing wood splinters.

A near miss did catch the post near Jacob, who felt a stinging sensation under his left eye as a large splinter struck him in the face. Caught up in the battle action, not truly feeling the injury, Jacob reached up, plucked the splinter from his face, and readied to give the order to fire.

"Make ready!" Jacob yelled out as the blood trickled down his face, mixing with the sweat.

"Take Aim!"

The British and the Loyalists continued to pour fire at the regiment as they formed their firing lines as the few chopped on the abatis.

"Fire!"

The muskets erupted in flame and smoke, the men trying for the heads poking up over the firing lip of the redoubt. The lip and air around the top of the redoubt were covered in dust as the balls impacting threw up dirt and dust in the face of the shooters, and a few fell holding their faces.

As the men labored, axes biting and woodchips flying, Jacob kept up a sustained rate of fire, having the men fire by files instead of volleys. This way, there was a constant barrage of muskets firing, but ready enough in case the enemy came over the top to engage them with bayonets. The air was getting thick with the grey smoke of musketry and cannon fire, and the layer of bodies at the bottom of the moat was beginning to get deeper.

After a few minutes, a few of the abatis poles were down, allowing more room for men to pour through, and Laurens motioned with his sword to charge. Yelling at the top of their lungs, men weaved through the openings. They charge up the sloped redoubt into the furious fire of the enemy.

Digging their feet into the slope, the charging infantry roared with their pent-up emotions and fear, Laurens urging them on. Several men snapped back, struck by the musket balls hit at point-blank range, their leather helmets falling and rolling down the slope, along with the bodies. The helmets would rest on top of the dead men at the bottom of the moat.

Shaking his head to clear his eyes from the dust and splinters, Jacob saw one of the men who were so caught up in the adrenaline and fear of the charge didn't realize his bayonet sling was snagged on a split abatis log. He kept trying to charge forward, legs churning and not going anywhere. Finally, pulling his tomahawk, Jacob cut the leather strap of the bayonet sling, and the man sprang forward, only to have his head explode as a musket ball went through, spraying Jacob's face in his blood.

Closing his eyes and shook his head to clear the blood off, not dwelling on the loss of the man he had just freed. Then, with a carnal roar, Jacob's anger boiled over, and he charged up the slope with more of the men following right behind him. The air around Jacob was full of loud sounds, the scream of the wounded, the shouts of the fighters, and the sound of musketry at close range.

The fighting almost became surreal, time slowing and the sound muffling as Jacob reached the top of the redoubt. Surrounded by smoke, it was as though Jacob was in a dream, or a nightmare, the silhouettes of men moving through the thick grey air. Sounds were dull, even the whizzing and snapping of the musket balls.

It was only momentary as reality snapped back into focus, the fighting very real, the sound and smell of battle assaulting his senses. A charging silhouette from the smoke, bayonet lowered, took a thrust at Jacob. The bayonet drove into his regimental coat, cutting across his abdomen and becoming stuck in the coat itself.

Using his free hand, he grabbed the musket and buried it in the head of the attacking Loyalist with his tomahawk. When he pulled his tomahawk from the dead man, Jacob looked closer, seeing the large white cockade and shirt outside of the coat.

"Damn, did I kill one of my men?" Jacob asked. Bending down to look, he saw that it was not one of his men; he was wearing a cocked hat and not a helmet. Somehow they knew of their plan.

"These crafty bastards!" Jacob yelled, "If they don't have a helmet, kill them! They're Loyalists and British!"

Jacob crossed the top of the parapet, joining in the close-quarters fighting. Then, like a stormy ocean, the blue wave crashed into the green wave, men locking in close combat where the action became primitive, biting, clawing, and punching their enemies, too close for the bayonet.

Jacob struck out, his tomahawk more suited for this style of fighting. In one motion, he caught a Loyalist at the juncture of his neck and shoulders, spraying blood on the already soaked ground of the parapet, before pulling it out in time to parry a sword swipe by a British officer from the 71st.

The officer pulled back his sword and attempted to slash Jacob, who once again deftly parried it with his tomahawk.

"Die, you damn rebel scum!" the officer yelled as he struck down at Jacob with all of his might. But unfortunately, he had put too much effort into the swing and was off-balance.

Jacob came under the downward arch of the sword to tackle the officer, taking both of them to the ground. As they fell, Jacob quickly placed his knee into the officer's groin, who let out a high-pitched scream, promptly ending as Jacob's tomahawk crunched into his throat.

Blood dripping from his tomahawk and smeared across his face, Jacob took stock of the situation. He saw the red and blue flags of the regiment had been planted on the parapet, and his heart soared, but for a brief moment.

Sensing they were about to break; Loyalist Major Glazier ordered the reserve of British Marines and the grenadiers of the 60th Regiment into the fray. Firing as they charged home, the balls smashed into the tightly packed men of the Second Regiment, knocking many of them down. A man in front of Jacob fell, the blow's force knocking them both down. The two rolled down the slope onto the piles of dead and wounded stacked high in the surrounding ditch.

The dead man landed on top of Jacob, pinning him on top of several dead French and regimental men. Jacob squirmed to make room, then pushed and rolled the dead man from on top of him. As he pushed himself up and untangled himself from the limbs and equipment of the dead, Jacob looked up to see Sergeant Jasper, the same Jasper who replaced the flag at Fort Sullivan during the battle, fall as he tried to save the flag once more.

As Jasper fell forward, the flag was tossed forward so it wouldn't fall on the redoubt. Lieutenant Bush grabbed for the falling blue colors from Jasper, turned, and was quickly shot down. Jacob started moving towards the colors, but it felt like he was in slow motion again. Then, finally, the green wave of green crested over the top of the redoubt. The Loyalists began to pour fire into the ditch and the men's backs.

A burning sensation pulled Jacob back out of his daze. A ball traveled along the top of his arm and exited from the back of his regimental. Jacob turned and began to run; his last sight was the regimental blue flag draped across the bodies of Jasper and Lieutenant Bush, surrounded by Loyalists. There was no way he could reach the colors now.

Shaking his head, Jacob leaped back down into the moat. Landing on top of the pile of dead, and leaned up against one of the abatis posts. He saw a few more determined men continue to fire up at the Loyalists, impervious to the death and destructions.

Jacob smiled, even in this bloody scene. "My brave, bloody fools!"

Making his way over to the stalwart shooters, he grabbed their shoulders and gave them the order to fall back and join with the other sections making a fighting withdrawal.

"I'm going for the rest of them," Jacob shouted over the din of fighting, "head back and tell them to keep up the covering fire!"

The men nodded, turned, and began to run back towards one of the sections forming a firing line, to support the rest of the men leap-frogging towards the rear. Then, taking a deep breath, Jacob plunged back into the vortex of shot and shell to see if he could find any more survivors and get them to fall back.

The British and Loyalists poured musket and cannon fire into the retreating men now that they were out in the open. The men were being hit from the front, the defenses' flanks, and the other redoubts. The crossfire was tearing men into bloody pieces and choking the ground with even more dead and wounded, the blue coats mixing with the white coats, all covered in red.

As Jacob weaved through the abatis, he found Colonel Laurens standing in the moat; his eyes showed his mind was gone, his arms stretched out to the side.

"Kill me, damn you!" Laurens shouted, "My honor does not permit me to survive this disgrace, and the dead demand it. Kill me!"

Sensing he had to do something quickly, Jacob slapped Laurens.

"This won't honor or save them!" Jacob yelled, "If you honor their sacrifice, live to fight another day! Avenge them!"

Lauren looked at Jacob sadly, "My honor does not permit me."

As another ball snapped past Jacob's head and the look that Laurens gave him showed he was lost, Jacob knew he had no choice. As Laurens turned, eyes closed, and faced what he thought was his execution squad, Jacob struck him across the back of his head with the flat of his tomahawk.

Taking Lauren's crumbled form, he threw him over his shoulder and carried him out of the moat and onto the field. As the musket balls skipped around his legs and cannon shot bounced about, Jacob labored with Laurens until he found a group of men from the other regiment.

"Take him to the rear!" Jacob ordered, and they nodded. After Laurens was passed, Jacob turned to weave through the gauntlet of death, looking for more men and making sure Jean and Samuel were alive. He also wanted to make sure Marion got away unscathed.

Cannonballs and scrap metal flew and bounced around them, the angry balls whizzing and snapping all around them as the men moved towards the ridge and the safety of the swamp. It seemed the fire intensified as they retreated, the British and the Loyalists showing no mercy. Although Jacob had to admit, this was much worse than what they faced at Carillon, much, much worse.

From what he could see, there were no longer any men from the regiment alive standing before the redoubt. All have been killed, wounded, or already heading back to the rear. Jacob felt a tug at his uniform as another musket ball passed through his coat but luckily had not hit him.

As Jacob was moving back, he saw a man trying to hobble back, using his musket as a crutch. Jacob moved up to him, placing the man's right arm over his shoulder and Jacob using his left arm to support him; the man was able to move faster. He looked over at Jacob and smiled, grateful for the assistance. Unfortunately, something hit the two of them with a heavy impact. The man to his left practically exploded as something heavy slammed into Jacob's left side, knocking the wind out of him and sending him to the ground.

The pain exploded up and down Jacob's body, starting in his side and traveling across his back, arms and legs. As he fell, Jacob found breathing difficult; no air was getting into his lungs. Finally, his body crashed onto the soft, swampy ground, bouncing as it came to rest. The pain started to lessen, but his vision was now a tunnel closing until the blackness finally took him.

CHAPTER 10

THE GREAT RETREAT

Jacob floated in a sea of white, with no sound, no movement, and no pain. Just a white light and a feeling of contentment. Slowly a face began to come into focus before Jacob; it was Maggie's face. As her face solidified, Jacob saw she was smiling at him.

"Maggie, what's going on? Where am I? Am I finally dead?"

"Shh." Was her only answer, almost an echo on the wind. Different emotions began to run through Jacob, not knowing what to think or what to do. But there she was, before him in a sea of white.

"I'm married and have a family now." Jacob stammered as he looked at the face of his long-lost love.

Maggie smiled and nodded, "It was about time you moved on; you're a good man Jacob."

"Maggie, am I dead?" Jacob asked; though Maggie smiled, she shook her head no.

Her face began to fade, the light began to cascade from white to colors, the pain was starting to reach out to Jacob, and the smell of tobacco smoke brought Jacob to his senses. He was moving, he could hear his name far off in the distance, but it was getting louder as Maggie faded away.

"Jacob, wake up!"

Samuel, arm bandaged, was shaking Jacob awake. His eyes fluttering, Jacob woke in reality, focusing his eyes and taking in his surroundings. He followed the smell of the tobacco smoke and looked up to see Peter with his pipe in his mouth. Samuel with a bucket of water in his hands.

"Peter," Jacob croaked, throat still dry, "where the bloody hell am I?"

Quickly looking down, Peter's grin grew.

"Thank Gott in Himmel!" Peter exclaimed. "We thought you dead; you looked terrible, my friend."

Jacob pulled himself up so he could sit up, saw he was leaning against a tree, and looked around to get a better view. When Samuel saw Jacob was awake, they put the bucket down, intending to dump it on Jacob to wake him up.

"Where are we?" Jacob asked, trying to settle himself more against the tree in a better sitting position. Pain shot through his side as he moved, and Jacob grimaced. "How did you end up here?"

"We brought down a load of supplies just as you started that foolhardy attack," Peter explained, "we stayed to watch the fight, and then you all came streaming back."

Peter paused for a moment, puffing on his pipe. "The army is destroyed from what I can tell, too bloody to fight again, or even more."

Another bought of pain raced up Jacob's side, and he winced but nodded his head in understanding. The images of the bloody, broken bodies in the bottom of the moat and on the field before the redoubt were still fresh in his memory.

"My side is killing me, Samuel," Jacob gasped, and Samuel replied, "I imagine so."

Samuel quickly moved over, grabbed a blanket, and then returned and placed it behind Jacob, trying to make him comfortable.

"A cannon shot bounced and took your mate in the back, smashed him to smithereens, and knocked you to the ground," Samuel explained, which to Jacob made sense. "Must have messed up some ribs."

"I think you're right, Samuel," Jacob gasped, "It sure as bloody hell hurts!"

Jacob saw the bloody bandage on Samuel's arm. "Nothing to worry about," Samuel explained, "just a chunk of meat knocked out will mend. I'll see if I can find some rum to take care of that pain."

Samuel patted Jacob on the shoulder, then turned and headed into the chaos of the camp. Peter winked, "I'll go see if I can find something with those other waggoneers that might help."

Jacob leaned against the tree but looked around at the camp. It was all in disarray, groups moving about, wounded being helped, and bodies being carried. Stragglers were streaming in, Jacob noticing that the men of the Charles Town Militia avoided and would not look at the broken Continentals, who gave them scathing looks for running so quickly.

Exhaustion took him, and Jacob closed his eyes and fell asleep. Then, a short while later, he was shaken awake by a surgeon's mate.

"Oh, sorry, sir, just seeing if you were alive or dead," stated a surgeon's mate and Jacob snorted then grimaced. "I think I am a little of both."

The surgeon-mate then asked, "Which injury is the worse?"

Jacob looked confused, then realized from what the surgeon mate saw, it must have been a horrific scene. Jacob realized he was covered in blood, some of it his, some of it from the men he killed.

"Ah, here. Believe I may have broken some ribs." Jacob indicated, pointing to his side.

The surgeon-mate probed with his fingers along Jacob's side, which caused him to grunt and winch.

"How did it happen?" he asked, and Jacob responded with "Cannon shot."

"Hmm," the surgeon-mate responded. "Ah, you're lucky, sir," the surgeon-mate said cheerfully,

Jacob gave him an odd look. "Lucky?"

"Just some broken ribs. You'll mend. No need for surgery, and the cannon ball didn't kill you. So you'll live."

"Oui, mon captain," Jean stated as he, along with Samuel and Peter, arrived, and the surgeon-mate moved on to check on the next causality.

They all sat down around Jacob, Samuel handing him a mug of rum. Jean had a bandage around his forehead, but only a small blob of blood could be seen. Jean could see what Jacob was looking at. "Just a small splinter. They took it out."

Jacob took a long pull of the rum, allowing the warmth to enter and fight off the pain of the broken ribs. "What is the butcher's bill on this one?"

Jean shook his head. "We lost about a third of the entire brigade; maybe two hundred and fifty are still lying before the redoubt. Still trying to get a return of the wounded and the survivors."

Jacob nodded his head and took another long drink. Samuel pulled a ceramic bottle out from his haversack and topped off Jacob's mug, then all of theirs.

"So what do our illustrious commanders want to do?"

"General Lincoln wants to continue the siege," Jean explained before taking a drink from his mug and staring at the cups inside. "D'Estaing had lost his will to fight. I think it's over."

Jacob shook his head. "So it was all for nothing?" Jean shrugged his shoulders and drank his cup dry.

"What about Marion, Moultrie? Did they make it out?" Jacob asked, and Samuel nodded as he refilled Jean's mug."

"They are," Samuel answered, "I am to report to them on your condition."

"When will you do that?" Jacob asked as he watched Samuel take a long drink from his mug and refill it.

"I am still determining your condition."

They raised their mugs to their fallen men, to William Jasper, all who gave the ultimate sacrifice and lay before the Spring Hill Redoubt.

"Well, I better go report to the General and Moultrie that you're alive," Samuel stated as he stood up with a grunt. Before heading into the camp, he held the bottle upside down to ensure it was empty.

"Get some sleep, my friend," Peter stated as he pulled a blanket around Jacob. "This is as good as a spot as any around here; we'll check on you in the morning." Peter stood and limped off to where the wagons and carts were.

"I'll go check to see if the final return of our men has been completed," Jean stated, "I'll let you know in the morning."

The exhaustion of the battle, the injury, and the rum had its effect, and Jacob fell asleep again. It was a fitful sleep, the images of the bloody. Broken men before the redoubt were there but would be chased away by the vision of Maggie. This went on all night, a nightmare of the blood and destruction and the image of Maggie chasing them away.

The following morning, under a flag of truce, they were able to negotiate a cease-fire to bury the dead. General Prevost consented, and the burial details went out to bury the dead and fallen. Around the Spring Hill Redoubt, they dug deep pits and buried the men in a mass grave where two hundred and three Frenchmen and South Carolina Continentals were laid together and in a smaller grave to the left of the redoubt, another twenty-eight.

The units were still having difficulties accounting for their men. Some of the wounded who could pull themselves to the swamp suffered the worst as their weakened bodies couldn't fight anymore, the marsh and mud sucking their bodies into the earth. But, on the other hand, some of the men kept going, not stopping at the camp, and began the trek back to their homes.

Once the men were buried, the British resumed firing their artillery at the French mostly, even though D'Estaing tried to parley for another truce. Still, General Prevost refused, having done the honorable thing of allowing the dead to be buried, but now it was time to get back to killing one another.

Jacob, having rested, was assisted by Jean and Samuel to return to their camp and his lean-to. He received a warm welcome from the survivors of the regiment, happy to see he was alive. Once in the camp, Marion came to check on him as he rested in his lean-to.

Marion motioned for Jacob to remain sitting and joined him on the ground. With Marion was Oscar, who had traveled out with the wagons to be with Marion.

"Jacob, it's good to see you are alive," Marion stated, "From what Sergeant Penny told me, broken ribs?"

Jacob nodded. "Surgeon-mate said I was lucky, will heal." Jacob held up his worn regimental coat. It now had a few bullet, fragment holes, and even large wooden and metal slivers stuck in the wool. "Very lucky. How goes the siege?"

Marion looked down at the ground, then back at Jacob. He already guessed it would be bad news. They could hear the French guns firing back at the British; it was not the same intensity as before the attack.

"We're broken. General Lincoln went to speak to D'Estaing, but our French commander ordered the camps broken, the siege lifted, and the army returned to Charles Town. They have had enough."

While Jacob knew it was coming, it was still like being punched in the stomach.

"We'll be on the march soon. Can you walk, or do you want to ride in a cart?" Marion asked.

Jacob gave Marion a stern look, not knowing if he was serious, joking, or taking a stab at his injury. Emotions were swirling around Jacob, but after taking a deep breath, he knew Marion was being kind and, due to his injury, wanted to save him from any more discomfort.

Jacob shook his head. "I'll bloody well walk out of here with our men, but thanks for asking."

Marion nodded and smiled. "Take care; we'll be back on the road soon."

With Oscar, who nodded to Jacob respectfully, Marion stood and turned to get the regiment's remnants ready to march. Samuel and Jean helped Jacob pack his gear and prepare everything for the march. Jacob hobbled around, his side still hurting from the broken ribs. The surgeon-mate had stopped by to wrap a thick bandage around his ribs, which did help support the bones from rubbing.

Once all was in order, Jacob rejoined the regiment or what was left of the regiment. Seeing many men's gear was loaded into empty wagons because they were gone was sobering. They could see at least half of the men were gone; about half of those standing in formation to march were bandaged in one form or another.

The army began their sullen march back to Charles Town. Jacob did see Lieutenant Colonel Laurens marching back with them as they were marching, though, in his eyes, you could see he was a broken man. It took all of Jacob's willpower to place his feet one in front of the other, his broken ribs making it difficult to move, but it reminded him he was alive, and he welcomed the pain.

The army wound its way through Georgia and back into South Carolina, a quiet army with no joking or the earlier enthusiasm that was part of the march there. The morale had suffered, and Jacob suspected the desertion rate would start as soon as they arrived back in Charles Town. The militia would make their way home anyways, but the word will spread of their defeat.

It was an uneventful march back; even the weather took mercy on the army, the temperatures were comfortable, and it didn't rain. They marched back to the city unmolested, the British celebrating their victory in Savannah. Due to his injuries, Jacob was ordered to rest at home; the city was already overflowing with injured.

Colonel Marion ensured Jacob went home by having Samuel and Jean escort him, staying with him and ensuring he rested.

"I need you healed up, Captain Clarke; I charged the sergeant-major and the lieutenant here to make sure you heal. The British will use this victory to embolden the Loyalists, and seeing our French allies have left with their fleet, we are open to attack, and we have no real army to stop them."

Jacob could see the seriousness in his eyes and knew he meant it. "I have a feeling I will need you soon, so rest up and be ready," Marion finished, then looked directly at Samuel and Jean.

"That also goes for you two. I need you both healed up and ready to go. We are short of good leaders, and Lieutenant Langy, I may need you to take a company as we lost many of our company commanders. So get healed up and get back here ready to fight the British. They'll be coming back soon, I fear."

Marion shook their hands and handed them their passes to head home on furlough. They signed out of the orderly room and secured their horses from the quartermaster. Jacob looked at his torn and tattered regimental coat. "Going to have to replace this when I am back," Jacob replied, looking over his regimental.

They spotted Peter with his cart and joined him for the trip back to their compound. Peter was offloading the gear he had brought from Savannah, mostly the equipment and uniform items from the dead men. Samuel looked for shoes that could fit him, taking a shoe and holding it up against the one he was wearing to see if they were the same size. Finally, he found a pair and changed them out with his old ones.

Once all was in order with the quartermaster, Peter led the wagons out while they rode next to him. Then, with pipe in hand, and a large grin, Peter happily exclaimed, "It's going to be a terrific Weihnachten dis year; die women will love having you home," Peter rejoiced, "for a change."

Jacob and Samuel arrived home to a very joyful family reunion, though he did get mixed messages from his wife. At one moment, Maria was happy to see him alive; the next, she was scolding him about being injured, then back to happy for him being home, and then back to being angry for not taking better care of himself.

Jacob ended it by sweeping his wife and kissing her intensely, after which she melted in his arms, and all was well. Then, with her hands on her hips, she stood back and looked at Jacob up and down.

"You look horrible; they are not feeding you well," She looked at his newly scared face and shook her head. "You're not sleeping and look like a beggar in that uniform!" Jacob pulled the tails of his uniform out, full of the holes the splinters and the balls went through.

"At least they didn't hit me," Jacob defended himself, "Doesn't that count?"

Jacob's children came out when they heard they had returned. Patrick was now as tall as Jacob; the work on the compound had made him a stout young man, along with his younger brother

Richard, who was also filling out. The two wolves came bounding from the garden, followed by Jacob's daughter Helga, bringing some freshly harvested corn.

As the boys charged up to hug their father, he put his hands up to ward them off, trying to protect his injured ribs. Helga walked up, placed her corn basket down, and stood next to Maria. She took the same pose as Maria, imitating her stance with both fists on her hips, the difference being that she stamped her foot and then walked up to Jacob.

As he bent down to hug his daughter, she punched him in the chest.

"You were supposed to be careful and not get hurt!" she yelled, once more hands on her hips and stamping her foot. "You promised mama you would be safe!"

Then, in faithful imitation of Maria, she turned toward where Samuel was with his family.

"Uncle Sam, you were supposed to take care of Papa!" she yelled. Maria tried to keep from laughing at her mirror image of a daughter.

"Sorry, darling," he replied, "But you know your father, always in the thick of it."

She turned and looked at her surprised father, sighed, walked up, hugged him, and kissed him. "I forgive you, Papa, though Mama may not. Oma will help you feel better."

Helga turned, still all business, grabbed her basket of corn, and headed to the house to finish her chores. The two wolves sat there, amazed at what they saw, then ran up with their tongues and tails wagging in the manner of wolf greetings.

"That is going to be a dangerous young lady one day," Jean commented, and Jacob nodded.

Maria walked up and gave Jean a hug. "Of course, she'll be dangerous," Maria commented, "She is my daughter!"

Maria stood back and once again inspected both Jean and Jacob's clothes, Jacob's much worse than Jean's. They both smelled, having not washed their clothes or themselves in a long time.

"No, this will simply not due. Get those clothes off. Boys, go get water and get the fire stoked up; your father and Uncles Sam and Jean need a bath!"

"But," Jacob started, but Maria stopped him by holding up her index finger with the look that said, "*Don't argue!*"

Jacob began to take his clothes off just as Maria's mother Gerda arrived, carrying a bag of herbs. She went straight to the wrappings after Jacob pulled off his shirt. She looked critically at the discoloration around the ribs. Then, she wrinkled her nose, "You need a bath!"

Jacob sighed, "Yes, ma'am, I have been told by Maria. Heading there as soon as we have some hot water."

Jacob, with Jean and soon joined by Samuel, headed to the barn where they work the skins. The boys were already there, the fires were stoked up, and buckets of water were heated. The water was poured into their vats, and Jacob climbed in. Helga arrived with a soap bar, "Mama said to use it." She also handed him a sponge to use.

Jacob had to admit, the warm water did feel good as the boys kept pouring in the buckets, and he began to scrape off the layer of filth and grime that he got used to as a soldier. "I do stink," Jacob remarked as he scrubbed with the soap and the sponge.

Helga returned with fresh clothes for Jacob. "I think Mama is burning your old clothes; she says she can't save them." Both Jean and Samuel chuckled from their vats as they scrubbed the dirt and grime from their bodies. Jacob scrubbed until his skin was a healthy pink, except where the bruising from the broken ribs was.

After pulling his new shirt over his head, Jacob walked to the house. Gerda was waiting and pointed to a chair next to the fire. Gerda's husband Gottfried was there with Peter, while Maria and Otti were in the kitchen. Jacob sat in the chair; Gerda went over and looked at the bruise now that it was clean.

Nodding, she went over and grabbed her bags of herbs. Helga was there, watching and learning as Richard brought a mug of flip over to Jacob. The fire helped dry from the bathing; Jean and Samuel joined him at the fire, pulling up chairs. After Gerda ground the herbs while explaining what she was doing to Helga, she made a poultice.

She placed it on the ribs, then Helga helped Gerda wrap Jacob's ribs and secure the herbs to his ribs. The scent was unique and had a distinct herbal smell to it. With the smell of the food being made, the fire, and the flip in his hand, Jacob had that warm feeling of being home and missing it.

Over the next few days, Jacob was only allowed to sit and heal, Helga making sure Jacob followed Gerda's instructions. Finally, his ribs were recovering, the color returning and the pain was going away. Friends and neighbors stopped in; all wanted to know about the defeat and check on Jacob. He told them of the assault and answered their questions.

"Do you think the British will come?" was the most asked, and Jacob was honest with them

"They have the advantage at the moment, and I believe they will."

***

Major Banastre Tarleton of the 1st Dragoon Guards made his way along the muddy and snowy streets of New York, having been summoned by General Sir Henry Clinton, the new overall commander of his majesty's forces here in the colonies. He expected a campaign was on the horizon, the excitement just below the surface. On the contrary, he was itching for action, hating to be in winter quarters.

His last action was back in 1778 when he had been wounded in action against rebel troops in Pennsylvania. Now that he had recovered, Tarleton was looking forward to returning to the field. However, garrison life was boring, and he was not suited for it. He approached a well-constructed house; the two guards posted at the door came to attention and presented arms when he climbed the stairs and entered.

Tarleton was shown to another room where other officers had been gathered, a large fireplace crackling in the center of the room. General Clinton was in the center of the room, standing over a large table, going over maps. Major General Alexander Leslie commanded the grenadiers and light infantry and was in quiet discussion with his deputy, Lord Charles Cornwallis.

Over in a corner was Brigadier General James Patterson, commanding the forces in New York, speaking with Major Patrick Ferguson. Also in the room were the German commander, Major General von Huyn, and Admiral Arbuthnot, who would command the fleet.

Tarleton knew they were in a sticky stalemate with these damnable rebels. With the loss of General "Gentlemen Johnny" Burgoyne and his army up near Saratoga, they had to retake the initiative. He moved over and took an open space next to the fire, the room a low murmur of discussion.

"Gentlemen, it is time to discuss our next objective," Clinton stated as he stood up and faced the assembled officers, "That being Charles Town. We have received dispatches that Campbell controls Georgia, and Prevost successfully handed these rebels and the French a decisive victory."

The assembled officers nodded and commented on the news they had also heard from Savannah. Finally, Clinton turned to address Admiral Arbuthnot.

"Admiral, have we confirmed that the French fleet has departed?" Clinton asked, concerned about the fleet as it would interfere with his movement of troops to Georgia.

Admiral Arbuthnot stepped up to the table, "Sir, my frigates have confirmed the French have departed, not wanting to be caught in any winter storms, and sailed for the Caribbean."

Nodding his head, Clinton felt better knowing the French fleet was no longer an issue. Then he turned to General Cornwallis, "How is our troop strength?"

Cornwallis turned to a smaller table and picked up a document, answering, "We have received the reinforcements from New York," indicating with the paper to General Patterson, "and we have the reinforcements consolidated from Philadelphia and Rhode Island, and home. We have about seven thousand men under arms and fit for duty, sir."

Clinton looked at the map as if it could speak to him and tell him what he wanted to know. "The rebels are smashed and demoralized, the French have left, and we have sufficient naval and land forces to take them," Clinton mainly spoke to himself, but loud enough for the assembled staff to hear, "and Lord Germaine wants us to shift the fighting to the south. Are the reports correct about the Loyalists who will flock to the colors once we arrive?"

Major Ferguson stepped forward. "Yes, sir, we have reports from the area that indicate Scotts and Irish will answer the call, Germans too," Ferguson nodded his head towards General von Huyn, who gave a curt bow, "and other Loyalists will support us."

That was enough to satisfy General Clinton, "Then gentlemen, you have your marching orders. Admiral, see to the feet and ensure it is provisioned and ready to sail before the harbor ices over. General Cornwallis, see to the men and ensure enough provisions and equipment are loaded. We will take Charles Town and bring the south under our control before summer; then this Washington will have to meet us on our ground."

Tarleton nodded and smiled; they were heading out on campaign and heading south once more away from this snow and mud. He had been part of the first expedition in 1776 as a cornet when they tried to take the damn fort outside Charles Town. So now they were heading back.

"Major Tarleton."

General Clinton had called his name, and Tarleton quickly responded.

"Yes, sir?"

Clinton pulled out a rolled document and handed it to him. "As you heard, Major Ferguson has indicated the Loyalists would flock to the King's colors if we can make them feel safe from these damn rebels. Therefore, I am promoting you to Lieutenant Colonel and charge you with forming a Legion once we arrive and secure Charles Town."

Tarleton came to rigid attention, "Yes, sir! Thank You, Sir!"

Clinton waved his hand at the salute. "Don't thank me yet," Clinton warned, "This is tough territory we're going into; recruiting and logistics will be challenging. Are you ready for this challenge?"

Once again, Tarleton came to rigid attention. "Yes, sir, I love challenges and accept this one!"

Nodding his head, Clinton dismissed Tarleton, who turned and departed the house. It took all of his willpower not to prance until he got outside and away from the view of the guards.

"I have my own command; I have my command!" Tarleton thought as he headed to his quarters. While his family had

purchased and secured his position as a cornet in the 1ˢᵗ Dragoon Guards, the rest of his promotions had been earned.

"Not bad for someone only Twenty-five!" Tarleton said aloud, thinking of the new honors he could earn on this campaign.

The army was loaded onto a fleet of ninety troop ships, which fourteen warships would escort. Once loaded, the invasion fleet sailed on the 26th of December, 1779, and made for the warmer southern colonies.

***

Jacob, with Samuel and Jean, along with all of their boys, spent several days hunting when Jacob's ribs had healed but were still sore. The wolves ran alongside, helping to track and spot the deer. Jacob, along with Samuel, watched their boys handle themselves. They rode well and were expert shots, cleanly taking deer on the run. Jacob smiled with pride.

"Reminds me of my younger days," Jacob commented.

"Which one, I hope you don't mean when you wintered that one year with the Mohawks, didn't you get into trouble with one of the war chief's daughters?"

Jacob shook his head and chuckled. "No, but close enough."

During the hunt, they passed through Manchester and headed up to Stateburg. Every place they stopped, the locals asked for news of the defeat at Savannah and information from the upcountry.

"Those damn highwaymen are back," a trader commented while loading goods at Sumter's store in Stateburg. "Heard from a few others they are spreading like locust from up country, may even be heading here."

Jacob nodded his head in concern. "Any word of the Cherokee?"

The trader scoffed, "That's the tale of it; I haven't heard anything on the Cherokee. No one has seen or heard anything on them in good time."

Thanking the trader, Jacob looked at Jean and Samuel. "Sounds like they are up to their old tricks and no good. So something must be afoot."

Samuel nodded, "But nothing on our local friendly Cherokee, and that's strange."

Nodding his head, Jacob made a decision. "Guess we'll go and ride up to the Catawbas and see if they know anything."

The boys smiled; they liked going up to visit the Catawbas. So Jacob led them out of Stateburg and headed towards the Catawba towns on the border with North Carolina. The days were crisp and cool, but not bad for being winter. The nights were cold, but they had a good fire and thick blankets.

After only a few days on the trail, they rode into the Catawba village of Newtown, where they tied their horses and brought some of the deer meat and skins they had taken to the elders. They met in the long meetinghouse in the center of the town, and their new leader General Green River was there.

Jacob was not surprised that the Catawba had a new leader; they were not happy with the previous, King Prow. However, King Hagler, the first Catawba leader Jacob had met, was hard to compare to, as he was one of the best they had.

In the meetinghouse was their old friend Yanabe, who came over to grasp each of their forearms in greeting, even the boys.

"It's good to see you; after we heard of the news from Savannah, we feared the worse," Yanabe stated, "We are glad the great spirit must have watched over you in that fight."

Jacob nodded in thanks and sat before General Green River, who nodded in recognition of Jacob, Samuel, and Jean. "Ah, Okwaho, It makes me glad to see you and your pack of wolves still live." He said, though, there was a twinkle in his eyes, "Your pups are growing into wolves, I see as well. So again, we thank you for your gift of meat and skins. Let's speak of things, and then we'll feast."

As with the other towns, Jacob was asked about Savannah, and General Green River wanted to know the truth from one who had been there. As Jacob described the battle and the assault, Green River nodded as he listened intently.

"This is bad news; I am sorry for your losses of good men," Green River stated. "Do you believe the British and their friends will be back on the warpath? We have heard the bandits are back, but they are staying out of Catawba lands for now."

"Yes, we believe they will back," Jacob answered. "Have you heard or seen anything of the Cherokee? Normally if the British move against us, they get the Cherokee and their allies to come in from up country."

"What you say is true," Green River stated, "But we have not seen them for some time now. Although we may have killed more of them than we thought, perhaps they have finally learned not to take up the tomahawk against us, Catawba!"

The men in the meetinghouse murmured their approval of Green River's statement, having no love lost on their hated enemy, the Cherokee. Jacob looked over at Yanabe, who shrugged his shoulders.

"Young warriors, they will learn."

Jacob nodded. He looked at his boys; they were taking everything in, and knew that their time would soon be here as much as he wished against it. Patrick and Richard were tall and stout for their age, excellent hunters and sharpshooters. Jacob joined the Rangers around when he was sixteen, and Patrick was not that far off age-wise.

Looking back at Yanabe, "General Green River has a good head about him," Jacob commented, "perhaps he can talk sense until they are needed. Then we'll see if they must take the warpath and the tomahawk."

Yanabe nodded his head slowly. "Then you think it will happen, that the British will come once again?"

Jacob nodded his head. "I do; everything I have seen and heard is pointing in that direction. They have the advantage, and they know it. They'll use our sign of weakness now, that it's time for them to exploit it. They're coming, though I believe it will be in the Spring. No one campaigns in the Winter."

"Hmm," Yanabe commented, nodding his head in agreement. "What you say is true; I believe you are right. I think we'll have a bloody Spring coming."

After a night of feasting, Jacob and Samuel watched young Catawba girls flirt with Patrick and Richard, as they were older than Samuel's boys Robert and Thomas, but not by much. Patrick seemed to like the attention; Richard wasn't sure yet but didn't mind.

"See, they are taking after you," Samuel commented as they watched the boys, "at least it's not a Mohawk chieftain."

"Perhaps we need to find out if one of them is related to General Green River, no?" Jean joined in on the ribbing, and Jacob shook his head but kept a watchful eye on his boys.

In the morning, they began their trip back to the compound. Finally, they received the answers they wanted, no Cherokee movement, so it seems only the bandits and the Loyalists are stirring up trouble in the up-country. After saying their farewells to Yanabe and the Catawbas, Jacob led them back out onto the trails.

The weather was cold and grey, a wind moving through the trees with a hint of sleet. Robert commented on the cold, and Samuel began to tell them stories of the cold scouting expeditions they did up in New York around Carillon. The boys listened intently as he spoke of the Battle on Snowshoes.

They passed through Pine Tree Hill to replenish some supplies. They learned of more burning and banditry above Ninety-Six at the shop. Some of these attacks were near the Cherokee lands, and some locals were concerned. However, Jacob settled their fears from what the Catawbas told them, which seemed to ease their worries.

The days varied, from clear and sunny to grey and cold as Winter and Fall wrestled for land control. Jacob admitted he missed the distinct change of seasons from up in New York, amongst those tall grey sentinels of the mountains and the multitude of colors as the leaves changed.

Continuing through Stateburg and heading towards Manchester, they came upon a mounted troop of South Carolina Cavalry. As they approached either on the road, Jacob stopped, and the cavalry leader raised his hand and stopped just before Jacob.

"Lieutenant Edward Brown, at your service," he indicated, nodding to Jacob. "May I ask who you are and what news from the north?"

Jacob nodded. "Captain Jacob Clark, with Sergeant Major Penny and Lieutenant Langy of the 2nd Regiment, on leave recuperating from injuries."

Brown seemed to recognize the name. "Colonel Horry speaks of you, sir, from time to time concerning your previous exploits."

Jacob smiled, "Send my regards and best wishes back to the colonel when you see him next. As for the north, brigands and possible Loyalist attacks up above Ninety-Six. We are returning from the Catawbas at Newtown; they have not seen any Cherokee activity. So it's these bloody bandits and cutthroats out again."

Brown nodded his head in understanding. "Thank you for the information; we'll ride up there and take a look."

"Any word from the South?" Jacob asked, and Brown shook his head.

"Would you believe quiet? General Lincoln is trying to reform the army, and the governor is also working on reforming the militia. Captain Polk and his Rangers are keeping an eye on the Savannah River."

Jacob nodded his head in thanks. "Safe journey, lads!" he called out as Brown waved their column forward, and the dragoons continued up the road. Once they rode past, Jacob led them in the opposite direction towards Manchester.

"You see those dragoons," Richard commented to Robert and Thomas. "I think I might want to be a dragoon. Don't have to walk everywhere."

Jacob snorted but kept his comment to himself. He knew a lot of work was involved in the dragoons, especially caring for the horse. All he had to take care of was his feet. They spotted no one else on the road except o few farmers bringing in late crops and some woodcutters.

Jacob and the others spent the next couple of weeks healing up and preparing the compound for winter. They also ensured enough dried meat and other foodstuff was stored, and a good number of the muskets, shot, and powder they had secured from the bandits during the Regulator War were serviceable.

"Might be a good idea to stash some smoked venison and other game, along with a few muskets, shot and powder up in the hunting lands," Jacob discussed one morning with Samuel, Peter, and Jean.

"If the worse happens, and the British takeover, they'll come looking for all of us. I also have a bad feeling that those loyal to the Crown, those troublemakers we saw up in Dorchester, will come out in force."

They all looked at each other and could see what Jacob was talking about. It was the reality that some of their leaders were unwilling to address, that they could lose and the British would resume control with a vengeance.

"They will search all of our homes, taking food and looking for weapons, calling it foraging, but we know what they are up to. So we must be ready to move the family and get away if we have to."

Peter patted the stonewall that ran between the barn and Jacob's house. A nice, strong wall ran around the entire compound, connecting the three houses, the barns, and the workshop. In a sense, the compound was a small fort built because of the Cherokee so the neighbors could come to in time of trouble.

"We can take care of ourselves," Peter stated, "with enough of the hunters and the neighbors if they come here, we can keep them outside."

They stayed home through December, enjoyed the German holiday of *Weihnachten*, and healed up. Jacob tried his arms and shoulders, moving them around. The ribs had healed nicely.no real deformity, and the pain was gone. The muscles and tendons around the ribs also recovered, and Gerda's herbs removed the bruising. Finally, Jacob knew it was time to return to Charles Town.

Putting on his new regimental coat that a tailor had sewed in Dorchester, Jacob gathered his gear and, spotting his old rifle leaning in the corner, decided to bring it with him. He had sent it home with Peter just before the campaign; now, he had a feeling he would need it.

Maria and Helga finished making a food bundle of dried meat, fresh bread, and cheese, items Jacob would need as Maria constantly mumbled how they didn't feed Jacob right in the army. Finally, Patrick had Jacob's horse saddled and ready to go. Jacob brought his gear to the waiting horse, the two wolves sitting, waiting expectantly.

Jacob looked down at the full-grown wolves, knowing they would be incredibly beneficial like what he had back up in New York during the last war. But this army and its regulations frowned on such activity, so the wolves had to stay home.

"Sorry, lads, perhaps later," Jacob commented, and the wolves cocked their heads to the side in the way of the wolves asking why.

Maria brought out the food bundle and secured it to the horse. She straightened out Jacob's uniform; he did not always pay close attention to settling his coat correctly on his shoulders. She wiped the dust off, stood back, and looked at him in his uniform.

"At least you look like the officer you are supposed to be," Maria commented. Then she walked up close to him, looking up into his eyes as Jacob looked down at his wife. Finally, she brought her finger up and placed it under his nose.

"You will stay safe!" she stated, emphasizing the "will" part.

"I will do my best," Jacob commented, "perhaps you need to tell our British friends."

"I just might!" Maria commented, reached up and kissed Jacob, then rested her head on his chest. Then she let go, straightened herself out, and nodded. She has already gone through this, Jacob leaving as he had done in the past.

Helga brought Jacob's helmet to him and handed it up to him. As he placed it on his head, she gave him a stern look and, in a perfect semblance of Maria holding up her finger, "You listen to Mama, you stay safe, Papa, don't get hurt out there!"

Then she hugged Jacob and gave him a mischievous smile, "Love you, Papa!" Then she stepped back and stood with Maria, who smiled and placed her arms around Helga's shoulder. After getting the horse ready, Richard stood next to Maria and Helga while Patrick held Jacob's rifle.

Jacob took a deep breath, then mounted up on his horse. Patrick handed Jacob his rifle, and Jacob nodded his head in thanks. Having completed the same ritual with his family, Samuel rode his horse up and joined Jacob. Even Jean was pampered and cared for like he was an adopted family member, and he joined them.

"You all take care now, and I'll watch over them here," Pater stated, motioning to the compound with his pipe in his hand.

"Make sure they feed you better in the army," Maria stated, with Otti nodding her head along with Helga, "Don't need to see you all skin and bones the next time you visit!"

Jacob took off his helmet in salute. "Yes, ma'am, I will do the best I can though I think I may have to speak to the quartermaster."

Maria blew a kiss to Jacob and then waved as Jacob led Jean and Samuel out of the gate and back to the road. They watched the three rides out before returning to their everyday lives in the compound while Jacob, Jean, and Samuel returned to Charles Town.

CHAPTER 11

1780: THE BRITISH ARRIVE

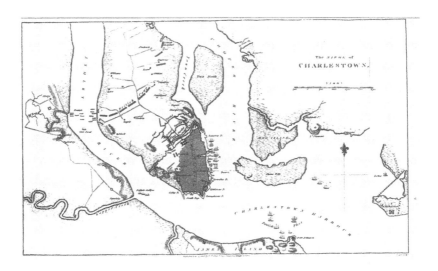

Siege of Charles Town

Charles Town remained a hub of activity between the reformed army and the constant trade flow in and out of the city. Although war may occur, trade continued as long as it did not affect business directly. Maclane, having returned from letting the brigands and thieves loose upon the up-country, now focused on gathering information on the activity there in Charles Town.

He was sitting in his office, having opened a shipping container with the hidden message from British High Command about the invasion force en route. Maclane looked outside through his window as a strong wind blew through the city, leaves, and trash moving in whirlwinds down the streets.

The message hidden in the package indicated that the fleet had sailed but had not arrived when they were supposed to. Maclane was concerned if the French had intercepted it. In addition, he had overheard some of the cargo captains speak of a severe winter gale out in the Atlantic. Maclane communicated with a trusted agent in Savannah using a small packet schooner, who indicated no ships had arrived.

Shrugging his shoulders, Maclane walked to the small fireplace in his office. He tossed the message into the fire to be consumed by the flames. He paced about the room, staying near the warmth of the fire, brooding. He knew this was the time to strike, while the rebel army was disorganized and their morale was low.

As Maclane thought, the crackle of the fire was the only sound; the muffled sound of the dock workers and the wind blowing a loose shudder was the only sound heard. But, in his mind, he was putting the details of the coming tasks he would be responsible for. General Clinton had sent him precise instructions to support the imminent invasion.

He had to continue gathering information on the strength of the rebel army and keep an eye on any reinforcements or news of significant desertions. In addition, he was to immediately report any sightings of the French Fleet in the area around Charles Town. Finally, General Clinton was concerned that his invasion force would be caught at sea, their military superiority negated in a naval battle.

The fact the fleet had not arrived on time did make Maclane concerned. Winter was passing, and spring was approaching. He knew this was the time to start the military campaign to take Charles Town and, as they did in Georgia, secure all of South Carolina before moving north. However, Maclane was frustrated as he could not know what delayed the fleet's arrival.

Once the siege began, Maclane had been instructed to sow discord and cause friction between the civilian and military leaders. General Clinton was adamant that there must be unity of command; the more fracture, the better. Maclane nodded to himself as he already began working on some of the critical city leaders who were not happy at the prospects of a battle. They were very concerned about the destruction of the city and the injuries or deaths of the civilians in the city.

Maclane had his agent in the State Assembly, Richard Pearis. He kept him informed on what the assembly was doing but had already begun sowing the discontent with identified members of the assembly who were more neutral and concerned over losing money than gaining their freedom. So he would use Pearis to keep them off balance.

Maclane moved over, sat at his small desk, and looked at the window as local civilians moved about the street. They had their heads down, holding their hats on in the strong wind, leaves dancing amongst them as they walked. A storm was coming, and he knew it; now, he just had to wait for the fleet to arrive so that the show could begin.

***

Scouts and spies in the north had passed the information about the fleet's departure as it sailed from New York. The scouts followed it along the shore until the fleet veered off into the Atlantic out of sight from the coast and the scout's loss site of it. What small ships they had run into the winter gale and were forced to turn back.

General Lincoln expected the British would bank on the success of their defeat of him at Savannah and capitalize on it. Knowing he would need time to prepare, Lincoln dispatched scouts. Colonel Daniel Horry and his South Carolina Dragoons, Captain Alliston and his Catawba Raccoon Company, and Captain Polk's Rangers. They were to scout and watch the Savannah and give them an early warning.

As the scouts kept an eye out for the British, General Lincoln knew he had to reinforce and build up upon their defenses across the Charles Town Neck that they had already built and make them stronger. So Lincoln started to recall the militia to support strengthening the fortifications. Many were refusing to answer the call. Instead, they were looking to evacuate their families and property.

This stopped when Lincoln instructed that any militia not answering the call to arms would have the property seized. This encouraged the militia to answer the call. Finally, Lincoln recalled all of his forces to consolidate in the city. It was about this that Jacob, Jean, and Samuel learned after arriving at the barracks in Charles Town.

"Well, that's not a good way to get the militia to return by using threats," remarked Samuel after learning what Lincoln had directed. "Isn't that type of threat that this war is being fought over?"

Jean nodded his head in agreement. "Montcalm did the same to us; when he was going after the British, he forced the militia to join if they wanted to or not. So so many joined and then quickly deserted and went home anyway."

After they signed in with the orderly, they headed over and reported to Lieutenant Colonel Marion that they had returned. Marion warmly welcomed them and inquired that they were healthy and ready for duty, to which they all nodded.

"Well, you look much better than when you left here," Marion commented, looking at the three men before him. "You even got new uniforms, all brand new men!"

Then Marion got down to business. "As you can imagine, after that battle in Savannah, we did a return of men who were healthy enough to remain in the regiments. But we suffered greatly and lost a good number of our men."

Marion paused, reflecting on the losses, the decimation of the proud men of the 2nd Regiment, considered a veteran regiment, was now reduced by half.

"What is left of our regiment has been consolidated with the remnants of the Sixth; we barely have enough men for all three regiments." Marion looked seriously at Jacob, Jean, and Samuel, "We have only two hundred and forty men for the entire regiment, and company strength is around twenty-five men."

Jacob looked to Jean and Samuel, not realizing the losses had been so high. Marion continued. "Because we had to consolidate the remnants of two regiments into one, as much as I want you to take command of a company, there simply isn't one available, Captain Clarke."

Jacob nodded his head in understanding. "What is to be our role, sir? Where would you have us, sir?" Jacob asked, to which Marion responded with a slight grin on his face

"While there is no regular company to give you to command, I have a special company that I call The Colonel's Company, where you will serve in your best capacity."

Jacob furrowed his eyes thinking, and asked, "Our best capacity?" Marion smiled, nodded, and answered, "Yes, your best capacity, conducting special tasks that I may need you two to perform, just like you have been doing so well."

"Tasks, such as?" Jacob asked, and Marion smiled once more.

"Raids, ambushes, and scouting. I want you to stay connected with our Catawba friends in the Raccoon Company and even the Rangers under Captain Polk. You will be our force to react and get ahead of the British or their Loyalist friends."

The three smiled; while not a traditional command, it was a command, and it was something they were more used to, non-traditional. Marion could see they were pleased with the assignment, having them in mind when he created the company.

"I will give you a handpicked section of light infantry, most of whom you know as you trained them or had been with us with Middleton. I am sending you up to watch Bacon's Bridge, as we all know the British will be coming soon if our information from up north is correct."

Jacob nodded, "How accurate is the information? When is the estimation of their arrival?" Jacob recalled this was similar to how it happened back in 1776 when the British first tried for Charles Town, having sailed down from New York.

"From our estimation, they should already be here; somewhere south, more likely, they sailed to Savannah," Marion answered.

"The rest of the deployments?" Jacob asked.

"General Lincoln deployed the First South Carolina Regiment to garrison Fort Moultrie on Sullivan's Island. The Third South Carolina Regiment, the rest of the Second Regiment, and the Charles Town Artillery are manning the trench and two redoubts across the neck."

"So we're back in the trenches again?" Samuel asked, and Marion nodded.

General Lincoln has put the rest of the militia and city workers on improving their defenses. But, the trees and brush were first cleared before the defensive line. This includes houses, so there was nothing but a clear field of fire."

"That should make the farmers happy," Samuel stated, "but I guess it's better than being caught in the middle of a battle. Would lose their homes anyways."

Marion nodded. "We are still finishing and strengthening the line across the neck to include the new Hornwork."

"Hornwork, sir?" Jean asked.

"A small fort built in front of the defensive line, following our example out on the island, constructed of the spongy palmetto logs, covered in the line and oyster shells, and armed with eighteen cannons."

Jacob nodded, "Sounds like he is at least doing everything he can to prepare for an attack. We can hold if we have strong defenses across the neck and can keep the British fleet out of the harbor."

"If providence smiles upon us," Marion stated, "the chosen men are waiting for you in the barracks area."

Jacob, Jean, and Samuel saluted, Marion returned it, and then he returned to get the regiment reformed. They headed over to where the chosen men were waiting, and when they arrived, Marion had been right. So many familiar and smiling faces greeted Jacob, Jean, and Samuel. All came out and shook their hands in welcome, and Jacob nodded his head to the men.

"Well, lads, good to see you all once again." Jacob began, "We're off to Bacon's Bridge to keep an eye out for our friends, the British. See you to your gear. Do we need anything from the quartermaster?"

"No, sir," answered one of the chosen men, "the colonel knew we would head out as soon as you would arrive, so we have a week's worth of rations, powder, and ball all packed and ready to go."

Jacob nodded his head in approval. "Well then, let's get our gear on, be ready to move."

The company of chosen men was insignificant; only fifteen plus the three made eighteen. They were excellent light infantrymen; many were long hunters and expert shots. Some had served with Jacob and Marion in Middleton's Regiment and knew light infantry and Ranger skills.

Jacob, along with Samuel and Jean, went to their barracks room; sure enough, their gear was waiting for them. Jacob went over his pack to ensure all he needed was in there. He was pleasantly surprised none of his items had "walked off mysteriously."

"Well now, this is a pleasant sight," Samuel remarked. "My pack somehow is brand new, a nice French knapsack, and it has no holes in it."

Jean checked his gear and noticed it was also a new knapsack with all of his belongings inside. He nodded, impressed with the new pack and his kit already packed. "The men must have watched out for us, no?"

Jacob nodded, noticing his pack was new as well. Securing their gear, they headed out to the waiting chosen men, each with a knowing grin on their faces. Jacob looked at them all and smiled back in return.

"Thanks, men, we appreciate what you did with us. Let's head out!" As the men were on foot, Jacob decided they would leave the horses behind and move on foot with the men. Following the road out of the city, they made their way through the work areas in the rear of the defenses. They passed numerous teams moving around, working on strengthening the walls or building gabions.

They passed through the redoubt they had manned against Prevost's bluff and could see this new fort, the Hornwork. They also saw another ditch and a double palisade wall built in front of the defensive line. Jacob looked over the ground with a critical eye and could see that the construction was intended to break up any neat British lines if they advanced against the earthworks.

Jacob had to admit that Lincoln's defensive plan appeared very sound. Along with reinforcing where the confrontation will occur out on the neck, to deny the British navigation aids, the tall white steeple of Saint Michaels blackened.

"Yes, sir, the general has kept everyone busy," remarked one of the chosen men. "The general even had boat crews head out and removed all of the buoys, and even had the old Fort Johnson was blown up to prevent it from falling into the enemy's hands."

Jacob nodded in understanding and appreciation of the efforts, having been involved in a few sieges in his time. Lincoln was making prudent decisions and work details that had to be done. Everyone was working. Militiamen, continentals, citizens, and Negroes worked long hours to prepare for the coming attack.

Hefting his rifle, Jacob led the small company out and headed towards the bridge. Once they reached the top of the neck, he turned to look back at the impressive site before them of the defenses being built. They all stopped to look and nodded in appreciation. Jacob looked over at Jean, who seemed to have a faraway look.

"Almost like your defenses on Carillon," Jacob stated, and Jean nodded slowly.

"But we had the guns of the stone fort behind us, not a city that can burn. But still an impressive sight."

Jacob could see his point and nod in agreement. "Well, we don't do anything if we're standing here gawking at the works," Jacob reminded them all, "Let's see to our business."

Taking up their rifles and muskets, the chosen men followed Jacob as he led them towards Bacon Bridge to keep their eyes and ears out for the British or Loyalists.

***

The admiral's cabin on the *Europe* was tight, as General Clinton held a council of war that now most of the convoy had arrived at Savannah. Tarleton didn't like the stuffiness of the room full of officers, even with the cabin windows open for fresh air. The senior leaders who sat around the central table had better access to the fresh air; Tarleton was up against a bulkhead as a minor officer.

The fleet had suffered from the beginning of the campaign, nearly being iced into the harbor as ice flows began to push into New York Harbor, almost crushing a few of the transports. Then, they ran into that terrible winter gale even after they made it out to sea, going further out to avoid being watched from the shore.

Eleven ships were reported missing, including the transport with all their heavy siege artillery aboard. Fighting the storm, a trip that should have taken only ten days instead, took five weeks. Food and water for the crews and the army started becoming scarce. Tarleton shivered when he thought of food; it had taken him a while to get used to eating again, the terrible weather making him and the majority of the army terribly seasick.

Now that the ships rode at their anchors, men began getting their stomachs back under control and getting supplies from Savannah. Though it was February, Clinton was very wary of the weather and wanted to start the campaign as soon as possible, so this council of war was called.

"Gentlemen," Clinton started from the center of the room, "I intend to use these inland waterways to get close to and then invest in Charles Town before the weather wrecks more havoc on us or the heat of the summer arrives."

Instead of sounds of praise, surprisingly, the sound of discontent echoed across the room. The officers did not like the proposed idea. Tarleton, leaning up against the bulkhead, watched and listened as the different senior leaders voiced their concerns. General Clinton had a surprised look as he heard all the low voices.

"Well, gentlemen, what is it?"

"Sir, we have no heavy guns," stated Major Traille of the Royal Artillery. When we lost the *Russia Merchant,* she had all our siege artillery and ammunition. How can we batter down the defenses without our heavy artillery?"

Clinton nodded his head in understanding, pursed his lips, and scratched his chin. Then an idea struck him as he looked above at the ceiling. Then, turning to look at Admiral Arbuthnot, "Admiral, can we get some of your heavy guns to be used in the siege?"

The admiral nodded in agreement. "Why yes, of course. The *Defiance* had foundered just south of here. We can salvage the guns, shot and powder, and get them to you, Major Traille."

Clinton looked over at the major, who nodded that the guns would serve as heavy siege artillery. Then, Clinton looked around the cabin at the assembled officer. "What's the next point of contention? There has to be more to it than just the artillery."

Tarleton looked around the room and saw what the officers were thinking, so he decided to bring up his primary concern.

"Sir, if I may?" he asked, and Clinton nodded. "Tarleton is it? What is on your mind?

"Horses, sir," Tarleton pointed out, "we have no horses, which mean I have no cavalry. No cavalry means you have no eyes and ears to find these rebels or their weak points."

Clinton sat back and nodded his head. Another victim of the gale. To save the ship, the panicking horses were thrown overboard. So, along with the cavalry horses, were the transport horses to drag supplies and artillery. Now they had no horses for scouting or moving equipment.

"Yes, the horses. That will be an issue," agreed Clinton. Although he began to see the officers' points, his plan was not as easy as he had thought. While using the inland waterways may make moving men and material easier, without knowing the land along the river, his ships could come under fire from hidden batteries.

"Right. Gentlemen, I see your points. It does not make sense, nor will I blindly blunder into the countryside and stumble around like a newborn babe. Seeing the men reel from the voyage, the army will camp ashore and recuperate from the travel. I will send for reinforcements and resupply of artillery, shot, and powder from New York and our holdings in the Bahamas."

Looking down at the map of South Carolina and Georgia, Clinton quickly thought before nodding. Then, he looked up at General Patterson, the commander of the Georgia British forces.

"General Patterson, you are to take your men and go after any holdouts here in Georgia. I want you to push these backcountry militiamen away from Charles Town and us."

Then Clinton looked at Major Patrick Ferguson. "Major Ferguson, you are to accompany General Patterson and support his engagement of these rebels."

Finally, he turned back and looked at Tarleton. "Colonel, I need your eyes and ears. You will also go with General Patterson, and I want you to secure mounts for your men from the local area by any means."

Tarleton stood up from his leaning, "Secure mounts by any means, sir?"

Clinton looked at Tarleton and nodded. "Yes, by any means necessary. When we begin this campaign to take Charles Town, I will have cavalry."

Clinton looked at Tarleton, who seemed to hesitate for a moment. "Is there a problem, colonel?"

"Sir, these horses won't be trained, maybe good for pulling a plow or fox hunting at best, not for being cavalry."

Clinton simply raised an eyebrow at Tarleton's statement. "Then you best see to train them before the campaign. The sooner you can secure the horses, the sooner you can train them."

Tarleton nodded in understanding. "And for men, sir? Am I to recruit from the locals as well?" Tarleton was to create a legion composed of cavalry, infantry, and artillery. Only the small detachment of the 17th Light Dragoons was with the expedition and the Georgian cavalry.

Clinton smiled and nodded his head. "Why, of course, you are. You and Major Ferguson are to recruit from these fine Loyal Americans who have gathered to the King's Colors and take the fight to these thankless rebels."

Tarleton nodded in understanding, "Yes, sir, it will be done."

Two days later, after General Patterson departed with Ferguson and Tarleton for their tasks, General Clinton couldn't wait and decided he would secure a beach head closer to the city instead of down in Savannah, which would require crossing the Savannah River. So, he ordered the fleet to raise anchor; they traveled north to the familiar area near Trench Island and Stono Ferry.

Clinton stood on the deck of the *Europe*, watching the longboats travel back and forth from the troop ships and the shore. His cloak pulled tightly around him as a cold, grey rainy day met the invaders as they waded ashore.

"I thought I left this all behind in New York," Clinton mumbled, the color of his cloak pulled high to protect his ears. He thought of his warm house in New York, his warm, crackling fireplaces, and of course, the young Ms. Mellish, his new mistress. His grenadiers and light infantry boats were making their way through the cold, miserable rain and securing the shore.

By that afternoon, his aid told him the landing had been secured. "Well then, let's get this business started!" Clinton headed to his waiting longboat, climbed down the rope ladder, and took a place in the middle of the boat. The crew lowered their oars and began the task of rowing his to the shore. It was a short trip, and soon the bow of the longboat scrapped on the sandy beach, and Clinton stepped onto Southern soil. It was February 12th, 1780, and the invasion had officially begun.

The rain began to pound harder, and Clinton moved to a spot under a large tree whose boughs did keep some of the rain off. General Leslie was experiencing the full force of the driving rain in the evening as his men, composed of the Thirty-Third Regiment of Foot and German Jaegers, pushed out towards the old battleground of Stono Ferry. Clinton found himself a comfortable place amongst the tree's large roots, pulled his cloak tighter around himself, and fell asleep.

He was woken a short time later by a messenger. Wiping the rain from his eyes, Clinton looked up at the messenger. "Yes, what is it?"

"Sir, a report from General Leslie. He has engaged a scouting party who had occupied our old positions at the ferry and chased them off with a few volleys; no fire returned. Have secured the crossing at Stono Ferry, controlling both sides of the river."

Nodding his head, "Excellent news, pass my best regards to General Leslie. The army will cross and continue the advance. Have the engineers repair the fortifications here. Tell the quartermaster we will establish our base of operations here and consolidate our stores and supplies."

The messenger bowed to Clinton, then turned to head off to pass the messages. Crossing his feet and pulling his cloak tighter around him, Clinton allowed himself to smile even as the rain dripped from his hat. His plan was working, and the campaign was shaping up. In the morning, he would push on once the sun rose, and hopefully, the rain stopped.

When the sun rose, the rain stopped, but the roads were muddy and passable. Without cavalry to scout and screen the army, Clinton used his light infantry to scout ahead and screened his advance. He was surprised that none of the rebels came out to stop or at least challenge the advance.

It was two days since Clinton crossed at Stono Ferry, and on February 15, Clinton stepped onto James Island, south of Charles Town. He was still concerned that the rebels were waiting to ambush him, as he still hadn't made any contact with rebel forces. In the distance, Clinton could see the church spires in the city, and he nodded in satisfaction. Then he shivered as a chill wind blew in from the west, and the first snowflakes began to flutter around and settle on the red and blue uniforms of the British Army.

General Cornwallis joined Clinton as he looked skyward at the snowflakes dancing on the cold wind.

"Your orders, sir?" Cornwallis asked, also looking with concern at the snowflakes. A winter campaign and fight is as bad and sometimes worse than trying to fight a battle in the rainy season.

"Have the light infantry conduct a sweep of the local area to locate any rebels who may be waiting to ambush the column. The rest of the men will set up camp here. Send quartermasters back to Stone Ferry to bring up supplies."

Cornwallis nodded and then turned to send out the orders. Clinton turned back and continued to look at the city in the distance, going over in his mind what it would take to secure the city. *"A good show of force may be enough to intimidate the city leaders into surrendering,"* Clinton thought. *"Better than what Prevost tried. Hopefully, the rebels are still broken from Savannah and have lost their will to fight. That would make it so much easier."*

***

As the snowflakes fell and swirled around them, Jacob, Jean, and Samuel smiled like kids as they watched the snowflakes dance in the wind. While they had been living in South Carolina for a while, they had to admit grudgingly missed the cold, brutal winters of the northern frontiers they had grown up in, Jacob more than Samuel and Jean.

"The winters around Montreal were brutal sometimes," Jean commented as he watched the snow lightly fall. "But it is nice to see snow again, as long as it doesn't stay long, no?"

Samuel shook his head. "I'm for no; I have become accustomed to the more comfortable winters down here than up in those mountains of New York. At least we don't have to worry about the ice flowing through the hut."

Jacob walked along Bacon's Bridge, his shoes clunking on the wooden boards, footprints left in the snow. Cold and grey Ashley River gurgled under the bridge, heading towards the coast.

As the three walked around the far end of the bridge, they looked at one another, noses red from the cold, and they smiled, laughing, making their wispy breaths curl around them. The soldiers born and raised in South Carolina looked at the three former northerners as if they were insane. Shaking their heads, they continued splitting their time, watching the approach and stomping their feet to stay warm.

Jacob stopped laughing as he spotted the dark green flash of a coat, followed by another in the woods across from them. They were moving low, trying to stay within the trees, but their uniforms were a different color, green. They were not of their army.

"To arms, to arms!" Jacob yelled, Jean and Samuel, spinning quickly to see what had drawn Jacob's attention. They, too, spotted the green uniformed German Jaegers moving through the trees at a crouch, their rifles held low.

The company quickly took up its arms and formed ranks. When the first section was ready, Jacob gave the order to present, aim, and fire. The muskets cracked and boomed, and the men automatically began to reload. The Jaegers took cover and began to fire back, but Jacob knew to beat them was to load faster, shoot more, and then drive them off.

Samuel took charge of a section, and then Jean the third, with Jacob, began a running fight, where his unit fired and loaded as Samuel's section loaded and as they loaded, then Jean's section. A tiny pause between sections and a constant rate of fire kept the Jaegers' heads down.

Then Jacob began to advance the sections in a leapfrog to close with the Jaegers, as a few of their riflemen got their shots off, and some of Jacob's men fell. Jacob pressed on, "Fire and load on the run!" he commanded, and the fight continued as they charged towards the Jaegers. The firing from the Jaegers slackened.

They broke through the tree line and noticed the Jaegers had left. Scanning the ground, they spotted blood trails and tracks; Jacob gave the order to follow them.

"Jean, hold the bridge, Samuel, take your section and follow the tracks heading south!"

Jacob led his section, personally tracking the blood and footprints while his men followed close behind, watching the woods around them. Finally, the trail led to a thick brush area, where he found a dead Jaeger sprawled face down in the dirt. Jacob's men quickly spread out to cover Jacob as he knelt next to the dead Jaeger.

Rolling the man over, Jacob saw the two large bullet holes from their musketry that had sapped his life away, giving them the trail they had been following through the light snow cover. Jacob quickly searched the dead German, found nothing of any military importance, but did secure his rifle and took his cartridge box and haversack. The rifle was shorter and slightly heavier than his rifle, but it felt good in his hands.

"Might be able to put this to good use," Jacob stated as he stood up, looking at the Jaeger Rifle. "Secure the dead man, and we'll bury him near the bridge." His men nodded, and four slung their muskets and picked up the dead German. When they arrived at the bridge, they went off to the side and placed the body next to two more that Samuel had found in an open space.

Samuel, with Jean and Lieutenant Parker, who had just arrived waiting. Samuel smiled and asked, "Found one, did you?" Holding the rifle up, Jacob nodded he had.

"We found one and followed a few trails, so they must have been scouting our positions." Samuel nodded towards Jean, "Jean and his men found a dead German over on the far right."

Jacob looked over at Jean, who shrugged his shoulders and nodded. "Oui, we found one but saw a few tracks heading away quickly. Found the cartridges they had used to load with."

"I guess we did our job and slowed them down some, right, Lieutenant?" Samuel asked Lieutenant Parker, who had just ridden from Charles Town with supplies and news from General Lincoln.

Lieutenant Parker smiled and nodded his head. Jacob shrugged and smiled, "Good job, everyone!"

Jacob yelled out, and the men cheered back, "Huzzah!" He then moved off to the side to speak with Lieutenant Parker while Samuel and Jean went to secure shovels to bury the dead Germans.

"General Lincoln believes the British are close and have started to scout out our defenses," Parker began as he nodded towards where they were burying the dead Germans. "Seems you have confirmed his suspicions."

"What is our commander planning?" Jacob asked.

"He has begun calling in the militia," Parker explained as he kicked some snow from the road. "However, when they arrived, they refused to enter the city. They said they feared smallpox because of the outbreak in '76. So they are manning the defensive line for now."

Jacob nodded, understanding why they would be afraid to enter, the disease tending to break out when people live so close together. Parker continued to update Jacob on the plan.

"The First Regiment is still holding Fort Moultrie, and as Fort Johnson is no longer in good enough conditions to be defended, was blown up. The lighthouse was also blown so that it won't help British navigation. However, we received reinforcements from North Carolina as General Lillington arrived."

Then, Parker had a concerned look on his face. "We have spotters up in Saint Michael's steeple, and they can see the British fleet to the south and campfires on Johns Island. So they are here; they must have arrived south of Stono Ferry."

"That makes sense, seeing scouts. So why aren't they using cavalry? Have any horsemen been seen?" Jacob asked, and Parker shook his head no.

"No horses; none of our cavalries has spotted any. So either they are holding them in reserve, or they don't have horses. That is the assessment from Major Maham of our dragoons."

Jacob nodded his head, still finding it odd that the British were scouting with light infantry than cavalry. Of course, during the French and Indian War, he had done many scouting and screening actions on behalf of the British Army. But then again, they had no cavalry with them.

Thanking Parker, Jacob went over to check on the wounded being loaded on a cart and taken to the city. Parker and his men would take them while they remained at the bridge. He wished them safe journeys and to get healed up as the cart headed towards the city. Snow began to fall lightly again, the sky a deep leaden grey.

The company remained at the bridge for another week, and during that week, the British probed again, but this time it was red-coated infantry. Using the same tactics, they split into three sections and fired upon the advancing British. Jacob led his section, except Jean went into action, and Samuel remained behind to secure the bridge.

Bringing his new rifle to his shoulder, Jacob liked the rifle's balance, making it easier to aim and track moving targets. He was rewarded when he tracked a running redcoat and, pulling the trigger, the man dropped to the ground, tumbling once.

Jacob nodded and began to reload the rifle while he continued to give the command to fire. Once again, the company drove the British probe away with little to no injuries during this skirmish. They tracked the blood trails and footprints as it had snowed again and iced the ground in some areas.

Jacob and his men were stalking through some brush, following a blood trail and footprints, when Jacob heard the sound of a man's labored breath and held his hand up to stop his men. They took a knee and listened, only hearing the wheezing sound of the unseen man.

Waving his hand forward, they slowly advanced; Jacob, moving a large bush out of the way with his rifle barrel to see a wounded British soldier sitting on the ground, leaning against a tree with a hand covering a wound in his side. He was breathing hard, eyes closed and the wisp of his breath curling around the tree leaves.

As Jacob rose and approached, rifle pointing at the wounded soldier, his eyes opened and focused on Jacob.

"Don't worry about me, mate," he wheezed, "I don't have me, Bess, and I am in no condition to fight. I am your prisoner." The man coughed a couple of times, wincing as he coughed.

Jacob knelt to look at the wound, the British soldier not interfering, just sitting and not moving. Jacob ran his hand along the injury and though bloody, could tell he had broken ribs, just like he had after Savannah.

"Ball must have creased and broke your ribs," Jacob stated as he stood up, "you're lucky to be alive."

The soldier tried to laugh, but the pain of his broken ribs made him wince again and groan.

"Luck, you say," he replied around a groan from the pain, "I think we have a different meaning of lucky!"

Jacob had the men help stand their prisoner up and helped him back to the bridge. Then, as it was a slow pace with the injured man, they ran into Samuel leading his section coming along their old path.

"Where the bloody hell have you been?" Samuel demanded before he spotted the wounded prisoner between the two men.

"Ah, I see. You bagged one."

The two sections returned to the bridge, and Jacob saw the man's injuries. Recalling what the surgeons did for him, he covered the wounds and then wrapped a tight bandage around the torso of the wounded man. He grunted a few times as Jacob wrapped, and Jacob chuckled to himself.

"I take it you have experience with this?" the wounded man asked, and Jacob nodded.

"Had broken my ribs at Spring Hill Redoubt outside Savannah, so I have been in your shoes."

The wounded man looked at Jacob as he finished wrapping the bandage. "Aye, I imagine so. That was a bloody day for both of us.

A new company under Captain Blake arrived from General Lincoln, told Jacob that they were taking over, and passed to him that the general was asking for information about the advancing British forces.

"General Moultrie wants more information, and the colonel thought you would be the best to go get it. They want the British found, the exact positions noted, and if possible, strength. They are already discussing this is another probe like the last time, or is it what we feared, an actual attack."

Jacob, keeping Jean and Samul plus the section he had led, would be the scouts. The other two sections with the wounded British soldier began their march to the city, using a cart to pull the injured British with them.

After Captain Blake took over the bridge, Jacob took a path that paralleled the route the British had used to probe to ensure they wouldn't run into more British or Germans, as they stuck to the woods as best as possible. The sky stayed grey, and the wind was cold, but there was no snow, and luckily. No rain was falling.

As they were closing on a stream crossing, they heard the sound of horses which Jacob hissed, "Take cover!" The men dove into the bushes. A troop of horse came trotting by, and they were not theirs.

The men wore dark green uniforms faced in black and wearing black leather helmets with black bearskin fur along the helmet's crest. The horses stopped, some watering in the stream as three men looked at a map and then pointed down the road.

"Our objective is that way, Colonel Tarleton, down that road." An officer nodded; Jacob suspected this was the officer named Tarleton, who gave the command to resume their ride. Jacob watched the horsemen ride past, placing the man's name in his memory for later.

"Well, it seems they have found some horses," Samuel whispered to Jacob, who nodded, "The general will probably want to know this."

Jacob continued to move his men along the river until they came to a point where they could see the advancing British. In the distance were the ruins of Fort Johnson, having been blown earlier. In and amongst the ruins, British soldiers could be observed.

A column of British redcoats was on the march and heading up the coastal road towards Charles Town.

"That's a lot of British," commented Samuel, and Jacob had to agree. "I don't think this is a probe. That's more than what we saw crossing the Savannah when they made the first push against the city. So this may be it!"

They moved away, headed back in a different route, along the Ashley River, and found the British were bringing up flatboats and longboats, stockpiling supplies. Once again, they went to the ground and slowly approached where they could observe the British from concealment.

"Looks like this is where they will ferry the army over," Jacob commented, "We better get this info back to General Lincoln."

Slowly, they backed away and moved towards the city. Like the sunset, Jacob felt it would be safer to spend the night on the field instead of try approach the defensive line in the dark. They found a thicket, and it rained on the men that night as they tried to rest. While it was miserable, it helped to hide them from the horsemen who rode past again.

Jacob watched the road, his blanket coat helping to conceal him and keep most of the rain off. This was not good; the British now had cavalry and were using them to scout ahead. They would have to be careful in their movement. Jacob turned his head as he heard someone approach, and it was Jean.

"You need to get some rest too, no?" Jean asked, and Jacob nodded his head. Jean had traded his white French blanket coat for one of their green ones, helping him blend in more.

"You look good in green, "Jacob commented, "It suits you."

Jacob could tell Jean was giving him a dirty look but played along as part of their ordinary ribbing from the old days. "If you can't beat them, join them, no? Is that not how it is?"

The two men quietly chuckled before looking out into the wet night. "Not like our war, is it?" Jacob asked, feeling odd that he could say "our war" as now they were on the same side.

"No, my friend, it's not," Jean replied, looking at Jacob. "Neither of us had to deal with horses; this is a different way of fighting; we have to be more cautious."

The following day, they returned to the city undetected and reported what they had observed to General Lincoln. Lincoln shook his head; this was not good news and thanked Jacob for the report. After that, Jacob and the section returned to the company and supported the construction of the defenses.

The British continued to move steadily, and more reports were coming in about these green-coated cavalrymen making it hard to scout and keeping most of their forces close to the city. Finally, as Jacob and his men were working on the Hornwork, they received news on the 22nd that Major Maham had led his cavalry on a scout of the British at Stono Ferry.

They had a run of good luck, avoiding these green uniformed cavalry, and captured a British picket of an officer and eight men. However, Maham did confirm the British were still approaching in force and would soon be on the neck itself.

On the 23rd, the weather made the digging more miserable by snowing, sleeting, and dropping icy rain that froze the ground in and around the defenses. Most workers were spending their time making fires to stay warm, while only a few men worked. The next day, the sun came out, the temperatures warmed, and the ground turned mud.

Jacob and the Second Regiment stayed in the city; only a few scouting parties had been sent out. They all waited for news from these scouts, especially about how far away the British were. News trickled to them that a small detachment from Pulaski's Legion engaged a British foraging party near Stono Ferry. They did kill or wound about half of the British before returning to the city.

On the morning of the 26th, as the morning formation was being conducted, the sound of heavy cannon fire could be heard from the direction of Fort Johnson. Not liking that the British had taken the fort, Lincoln sent the South Carolina Navy to deal with the British, even if they were in ruins.

As Jacob and his men strengthened the defenses and drilled with their muskets and the guns in case the artillerymen needed help, the navy bombarded the old fort. The naval gunfire went on for a week; Jacob, Jean, and Samuel, along with some of the men, would go to a vantage point to watch, using Jacob's telescope.

They could see the British were building new earthworks in ruins, and the navy was trying to knock them down. Jacob also observed the British had brought up their cannons, and an artillery duel was in place. The two sides were trading shots, and Jacob started to chuckle.

"What's so funny?" Samuel asked.

"Now the shoe is on the other foot. We are bombarding their redoubt while they did the same to us back in '76. It seems history repeats itself, except we are on different sides of this fight."

***

General Clinton observed the action from the tree line as the rebel ships fired on their redoubt built within the ruins of the old Fort Johnson. He looked at the tumbled piles of tabby and old Palmetto logs, appearing as the ribs of a great dead beast.

Between these mounds and just behind was where they were building the redoubt.

The cannon balls screamed and crashed around the redoubt, causing minor damage. Nevertheless, the British engineers and German grenadiers from General von Kospoth continued building the redoubt and moving up two heavy, 24-pound cannons to fire on the rebel ships.

Their redoubt was built on the only open space; however, as they dug the earthworks, remains of the dead had been dug up. General Clinton later found out the space had been an old cemetery for two regiments of British soldiers who had garrisoned a now destroyed barracks. He had them reburied in a mass grave nearby, having a chaplain say words over the remains, not wanting any bad luck to interfere with the campaign

Clinton scoffed with the thought that he was not usually a superstitious man, but why to take the chances. Then, turning to an aide close by, motioned for him to come up to receive instructions.

"Take this to Admiral Arbuthnot; have the fleet approach the bar as we have moved artillery to cover his approach. He is to drive these rebel ships away."

The aide took down the message and then turned to deliver the message as Clinton returned to watch the action, pacing slowly with his hands behind his back. Looking over the point, he saw the city in the distance, his goal. Everything proceeded to plan; his light infantry was already on the mainland and securing a bridge while skirmishing with rebel infantry and cavalry.

He then looked to the other side of the city, on the peninsula where the real work would begin. With artillery posted here, and the Royal Navy to take position off the city, he will be able to move the rest of the army to build siege lines and invest in the city. Then, as he had hoped, perhaps his overwhelming force would be enough to intimidate the city leaders into capitulating instead of fighting a prolonged siege.

"We will just have to wait and see," he muttered as he continued to pace and watch the cannonade. "We will have to see."

CHAPTER 12

THE SIEGE OF CHARLES TOWN

The troop of horses followed in a staggered column along the road before Tarleton held up his hand to halt the horsemen. They had crested a hill, and he wanted to look at the countryside ahead, concerned they would run into rebel cavalry. But, as he tried to look with his telescope, the horse he rode kept shifting and swaying, making it hard to look through it.

"Come now, you nasty brute!" Tarleton growled at his horse as he pulled the reins to settle the horse. "You work with me, and I'll work with you!"

He had led his Legion into Beaufort and secured all the horses they could find. Granted, now his men were mounted, but these horses were more for the farm pulling plows than the fine horses they had loaded in New York but now rested at the bottom of the Atlantic.

As Tarleton scanned the area, the horse stopped shifting and bent its head down to nibble on some tall grass. He had been tasked to locate the rebels while he rode to join General Patterson's division, who was already ahead of them near Charles Town. As much he wanted to run into either this Luzon's and his lancers, or any of the rebel cavalry, he knew that his horses were no match and could be a decisive factor in whether or not he would win the encounter.

"We bloody have to get these brutes bloody well trained up before we engage these rebels," Tarleton stated to Captain Lindsey, who rode next to him. "How would it look if we were beaten by these rebels back in England?"

"Not very well, sir," Lindsey replied, as he nodded his head in agreement, "Not very well indeed."

"Still, we have a job to do." Tarleton continued, "let's see to completing it!" Waving his hand forward, the column began trotting down the road towards Charles Town. It wouldn't be long before they rejoined the army; they could hear the sound of the cannons from their location, motivating them to get into the action.

***

General Lincoln looked out upon the defenses before him, then down at a map showing the general fortifications of the city. Then, taking up his telescope, he could see the British redoubt and artillery occupying the old Fort Johnson ruins. He also knew from his scouts that the British had crossed the Wappo Cut and even repaired the bridge.

Lowering his telescope, he looked at the activity of the men finishing the final sections of the defensive line. It looked strong, well-dug earthen work tied into small redoubts and the Hornwork. The Hornwork is an 18-gun earthen fort designed to anchor their defenses, taking the neck into their deadly firing arcs.

"But will it be enough?" he asked softly, "will it hold when the siege begins?" Lincoln knew the British would not foolishly do a frontal assault on his defensive line, nor did he think they would try an amphibious landing on the city.

"No, they will do a proper siege, digging their approaches until their artillery is close enough to pound us and the city into dust."

He had issued orders that the sentries be ever watchful, and they were to be relieved every half hour. To help this, he had directed that the steeple bell of Saint Michaels ring every fifteen minutes. Finally, the sentries were to call out "all is well" to the sentry, who repeated the call-up and down the line.

Learning from the Prevost attempt earlier in the city, Lincoln ensured no one would accidentally fire their muskets at friendlies. He strictly forbade the firing near the lines or camps. He even went to the decree patrols were to go through the city and, without firing their muskets, kill all of the stray dogs so their barking may not cause the defenders to think the British were attacking.

"*Those city leaders didn't like that order,*" Lincoln thought as he weighed decisions on how to defend the city. "*I must do what I feel is right to protect this city and defend it to the best of my ability!*"

He did have some good news; at least more reinforcements had arrived from North Carolina, and 600 Continentals under General Hogun had arrived. These veterans had fought with Washington, and Lincoln would put them to good use. Moreover, he knew the attack was coming soon. The previous night the British had launched rockets that had landed in the city and set some buildings on fire. Thinking this was a signal to attack, the men took up their positions in the line, but no battle occurred.

"*What are you up to?*" Lincoln thought, "*You have the advantage, I must admit.*"

He had just learned that the British occupied the old lighthouse that he had blown up and were emplacing cannons. Those guns with the redoubt on Fort Johnson could hit the city and cover the river. The British had burned down a house on Fenwick Point; he assumed it was to clear fields of fire.

"*Their warships have not attempted to cross the bar, which is very strange.*" So Lincoln thought, looking out to sea passed the point where the ruins of Fort Johnson lay. His small fleet of South Carolina and a few Continental Navy frigates were still no match for the Royal Navy. Turning, Lincoln headed towards the city, "Need to go have some words with Admiral Whipple on how we're going to deal with the Royal Navy."

Mounting his horse, his aid and a few staffers mounted their horses and began to ride towards the city and speak with the admiral. "Need to see if we can hold this Five Fathom Hole or not."

***

Jaeger Johanne Kleist crouched low in the flatboat; the sun was just clearing the top of the trees as the morning arrived. For a spring day, it was still cold in the morning before the heat of the day warmed them. Kleist watched the shore as his mind was back in Germany, comparing the morning's cold with that of his home.

"At least home, I don't have to deal with these damn deadly snakes near water or in the fields, and these damn dragons we find in the swamps!"

Kleist shook his head and returned to focusing on the task at hand. They needed to find a landing point on this Ashley River for their army, and they were sent to find it. They had several flatboats filled with his company of Jaegers, plus British Light Infantry. For support, an armed row galley escorted them.

"Crack! Whiz!"

Kleist automatically brought his rifle to his shoulder, looking for the shooter. Instead, they were passing what he had been told during their briefing was Drayton Hall.

"Crack! Splash!"

Another ball flew the ball, landing in the water near Kleist. He scanned, looking over the short barrel of his rifle, and just caught the puff of grey smoke in some bushes near the house.

"Damn American Long rifles!" growled Kleist. They had better range than his rifle, but he was easier to use in the woods because of its compact size. He had learned it was German immigrants who were gunsmiths, had settled in Pennsylvania that had brought their design with them, and made the long rifles that now fire on them.

They kept watching the shore, but no more fire, and the expedition continued along the Ashley River. Finally, after going about four miles, they spotted what appeared to be a good position for their army on a raised bank. They could see a house on the bank, and seeing they had already been fired upon, the row galley came up and fired its cannon into the house.

While no rebel artillery fired back, men scrambled from the house and began to fire their muskets at their flatboats. The balls whizzed by but caused no damage.

"Have at them!" was commanded, and the boats began to head towards the shore, "Commence fire, fire at will!"

Kleist brought his rifle up to his shoulder and, seeing a rebel loading his musket, took aim and fired his rifle. Through the grey smoke, he could not see the rebel from the bank but just began to load his rifle. Kleist and his fellow Jaegers spread out when the boat hit the shore, sweeping to the right side of the house while the Light Infantry went to the left.

As Kleist advanced around the house, he could see horse tracks and some paper cartridges from where the rebels had loaded their muskets. They met on the other side of the house with the light infantry, who shook their heads no, not finding any rebels.

"Sir, look over there!" one of the light infantry yelled, pointing in the distance. The commander of the light infantry pulled out his telescope and looked at where the soldier was pointing.

"Some negroes watching us, that's all." He commented, lowering and closing his telescope. "They appear to be watching more than engaging. Let's see to securing this site for the army."

***

Jacob's blanket coat flapped in the cold wind as the rain came down in sheets, covering the sound of their footsteps as they crept through the woods and headed towards Fenwick Point. They had been sent out to scout what the British were up to and determined strength and intent.

He hoped it would be enough to keep the primed powder dry by using his old mittens to cover his lock on the Jaeger Rifle he carried. The rain helped blend the colors of their coats with the trees and brush, allowing them to blend in. The daylight was fading, which also helped.

The scouting party was Jacob, Jean, and Samuel, plus three other men from the Colonel's Company, all veteran scouts who crept through the trees. They moved in a single file, watching and listening to their surroundings, as they knew they were getting close. Since they departed Bacon's Bridge, they had been watching for the green uniformed cavalry but had not seen them.

The trees and brush were starting to thin out, and the scouts began to crouch down and move more slowly until they came out to a tree line. Jacob knew they were close, but not at the point yet; taking his bearings, and led the scouts back into the woods before continuing in a more westerly direction.

Dusk was settling, and the light faded when Jacob spotted the twinkle of campfires in the distance. He turned back and motioned with his hands to be careful before crouching low and moving forward. The rain had stopped, so they had to be more cautious not to make any noise, though the ground was soft and wet.

As they got closer to the fires, they could hear voices speaking from the direction of the fires, English voices. There was a scent of char in the air, Jacob believing they must be listening to the burned-down house on the point. They lowered themselves to hands and knees, crawling forward until they came to the tree line before sinking to their bellies.

Four camp fires could be seen, the flicker of the fire growing as British soldiers were stacking more wood on the fires, building them up. Jacob looked around, using the firelight to see what the British had built there. From the glow, he could see boxes and barrels and what appeared to be wooden platforms.

"What do you think they built here?" whispered Samuel, and Jacob shook his head, still taking in the area. The British soldiers were talking; no muskets were seen in their hands or near them.

"Bloody wet and cold, can't tell you how much I hate this," one soldier grumbled, and the other two standing around the fire nodded their heads in agreement.

"Aye, but it's better than that bloody cold New York; much better down here it is." Again the three men nodded and continued with their small talk. Jacob was still trying to determine the position when he heard the command of "Load!" come from the far side of the fires.

He could hear the scraping noise of a worm going down a barrel of a cannon, and from the tone of the scrape, it sounded like a big one. He could barely distinguish the shapes of the men moving to what Jacob suspected was the loading of guns. Then in the dark, the tiny pinprick of a glowing ember of a linstock was seen.

"Give, fire!"

Four large cannons roared, and one gave a loud thump of a howitzer went off. The flash of light of the muzzle silhouetted the crew and the shapes of the guns. Jacob nodded; he knew now what the British had built, a battery.

"Looks like a pair of 32-pounders, perhaps a pair of 24s, and I think a howitzer," Jacob whispered to Samuel, who nodded in agreement. "That's why they must have burned the house so the guns would be lined up towards the city and the defenses."

"They're big enough to hit the city from here, so I am guessing this is where they'll start their siege lines from," Samuel commented, and Jacob nodded in agreement.

"Let's pull back and see what's west of here on the Wappoo Neck. That will give us a definite answer." Jacob crawled back until they were deeper in the woods before standing up and leading the way to the west. They moved through the dark, finding a path that allowed them to move quicker.

The night sky became clear and cold, and though his blanket coat was still damp from the rain, it did keep some of the chill off. So Jacob led them through the night until they arrived at the Wappo and began to follow it southward. As dawn approached, the sky was starting to become pink, then orange. So far, they had not heard or seen anyone.

As the sun rose and the light became more substantial, Jacob spotted what he had assumed would be British crews lashing flatboats together into a bridge across the Ashley River. Longboats would help push the flatboats into a position where they would be lashed together. So far, it appeared they were about halfway across the river.

"Well, that settles it," Jacob commented in a low voice to Jean and Samuel, kneeling next to him, "This is where they will cross, and they already have a battery up at Fenwick. Moreover, those flat boats look sturdy enough for men and artillery to cross."

"Could General Lincoln lead the Army out, stop them here?" Jean asked, making a good point about their position. "With artillery and infantry, maybe some of the warships coming up the river, we could hold this line, no?"

Jacob looked at the position and nodded his head. "It makes sense, but will our commander see it?"

Jean shrugged, "We won't know unless we get back and tell him, yes?" Jacob nodded, then turned and led them back towards their line at a quick pace. But, first, they had to get their information to the general so he could devise a plan to stop the attack.

***

Lincoln fumed, pacing his office, shaking his head, and muttering about the disloyal militia. He had just learned that Lillington's men's enlistment had ended, and they were heading back to North Carolina.

"Ungrateful bloody militia!" Lincoln yelled at the ceiling as he paced. He had even learned that Governor Rutledge had offered an extra three hundred dollars and new clothes, and they still refused except for about 150 who stayed. Lincoln shook his head in frustration.

Then there was this fear of smallpox, keeping most militia companies outside the city. Only one company overcame their fear, joining the city's defenders. Lincoln walked over to his map and tried to guess where the British would strike first.

With the bad weather during the night, one of the town's provosts found a large, 32-pound cannon ball at Cumming's Point and another in the Sugar House. *"They must have fired during the night, and we didn't hear it."*

Lincoln's eye traveled to the map and the mouth of the Ashley and Cooper Rivers, then down to the bar and Five Fathom Hole and the open ocean. Lincoln began to nod, *"The Navy. They will move their Navy over the bar as they tried back in '76. Then, with the Navy from the ocean, batteries at Fort Johnson, and coming down the Neck, they'll have us mostly surrounded."*

"Orderly, take a message!" Lincoln called, and quickly an orderly came into his office.

"Sir?"

"Take a message to Admiral Whipple; I would like to know his plan in defending the city."

The orderly nodded, then turned and headed off to deliver the message. Lincoln returned to look at the seaward side of the city.

"If Whipple can't stop them, we'll be in a bad position," Lincoln stated as he looked at the map and shook his head. "We may already be too late."

***

They have received confirmed reports of the British fleet finally moving up the coast, as the recent bad weather and the strong southerly wind blew against the British ships. Now the Royal Navy was approaching the bar, and Whipple assumed they would try to get their ships over the bar close to the city.

"Gentlemen, as you know, the Royal Navy is approaching, and we must be ready." Whipple started his council of war, "What I am looking for is options. How can we stop their ships that we know are bigger and better armed than ours?"

"We can use the same plan back in '76, now that Fort Moultrie is fully built. Tied in with the southern battery in the city, we can place our fleet to support the fort and battery, to meet the approaching ships." Captain Simpson of the sloop *Ranger* stated. There was a murmur as the captains discussed the idea.

"We must sail out and attack!" a voice shouted from the back of the room. All turned to see who had made the statement. Captain Crawley of the galley *Marquis de Brittigney* came forward to show his idea to the admiral and assembled officers.

"We must not take a defensive stance here; we must attack!" Crawley stated, and a few of the captains chuckled at the idea.

"What, against those ships of the line, that's suicide!" one of the captains retorted, but Crawley continued.

"Those damn ships of the line are too heavy to get across the bar, just like back in '76. I believe they will use their smaller ships, much like ours, to attempt to cross over the bar. To do this, they will have to be made lighter, so they won't have all their cannons and shots."

Crawley looked at the assembled officers who were following what he was describing. "We have the advantage, not them! We take up position on our side of the bar, and when they attempt to cross, we concentrate our fire, and if we can sink them on the bar, it will block the harbor."

"Bold but risky plan," Whipple commented but shook his head. Even if we could form a line of battle and fire on the approaching ships, while their ships of the line can't cross the bar, they can sure bloody well blast us out of the water from the other side, covering their crossing."

Once again, the men murmured and talked, but Crawley shook his head.

"Perhaps, sir, but we must face them there, where we have the advantage. If we keep the fleet back, hoping they come towards us after crossing the bar, they will only be engaged by the fort and the batteries. What's to keep them from just sailing up the Ashly away from us, forcing us to pursue and come within range of their ships of the line?"

"Well then, let's decide," Whipple stated. "All in favor of supporting Captain Crawley's idea of meeting them at the bar, raise your hand."

Crawley's hand shot up, but he was the only one raised. Whipple raised an eyebrow, "Those in favor of supporting the defensive plan, raise your hands." The rest of the officers raised their hands, and Crawley shook his head.

"This is a mistake that will cost us dearly," Crawley stated, but no one was listening as the other captains and Whipple finalized how they would move back towards the fort.

**

The swamp was cold; Jacob shivered as he was trying to both not sink to his knees but not make any noise. Once again, he and some of his men were sent out to get more information concerning the British; General Lincoln wanted more details on who he was facing.

The swamp was not too deep, mostly knee-deep in some areas. They were moving through the area near what Jacob was told was the Drayton Plantation near the Ashley river; they had used some of the South Carolina Navy's longboats to move up the river to where they landed.

Now on foot, his men had to watch for British sentries and those large Alligators he had learned from the locals, a name derived from the Spanish meaning "Large Lizard." From the few Jacob had seen, they were enormous. Unfortunately, however, these great lizards were usually not about on a cold day.

Jacob, with a small detail of scouts from the company, moved towards the plantation; the light was low as they approached at dusk, using the deep shadows to conceal their movement. In this swamp, though, Jacob had to admit there were enough palms and other bushes that still had their leaves to help hide them.

The black swamp water curled around their legs, the soft sound of feet gently lifting and placing without making the "sucking" sound of the mud. They moved quietly enough that the birds and herons did not fly away, only watch curiously.

The glow of fires began to appear in the dusk, showing they must be approaching the camp area where they believed some of the British were encamped. Crouching low, keeping his rifle clear of the water, Jacob approached the bushes, thankful to be out of the cold water. The trees were heavy with this Spanish Moss, which he used to his advantage.

Lowering their stomachs, the men slithered and crawled forward under the bushes by gently moving their leaves. When Jacob could see the camp, he stopped moving and took stock of the situation. They were behind the house, a well-constructed two-story house, where rows upon rows of white tents were aligned in perfect British style.

They arranged with company streets, the officers and command tents to the top, and the field kitchens and supplies at the bottom. Jacob shook his head in appreciation, well versed in this standard layout from the early days up in New York. His men watched the flanks and rear, their feet touching one another in a circle, so they could tap one another if needed.

Jacob took in all he could see, the number of tents, artillery, and supplies. Using the math of five men per tent, he was getting that there was at least a brigade of British soldiers here. Many men moved around the camp in shirts and breeches, though Jacob saw sentries moving along the perimeter and near the house.

"Must be where the commanders are," Jacob thought, *"They always take the homes from the people."* The amount of bales and bags and the several field kitchens already dug meant these men were ready for a prolonged siege. It was enough information that Jacob needed; tapping the men's feet, they backed away and made their way back to their boat.

Not seeing any other British along the way, they arrived where they concealed their longboat, and the men took their places. The last man pushed the boot in as he kicked them away from the shore. The men passed their oars out, and after turning the boat to face south towards the city, the men began to row. The water grass was tall enough; it was above the boat and helped conceal their movement.

As Jacob sat in the rear of the boat, he thought about the situation. The British now have a camp between the city and Bacon's Bridge, though he had not yet received any word they have come across the bridge. If that was only one of their camps, the British would have them encircled, and if they didn't do something soon, they might be unable to fight or escape.

When the longboat approached the beginning of the neck, one of the sloops stationed on the river to protect their fortifications challenged them as they approached. Jacob called out the password, and the sailors let them pass. As they rowed past the defensive line, it was lit up with fires and torches so they could see the approaches to the line. Jacob had to admit; that it was an impressive sight.

After arriving at the dock, the boat was turned over to the navy; Jacob and his men made their way back to the barracks so that he could report his findings to Marion and General Moultrie. He thanked the men for a good scout and released them back to the barracks to clean and dry their clothes; Jacob headed to the headquarters. Marion was still up when he arrived; he smiled when Jacob entered his office.

"So Jacob, what did you see?" Marion asked.

"We're in trouble, sir if we don't do something soon," Jacob answered. "We saw near this Drayton Plantation about a brigade of British regulars, well supplied with tents, field kitchens, and supplies. They are here for the long haul, ready for a sustained siege."

Marion nodded, thinking about what Jacob said. Then, he looked back up at Jacob. "Is it that bad? Are we already encircled?"

Jacob shook his head. "No, sir, not yet. I strongly suspect they will soon have enough forces to begin a by-the-book siege of the city."

Marion nodded, then looked at Jacob. "What's on your mind? What else are you thinking?"

Jacob thought about it before answering. "The Royal Navy, sir, where are they?"

Marion nodded, understanding Jacob's concern about being caught between an attacking ground force and a supporting naval force.

"We have scouts reporting they are still waiting to the south," Marion explained. "They may be trying to time the rise and fall of the tides to get their ships over and the ones that can't, to get close enough to bring their heavier guns to bear."

Jacob had a look of concern across his face. "What about our navy? What are they doing?"

Marion let out a deep sigh and tossed a quill onto his table. "Ah, our illustrious navy. From what we learned earlier today while you were scouting, the admiral will not hazard his ships against, using his words, a more superior fleet. So they are falling back to the safety of our batteries, sinking old ships to block the entrances, and transferring their gunners and marines to serve in the defenses."

Jacob stood in shock as he heard the news. "That is bloody insane!" Jacob stated, "The batteries or the fort won't protect them. Those man-o-wars have heavy 32-pounders; they'll sit back and still blast our ships into driftwood. What the hell is the admiral thinking? What about General Lincoln? Does he support this?"

Marion bit his lower lip and nodded. "Yes, he does."

Jacob held his hands up in desperation, shaking his head. "Well, that's bloody typical!"

Jacob stood, shaking his head, then looked up and took a deep breath before letting it out. "Sorry, sir, I didn't mean to be disrespectful to our commanding general. But, unfortunately, our situation is getting worse."

Marion nodded in understanding, "Well, I hate to break it to you, but it may be getting worse."

"Worse?" Jacob asked, "How could it get worse?"

"Most city leaders have complained to the governor and General Lincoln about the upcoming siege. They prefer surrendering the city to save it from damage instead of fighting it out."

Jacob shook his head in disbelief. "Just like last time when they tried to bluff us, how the city leaders would surrender if the British would allow them to be a neutral, open city. Is this what they are thinking again?"

Marion shrugged. "I have only heard rumors, but from what you describe, yes."

Marion nodded in understanding of Jacob's frustration at the situation; he knew Jacob was a man of action, much different from these weak city leaders.

"Go get some rest; I'll see your information gets to General Moultrie and up to Lincoln." Then Marion wrinkled his nose. "May want to get that swamp smell out of your clothes."

***

Tarleton led his cavalry troop across the floating bridge that had been finally completed at Wappoo Neck. As his horses clomped across the wooden planks, Tarleton had to admire the ingenuity it took to construct this bridge. Their engineers and men had to float all these flatboats passed rebel batteries in the middle of the night with muffled oars. Tarleton snorted at how easy it was to move seventy-five boats past these rebels, *"Must not be very vigilant on guard duty."*

After crossing the bridge, Tarleton led his cavalry troop to one of the campsites. Tarleton reflected on the action so far, amused that many of these rebels thought he and the 17th would not find horses locally, and was greatly disappointed how easy it had been. Granted, he admitted, they were not top quality but will make do.

"Rather amazing a bag of jingling coin can do for the effort," Tarleton commented on how some locals who may not be directly supporting their rebellious cause took English coin. However, reflecting on his first meeting with the rebel cavalry near Rantol's Bridge, he reevaluated his thought on their abilities. He had learned they were under the rebel command of Washington and Bland, along with Hussars from Pulaski.

"They did capture Lieutenant Colonel Hamilton of the Provincials," Tarleton thought, *"Nearly drew the advance guard who pursued into an ambush. The fight was a draw."*

When the troop arrived at the camp and supply point, he had his men dismount and see to their horses.

"Lieutenant," Tarleton shouted, "See to the horses and men, replace any item or rations we need from the quartermaster."

"Yes, sir!" The lieutenant answered before going off to form a detail. Tarleton headed to where he could see what the army was up to. From a vantage point, he could see a large work party of men digging and creating two large redoubts and siege lines. Tarleton shook his head, not liking a fixed fight. He was a cavalry commander; maneuvering was his business and how he will meet his foes on the field.

From his estimation, they were about eight hundred yards from the rebel lines; they had begun construction on the 1st of April. First, along with the men digging the zig-zagging trenches, the gun crews moved the large artillery pieces into position in the redoubts. Then, looking off to the side, Tarleton saw men working on getting a large siege mortar ready for action.

"Gove me the open fields where I can charge and crush my enemies instead of sitting behind a wall, waiting on one of those damnable shots and exploding balls land on me!"

In the distance, a few cannon shots could be heard firing at their position, but to Tarleton, they appeared to do nothing except make some noise.

"We'll see how this all works out in a few days," Tarleton spoke to himself before turning and heading back to where his men and horses were being tended.

***

Jacob and the Colonel's Company took turns in the defensive lines and the Hornwork. Jacob focused on the British in the distance using his telescope as Jean and Samuel joined him. They could see the British working on their trenches and redoubts, shovels of dirt, sand, and mud flying. From this right, Jacob heard the sound of cannons booming, sending their shots toward the British, but Jacob knew they were out of range for now.

Hearing footsteps approach, Jacob turned to see a messenger approach. "Captain Clarke, please, you and Lieutenant Langy are to accompany me."

Jacob looked over at Jean, who shrugged; Jacob motioned for the messenger to lead on.

"Should I get ready for another scout?" Samuel called after them, seeing every time they got a particular assignment, Jacob would get the task while he and Jean would get their gear ready.

"Who knows, Samuel, but be ready just in case," Jacob called back before waving and turning to follow the messenger. Then a strange feeling came over Jacob, and he stopped, turned, and looked back at Samuel, who was returning to checking on the men and their position in the Hornwork.

It was a strange feeling of impending danger that surrounded them and Samuel. Jacob couldn't place his finger on it, shrugged it off as too much time in the trenches, and continued to follow the messenger.

"Is everything good?" Jean asked, and Jacob shrugged.

"I don't know, just a strange feeling of impending danger came over me. I just don't know why."

The messenger did not take them back to the barracks but to a house near the docks. The messenger knocked on the door, which a man looked out and, after seeing who it was, opened it and hustled Jacob and Jean into the house before closing the door. They followed the door attendant, who led them to a back room, where once again he knocked, and another man opened the door.

When the door opened wider, Jacob could see it was Christopher Gadsden. Jacob knew Gadsden, the same firebrand they had served with in Middleton's Regiment. "Good, they found you," Gadsden remarked as he hustled Jean and Jacob into the room. Again, Jacob was surprised who was in the large bedroom. In the bed, Marion was bandaged with his leg on pillows, attended to by Oscar. Governor Rutledge was there, and so was General Lincoln.

Marion had a very dejected look on his face; arms crossed across his chest. Governor Rutledge had a hard look, and Lincoln had a desperate look.

"As I was saying, governor," Lincoln stated, "You must leave the city before it's too late. You are the Civil Authority; if the British capture you, South Carolina falls. So we must continue to resist."

"My job is to be here!" Rutledge fired back, "I may be the Civil Authority, but I will be damned if I abandon my people during this fight!"

"You are not abandoning your people," Lincoln tried to explain. "In fact, you would do more for your people if you continued to fight and support us from the upcountry. Inspire the people; make sure they don't give up!"

Rutledge sighed and nodded his head, "Who will run the government if I am away?"

"I will," Gadsden stated. "I will stay behind as your Lieutenant Governor and see to the people however happens."

Rutledge looked at Lincoln. "If the city falls, you will become a prisoner. The British may accuse you of being a traitor and hang you."

"Let them try!" Gadsden fired back. "I have no fear of dying as a patriot!"

Rutledge nodded his head, accepting what must be done.

Then Lincoln looked over to Jacob and Jean.

"Captain Clarke," Lincoln began. "Jacob. You saved my life all those years back, and I owe you. But I need of you again, and it will be a debt I may not be able to make again."

Jacob began to piece everything together, looking at the dejected Marion, who was staring at a wall, and a depressed Rutledge.

"I am asking you to get the governor and Colonel Marion out of the city, see to their safety, and get them as far away as possible. We must keep the fight alive, or liberty dies here with us."

"And you, sir?" Jacob asked, "What of you?"

Lincoln shrugged his shoulders. "I am going to hold out as long as we can, resist both the British and these damn cowardly city leaders who want to give everything away quickly. I will stop them, both of them, and even if providence smiles upon us, may even force these British back to Georgia!"

Jacob doubted he could beat the British, but he understood why he had to get the governor and Marion out of the city. "We'll get clear and move to a friendlier area until we're needed or ready."

Lincoln nodded as he headed towards the door, and Gadsden joined him. "If it comes to past we fail, and the city falls, they will come after you as traitors, hunting you down."

Jacob nodded, "Yes, sir, we expect they would. They won't catch us where we're going."

Surprising Jacob, Lincoln reached out and shook his hand. "Good luck and Godspeed!"

Lincoln and Gadsden departed the room, and Jacob went to where Marion lay on the bed. He looked up at Jacob and sighed.

"I bet you wonder why I am here with a bandaged leg?"

"It did cross my mind," Jacob answered, "Sir."

Marion shrugged once more. "I think I broke my ankle."

Jacob raised his eyebrows, "Broke your ankle; how?"

"All senior officers were invited to a dinner party hosted by Captain McQueen. I tried to explain that I don't touch those vile spirits, but everyone seemed to be drinking like it was the end of days."

Jacob nodded, and Marion continued.

"Well, I tried to leave and found all the doors and windows locked on the first floor. No one seemed to notice or care; they were more caught up in drinking games and singing songs. So I made my way up to the second floor and found an open window."

Jacob could see where the tale was going but began to work hard on not smirking.

"So I went through the window and down the eave until I got to the edge. I was getting ready to swing around and drop from the roof." Marion paused, and a depressed look crossed his face.

"I lost my balance and fell, not ready for a good landing, and when I hit the ground, I heard my ankle pop like a musket being fired. I limped back to the barracks, and the regimental surgeon confirmed it was broken. Therefore, they splinted and bandaged it up, but it hasn't healed, so I have been found unfit for duty. So here I am."

Now Jacob understood why he looked so bleak. "We'll make the arrangements and secure supplies. I will also have to make some contacts so we will be met and helped."

Both Marion and Rutledge nodded; Jacob motioned for Jean to follow him, then left the room and headed out into the city.

Oscar handed Marion a cup of tea, "Here, sir, take some tea. Captain Clarke will see us all to safety, don't worry."

"Go get supplies, food, and some powder, anything we can get from the quartermaster. I will secure a longboat and see if I can get help from the Raccoon Company." Jean nodded and headed towards the barracks while Jacob ran to the docks while numerous thoughts raced through his head. Finally, a plan began to form, and Jacob nodded to himself, for it just may work.

Jacob could secure a longboat from the navy just like before, as there was no need for them. Then he headed towards where the Catawba Raccoon Company was garrisoned. As he moved through the city, columns of wounded, sick, and other invalids were being marched out the north gate, trying to get them away from the siege, being moved over to Sullivan's Island.

Jacob returned with two Catawbas, Winnatoo and Olshatahan, while a third named Yalangway had already headed over to Charles Pinckney's Snee Farm, where he would secure mounts. Jacob had Jean move the supplies to the boat and wait for them there as he moved Marion and Rutledge over by a closed carriage. He didn't want anyone to see they were moving.

Helping Marion hop to the carriage, Rutledge was already inside; they moved to the dock, and after stopping in an alley where they could not be seen, they left the carriage and helped Marion to the longboat. Jean and Oscar carried the bags of supplies. After getting Rutledge, wearing a cloak with the collar up to conceal his face into the boat, Marion was loaded.

His face was red from the broken bones' effort and pain. Once everyone was loaded, they slipped the oars and began to row across the Cooper River. As they began to cross, the British started a heavy bombardment of the city. Shot and exploding balls flew in an arc and crashed into the defenses and Charles Town.

Jacob was in the rear steering while the others pulled on the oars. Marion continued with his dejected look, and with the sound of the heavy bombardment, Rutledge shook his head. They made their way across the Cooper and had no issues. They landed at Snee Farm and transferred to a barn. Yalangway had not returned with mounts, so they had to wait.

With Jacob, Jean, and the governor, Marion watched the siege across the river while the Catawbas kept watch for any British. The guns boomed and thundered all day and into the night. The city glowed from the fires, and the traces of the burning fuses could be seen in the night air. It reminded Jacob of the attack on Fort William Henry, where he watched that siege unfold.

"Do you think Lincoln will try to evacuate just like we did, get the army out, and fight the British on a field of his choosing?" Rutledge asked.

Jacob looked at Marion, who shook his head slowly, and Jacob had to agree. "No, sir, to be honest, while we can get small parties across at the moment, if he tried to evacuate the army, the Royal Navy would swoop in and take them under fire."

Rutledge nodded his head, knowing Jacob was right. In the morning, Yalangway arrived with mounts, and they loaded the extra supplies and gear on the horses.

"It was not easy getting horses," Yalangway commented, "British cavalry have been buying them all up."

"Did they describe these cavalrymen wearing green uniforms?" Jacob asked, and Yalangway nodded.

"They did."

Jacob shook his head and, along with Oscar, helped Marion mount his horse. He gritted his teeth went he mounted, then nodded he was good. Next, Jacob mounted his horse and laid his Jaeger Rifle across the pommel.

"I will take the trails we know and start heading up along the river towards Goose Creek, and then we'll see where to go from there. We know those still loyal near Dorchester, so we'll have to be careful."

"We can go to the hunting site near the falls," Jean stated, "We have the shelter and supplies still there.

Jacob nodded. "My same thoughts; we could start there and see where we go next."

They all turned to take one last look at the city across the river. The British guns barked and boomed, the defensive line firing back in kind. The flames were starting, the glow and flicker reflecting off the water, and the howitzer shots arced between the fighters.

Governor Rutledge looked and shook his head in anger and frustration. "I will rally the militia and strike them from behind, so help me God!"

Marion settled himself more comfortably in the saddle, favoring his good leg. Then, nodding his head in agreement with Rutledge, he set a determined look on his face.

Having seen this all before, Jacob knew there was nothing they could do now. They would have to bide their time, gather their forces, and strike when right. If not, all they would be doing is throwing good men away.

"We need to get moving while the night covers us," Jacob commented, and they all agreed. So Jacob turned his horse and led the small column into the woods while in the background, the sound of booming and crashing as the artillery bombardment increased.

CHAPTER 13

THE CITY FALLS

Samuel, with some of the 2nd, hunkered down in the Hornworks as the British artillery pounded away at their lines. He gazed out before their lines, admiring all of the hard work they had put into it. No house, no tree, no bush stood in front of their line, giving them clear fields of fire.

He ran his hands over the redoubt, made from the same tabby, lime, and oyster shells formed over logs, making it as hard as a rock. Before the works was a deep ditch to slow any attacker who tried to charge them as they went through at Savannah, they had two smaller redoubts covering their flanks would see no attacker would get that close.

Before the Hornwork, the first line of defense stretched from the Ashley to the Cooper River, composed of redoubts and batteries connected by a wall or a trench. A redoubt at both ends covered the approach from the rivers. The Cooper River Redoubt was actually in front of the line to fire across the line, catching any attacker in the flank.

Both river redoubts were constructed just like Fort Sullivan had been back in 1776, with the spongy Palmetto Logs and sand. They were sixteen feet apart and impressive looking, redoubt Samuel thought. I ditch ran along the entire length of the line, six feet deep and twelve feet wide.

If that wasn't enough, they had constructed a double palisade along the bottom of the ditch and sharpened stakes facing out at an angle. A flooded canal further out in front of the line was another obstacle. Finally, a forward redoubt on the Ashley side of the line covered the ditch, called the half-moon battery.

To Samuel, it almost looked impenetrable. Defending the left side were the Virginian Continentals, along with the 2nd and 3rd South Carolina. The North Carolina Brigade was on the right. Colonel Laurens Light Infantry was in reserve behind the Hornwork.

At the moment, they were all taking a beating from the artillery, everyone staying low and behind the walls. Numerous times Samuel ducked as he spotted a ball bouncing in their direction before striking the wall of the redoubt. Sometimes the ball stopped and rolled down into the ditch; sometimes, it would hop again and fly over their position.

This went on for days and the constant bombardment that went on, day and night. Finally, Samuel moved about the men, reassuring them and telling them to keep their heads down. He could also see that their nerves were being stretched thin, and their resolve was beginning to waver. So he gave them words of encouragement, though he wondered where Jacob and Jean had gone to.

"Stay easy, lads; this was no different when we were in the fort, being hammered by the Royal Navy. At least the dust isn't falling on you, and it's much cooler than what we have. Stay easy!"

There was a lull in the fighting on April 8th, when the Royal Navy moved into the harbor. The warships sailed past Fort Moultrie, more successful than it had tried in 1776. A massive cannonade occurred between the city's warships, the fort, and the batteries. Both sides on the neck stopped to watch the fighting. This time, the Royal Navy was successful.

The British warships took positions next to the old Fort Johnson ruins and began to fire on the city. Over the next few days, more gunboats and other vessels secured more of the waterways, and a great exodus of small boats could be seen leaving the city as many of the civilians were trying to escape the coming carnage. The city's morale was plummeting, and the men in the trenches were not doing any better.

***

As the cannonade rattled the windows of his command house, General Lincoln looked at the updated positions of the British on his map. The new siege positions were now close enough for their heavier guns to damage the defensive line seriously. Then there was the Royal Navy now to contend with.

"Why in the bloody hell didn't Whipple stop them at the bar!" Lincoln growled at the map, "that could have made the difference; now look where we are at."

More English ships had crossed before Fort Moultrie, surviving the cannon fire to reinforce what warships were already anchored in the rivers. He looked closely at the map, knowing success for his defense was to keep the northern approach from the Cooper River had to be maintained so he could get supplies and, hopefully, reinforcements from Rutledge.

"I can't rely on the log boom that is stretched over to Folly Island; I am going to need more," Lincoln spoke to himself as he thought. Then having made a decision, he stood and faced his orderly.

"Take down these orders," he commanded, and his orderly prepared the documents.

"To Colonel Malmedy, you are to take your North Carolina Militia and secure the passes across the Cooper River. To do this,

I will supply you with cannons from Fort Moultrie as you build a redoubt to cover the approach. In addition, I will send you more men to reinforce your position."

The orderly wrote it down, then looked up for the next one.

"To Colonel Laurens, you will take your detachment of light infantry and reinforce Colonel Malmedy at his new position on the Cooper."

The orderly finished that order, then prepared for the general.

"To General Huger, you will take all of the cavalry, consisting of the 1st and 3rd Continental Dragoons, what is left of Pulaski's cavalry, and Colonel Horry's State Dragoons. You will secure Biggin's Bridge to keep it open for reinforcements and supplies."

Lincoln nodded. He was done, and the orderly finished with the orders before bringing them to the general to sign. Once complete, the orderly departed to have the orders issued. Lincoln returned to his map and looked at the red lines showing where the British siege lines were located and the warships. To him, a hangman's noose was tightening around his neck.

***

The siege continued without let up, and no reinforcements arrived. The British line was now only three hundred yards away, and they had posted their riflemen to take shots at the Patriot artillerymen. When the gun crew would begin to load, the German Jaegers would fire at them through the embrasures.

Of course, the Patriot riflemen would fire back as well, and soon a deadly duel between sharpshooters began; the gunners and any unfortunate infantrymen were the game. Samuel, with a detachment of riflemen, would take up positions near the British line during the early morning, and they would begin their deadly game when the sun rose.

Samuel's game for the day was the green uniformed Jaegers firing on their artillerymen. Making himself a good firing position, he laid his rifle on a soft bag filled with dirt, with another man spotting for him. After the sun rose, Samuel began scanning the British line; he and the other riflemen were waiting for a target to pop up.

"Just like hunting deer," his spotter mentioned as he used a small telescope to look at the British line. "They never show up when you need them to."

Samuel chuckled as he scanned. Then, off to his right, he saw movement and slowly aimed his rifle at the movement. He was rewarded when a flash of green, a Jaeger, was slowly moving up the lip of the berm, his rifle at his side. It appeared he was also looking for a target, not knowing he had become one.

"You got him?" Samuel asked his spotter, and the spotter replied, "Got him."

Settling his rifle deep into his should, getting a good sight along the barrel, Samuel cocked his rifle to full. Then, letting out his breath slowly, he gently squeezed the trigger, and his rifle barked. The ball caught the Jaeger in the side of the head; he tumbled back into the trench.

"Good shot!" the spotter commented as Samuel reloaded his rifle. Then, as he began to ram the ball down the barrel, Samuel thought, "*How many was that, 6, or was it 7. Sometimes hard to keep track.*"

Once ready, he brought his rifle to half-cock, and returned to watching his area. To his left, a rifle barked from the British side, quickly followed by a groan as a Patriot been hit. Samuel shook his head and then returned to scanning. "*We get one; they get one. Eventually, no one will be left.*"

***

From his vantage point, General Clinton and Cornwallis observed as the heavy mortars finally went into action, lobbing their shot over the rebel defensive lines and into their rear area. Having learned from their bloody riflemen, he had ordered the Jaegers to build sandbag positions to protect themselves. These bags were made from cloth, two feet long and one foot thick. They did the trick; they were not losing as many of their Jaegers, which helped morale.

Using his telescope, Clinton looked across the field at what he considered a textbook example of how to wage a siege. Well-constructed artillery positions were covering the siege lines. The approaches zigzagged, so their men were protected as they reached demi-parallels, slowly moving forward.

"I am rather surprised these rebels hadn't tried to sally forth and engage our lines," Clinton commented, noting how close the lines were.

"What do you expect, sir," Cornwallis replied, "They know not how to wage war."

Clinton nodded. "How are we set for 24-pound shot?"

Cornwallis walked over to a field desk and found the report after shuffling through some papers.

"Sadly, we are running low; unless they surrender or we attack, we may not have enough shot for the 24-pounders to support either."

Clinton grimaced; he didn't like the news. "What about the navy? Surely they are not using their guns as much. Can we get shot from them?"

"We have sent a request to the admiral," Cornwallis responded, "He is gathering what spare he has and should be shipped over to us later today."

Clinton nodded; that was better. Most of his heavy artillery was 24-pounders, and he needed them to batter down these bloody tabby walled redoubts and spongy logs. Cornwallis stood back and glowered at Clinton. He detested the man and, somewhat not professional, hoped a rebel cannon shot would do him the favor of removing him, allowing his rise to be the overall commander.

With all of these efforts, the rebels had not fallen, even if this was a textbook siege; if they failed again in taking this city, he feared his good name and honor would be dragged down with Clinton if they failed. *"I must distance myself the best I can from this wretch,"* Cornwallis thought, *"Perhaps fate would favor me. Already a rebel cannon burst almost took him."*

"Any word on the whereabouts of Colonel Webster?" Clinton asked, pulling Cornwallis back into reality.

"No, sir," Cornwallis replied, "We have dispatched the 23rd to search for Webster's Brigade. We are still waiting on the word to see if they have been located.

Clinton nodded and returned to look over the field. He had dispatched Colonel Webster's Brigade to attack the rebels on the east side of the Cooper River, driving them away from their redoubts and opening the way for an attack.

"Sir, an envoy, is here: an orderly stated.

"An envoy, from who?" Clinton asked.

"Believe he is a Chief of the Lower Creeks, sir."

Clinton turned, and before him stood a well-dressed and decorated Creek Indian. He wore a blue coat with red lapels and a collar; sandals on his feet but no breeches or stockings. His head was shaved except for the crown as it was their style, his face pained on red in several places, and he had two silver rings in his nose.

A silk scarf was wrapped around his head, held in place by a silver clasp. On his chest, he wore a silver ring-shaped collar; around both arms were silver shields held on by red ribbon. Hanging from his ears were silver pendants of swords and pistols.

"Great war chief," he stated in English, a deep resonated voice, "I am Ravening Wolf of the Lower Creeks, and I have come to see how you make war."

Clinton bowed in respect, and Ravening Wolf bowed in return.

"Does this mean the Creeks are answering the father's call to take up the tomahawk?'

"No," was the simple answer Clinton received. So the Creek walked over and looked out over the field to watch the bombardment.

Clinton looked over at Cornwallis, who only shrugged his shoulders. Then, shrugging his shoulders, Clinton quickly ignored the Creek and returned to look at his map, the freshly drawn positions of his men, and the estimated positions of the rebels.

***

The house shook, and the windows rattled as the officers had gathered to hold a council of war. General Lincoln looked through his reports, and it all summed up into one situation, grim. They had now been under siege for twenty days. While they were holding, causalities were mounting, and morale was suffering.

Lincoln stood with the reports in his hand and faced his assembled officers.

"As you are all well aware, our situation is not looking well," Lincoln began as he held up the first report.

"We will receive no more reinforcements from Virginia, and Scott's Brigade promised us, will not depart."

Lincoln shuffled the reports and brought up the next one. "We asked North Carolina for some twenty-five hundred militia;

we received only three hundred." He shuffled to the following report, perhaps the grimmest.

"Based on our last return of able-bodied men to defend the city, we have about four thousand left for duty. The rest are either wounded, sick, dead, or have deserted."

"What is the estimated strength of the British?" Moultrie asked.

"At least twice that many, if not more," answered Lincoln, and the officers talked amongst themselves.

"What about the Royal Navy? What is being done to move those ships away from the city?" asked McIntosh.

Lincoln frowned and shook his head. "Admiral Whipple, in my opinion, has failed to do his duty, for he won't' even venture out to defend the rivers, let alone engage the British ships anchored off the city. Therefore, he cannot be relied upon."

"So, what options are left?" asked Colonel Parker from Virginia.

Lincoln took a deep breath before answering. "We can evacuate; the militia would hold the city as a diversion while we move as many of the army across the Cooper."

Then he paused before he stated the worse of the options, "or we surrender the city."

The officers' voices rose in disagreement about surrendering, except for Colonel Laumoy, who supported the idea of surrendering.

"If we surrender the city, General Clinton, an honorable man, would grant us favorable terms based on our heroic defense."

As the very heated debate began, sitting in the background was Gadsden, who shook his head in disbelief. Then, he stood and faced the officers.

"Honorable officer, you say?" he began, "Favorable terms? How dare you, of all things, officers of our army, look to surrender our city to the likes of him. Do you know what the British will do when they enter the city? First, they will plunder it as punishment for this heroic defense. Then they will destroy the city; that is not what I call favorable!"

The officers went back to arguing; the majority wanted to fight on, only a few thought surrendering was the key. Gadsden once more shook his head.

"I will have to consult with the city leaders and see what they desire," he shook his head once more before departing.

***

When Gadsden passed what was being discussed with the army officers, they too exploded into heated debates. Thomas Ferguson held his hands up to get the attention of the city leaders.

"If Lincoln and his bloody army abandon us to the British and flee across the river, I promise I'll be the first one at the gate to open it to the British before I see any more of the city burn or the people suffer! I'll even lead the British right to where Lincoln and his brave men are crossing the river, and I will help them attack these soldiers before they get into their boats."

The idea of opening the gates was a shock to Gadsden, as the Privy Council of the City debated what they should do. Mostly they wanted to surrender, but if they followed Ferguson and attacked the army, it would be what he feared. A civil war would break out between the army and the people they were here to defend. He shook his head in despair.

***

At a later council of war, Lincoln and the officers learned what had been discussed in the Privy Council and Ferguson's threat.

Lincoln now knew they were left with only one option, to surrender.

"Well, gentlemen, have you all learned about the intent of the city leaders? We have no choice, it seems. As evacuation now appears to be out of order, do we continue the fight, or do we surrender?"

A low murmur as the officers spoke amongst themselves before they all nodded. "Then I take it we all agree, as distasteful as it is, to save lives, we must surrender the city. Then what are the terms will we ask for?"

The men discussed and proposed that they agree to surrender the city and the forts to the British as part of the terms. The Continentals, militia, and navy keep their arms and ammunition and have thirty-six hours to evacuate the city. Once the army was cleared of the city, the British were to give them a ten-day head start before any pursuit began.

Moultrie listened to the terms being discussed and shook his head. There would be no way Clinton would allow them to keep their arms and ammunition and be given a head start. He wouldn't allow his enemy these terms if he were in command. He suspected Clinton wouldn't accept them either.

The following morning, the drum beat for parley was sent, and their terms were sent over to the British lines. Along with their terms for surrender, Lincoln had requested a six-hour cease-fire. However, the guns quickly resumed firing, Clinton not granting a cease-fire at any cost.

Clinton passed the terms to Cornwallis, who read them, and once complete, he handed them to Admiral Arbuthnot.

Clinton had a smirk on his face, "Gentlemen, thoughts? Do we honor these terms for surrender?"

It was the admiral who answered first. "Bloody hell no, that's my thought. We have the advantage; either they surrender, or we level the city!"

Clinton nodded, then turned to Cornwallis, "Your thoughts?"

"Same," was his reply, "No terms."

Clinton nodded and sent a reply back to General Lincoln. "You have until ten o'clock this evening to surrender."

The message was sent over to the American lines. Clinton waited while he had the artillery orientate towards the Cooper River. If they were going to evacuate, it would be over in that direction. When 10:30 arrived, and the city had not surrendered, Clinton nodded.

"Right, tell the batteries to commence fire!"

The heavy 24-pound cannons, siege mortars, and howitzers boomed in a thunderous roar, taking the area near the Cooper River under heavy fire. From his position, Clinton smiled to himself, impressed by the amount of fire falling on the rebels, the most he had seen so far.

"Perhaps our men tire of this game and want it ended too."

"You make war well, great chief," a deep voice stated behind him. Clinton turned to see the Creek chief admiring the cannonade, a gleam in his eye and a smile on his face.

"Very well indeed."

***

As the horses moved along the road, the sound of the cannonading at the city could even be heard up there north of the city. Tarleton was pleased, no longer bound to sit with the army in their trenches. Cavalry was meant for the field, not a siege, and soon he would prove their worth.

General Clinton had learned the rebels had cavalry and some militia holding a bridge north of the city across the Cooper, which was one of their last lines of communication. He wanted this distraction dealt with to complete the encirclement of the rebels. Tarleton smiled to himself; rebel cavalry! Finally, a real fight!

The Legion infantry and cavalry troop marched into Goose Creek, and Tarleton held up his hand to halt the column. He was ordered to meet his reinforcements there. When they entered the small town square, Major Ferguson and his sharpshooters were already waiting. After passing his reins to one of his troopers, Tarleton dismounted and went over to speak to Ferguson.

"Any new word on our rebel friends?" Tarleton asked, and Ferguson nodded.

"Local loyal subjects have seen rebel horsemen near a bridge next to a place called Monck's Corner; I believe they call it Biggin's Bridge," Ferguson explained, and Tarleton nodded.

"How many rebels are there?"

"Our sources said they saw three distinct uniform differences and some militia infantry at the bridge," Ferguson explained, and Tarleton smiled.

"When Webster gets here, we'll go pay a call on our rebel friends." Ferguson bowed in response as Tarleton turned and headed back to his cavalry, and Ferguson went over to his men. But, watching all from Mr. Marshal's Mercantile were Peter and Patrick.

"Easy lad, sit still," Peter advised Patrick, excited at what he saw. "We're here on business; if we leave them alone, they leave us alone. Keep your eyes open, though."

Patrick nodded, then took a deep breath and tried to relax. The British, they were right here in Goose Creek.

"If they are here, then we must not be doing good down in the city," Patrick whispered, his eyes never leaving the green uniformed dragoons. "I hope Papa is doing well."

"Aye, lad, so do I."

A short time later, the drums could be heard, and Peter quickly recognized British drums with a marching beat. Then, red-coated British infantry appeared from a different direction as Colonel Webster arrived at Goose Creek. Tarleton and Ferguson approached Webster.

Patrick was getting excited again, and Peter reached down to squeeze his arm to settle down. Then, as they were watching the British, Mr. Marshal came out to tell them they were all set; everything had been unloaded when he saw all of the British.

"My word, now that is a sight?" he asked, and they nodded. Then they stood up and headed for the carts to return home so Peter could pass what he had observed.

***

Tarleton and Ferguson bowed to Webster, and he bowed back before dismounting. "These bloody roads are going to wear my backside off," Webster grumbled before shrugging it off. "What word of our rebel friends?"

Tarleton explained how Clinton wanted them to remove the rebels from Biggin's Bridge, and Webster nodded in agreement. "Makes tactical sense, not to leave your enemy behind you and to finish the encirclement. Do you have a plan?"

"Yes, sir," Tarleton began. "With Major Ferguson's marksmen, we will attack the bridge at night, catching the rebels by surprise. We'll catch the whole lot or remove them. In either case, we will hold the bridge and disperse these rebels."

Webster nodded his head in agreement. "Then to it, colonel, I wish you both good hunting. I will lead my column along the river, so what trouble I can flush. Should be a good day for hunting."

Tarleton and Ferguson moved off to the side to go over his plan. "We will move once the sun begins to set. Silence will be maintained at all cost. Then, once we get close enough to determine their sentries, we attack in the middle of the night with saber and bayonet."

Ferguson nodded, though he wanted to use his sharpshooters for what they were designed for, expert shooting. For now, he will follow Tarleton's plan. After resting and checking the gear, Tarleton ordered the troopers to mount, with Ferguson following.

Except for the soft sound of the hooves on the dirt, Tarleton's cavalry moved at a leisurely pace so the infantry could keep up with them. An advance guard had been sent out as an early warning; other than that, no sound was heard. The men maintained their strict, no sound command.

The sun had fallen, and the darkness of the night was settling when the advance guard brought Tarleton, a Negro they had intercepted. Tarleton halted the column, "What's this?"

"Sir, we came across him, and when he saw us, he made for the trees. When we secured him, we found this letter which may be of interest to you during the search." After seeing a home close by, Tarleton nodded and moved the column there to read the letter and speak to the Negro.

Tarleton, Ferguson, and a few of his men were in the house's main room. It was now well-lit with candles as the family who owned the house, we're kept in their bedrooms. Tarleton opened the letter and was surprised to see it had been written by an officer in General Huger's command.

"Well, what do we have here?" he commented as he read the letter. The letter had been intended to be delivered to Charles Town and described the disposition of the rebels at the bridge.

"It appears, gentlemen, some good fortune has fallen in our laps. This letter explains that the rebel cavalry is on our side of the Cooper River. The militia is in a meeting house across the river, covering the bridge from there."

Tarleton looked at the Negro, a field hand by his dress. "What instructions were you given?"

With a trembling voice, the Negro responded with, "I...I was to take to the barracks in the city, pass to officers there."

Tarleton nodded and asked, "Were you given a password for the rebels?"

The Negro nodded his head, "Liberty."

Tarleton chuckled and then shook his head. He turned and headed towards his men. "What are we to do with this man?" One of his officers asked.

Tarleton turned and said, "Pay him and let him go."

As Tarleton and Ferguson returned to their men, Tarleton quickly formed a plan in his head. "We'll have to move fast if we are to catch them."

Ferguson nodded, excited for the coming action, "We'll keep up!"

Quickly forming into their columns, they continued down the road at a quicker pace but maintained silence. In time, they arrived at the edge of the woods, and the bridge could be seen in the moonlight. It was roughly three in the morning, and Tarleton smiled to himself. Ferguson joined him, standing at his knee.

"Couldn't ask for a perfect time to attack," Tarleton stated, "This is when sentries are not at their best, and the rest are deep asleep. But, oh, this is going to be grand! We'll lead the charge, and you follow."

Ferguson nodded, "Bayonets only?"

"No, we will achieve surprise, so you may fire on your targets when you see them. Try to take some prisoners, especially officers."

Ferguson smiled; for now, he would be allowed to do what they are good at. He stepped back as the cavalry began to walk forward slowly. Then, without a word, Tarleton drew his pistol and held it up, his men following suit.

***

The sentry yawned so largely that his jaw creaked. A horse shook, its bridle making a jingling sound. After that, there was no sound except for the sound of the water passing under the bridge. The cannonade off in the distance reminded him of a far-off thunderstorm. He shook his head to clear it when he heard the approaching sound of hooves walking.

Bringing his musket up, he shouted, "Halt, who goes there?"

"Friend" was the reply from the dark.

"What is the password?" the sentry challenged.

"Liberty"

Feeling relieved, the sentry lowered his musket. "Advance, friend!"

It would be the last thing he did as Tarleton himself rode up, and just as the sentry realized they were not friends, Tarleton lowered his pistol, pulling the trigger. The ball tore through the sentry and knocked him back into the river.

Tarleton's dragoons kicked their horses at the sound of the pistol, and the charge was on. They rode across the bridge, firing their pistols at close range at the Continental and Luzon Cavalrymen before drawing their sabers. Tarleton whirled his men around and was happy to see some of the fancier dressed cavalrymen were mounting to challenge.

Raising his sword, Tarleton gave the command of "Charge!" His horsemen surged forward and slammed into Luzon's Cavalry before they could initiate their charge. Sabers flashed in the moonlight as Ferguson's sharpshooters began firing on their targets. The blades clanged against one another, Tarleton himself locked in combat with a Luzon. He overextended, and Tarleton ran his sword through the opening. The man fell from his horse, blood spurting from his mouth.

Tarleton broke contact to take in the situation and saw hundreds of rebels running for their lives into the swamps and woods. His infantry under Major Cochran, supported by Ferguson's sharpshooters, were charging the meeting house. The militia had no chance as they spilled out of the house or tried to fire from it. Cochran's bayonets and Ferguson's sharpshooters made short work of the militia.

As the sun began to rise, Tarleton took stock of the situation. He had achieved his goal; they had secured the bridge and drove off the rebels. "Give me a return of our wounded and what we have captured," Tarleton ordered as he dismounted and stretched his legs, still full of the adrenalin from the fight.

About ten minutes later, one of his officers reported. "Sir, five horses, are dead, one officer and two men wounded."

Tarleton nodded, then walked over to where the rebel cavalry horses were picketed. This was the most significant prize he could ever have wished for, trained horses! He had captured all of the rebel and officers' horses, numbering about four hundred. These horses his men badly needed.

"Quartermaster!" Tarleton ordered, and after a short moment, he arrived.

"See the men exchange these plow horses with a real cavalry horse and get their gear transferred. Then take stock of the other rebel arms and equipment we captured."

The quartermaster nodded his head, "Right away, sir!"

Tarleton spent the day having his cavalry exchange horses with the captured mounts and had their tack and equipment readied. Colonel Webster, having heard of the taking of the bridge, arrived around midday and congratulated

"Well done, sir, well done!" Webster exclaimed as he shook both Tarleton's and Ferguson's hands. "Bloody wonderful job you did here, excellent work. His lordship will be pleased when he learns of it."

Tarleton and Ferguson both bowed at the praise. "Now, we must see to completing this investment in the city. We have a lot of crossings to watch to make sure none of these rebels get help," Webster paused for a moment before smirking, "or escape."

"Tarleton, you are to secure Bonneau's Ferry, another one of these bloody crossing points. You and Major Ferguson are to move along the river and secure any boats you find so the rebels may not use them. I will continue to move along the river and engage any rebel forces."

He then turned and addressed Tarleton directly. "Send out scouts; we need to learn of the countryside, the dispositions of any rebel forces, and if possible, capture them. We have learned that some of the city leaders may have escaped."

Webster moved very close so Tarleton could see the seriousness in his eyes. "Hunt them down!"

Webster moved off with Ferguson, smiling, and Tarleton smiled a large, wolfish grin. "This is what I was meant to do!" He headed off in a trot to his command to issue orders.

**

Jacob and the others moved cautiously along the trail. So far, they had been lucky and seen no sign of anyone, not even farmers or fellow hunters. Jean rode next to Jacob, their horses slowly plodding along the path. Looking over his shoulder, Jacob saw Rutledge and Marion's heads together in quiet conversation, Oscar just behind them and Yalangway bringing up the rear. Winnatoo and Olshatahan were just up ahead as scouts.

"Does this seem odd to you?" Jacob asked Jean, "No one is out, no farmers, no people, simply no one. I know we are on a trail, but you know the hunters use it as well as I do. This is spring, time for more meat and skins to be brought in."

Jean nodded, "You may be right; something does not feel right; I don't know what it is."

The musket fire was heard from their front, followed by rifle fire. Jacob and Jean kicked their horses and quickly emerged on a dirt road. Both Winnatoo and Olshatahan lay behind their fallen horses, loading their rifles. Looking down the road, Jacob saw what had shot their horses, enemy cavalry.

Jacob and Jean quickly dismounted and brought their rifles up while still holding their reins. Jacob sighted on a green dragoon who was drawing his saber to charge and fired. The rifle ball took him square in the head and knocked him out of his saddle, starting the other green-uniformed dragoons. A few fired their pistols at them, but to no effect.

Jacob reloaded as quickly as he could, ramming the tight ball home. This shorter rifle made loading quicker, and no sooner than he finished priming, Jacob looked up to see a green dragoon charging at him with his saber raised. With no real time to react to the closing horseman, Jacob brought the rifle up at an angle in front of himself as the ground shook from the approaching hooves.

Luckily the dead horse in front of Jacob caused the charging horse to veer away, the downward arch of the saber only connecting with the rifle stock. However, the force was still hard enough that it knocked Jacob over. Continuing the roll, Jacob came back up on his knees, turned, and fired, but his aim was off by the acrobatics and only hit the dragoon in the shoulder. Winnatoo fired and finished the job, knocking the wounded dragoon off his horse.

"Go, get out of here!" yelled Olshatahan. "Get those men to safety; we will hold them off." Jacob knew they were right; they had to live to fight another day. Jacob nodded to Olshatahan, who nodded back. "At least I can get more scalps this way without competing with you!"

Jacob shook his head and ran over to where Jean had already mounted and had retrieved Jacob's horse. Yalangway arrived, brought his rifle up, and fired, dropping another dragon in the distance. "Go, I will stay and fight. We will see you again!"

Moving back, Marion and Rutledge were already waiting and followed Jacob as he began to trot down the trail in a different direction. Marion clenched his teeth from the pain but picked up the pace to get away.

**

April turned into May, and the siege continued. Mother Nature became involved as the heat rose, the men suffered from bad water, and now the various swamp insects feasted on friend and foe alike. The German Jaegers had now become so efficient that the rebels could only load their cannons at night and fire them once during the day. An invitation from a Jaeger Rifle's ball was to try to load again.

Clinton looked down on the field, their third line now ran parallel with the canal, and his engineers were able to destroy the damn that kept the water in it, and it all drained out. It was no longer considered an obstacle. So now, he had to decide whether to continue the siege or launch an all-out assault.

The men's morale was starting to strain, though they seemed to be causing more damage than receiving. The water was getting worse, and these damn insects were making their lives horrible and sleeping even more. He may have no choice.

"Why won't these bloody rebels see reason!" Clinton exclaimed finally in desperation. "Are they simpletons, blockheads? Don't they know they are beaten? Do they want me to send in assault to put them all to the bayonet?"

Clinton gave out a loud sigh and shook his head. Then he turned and looked at Cornwallis. "Have the army prepare for an assault."

Cornwallis nodded. "Then, if I may, sir, if we are to assault these rebels, I request to do it with my old friends, the grenadiers and light infantry."

Recalling the horror back at the beginning of this mess, at a place called Breed's Hill outside of Boston, any officer leading an attack would likely be killed.

"You do realize what you are asking?" Clinton responded, and Cornwallis nodded. "The success of this storm hinges on our navy and may be in doubt."

"I do," Cornwallis replied, "That's why I want to be with the grenadiers and the light infantry. Perhaps it will be the turning point that decides this attack."

Clinton nodded slowly, "See to the preparation."

The following day, good news arrived. Fort Moultrie had surrendered without a fight. Clinton moved to where he had a good vantage point and, after pulling out his telescope, saw the Union Jack flapping in the wind.

"Ha, that will knock them down a peg," Clinton exclaimed. "Orderly, send a message to General Lincoln, tell him I demand his unconditional surrender!" As the orderly penned the message, Clinton addressed Cornwallis, who had just arrived, having learned that Fort Moultrie had surrendered.

"I do not trust these bloody rebels as far as I can throw them," Clinton grumbled, then he looked at Cornwallis. "Cover the Cooper River, make sure they are not trying to deceive us. I will give them a ceasefire until midnight, then we will see."

***

Lincoln looked at the dispatch from Clinton and shook his weary head. While he always had a sleeping problem, the siege had worsened, and he was physically and mentally exhausted. The council of war held at the Citadel contained every regimental officer, ship captain, and civilian leaders.

The silence was eerie, having not heard it for so long. Lincoln knew he had no choice now; they had to determine the terms of surrender. He had requested that the ceasefire goes until eight in the morning, and Clinton had agreed.

"Gentlemen, we are in a very dire situation. We have no more food, no reinforcements, and we're surrounded. So, by vote, do we surrender or continue the fight. All in favor of surrendering?"

Of the officers assembled, fifty voted to surrender. When the call for fighting was asked, only twelve raised their hands. The army had enough and was at the breaking point. The twelve officers who wanted to keep fighting were from South Carolina, and they had disgusted looks on their faces as they drew up the terms.

Before the sun rose, the terms had been delivered to Clinton. Lincoln had requested a ceasefire until the negotiations of the surrender were complete. Samuel, scarred from numerous near misses, snored deeply as he sat back and leaned against the wall of the Hornwork. The quiet that finally settled over the field, many men just collapsed where they were and fell asleep. Had the British launched a surprise attack, they could have quickly taken the line.

In the terms, Lincoln had requested the army the "Honors of War," allowed to march out with flags flying and bayonets fixed in the time-old tradition. The city and fortifications were to be surrendered to the British. Private property remained with the owner, and the civilians were allowed to leave the city.

Clinton read over the terms and shook his head. "Honors of War? Is he bloody daft! Like bloody Hell, I will allow him the

Honors of War. They will surrender their ships; the militia will return home as prisoners on parole, and officers will give up their horses. That bloody army will march out with colors cased and no Honors of War. These civilians are traitors and criminals and will be treated as such!"

Clinton sent his response back to Lincoln and waited on his answer. He received it at nine in the morning, when the church bells rang, the men cheered "Huzzah" three times, and the cannons began to fire in random order.

"Well, that's how he wants it!" Clinton yelled, "Have our batteries open fire!" Once more, the cannonade opened fire, killing the blissful silence once more.

***

The cannonade continued into the night, Samuel stumbling around in the Hornwork. He was stretched thin as far as his mind and body could go by the constant firing, no sleep, and poor diet. Nevertheless, he was tired enough that even in this maelstrom of fire, he did find a spot on the wall and slept, his body too tired to care.

The balls and shot whizzed and hissed as they flew, finding the powder stockpiles or supply points, causing volcanic explosions within the city and the defenses. Samuel cautiously looked over the lip of the Hornwork and could see the British had dug to within twenty-five feet of their first line.

"Anytime now," he whispered, "they'll come over the wall, and we'll have it up close and personal. At least I can bloody well wrap my fingers around someone's throat instead of ducking all the time!"

By morning, the British changed to heating their shot red hot before lobbing them into the city. Houses quickly caught fire, and several heavy and thick columns of smoke rose and danced in the wind. The city was dying. To make matters worse, the Royal Navy was close enough to fire down the streets in the city, so nowhere was it safe.

Gadsden approached Lincoln, who looked like death warmed over. Gadsden simply shook his head. "They have had enough," he advised, "None of the remaining city leaders want to fight; they will agree to anything to stop this madness." He handed Lincoln a petition from all the prominent citizens and militia members still in the city, begging him to seek terms.

Lincoln ran his hands through his hair and shook his head. He had been holding out to give these same citizens and militia good terms, but they now indicated they have had enough. Then, walking over to his table and taking quill in hand, Lincoln wrote his message to Clinton, detailing their desire to surrender.

Samuel was snoring loud and steady, though the guns going silent went unnoticed by himself and a good number of the men who also had fallen asleep in the silence. Samuel was dreaming of his family when in the distance of his dream, he could hear "Sergeant-Major, sergeant-major, wake up!"

Samuel woke to a rocking motion, and as his eyes opened, he saw one of his corporals kneeling next to him. "Who, what, are they attacking?" Samuel began to scramble for his rifle when he noticed it was quiet. As he looked around, he could see others fully standing and looking over the walls.

Samuel slowly raised all the way, having been in a crouch for nearly forty days. It felt strange to stand. Looking out onto the shattered and chewed-up field between the lines, he could see the blue-coated officers with a white flag speaking with red-coated officers. Samuel felt a rock settle in his stomach.

"They surrendered, they bloody surrendered." He stated, and the corporal next to him nodded.

"They are figuring the terms right now, and Lieutenant Baker wanted us to be ready when the final decision is made." Samuel nodded, then turned to gather up the rest of the survivors of the 2nd. From what Samuel was able to gather, less than two hundred remained. By midday, the orders arrived to head to the city.

It was a shabby-looking regiment, uniforms and frocks torn and dirty from the siege, muskets dingy. Samuel and what few officers were left got the men organized and into a column with the other survivors near the Citadel. Samuel turned to Lieutenant Baker, "What day is it?"

"May 12th," replied Baker, "It's May 12th." Then the sound of fifes and drums could be heard, and the city's gates opened wide. A company of German Grenadiers and a company of British Grenadiers marched in all of their fineries with their flags flying. All of their colors had been cased as directed by the terms of surrender. The grenadiers marched into and took charge of the Citadel.

The command to march was given, and on horseback was General Lincoln; walking next to him was General Moultrie, and they led the remnants of the Southern Army out of the gate. Arrayed on either side of the road to the canal, the British Army was posted, while others observed from the top of their redoubts.

As part of the terms, they could not play any British marching music, but instead, the Patriot drummers beat out the "Turkish March." Halfway down the road, they were met by a detachment of British Light Infantry and German Jaegers, who led them through an opening in the abatis onto open space. As they couldn't fit, they were split into two columns and then marched out onto the area.

There, the command they were dreading was issued. "Ground Firelocks!" Samuel and the other regiment members shook their heads as they knelt and placed their muskets and rifles on the ground before standing erect.

"Drop cartridge boxes and bayonets!" The men slid the shoulder straps of their boxes and bayonets, allowing them to fall to the ground. In the city, the Union Jack rose, and from behind the men, the British fired a twenty-one gun salute and cheered. Samuel could see many men weeping, tears making long streaks down their dirty faces. He wondered what would happen to them next.

EPILOGUE

Maclane walked through the ruins of his office, picking through the papers and other items that could be salvaged. But, as fate would have it, some of the Royal Navy's cannon fire had found his office and warehouse near the docks, and not knowing friend from foe, promptly knocked massive holes through the roof and structure, which was followed up by a small fire caused by the hot shot that dropped into the city.

Maclane picked up a leather-bound ledger and brushed the debris off. Opening, he saw that, to his relief, the information it contained was intact and not damaged. He was relieved it was still intact.

"Sorry to see what happened to your office," a voice said from behind Maclane, "fortunes of war and all."

Maclane turned to see Major Bedlow stepping through the door, except this time he was wearing his regular British officer uniform, instead of the plainclothes he usually wore. Bedlow looked around, scanning the damage that cannon fire had done, nodding.

"Don't worry; we will ensure your place of business is repaired so you can continue your duty to the King."

Maclane looked at Bedlow and nodded his head in agreement. "Until then, what do you require of me?"

Bedlow nodded, "Straight to the point, good." He approached and stood before Maclane.

"We are now responsible for bringing this rebellious state back under our firm control. I am aware you have your sources." Bedlow had a distasteful look on his face, not favoring that Maclane uses brigands and thieves.

"We need to root out these rebels and their supporters. We are also aware from loyal subjects here in the city and other sources that some city leaders escaped to include the governor. So we must capture this Rutledge and bring in all of those other traitors."

Maclane nodded, "I will head up country and get my sources busy; I am sure they will be more than willing to hunt these people down." He paused for a moment before continuing. "For the right price, of course."

Maclane stared directly at Bedlow, who saw his meaning and nodded. "Of course, I'll see to it before you go."

"Then I'll get to it, get my sources searching the countryside, and find you these rebels."

Bedlow nodded, "Good hunting, keep me informed." Placing his well-made officer tricorn on, Bedlow departed and headed into the city

Over on the far side of the city, in a strange irony, the captured Patriot muskets were placed back in the city powder magazine. The quartermaster recorded the number and type of musket, bayonet, and cartridge boxes. He shook his head at the different models and the logistical nightmare he inherited.

First and second model Brown Besses shouldn't be an issue. It was all of these French Charleville muskets and bayonets. They used a smaller size ball than what they used in their muskets. He would have to scrounge the city for casks of French musket balls.

"I can always issue them to these Loyalist volunteers, let them have to deal with it," he remarked as he continued to record the information in his ledger. Then, he looked up to see a German officer approach him, and he bowed to the officer.

"How may I be of service, sir?" the quartermaster asked.

"Are you sure these muskets are unloaded," the German Officer, a major, asked.

The quartermaster didn't like someone, especially a foreign officer, to question his performance.

"With respect, sir, I believe I know what I am doing. I have been taking care of this army for years now. They are unloaded."

The major shrugged and walked off while the quartermaster shook his head and returned to work.

"Who the hell is this officer questioning my abilities." It would be the last thought he would have.

As the captured muskets were being stacked, one fell over and went off. The ball struck a barrel of powder, which in turn caused one hundred and eighty barrels of powder to explode, which caused five thousand loaded captured muskets to all discharge.

A giant mushroom-shaped cloud of fire and smoke rose over the city, the shockwave shattering windows and shaking tiles off of roofs. The explosion killed two hundred civilians, six houses were destroyed, including a poor house and a brothel, and thirty British soldiers were killed.

***

Like the powder magazine explosion rocked the area around the city, the call for Loyalists to flock to the King's Colors went out, and soon they began to arrive in droves. Though concerned about the loss of the powder and muskets, General Clinton still basked in the glory of his victory.

"These rebels are finished; I broke them!" he yelled at the ceiling of his headquarters and laughed. There was no need for him to remain here in this broken city. He could return to New York and leave this festering wound to General Cornwallis.

Before he left for New York, Clinton gave his instructions to Lord Cornwallis. "I leave the south in your capable hands," Clinton began, though in his mind, he quipped, *"Better you than me!"* Nevertheless, Clinton continued with his instructions. "Your primary task is to hold and safeguard our new possession of Charles Town and prevent any rebels from rising. At no time are you to march the army northward to North Carolina; I will take care of that."

General Cornwallis nodded his head. While he had received his wish of being in overall command, except it had not expected just here in the south. As Clinton droned on with his instructions, Cornwallis accepted, *"Go back to your mistress; at least you will be away from me."*

Clinton continued. "To meet your task, you are authorized to use any means at your disposal to raise and equip Loyalist militias and see to their training. Organize them and strengthen your position here. In time, when you have gained sufficient forces, I will call upon you to march in a coordinated effort to take North Carolina."

Once again, Clinton thought, *"It will be a cold day in hell before I call on you; the glory will all be mine!"*

On June 3rd, 1780, Clinton wrote and proclaimed, "All men who were paroled for their actions against the Crown, are released from the state. They are to swear an oath of loyalty to their King, and when called, serve the crown as loyal, royal subjects to defeat these rebels who would usurp their rightful King."

The proclamation was sent out across South Carolina and angered many militiamen. While they were paroled, they refused to serve the Crown. They decided to violate their parole, seeing in their mind that the proclamation violated the terms of the parole anyway and will fight again. All they needed was someone to organize and lead them.

The day General Clinton departed, Cornwallis observed from the dock as Clinton and his staff loaded the longboat to be rowed out to the waiting warship. So turning, Cornwallis watched the other longboats ferrying a good portion of the army back out to the troopships.

General Cornwallis began to take inventory of their supplies and personnel and knew he would need help organizing the Loyalist militias. He took over Clinton's headquarters in Charles Town, moving his personal items and staff into the now vacated house. He looked at the map prepared for him, showing the circled areas where they believe rebels are hiding.

Cornwallis called for Major Ferguson and Lieutenant Colonel Tarleton to the headquarters; he had specific tasks for them to perform. Both officers arrived and reported to him. Cornwallis returned their bows, "Gentlemen, we have work to do." He led them over to his map with the circled areas.

"Major Ferguson, I am appointing you my Inspector General for Militia as these loyal subjects are answering their King's call and gathering to the colors. You will see to their training and equipping, though I am afraid losing the main powder magazine may take some time."

Major Ferguson nodded, accepting his duties. Cornwallis Continued. "Once you have a force you feel is trained and ready to fight, you are to head up country and bring these rebels to heal as you see fit."

Major Ferguson again nodded his head in agreement. Cornwallis nodded back, then turned to Tarleton.

"My dear colonel, as you have demonstrated so far your ability to move rapidly against the rebels, you are to take your Legion and scour the countryside for these rebel leaders who escaped and bring them to justice. When we learn of their location, I want you to move quickly to engage and, if possible, eliminate this threat to our control."

Tarleton smiled and nodded his head in agreement. "Yes, sir, as soon as my Legion is reconstituted, we shall move. Where should I lead my command?"

Cornwallis looked at his map at the circled blocks and pointed to the area around Georgetown. "Secure the King's Highway along the coast, keep our lines of communication open. Any rebels dare attack our supply lines; I want you to deal with them."

Continuing to smile, Tarleton nodded his head in agreement. Cornwallis looked at both officers. "Sadly, it seemed, our former commander took a good portion of the army with him; as soon we receive reinforcements, I will make sure you both are supported as I build the army to secure South Carolina before we move against North Carolina.

***

Francis Marion, resting at home with his leg resting on pillows, received word of the city's surrender and the army, plus the Clinton Edict, from Gabriel, who had brought the message. Both Jacob and Jean, who was with Marion, heard the news and thought of Samuel and wondered if Samuel was still alive or not.

Marion leaned back on his bed, his black and blue swollen ankle unfortunately not healing quickly for all of the movement they have been doing, staying ahead of these green-uniformed dragoons. They would only spend a night at a location, either one of Jacob's hunting lean-tos or a barn, until they arrived at Marion's home in Saint Mathews.

"Is it over then, Marion?" Gabriel asked Marion's nephew.

Marion looked sharply at him. "It is certainly not; as long as men have the will to resist, the cause will continue!"

Then Marion slumped back against his pillows, "It's just the cause will have to wait a little bit, or until I can heal up." Gabriel nodded and took a seat in a chair across from Marion. So Jacob thought, and Marion was right; for the moment, they had to stay out of sight and be patient.

"The oxen are slow, but the earth is patient."

They turned to see Oscar bringing a cup of tea to Marion. "My grandmother taught me that when I was younger."

"So, what do we do now?" Gabriel asked, and Marion thought about it.

"We're going to need men, men to fight and men to lead. We can trust men, which will be tough with this proclamation. This proclamation will hurt us," Marion thought, "and it will help us. It will anger many militiamen, and they won't stand for it and fight."

Jacob nodded his head in agreement. "We just have to wait and bide our time and find some leaders we can trust. The problem is, many of the officers were captured with the city."

Taking a deep sigh, Marion looked out the window and thought about it.

"Not every officer was taken with the city," Gabriel commented, and Marion looked at him, thinking Gabriel meant himself.

"Horry was leading the State Dragoons at Biggins Bridge; I heard he escaped and is in hiding. Then, of course, the other militia officers served like you against the Cherokees.

"Well, once my ankle heals up enough for me to move, we'll start organizing and finding good, trustworthy men. The time may be dark for now, but the light of liberty will burn bright again; just for now, the flame is low. It will grow."

Marion looked over at Jacob and Jean. "Nothing for you to do here; I don't need you two to nursemaid me. Go home, get men ready, and when I call, answer, and we'll take the fight back to the British and drive them back to the sea!"

Jacob saw the enthusiasm and dedication in Marion's eyes. "We're still officers of the Continental Army, and we have not surrendered. Our duty is to fight, and once the new Southern Army is formed, we shall meet them and lead them to victory!"

Jacob nodded, then rose and approached Marion, shaking his hand. "We'll be ready." Marion nodded, then Jacob and Jean departed, headed out to their horses, and mounted. Looking over to Jean, "Well, old friend, strange but exciting times are upon us."

Jean smiled and nodded, settling his rifle across the pommel of his saddle. "It's like when you came to Quebec; we must get small groups of men and women dedicated to defending their homes. That will make a difference."

Jacob looked over, "Women?"

"Oui, my friend," Jean answered. "Most English ignored our women during the war in Quebec, but they were our eyes and ears. That's how we tracked your movement."

Jacob looked in disbelief at Jean and then laughed. "That makes sense now, and you are right. We must gather good men and women to carry on the fight."

Jean nodded, and then the two turned and headed their horses into the woods, heading back to their home in Goose Creek.

***

Andrew Devaux sat in the darkened back corner of the Swooning Maid, sipping on his tankard and watching the commotion around him. Men were cheering and boasting about how they had the rebels beaten, and the Crown had regained control of Charles Town. "Long live the King!" the men chorused and drank noisily from their tankards, in which Devaux raised an eyebrow and said, "Not a bad idea."

Finishing his tankard, he whistled and raised his empty mug to the serving girl, who nodded her understanding. Devaux was still watching the swishing hips of the serving girl walk away when the sound of a bottle clunking in front of him made him jump, pulling a knife halfway out of its sheath.

Maclane had set the bottle of rum before McGirtt and took a chair across from him. "Bloody ass, you almost got yourself stabbed," Devaux growled; Maclane shrugged and replied with a "Maybe."

Devaux leaned back just in time as the serving girl brought a new tankard of ale and placed it in front of him. He took a long pull from the tankard, then wiped his mouth on his sleeve, looking at Maclane in the eyes.

"To what honor do you sit with poor old Andrew?" Maclane smiled, picked up the bottle of rum and pulled the cork with his teeth, and spit it onto the floor.

"I am here to honor you, my friend, for following your orders and staying out of sight," Maclane explained, though he knew good and well that Devaux and his men, from time to time, raided and robbed, but at least remained discreet, by leaving no witnesses. Besides, he was easier to control than Big Harpe.

Devaux made no indication that Maclane knew of his indiscretions, shrugged, finished off his tankard, and concluded with a loud belch before setting it down. "Get to the point and tell me what you want, Maclane, so I can get back to drinking and celebrating our victory over the rebels."

Maclane leaned back in his chair and smiled, "To the point, as you wish."

Maclane leaned forward and placed his hands on the table. "For your undying Loyalty to the Crown and your patience, I want you to do what you do best."

Devaux leaned forward, placing both hands on the table, and looked at Maclane in the eyes, "and that is?"

Maclane smiled and replied, "Mayhem, death, and destruction. General Cornwallis, commander of Charles Town, wants the area pacified and to prevent the rebels from organizing and fighting. He was told by his commander General Clinton by any means at his disposal, which means you."

Devaux continued to listen; his interest peaked, "Go on."

Taking a deep breath, wondering if he was letting another devil like Harpe loose upon the world.

"You Devaux are to ensure the rebels will never fight the Crown again. Rob, pillage, burn, do all that you seem best suited for. No mercy, men, women, children, make them all pay. Their homes are yours; their property is yours to do as you see fit. If you hear of any gatherings, kill them and make examples of these rebels so others will take notice of what will happen if they continue to resist. Either they accept the King as their sovereign lord, or they die. Simple."

Leaning back, Maclane pulled a document out of his pocket and handed it to Devaux, who picked it up and turned it over a few times before looking at Maclane.

"What's this?"

"Your license charging you to do this on behalf of the King," Maclane explained. "It's your commission in the militia as a Major to raise men and secure horses to meet your needs. So take the fight to these rebels."

Devaux reached across the table with visions of plunder, fire, and wanton destruction he would release upon these hapless rebels or anyone who didn't support him; Daniel raised the bottle of rum and saluted Maclane.

"They will rue the day they ever took up arms against the King or failed to show proper respect and obedience to the Crown. I will make them pay, oh yes."

Devaux took a long pull from the rum, closed his eyes, and savored the burning sensation as the rum went down his throat, "I will make them surely pay."

Maclane reached over and saluted Daniel with the bottle, "To your triumph, my friend," and took a long pull from the bottle. The scourge has begun.

***

Samuel sat in the boat; he had a cup, a horn spoon, a wooden bowel, a blanket, and the old clothes on his back. He, along with other men from the army, was being rowed out to an old cargo ship with some masts but nothing else anchored out in the Cooper River. The longboat bumped up against the side of the hulk. Samuel and the others had to climb up the ladder to the main deck.

Stepping onto the old main deck, there were four guards with bayonets fixed, directed them towards an open hatchway. Samuel and the other prisoners entered the hatch and climbed down the wooden steps into the main deck. There were already prisoners sitting on the wood with shackles around their ankles.

Samuel and his group were moved to an open area, where two men with shackles were waiting. First, the prisoners were forced to sit down while the other men shackled Samuel's ankles. Then, they moved down the line, shackling the other prisoners. Samuel reached down and pulled on the chain attached. It ran from his shackle to a large eyebolt on a thick beam.

The chain gave him some limited space to move. Samuel placed his personal items and blanket on the deck and looked around the dark interior. Already, sweat was starting to spread under his shirt, the heat of the day building. Only a few open old gun ports let in only a little air, but it wouldn't be enough.

Samuel took in his situation with a deep sigh and shook his head. While he was alive, he would have to figure out how to escape. *"I will try and figure out a way to escape."* So Samuel thought as he looked around the interior.

The other prisoners found a space, some accepting their fate; others, like Samuel, were looking to find a way to escape. He saw a few men with a chain length look at a gun port. While they could fit through, they had no way to break the chain or shackle. Then there was the swim across the river into British-held territory.

Samuel leaned back against the bulkhead and nodded his head. *"I must survive."* While he still thought about Jacob and Jean if they had escaped, he mostly thought of his family.

"I will survive for them."

A new line of prisoners began clumping down the stairs, the red-coated guards with their muskets herding them. Samuel gave the guards a hard look.

I will survive, rise and fight again, you bastards! I am not done yet! I survived a scalping, I will sure, and hell bloody survive this!"

Review Requested:

We'd like to know if you enjoyed the book.
Please consider leaving a review on the platform
from which you purchased the book.

Ingram Content Group UK Ltd.
Milton Keynes UK
UKHW040709080323
418175UK00001B/14